The Foul Out

BOSTON REVS THREE OUTS BOOK 3

Jenni Bara

The Foul Out

Boston Revs Three Outs Book 3

Line Copy and Proof Editing by VB Edits

Final Proofreading by Jeffrey Hodge

Interior formatting Sara Stewart

Cover by Cheslea Kemp

ISBN: 978-1-959389-16-3 (ebook)

ISBN: 978-1-959389-21-7 (paperback)

ISBN: 978-1-959389-24-8 (hardback)

Jennibara.com

DEDICATION

For all the moms raising your
neurodiverse kids, feeling alone
and exhausted, but trying to
keep it all together—
Harper and I see you.

BOSTON REVS BASEBALL CLUB

REVS | HEAT
OCTOBER 11TH | 6 PM

LINEUP

COACH: TOM WILSON #49

1 KYLE BOSCO #29   RF

2 JASPER QUINN #16   1B

3 EMERSON KNIGHT #21   3B

4 ASHER PRICE #5   C

5 SCOTT ADAMS #4   2B

6 EDDIE MARTINEZ #30   SS

7 COLTON STEWART #23   DH

8 TRISTIAN JENNER #27   LF

9 MASON DUMPTY #22   CF

P CHRISTIAN DAMIANO #35   P

B

Playlist

◄◄ ⏸ ►► ⟳

Lonely Eyes - Chris Young

Collide - Howie Day

Teenage Dream - Katy Perry

Only the Good Die Young - Billy Joel

You May Be Right - Billy Joel

Why - Sabrina Carpenter

Daughters - John Mayer

Fight Like Hell - Warren Zeiders

Rewrite the Stars - Zac Efron & Zendaya

She Used to Be Mine - Sara Barielles

Sun to Me - Zach Bryan

Feel Again - One Republic

One Call Away - Charlie Puth

PREFACE
KYLE

It doesn't take long for life to do a complete one-eighty. Trust me, I know.

Three months ago, I ran away as fast as I could, because the last thing I wanted was any responsibility outside of baseball. Now? I wish I could go back and do things differently.

I scanned the field, my focus snagging on a shock of red hair. Lots of red hair. For one beat, utter joy overwhelmed me. Maybe everything would be okay. But as a smile crept up my face, she turned and beamed at the man stepping up next to her. The smile dropped from my face. My heart clenched, and my breath stopped. All I could think was no. No fucking way. My world tilted too.

Mason grabbed my arm as I stumbled, but I couldn't stop my legs from continuing toward the stands.

"Jeez, Streaks. You're going to bust your ass," he growled, hustling to keep up with me. "Breathe. You don't know what's going on."

But I couldn't breathe. I needed to move. Be faster. Undo the last month. Hell, go back in time and undo the last three months. Because fuck all of it. I should have made better decisions every step of the way. Everything that mattered—really mattered—was abundantly clear in that moment.

"Breathe," he repeated.

I sucked in hard. Yes. Breathe. If I didn't, there was no way I'd make it across this damn field to the three people who mattered more than I wanted anyone to matter.

Because even after everything, I couldn't find it in me to want a life that didn't include them. Hopefully I hadn't already fucked it all up.

Harper
1

FOUR MONTHS *Earlier*

Don't let it be a heart attack. Or a stroke. Or even a broken hip. Let the reason for pressing the panic button be a dumb one.

As the director of Boston's most reputable rehab and assisted living complexes, I couldn't pass a resident's emergency off on anyone else. The thought pulsed rapidly through my mind before the guilt kicked in. Dammit. I truly was the most selfish woman on the planet.

Mr. Roper, although difficult and grumpy, meant well—most days. Plus, I *should* be worried for his well-being, but honestly, I was terrified that his emergency would make me late to pick up my daughter.

It was Friday.

The Friday.

The day she'd been waiting for since her birthday. And I couldn't be late.

With my seven-year-old, schedules and pickup times mattered. When anything went even slightly off plan, she didn't handle it well. And in the moment, I feared that what should have been the best day of the year for her would turn into a nightmare for both of us.

I hardly gave the courtesy tap on the studio apartment door before I burst inside.

"Mr. Roper," I called when I didn't immediately see him. Rooms here weren't big, but the area past the bathroom wasn't visible from the doorway. Thankfully, panic hadn't set in as I turned the corner and found him sitting comfortably in his green velvet La Z Boy.

"It's the wrong one again." He shook his head, his frown one of annoyance as he glared at the TV. He didn't even look pale.

I skidded to a stop, my heart still pounding. My brain was warring with itself. On one hand, I was happy that this wasn't an emergency. But on the other, I was irritated because *this wasn't an emergency.*

"No need for a bus," I said into what was basically a walkie talkie.

"Damn television box. Never plays the right show. We saw this one last week." The eighty-eight-year-old jabbed the remote into the air, pointing it at the screen and furiously pressing buttons.

For employees in assisted living facilities like Boston Lights, technology was both friend and foe.

I sighed, my shoulders dropping. "You hit your panic button." *Again.*

"Yes." The wrinkles on his forehead deepened as he lifted his brow. "I called for help because I currently need assistance."

When the board had approved panic buttons on wristbands for every resident, they clearly hadn't considered all the ramifications. The ability to contact staff quickly in an emergency was great, and the GPS component assured we could easily locate everyone. However, for every one genuine emergency, there were at least one hundred instances where the button had been used as if it was a flight attendant call button.

"Mr. R—"

"Henry," he corrected with a glower. "And don't tower over me like the Redwoods."

"Henry." I kneeled next to his chair and rested my palm over the back of his veiny hand. I lightly tapped the square device that sat on a rubber bracelet. "This is for emergencies."

"Missing Kevin and Tommy fixing up the Glen Ridge Place *is* an emergency." He harrumphed.

I squeezed his hand and turned back to my com. "Can someone send tech support to 2203, please?" As I focused on him again, I tapped the gray rubber. "This is for actual emergencies. Use your phone to call for TV help. It's set to speed dial."

"Not interested in pushing damn buttons on the phone. I can't remember who is eight and who is four. You know how many times I've asked the kitchen why the six-o'clock news isn't working on my TV? What is this world coming to?" he muttered. "And no one my age can make out that tiny-ass writing on the number pad."

I sighed.

"At least I'm not like Charlie. He called for help with his pants." He burst into laughter, which quickly turned into a choking cough.

I gave him a quick pat on the back.

I hadn't found Charlie's "emergency" funny. Not when I arrived, heart pounding, to discover that the problem was his shirt had been caught in his zipper.

"There's no bigger emergency than lunch not sitting right and your damn zipper not opening." Henry was still half laughing, half coughing as he shook his head.

"That was unfortunate." Scissors had saved the day. Otherwise, we would have had a big mess on our hands.

"That was a shitstorm." He clapped.

I frowned and fought a shudder. "Not literally, thank God."

A tap sounded on the open door. "Tech support, Mr. Roper?" Lexi peeked into the room.

"Henry," he answered, the smile sliding off his face. "This damn picture box is playing the wrong show again."

"I hate when those damn picture boxes do that." The twenty-two-year-old practically skipped into the room and took the remote out of the old man's hand.

He narrowed his eyes at her. "Don't you sass me."

"Wouldn't dream of it." Her expression was the exact opposite of his, all sunshine and rainbows. Clearly, it was an effective way to mess with the guy.

I left them to it and headed back to the office to turn over control of the five hundred–resident building to the night manager, Jacki, who had come in more than an hour early to cover for me today.

"Have fun at the game," she said, taking the radio from me. "I'm sure Piper is excited. So don't be late. I've got this." Jacki was a mom of two herself, and although she didn't fully relate to my struggle with Piper, she was supportive and a great listener.

"Thanks," I rushed out. My stomach burned. Even with the shift change, I was behind schedule. I grabbed two Tums from the roll in my pocket, hoping to settle the scorch of stress, and headed out.

Fate wasn't on my side today. A car accident and the subsequent rubberneckers slowed me down. Thirty minutes later—twenty minutes late—I parked at the daycare center. I popped two more Tums and swallowed down the dread threatening to overtake me. The unknown always did this to me, and I never knew what kind of day my child may have had.

The car door wasn't even closed behind me before Doreen, the facility director, was pushing through the front entrance.

My stomach sank. That was a bad sign, if experience had taught me anything.

Sam, my three-year-old, spent almost nine hours here each weekday though he was never the issue. It was always Piper. My daughter only spent two hours at the YMCA's day care program after school each day, yet she managed to cause mayhem.

I braced myself.

"I warned you." Doreen crossed her arms.

She had warned me, probably four times, that Piper was on her last chance. I'd used up any good grace she had offered. Piper wasn't being difficult for the hell of it. Her behavior was a neurological response. Her body didn't produce the dopamine needed for her to feel comfortable. She was living on the edge of fear. Unfortunately, despite how many times I'd explained it, most people only saw a poorly behaved child.

"What did she do?" I tried to keep the hesitancy out of my voice. It was a challenge, though, because I wasn't sure I wanted to know. But I had to face the music. Because as much as I wanted to give up some days. I couldn't. There was no one else. So I pulled my shoulders back and waited.

"You're late." She cocked a gray brow.

I winced. There was no denying it. "Di—"

"We tried your trick. We removed the clock from the room." She shook her head. "Not only was it ineffective, but it became a sticking point. She fixated on the fact that it was missing."

My chest tightened with dread.

She tapped her fingers against her arm, drawing my attention to her opal-colored nail polish, one brow raised in expectation of my response.

Piper did tend to fixate, and when she was unsettled, things never ended well. "And she wouldn't let up until you told her the time."

"Clearly." Doreen's lips flattened, the lines around her mouth deepening.

"And?" I asked, trying to pretend I didn't want to disappear into the pavement.

"At four o'clock, when you weren't here, she became agitated." Her lips turned down, her eyes hardening.

Agitated. That was a nice way to say she'd thrown a fit.

"And by four ten, she was hysterical. We tried to settle her, but when Joy touched her shoulders, Piper bit her."

My shoulders slumped, and my heart squeezed painfully.

"Thankfully, she didn't draw blood this time."

Shame flooded me, weighing me down heavily. I did everything I could to help my daughter. Creating schedules so she knew what to expect, giving her warnings when things were going to be different. I'd read every book I could get my hands on and I listened to the advice of every doctor. I was exhausted, and it still wasn't enough.

"She's calmed down now. She's in the office with her iPad and headphones."

"Thank you." That eased a little of the trepidation that seemed to be a constant in my life.

She frowned. "Harper." Man, she sounded exactly like my high school principal calling me into her office.

My skin crawled, and the modicum of calm I'd found fled. Dammit. I knew what was next.

"We understand there are special circumstances here, but we can't keep doing this." Her tone was soft, but her expression was firm, unwavering.

I swallowed and nodded. "Right." Another day care down.

"You'll need to find other arrangements moving forward."

I blinked hard, fighting back the heat building behind my eyes. It was Friday, thankfully, which meant I had two days to find another day care willing to take a neurodiverse child. No problem.

"Come on. She's waiting for you in my office."

Silently, I followed Doreen inside, and as we strode down the hall, the only sound was the clicking of our heels against the tile floor. In the small outer office, Doreen's assistant sat at her desk, avoiding eye contact. On the other side of the space sat my daughter.

Piper's back was to me, so all I could see were her red pigtails under her royal blue headphones. If I had to guess, she was listening to one of the Boston Revs' most recent games. She'd watched each multiple times. It was the only thing that kept my poor child calm. The headphones weren't completely noise canceling, but they at least took the edge off for her.

Knowing better than to surprise my daughter with any kind of physical sensation, I didn't touch her. Instead, I circled around her and stood where she could see me. Her eyes drifted to my shirt and stopped there. Then she pulled the headphones off.

"We are going to be late," she accused without meeting my eye.

"No, Pipe, we aren't. I told you that as long as we leave by 5:45, we'll make it to the stadium in time to find the seats before the game starts."

"Uncle James said we were sitting on the field." She blinked, her lips turned down.

"No, he said our seats are in the first row on the first base line," I reminded her.

I'd better make that clear now. The last thing I wanted was for her to melt down at the stadium when she realized we couldn't sit in the grass. And I had no interest in explaining to James that we'd missed the game after he spent God knew how much on this birthday present for Piper. Seriously, who gave a child tickets to game seven of the American league championship?

But Uncle James excelled in the art of buying my kids' love. My jaw locked, and a niggle of guilt ate at me. That wasn't entirely fair, especially with our complicated relationship, but it also *wasn't* inaccurate. He'd meant well when he gave her these tickets, but very few people understood my child and the challenges that came with her. A game sounded like fun on the surface. But he was clueless about all the details, all the difficulties associated with changing her routine, taking her somewhere new, putting her in a place with so many people and so much stimuli.

Piper nodded, still not meeting my eyes. "Yes. It's going to be the best."

I wished I could agree. But in my heart and in my head, I knew it would be exactly the opposite.

KYLE
2

A LOUD WHOOSH of air escaped Mason Dumpty as the center fielder spit a sunflower seed across the dugout.

No one commented.

Normally, the mood on the bench was lighter, teasing. Normally, we were a bunch of smiling assholes.

But today was too important. And we were all feeling it.

"*Striii,*" echoed from the plate.

"Fuck," Mason muttered into the silence.

"We got this." Emerson Knight, our third baseman, assured him, sounding far too unaffected by the tension in the air. I loved the guy, but despite the couple of years I'd known him, I still couldn't understand the source of his constant state of positive chill. "Angel Boy's bat has been on fire the whole series."

Emerson wasn't wrong. Our catcher, Asher Price, had led the team's bats this season. He'd been a one dot for the last month. During the playoffs, that was nothing short of a miracle. With that on-base percentage and his slugging, it was likely he'd score. But it was the bottom of the eighth, and we were only ahead by one.

"We need a bigger lead, since I won't be controlling the ball." Christian Damiano kept his expression neutral, even though we all knew he'd prefer to be outright glaring at our head coach. Not that long ago, he'd have lost his shit the second Coach Wilson pulled him. But that was before Christian's fiancée, Coach Wilson's daughter, wrapped our pitcher around her finger.

Not that he was alone.

At the start of the season, Eddie Martinez had been the only guy on the team in a relationship. Then the owners brought in family-man Asher Price, and slowly, a few of the guys coupled up.

Not long after Christian and Avery got together, Mason had fallen hard for the Revs' trainer and had swiftly moved her into his place. Earlier this week, Emerson had proposed to Christian's sister. That potential clusterfuck turned out way better than I thought it would when I first discovered our third baseman was hooking up with Gianna behind his best friend's back.

I shook my head. It had better not be something in the water cooler here. I had no intention of settling down ever, let alone this year. My role as a professional baseball player was all the responsibility I could manage.

"You've thrown too many pitches already this week, Dragon," Mason, our team captain, reminded him. "You're lucky he left you in through eight."

Christian crossed his arms and glared at the field. If Tom Wilson let him, the guy would pitch every game in its entirety.

The sound of wood shattering startled me, and I jumped to my feet. It was the opposite of the good type of crack. This was the sound of a bat that had met its end. The shattered pieces of wood flew farther than the ball, which hardly rolled into the infield, making it easy for the catcher to scoop it up and toss it to first long before Asher Price made it to the bag.

Out number three.

I tamped down on the nerves skittering through me.

"We've got this, guys." Emerson, always the peppy cheerleader, clapped his hands. I had a mind to punch him, but he was too damn happy, and if I did that, I'd feel like an ass. If he could find it within himself to grumble a little, maybe I'd be able to smack him when he was being annoying. That'd never happen, though. He was too supportive and positive to ever get outwardly angry or even frustrated. "Leading by one into the ninth is a great place to be."

"Leading by five would be great," I muttered.

With a shake of his head and a smirk, he grabbed his mitt and headed to third. Annoying as it was, I envied his ability to smile. There was no way I could force my lips up. Not with so much on the line.

I climbed the stairs and stood in the grass with my team as the crowd cheered around us. The deafening sound sent a chill down my spine. Five years ago, when I joined this team, I couldn't have guessed that we'd ever be this close to the big game so soon, and yet here we were. As I trotted out to right field, I took in the moment. The fans, the guys. The score board. The night. We were just three outs from the dream I'd been chasing for most of my life.

Three outs, and the Boston Revs would secure a spot in the World Series.

From center field, Mason tossed the ball to me. I settled into my position in right field, then threw it back. After four more warm-up throws, Mason turned the crowd, searching for a fan to toss the ball to. His head moved from side to side as he scanned the bleachers of deep right field, where fans waved and screamed, hoping to be chosen.

So much excitement. Unlike some guys, I never promised a fan that I'd get them next time. When the inning started, my mind was focused on the game only, and a lot could happen between then and the next time I took the field. The last thing I'd want to do was forget someone. It was a simple thing, a baseball, but in a setting like this, one given to a person directly from a member of the Revs was a big deal.

Even when I'd just joined the team and we'd lost almost 70 percent of the games we played, fans still shouted to us from the stands, always clapping and cheering. Now, five years later, we were finally about to prove that we'd been worthy of their support all this time.

A teenager jumped up to swipe the ball Mason gently tossed to him, cheering as he did.

It was hard not to smile at the glee in his expression. But I reined in the emotion and spun back to the plate as the fans settled into their seats. Shutting my eyes, I took a deep breath, and when I opened them and recentered, I focused on Tugerot, who was digging his foot into the sand of the mound. We really could have used Dragon for our final inning. No one threw fire better than the first guy in our rotation. But he'd spent the playoffs killing his shoulder, and with the possibility of going to the World Series so close, he'd have to rest that arm. I couldn't disagree with Wilson's decision to pull him after the eighth inning.

I scanned the stadium, zeroing in on the box where the men who controlled our team stood watching. Beckett Langfield and Cortney Miller. They were by far the best leaders in major league baseball. We were lucky to play for them, and we all knew it. They wanted this win almost as much as we did. Or close to it. I wasn't sure anyone could want it as much as I did. My desire to step onto the field at the World Series was so strong I could taste it.

When the first batter went down swinging, I let myself start to believe this could be real. A pop fly made it more possible. Even the base hit didn't get me down. We only had one more out, after all. We could do this. Just one more. The guys tossed the ball from base to base before it ended back in Tugerot's glove.

Heart pounding, I beat my fist into the leather of my own mitt. We had this.

The first pitch was followed by the ump's strike call. Two more.

The batter swung at the second pitch and made contact. The wooden bat cracked against the leather, sending the ball flying. The sound was the kind we all paid attention to. A solid hit. And in a blink, it was headed my way, and I was running. As it flew over Emerson's head, I sped up. Before I could worry about the bounce, it turned foul and hurtled toward the stands. If I made this catch, that'd be it. Game over.

My heart pounded as I pumped my arms and legs faster. The win was in my hands.

My quads burned as I passed the white line in the dirt, heading for the stands. With my gloved hand in the air, I tracked the ball over my shoulder. I was right there. I had this. Quickly, I risked a look at the people in the stands above the padded blue wall.

I wasn't at all prepared for what I saw just two feet away. Red pigtails, blue headphones. The little girl was maybe six. The mom was…not six. I couldn't help but take in the smooth column of the woman's throat or her amber eyes. The breath rushed out of my lungs.

Lonely eyes.

It was a term people tossed around often. But I'd only seen an expression this sincerely lonely on one face in my entire life. Staring into the deep amber-brown eyes shorted out my thoughts.

It was only a blink, hardly a hesitation. But it was just long enough that the woman moved. Her hand came up to block the ball headed for her kids. And before I could get my mitt up to make the final move to catch it, she'd swiped it out of the air.

A collective gasp echoed around us.

She grimaced and shook her hand, causing the ball to teeter and then slip out. In slow motion, the ball bounced. And a small boy bent to pick it up.

The stadium grew eerily silent, the crowd shocked. This woman in front of me had caused the ball to be foul. The ball that would have been the third out. The ball that would have sent the Revs to the World Series.

The young girl with pigtails and sporting Revs pinstripes called out. Though her lips were moving in a way that looked like she was saying my name, I couldn't hear her. I couldn't respond. Headphones. Sad eyes.

No.

Violently, I shook off thoughts of them. Two seconds of distraction had already ruined what should have been an out. I spun from them, searching out the first base umpire behind me.

"Fan inference," I demanded.

He shook his head.

My hands trembled, and my knees shook. "What the fuck, man? That was catchable."

"Was," he agreed. "But you didn't catch it."

Chest puffed, I took a step toward the guy, but before I could do more than that, Emerson was in my face.

"Step back," he demanded.

"Move," I sneered, lit by a burning need to blame someone for the play. And the man in white and black was an easy target.

Emerson pushed my shoulders, sending me stumbling back a step. "I'll let you hit me before I let you get ejected from this game." Shrugging, he pasted on a smile that was all wrong after the play hadn't gone our way. But the fucker was always happy.

"Field," Tom Wilson barked at me as he stepped into my fight. "This is my job. Get the fuck out in the grass. If we need the bottom of the ninth, you need to be at bat." With a quick shove to my arm, he turned to the umpire.

I glanced back over my shoulder. To the family of three. The little girl's arms flew, and her face was red. She was yelling, and if I wasn't mistaken, she landed a hard kick to her mother's shin. Rather than getting upset, her mother kept her expression neutral, though she was entirely focused on her daughter. The little boy beside her was just blinking at the white ball in his hands.

My temper spiked. That ball should be in my glove. I should have caught it, and then, with a smile, I should have fucking tossed it to the little man. Because I *would* have caught it if not for the woman who didn't trust that I could. If she hadn't ruined my chance...

Clenching my right hand, I stormed back to right field, anger brewing in my gut. That quickly turned to rage when the umpire waved a hand, ordering Tom Wilson out of the game for finishing the fight I'd started. The emotion only compounded when the next pitch was a two-run homer. Then when the Vegas Heat scored one more run. It didn't cool when we only got a single run in the bottom of the ninth. Or when I barreled into the locker room. It sure as shit burned hot when the microphones were shoved in my face.

The fuckers had the audacity to ask how I felt about the foul ball call.

What did they expect me to say? *Wonderful*? No. They wanted a sound bite they could run with. And I was primed to give it. Primed to blame anyone but myself. Ready to let the Boston fans take care of the issue.

"Want to know the truth?" I glared into the camera. "We lost this game because of one person, and it isn't the umpire who clearly needs glasses. No." I shook my head and let a dark chuckle pass through my lips. "Want a villain, Boston?" I smirked. "You've got one. A redheaded villain dressed in a white button-down." I tipped my chin up. "Hopefully she knows better than to show her face in our city again."

I was too mad to feel even the smallest bit of guilt when the Boston media ran with my statement.

Harper
3

WITH SAM ON MY HIP, I attempted to wrangle Piper into the elevator. We'd already let two go without us. But Sam needed to get home. It was well after ten, and he was practically asleep, with his head on my shoulder. Piper, in true form tonight, wouldn't budge.

"Too full." She stomped her foot. "As stated on the wall on our way up, the weight limit is twenty-one hundred pounds." Her words were robotic. "Assuming an average weight, that is twelve people. Limits protect the occupants. Too full."

My daughter sounded anything but seven. In some ways, her brain was light-years ahead of mine, and in others, it wasn't as mature as her younger brother's.

I sighed. "You and Sam each count as half an average person, and by your standards, even I don't weigh enough to be considered a full person."

"Too full," she repeated.

With a defeated sigh, I gave up.

Seven opportunities to step onto that elevator and a million dirty looks later, we made it down to the car and headed back to our apartment.

By the time I pulled into the lot by our building and parked in my numbered space, I was exhausted. But I lifted Sam out of his seat. Piper, of course, was still awake. On a night like tonight, sleep wouldn't come easily for her. Getting her to settle took routine, and we'd messed that up by going to the game. The Revs' loss only made it worse.

Catching a foul ball should have been exciting. Most kids begged for balls from the players. But in her mind, when I caught that foul ball, I committed treason. I didn't get it. She had a ball from the team she adored. Win or lose, I wished she'd just be happy.

Now, somehow, it was my fault that the Revs hadn't won. The team wasn't to blame, nor was the guy who'd almost let a foul ball hit my three-year-old. Couldn't blame the batter who went down swinging to end the game either. Nope, just me.

She hit me with a glare as she stepped out of the car, those brown eyes hard, then turned away from me.

Sam settled onto my shoulder again, hardly waking even after all the effort it took to get him out of his car seat. He was such a good sleeper. Hell, he was just about the easiest kid on the planet.

"My legs are tired," Piper complained.

"Mine too," I agreed. It had been a long day. And I wasn't even a baseball fan.

The couple who stepped into the elevator with us kept their distance, giving us the side-eye.

Judgment. It was late, and my young kids were up. I got it. I'd been twenty-five once. Back then, I thought I was an expert on so many things, including parenting. My kids would be in bed early. They wouldn't use iPads. They would eat vegetables and behave. I'd raise angels.

Then I had Piper and was almost immediately humbled. It didn't take long to understand that people who didn't have kids had no right to be the judge and jury. This shit was hard. And as much as I wanted to be that perfect mom, the one whose kids went to bed easily and slept well, ate three perfect meals that didn't include sugar, and never went on social media, I lived in the real world.

I did my best.

And today, my half brother had blessed me with extra work.

Not fair, my brain chided.

He'd meant well, but buying tickets to a game he wasn't taking the kids to see himself, on a school day, on a workday, without asking me, meant the activity was more challenge than entertainment. And since I tried my best to be the type of mom who rolled with everything, who was fun and admired for her easygoing nature, I'd agreed to take the kids, even going so far as to tell my brother and my daughter that the plan sounded great. Inside though, misery quickly consumed me.

Which made me feel even shittier. When had I become *this* person? And why? There had been a time when I actually was fun. But that part of me had long ago been buried under a mountain of pressure and responsibility. Now, I was stuck with doing what I needed to do to get through this phase of life.

"The Revs won't have another chance to make the World Series for another 372 days." My daughter was clearly a numbers person.

I shifted Sam, wincing as I used my injured hand to prop him a little higher on my hip. I hadn't truly understood how fast a baseball could travel until I'd put my hand up to save him from being hit with it. It was already swollen.

Once the elevator had stopped on our floor, we headed down the hall to our apartment. I paused outside it, and my heart sank as I took in the slimy substance running down the door. Had someone seriously thrown an egg? Boy, wasn't this a super fun way to end a long day.

"What is that?" Piper asked.

Long ago, I'd learned not to lie to her. She was smarter than me, after all. "Egg."

She cocked her head, her red pigtails wobbling. "Who put egg on the door?"

Likely a random person in the building. I'd lived through more than one big loss for a Boston team. Tonight would be a rough night. All over the city, people would riot. Passion was a big emotion. And the fanatical Revs fans had it in spades. The Revs sticker logo on our door, courtesy of my daughter, had probably made us a target.

"Don't worry," I said as I ushered her in. "I'll clean it up."

Quickly, I changed Sam and got him into bed. The poor kid didn't even open his eyes. Once he was tucked in, I got started getting Piper settled. It took longer than usual, and when I came out and found my phone in the kitchen, I had three missed calls, all from unknown numbers.

For the love of God, please don't let some random website have sold my information to the world.

Two years ago, I'd received endless texts and phone calls for months. Jace had been sure I was hiding something because of all the unknown numbers. At least he was no longer around to make a bad situation worse again.

I sighed. I needed to get over my anger at my ex-husband. He had been trying lately. Jace struggled with Piper, but that didn't mean he didn't love her and Sam. We had to co-parent for the rest of our lives, so letting the past, the lies, the betrayal, the hurt go, was in my best interest. If only it weren't so difficult to put into action.

I set the phone on the counter and opened the fridge. I needed a hard cider after such a long day. As I grasped the bottle, pain shot up my arm.

Yanking my hand back, making the bottle wobble on the shelf of the fridge, I opened and closed my fist. My palm and fingers were already turning purple. My whole hand ached, but I hadn't had time to really focus on it. I probably needed to ice it, but I'd have to clean the door first.

With my left hand, I pulled out the cider and cracked it open. As I sipped, I closed my eyes and relished the cold, crisp flavor. Egg sucked. That slimy shit never came off easily. And I had plenty of experience. Piper had broken plenty in her seven years.

As much as I wished I could collapse in bed and put it off until tomorrow, if I didn't deal with it now, it would eat away the paint, and the last thing I needed was the super yelling at me. We got complaints enough because of Piper's tantrums. Time for some Bounty and good, old-fashioned elbow grease.

I propped the door open and swiped the surface of the door with a dry paper towel first, hoping to remove any excess slime. It did very little, so I stepped back inside and wet a few towels.

Back out in the hall, I got to work, only to be startled by a deep voice behind me.

"If it isn't Boston's newest villain."

Heart thumping, I turned around. Instantly, though, I relaxed. The owner of the voice was my neighbor Trevor. He was propped up against his doorjamb, arms crossed and smirking.

"Villain?" I asked, turning back to the door.

"Did you not go the game tonight in a very tight white button-down and catch the ball that should have been the third out?"

I rolled my eyes. "Ugh, not you too."

Piper had been awful when I'd caught the ball, and half the fans around us had muttered about it. But what was I supposed to do, trust that the frozen baseball player would snap back to reality in time to stop the ball from knocking my son's teeth out? Kyle Bosco was an overpaid, over-sexed, whiny, pretty-boy attention whore. There was no way I'd allow my son's fate to rest in that man's hands.

Trevor came up behind me, crowding my space, and took the wet towel out of my hand. I let him have it and snagged the second one I'd brought out. While he worked on the top half of the door, I kneeled and scrubbed at the bottom half.

Without stopping, I glanced up at the good-looking man looming above me. Trevor was nice enough. A single dad with two preteen girls. I'd probably like him more if women weren't always fawning over him because he took care of his girls every other weekend.

Maybe I was jaded, or just a bitch. But being a parent every other week for forty-eight hours didn't seem worthy of all the praise he received. Yes, it was nice that he loved his girls. But he got a lot of time to himself too.

Me? I got none.

I shut my eyes and took a breath through my nose. I inhaled until my lungs burned, then let it out again. Trevor had been fighting for more parenting time. That was more than admirable. And my situation didn't give me the right to hate on him.

He cleared his throat. "I guess you didn't watch the postgame."

"No, why?" I asked.

He paused his movements and tipped his head, frowning at me. "Streaks put a bull's-eye on your back, babe."

I peered up, making my bun wobble. Quickly, I dropped the paper towel and adjusted my hair. "What?"

"Kyle Bosco"—cringing, he turned his attention back to the door—"otherwise known as Streaks, told all of Boston that you were single-handedly responsible for the Revs' loss."

That wasn't shocking. From what I'd seen over the last couple of years, the guy never took responsibility for a bad play. Why would he suddenly change his ways now?

Trevor shook his head. "The guy's an ass."

I didn't necessarily disagree, despite how much my daughter loved the baseball star who danced around the field and scored runs.

I lifted a shoulder. "He wasn't catching it. Everyone there could see that." Unconcerned about a grown man's temper tantrum, I rubbed at one last smear of egg and then pushed to my feet.

"I hope you're right." Trevor stepped back, frowning, and handed me his towel. "If you need anything, call me."

"Thanks." With a smile, I stepped inside.

Trevor leaned on the doorjamb again, assessing me. "You doing anything this weekend? Maybe we could grab a drink."

Trevor and I had this conversation every other weekend. Though Jace had our kids every other Friday night, our free nights never lined up. Honestly, even if they did, I didn't have the energy. I barely kept up as it was.

"Trevor. There have got to be eighty gazillion women from those apps of yours lining up to have a drink with you."

He chuckled. "I'd still like to buy one for you."

I rolled my eyes. There was absolutely no chemistry there, but I tried to be flattered by his persistence. "I have the kids this weekend."

"Too bad." He tapped the doorframe with his knuckles and pushed back. "Call me if you need anything," he said again.

With a nod, I closed the door quietly and exhaled. I needed a solid ten minutes to relax before I crawled into bed. I tossed the gross egg-covered paper towel into the trash, then snagged my cider and phone from the counter. At least the kids hadn't had time to destroy the apartment today. Since I didn't have that mess to clean up, I sank onto the small sofa in the living room and took another sip of my drink.

My phone vibrated on the cushion beside me. Another unknown number. For fuck's sake. I slid my thumb over the screen to answer, intending to tell them to take me off their list.

"I'm not interested in whatever you're selling."

A female chuckled, her laugh sharp. "I'm not interested in it either, but this is what I'm paid to do. Is this Harper Wallace?"

I took another sip of my cider and swallowed back my nerves with it. "Maybe."

"This is Hannah Erickson. I'm the head of public relations for the Boston Revs. I can understand if you're upset with us. I know I am. Bosco and Quinn are going to drive me to search for a new job," she huffed. "Anyway, I'd love if you could give me two minutes of your time."

My heart leapt into my throat. Why were the Revs calling me? "How did you get my number?"

Hannah sighed, making the phone line crackle. "When Beckett Langfield wants something, he gets it. I've learned not to ask questions."

Okay.

"I know it's late, but I want to apologize for Mr. Bosco's statement. Please know he wasn't speaking for the Revs organization."

I pressed my lips together and hummed. What the hell did this guy say that warranted a call from the head of PR for a professional team? "Right."

"I have a plan to make this better for everyone, so hear me out. This is what I'm thinking…"

I listened as she explained, and although I was tempted to tell her I had no interest in helping the Revs out, I couldn't say no. This would make Piper's year. So, ridiculously, I agreed to swing by Lang Field the next day.

KYLE
4

"YOUR FAVORITE TREAT. S'mores coffee with the extra whip,"
Cameron said, his far too chipper voice echoing around my dark room.

"No," I muttered into the pillow. Last night, my dream of making it
to the World Series had ended. The last thing I wanted to do was face
the light of day, especially this early. I didn't need a clock to know that
I hadn't been asleep for six hours yet.

"I get that it was supposed to be a sleep-in day, but Hannah rang,
and when that girl calls, I answer."

"Time to learn to hit the red *Ignore* button." I pulled the thick goose-
down comforter over my head.

"Time to learn to control the word vomit." He was too damn
cheerful.

A high-pitched beep pierced my skull, and then the darkness under
the blankets wasn't so dark anymore. The asshole had opened my
shades. Whatever the fuck time it was, it was too early. My alarm was
set for nine, and it hadn't chirped yet. Cam could fuck right off. I was
tired. I'd fallen into bed sometime around three. Maybe four. Either
way, it was still too damn early for my assistant to be yapping at me.

"You're lucky it was Hannah and not your mother. I'm surprised she's not blowing up your phone and lecturing you for acting like a jerk."

I winced. If not for the fact that she and her best friend were on a cruise I'd sent them on, she would be screeching in my ear. "Lucky me," I muttered.

The blankets were yanked away, and cool air washed over me. "Have a cup of the nectar of the gods. Then you'll feel more like hearing me sing."

I blinked at the brightness, wearing a scowl. I had no interest in being tortured with Cam's singing, but the coffee he'd brought could never be the worst part of my day.

"You get this one fun cup. After, you'll have to pretend to love dark roast, no whip, no sugar." The fucker had a point. Only he knew I wanted all the fun shit. The guys would be relentless if they knew I preferred coffee that tasted more like a milkshake.

"Fine." I reached for the coffee, my eyes still mostly closed. *He better not be lying.* The warm cardboard settling against my palm was a momentary relief. "Why are you here?" Propped up on one elbow, I lifted the cup to my mouth. I tried to keep my scowl going while the burst of yummy goodness hit my tongue, but as a plastic bag hit the side of my head, I couldn't stop it anymore. "*Aw,* you brought M&M's."

"My little man always smiles for the baseball-colored candy."

I might love it, but Cam was the one who bulk ordered them in the baseball design. He thought himself a comedian.

"I'm not ten," I grumbled, even as I tore open the pack and dumped a few into my palm. One at a time, I tossed them into the air and caught them in my mouth.

"Says the man-child having whipped cream and chocolate for breakfast."

He palmed my head, but before he could mess with my hair, I reeled back and batted at his hand.

"Don't touch the hair."

"You just woke up. How do you not have bedhead?"

"It's a gift." I tossed another candy into the air. "What's with the candy and whipped cream? Are you here to bribe me?"

He propped himself up against my dresser, his own coffee sitting on its surface next to his hip. "Not me, man. Hannah."

Eyes closed, I groaned. She hadn't been thrilled with the statement I gave last night. And in the morning light, there was no way I could deny that I'd been an asshole. No one should be surprised by that, though. Least of all Hannah. I said dumb shit all the time.

"Moan all you want as long as you're getting your ass out of bed and getting dressed. Car service will be here in"—he glanced at the silver watch on his wrist—"less than twenty."

"Fucker," I mumbled. No wonder he was dressed up. Normally, Cam drove me around in my Escalade, but when he wanted to make sure I got my ass in gear, he'd call the Revs car service. The asshole knew that if the car was on the way, I wouldn't say no.

"It's why you pay me the big bucks." Smirking, he lifted his coffee into the air, then strode out of my room.

I tossed the covers off my legs and forced myself up. Fuck, I wanted to curse Cam again, but honestly, I couldn't do life without the guy. I'd hired him as my assistant a few years ago, but since then, he'd become one of my best friends. Now he was my roommate, and he managed most aspects of my life. As annoying as he was, I couldn't kick him to the curb. Something I reminded myself the entire way to the stadium as he laughed while showing me clip after clip of people calling me an asshole.

"Bosco." Hannah snapped the second my ass hit the chair.

Head bowed, I rubbed my temples.

"Are you still drunk?"

"No." I wasn't drunk to begin with. I nursed beers and a bad attitude until I finally gave up and bowed out at the second club. "If you want to harp on someone, call Jasper. When I left the VIP area of Dreads, the kid was ten seconds away from pulling his dick out."

Hannah gritted her teeth. "He'll get his turn. But shockingly, our first baseman isn't my biggest issue today."

I rolled my eyes. Most of the media was bashing my statement. Not in Boston, though. Revs fans had my back. But around the rest of the sports world, as Cam had so cheerfully pointed out in the car on the way over, I was being called a jack wad. I got it. No one wanted some cute little redheaded kid to get smacked in the face. Even I could see that would have been a shit show.

Hannah slammed her hands onto her desk. "Are you even listening?"

I nodded, even though that wasn't entirely true.

"Look at this." She pointed a black remote at the screen behind me and another talking head appeared, throwing me and the Revs under the bus for once again showing how much we hated kids.

"It's like I live in freaking *Groundhog Day*," Hannah said. "For the love of God, how many times can this team show the world that they hate kids and birds and dogs, and act like assholes?"

I blinked.

"Well?" she asked, brows lifted into her hairline.

"That was a question for me?" I cocked my head. "I think Jasper's the real issue. Or maybe Tristian."

She scowled. "Bosco," she said through gritted teeth.

No one liked Tristian Jenner. We'd all been hoping that Miller and Langfield would trade the left fielder.

She moved around the desk to stand in front of me and crossed her arms. "The family is coming here."

"Family?" I asked.

"Yes, the poor woman you turned all of Boston against. And her kids."

I swallowed past the lump in my throat. Shit. I had to face this woman? Today? "Why?"

Her eyes narrowed. "To fix the situation. Asher and Zara are coming to help." Asher, the Revs' catcher, and his wife were not only well-known to most of the country, but they were two of the most outgoing people I'd ever met. It made sense that Hannah would invite them to be the friendly faces in the group. "And bringing their kids, since they're close in age to Sam and Piper."

The names tickled something in the back of my mind. "Who?"

She closed her eyes and lifted her head for a moment. After a long breath out, she zeroed in on me. "The kids who almost got their teeth knocked out." Typical Hannah, bringing all the drama.

I slumped in my seat, scowling. "Never would have happened."

"Not how it looks when you watch the tape."

I fought back a wince. I'd seen replays a few times at this point. Though it stung to admit it to myself, she might be right.

"Avery and Chris are picking up Puff and bringing him over."

That lifted my mood a fraction. It was hard not to love our favorite feathered friend. Although when Damiano struck the bird with a pitch, it had seemed like a disaster, now we all agreed we couldn't do without the little puffin in our lives.

"Emerson and Gianna are coming too."

"Of course you want Bambi. You're filming this shit, aren't you?" I chuckled. Our third baseman always put on a good show. "Sounds like you don't need me."

"This is not a joke." She pinched the bridge of her nose. "You'll be there. Not to be the fun or entertainment for the kids, but to apologize. You'll *grovel* if you need to."

My spine snapped straight as annoyance burned in my veins. "Like hell I will."

"You will."

Gripping the armrests on either side of me, I scowled at her. She glared right back, eyes hard, like she wasn't at all intimidated by me. She probably wasn't. The girl had grit and an iron will. But I didn't back down.

This moment had the potential to turn into the world's longest staring contest, but a knock behind me broke the tension and had us both turning.

"Sorry, Hannah, babe, but I need my little man a minute." Cam stepped into the room. His charming-as-fuck act even got a smile out of our PR boss woman.

"Maybe you can talk some sense into him." Her tone with Cam was nothing like the verbal daggers she had been hurtling my way.

"That would be a first," Cam joked. His light expression dropped quickly as he held out his phone. "It's JJ."

My stomach sank. I had ignored two calls from him already.

"This is a real thing." Cam cocked a blond brow.

His tone instantly had me on edge. "Is everyone okay?" If something had happened to my aunt, JJ would be losing his shit.

Slowly, Cam nodded, pushing the phone my way.

I took it hesitantly and swallowed past the lump in my throat. "Sup man?"

"You promised me." JJ's tone had a bite I didn't understand.

I ran my hand through my hair. "I have no idea what we're talking about." I promised him a lot of shit. And I always followed through. He was my boy, and I'd do anything for him. Still, I had no idea what he meant.

"You promised you'd help me with the Harper stuff. I know I fucked up, and she got the shit end of the deal, but you promised you were going to *help* me."

I rolled my eyes. What the hell had happened this time? "Yeah, and I will. I told you that as soon as the season was over, we'd smooth stuff over."

"So why in the name of God did you make her the target of the entire city's wrath?"

My heart stopped, and ice ran through my veins. I'd put a target on someone, sure, but that couldn't be who JJ was talking about. "What?"

"White shirt, red-haired devil, *she hopefully knows better than to show her face in Boston again.*"

I swallowed. I'd seen the clip enough to know he was dramatizing my words a hair, but the point was the same. "Harper...*Your Harper*..." I shook my head. No way fate would do this to me. It wasn't possible. "She was the one who caught my foul ball?"

"Yes. And now, because of you, the kids got kicked out of day care, people are egging her apartment door, and some dickhead let the air out of her tires."

Fuck me. I sighed.

"You need to fix this."

I nodded like a tool bag, even though he couldn't see me.

Cam cleared his throat, garnering my attention. With just a glance at his face, it was clear to me that he knew the story already. With his lips pressed in a firm line, he crossed his arms over his chest.

"Well?" he mouthed at me. "What are you doing about this shit show?"

I wanted to say *nothing*. Two minutes ago, I'd told Hannah that this wasn't my problem. But I loved JJ, and I had promised to help with Harper. Though I couldn't have guessed that she'd ruin my World Series run when I said it.

Still, I turned to Hannah, and through gritted teeth, I said, "Harper and the kids are coming over to Lang Field today. Hannah has a plan. I'm…" I cleared my throat. "I'm apologizing." The phrase tasted like acid on my tongue, and it took a concerted effort to keep myself from grimacing. "We'll fix everything."

Hannah's smug smile made me detest the words leaving my lips all the more, but I didn't have a choice. I'd made a promise, and now I had to keep it.

Harper
5

"WAIT A SECOND, PIPER." I snagged one booster seat from the back of Trevor's car and set it on the ground beside me, then I grabbed the other, all while I kept my hand locked around Sam's wrist to ensure he stayed at my side. The pain that still throbbed in my bruised hand shot up my arm, but I didn't let go. I only needed another second. "Thanks, Trevor." I smiled at my neighbor, who was perched in the driver's seat.

Asking for help had not been on my bingo card this morning, but desperation had me begging him for a ride to Lang Field. Honestly, I should have called Hannah and told her we couldn't make it, but if there was any hope of Hannah's plan working, then we needed to be here.

Last night I thought Piper and Trevor were overreacting about the foul ball thing. But it was very clear now that Boston was madder at me than even Piper was.

"Want me to come in with you?" His offer was sincere, but he'd already had to get up early and drive across town.

"We. Are. Late." Piper's voice was laced with desperation as she stomped her little foot with each word. She was hanging on by a thread.

Being behind schedule was difficult for her. I got that. But getting here hadn't been easy. I worked hard to understand her brain, but I was also exhausted. This morning, I found my car covered in spray paint with deflated tires. Both Ubers I scheduled left without us when they discovered that I was the passenger. It was still early, yet I was already done.

"We'll be inside in two minutes," I assured her, then turned back to Trevor. "We're good. Thanks again."

He nodded, his mouth turned down in a concerned frown. "Call if you need a ride home."

I couldn't think that far ahead at this point. I just wanted to get through this.

"Ms. Wallace?"

I turned at the sound of the female's voice and was greeted by a gorgeous brunette sporting sky-high heels with the red bottoms.

"Hannah?" I asked.

The smile she gave me was genuine. "Thanks for coming. Again, we would have sent a car."

She'd told me that when I called to let her know we were running behind. She'd even offered to have one of the players, Emerson, I think, stop on his way. But the fanfare was all too much. Hannah tipped her head my way, and a big man dressed in a polo that said *security* stepped forward and took the booster seats from me.

"We'll hang on to those for you," he assured me.

Hannah crouched so she was at eye level with my daughter. "You must be Piper."

Piper stared over the woman's shoulder. "Last night there were thirty-nine thousand people here. It was the largest crowd Lang Field has had in the twenty-six years it has been open. The added standing room near the outfield was a wise choice."

Hannah's blue eyes flicked to me for a beat before refocusing. "You're a smart girl."

My daughter blinked at the stadium. "Can we go in? We are late."

"I hungry," Sam said. Although he'd had toast, a banana, two drinkable yogurts, and a scrambled egg since he'd woken up four hours ago, my almost four-year-old was always ravenous.

Hannah gave Sam a soft smile. "We have fruit and bagels set up in the team room."

My son's eyes widened when he realized Hannah was speaking to him, and he pressed his face into my hip, hiding.

I smoothed his soft red hair, my heart warming. He was shy, especially with unfamiliar adults. Day care been good for him, and his apprehension when kids were around had lessened, but now that the kids were no longer welcome there, I was pretty certain I'd have to bring him to work and keep him entertained in my office. Although he would love being with me all the time again, it would only set back the progress we'd made with his separation issues.

I bent and lifted Sam into my arms, silently reassuring him that I wouldn't leave him. His little body relaxed a fraction in my hold.

Hannah gave me a sheepish smile, surely realizing that her attention had made Sam uncomfortable, and focused again on Piper. "You're right on time. We're just waiting on Christian Damiano. He had to stop on his way and pick up a friend. He's bringing Puff to play. Did you know that we're the only major league team to ever have a puffin?"

"Puff is an Atlantic puffin," Piper said. "They are common in the northern Atlantic coastal regions. Westman Island lighthouse currently holds the record for the most puffins. About fifty-six thousand puffins were on that island at once. Not just one, like in Lang Field."

Hannah tilted her head and glanced at me, causing Sam to bury his face in my neck and rub his freckled nose against my collarbone.

"But you get to see one up close and personal here, Pipe." I sighed.

The poor woman was struggling to understand how to interact with my daughter. Most people did, so I couldn't hold that against her.

"Lang Field holds the record for the most no-hitters. Sixteen total. Kyle Bosco holds the record for most runs scored at Lang Field. He's been with the team for five seasons, and he has already scored 485 runs at home. Emerson Knight beat him this season with 113 runs."

"I think you know more about the team than I do," Hannah said.

Piper only blinked, gaze averted.

"She loves the stats," I said.

"Can we go in now?" Piper asked.

Hannah led the way, talking to Piper over her shoulder. "I hope you're excited to meet the players. We have Damiano and Puff, along with Knight, Price, and Bosco coming to hang out."

I'd heard the names. How could I not? My daughter spit out facts about them on the regular. But other than Kyle Bosco, whose poster hung above her bed, I couldn't pick any of them out of a lineup. And I couldn't say I was thrilled at the idea of the bird. He was adorable in the pictures and videos that Piper had watched eight hundred thousand times, but I didn't want to pass on my irrational fear of birds to my kids. So I tried to avoid situations where I'd be near them.

"How does that sound?" When Piper said nothing, Hannah glanced over her shoulder again, giving me a genuine smile. "Ready to go in? I promise everyone is happy you're here."

I held back a snort. I doubted any of these baseball players cared that we were here. But hopefully Hannah's footage of us together would put a stop to all the hate.

Piper peered from side to side as we walked through the wrought-iron gates to enter Lang Field. Through the brick archways, we made our way into the stadium. The place was eerily quiet without the people.

When Piper took off running toward the wall of balls, I hollered for her to stop. But she paid me no mind.

"It's okay," Hannah assured me, hurrying after her. "Everyone gets excited to see the signed balls."

With Sam in my arms, I struggled to keep up. At almost fifty pounds, he was really getting too big to be carried like this. But I couldn't deny him. It often felt like he'd gotten the short end of the stick. While Piper required a great deal of attention, Sam was a go-with-the-flow kind of kid. Unfortunately, that meant he didn't always get the attention he deserved. So if he wanted to be carried, then I'd do it for as long as I could.

Piper stopped toward the end of the wall and pressed one little finger to the glass.

"Kyle Bosco, number 29. Ball number 857."

"We saw these yesterday," Sam mumbled, giving me a small frown.

"We had to come back because Mom ruined the game. She has to say she's sorry to the team." Piper didn't even look at us.

That wasn't at all what I'd told her, but she refused to believe a word I'd said about not ruining the game. So I'd finally just sighed and let it go.

Hannah's eyes narrowed, but I waved her off. I didn't want a fight.

"How many balls are there on this wall?" I asked.

Piper moved to the row where the last two were placed. "Asher Price, number 5. Ball 869. Jasper Quinn, number 18. Ball 870."

"You might be better at Revs trivia than anyone I've ever met." Hannah smiled at my daughter.

Piper blinked at the glass and shifted back two rows of balls to number 857. "Kyle Bosco's favorite game is trivia."

Hannah nodded. "Want to go down and meet him?"

Piper turned and tilted her head up. Rather than focusing on Hannah's face, she looked at a spot somewhere near the neckline of her black fitted dress. "Yes."

Rather than gushing with excitement at the idea of meeting their favorite athlete like many kids would, my daughter responded with a single succinct word.

Hannah lifted a brow, as if in anticipation of that excitement. But after a moment, she gave Piper a nod and led us toward a heavy door that opened to a set of stairs. At the bottom was another hallway. We walked in silence down the long cinderblock tunnel that took us deep into the heart of the stadium. Clearly, Hannah had given up on making small talk with my daughter.

A set of double doors stood open, leading to a bright room. The space was filled with couches and tables and close to twenty people. Most were adults, but I spotted a child here and there. The group was milling about, and a few people hovered around the table filled with muffins, bagels, fruits, and other pastries.

"Can I have strawberries?" Sam straightened in my arms, his eyes locked on the massive bowl of his favorite fruit.

"One second," I assured him.

Patience wearing thin, he squirmed in my arms, so I set him down at the threshold, then stepped into the room.

Multiple sets of eyes landed on us as the noise in the room quieted to a hush.

"We've all been expecting Harper. There's no reason to make the poor woman more uncomfortable than Kyle already has." A light voice cut through the silence, the woman's British accent slight. She was petite, and a young boy kept close to her side as she moved my way. "I'm Zara Price, and this is my son Greyson." She gave Sam a small smile. "Greyson also loves strawberries."

"Unless they're mixed with bananas." Greyson yanked on Sam's arm playfully. "Don't call me Greyson. Just Grey. Let's go eat the strawberries before Dad and his friends take them all."

Sam tilted his head back, looking up at me, eyes wide.

I nodded. "I'm not going anywhere. You'll be able to see me from the table."

Hesitantly looking over his shoulder twice, he allowed Greyson to drag him toward the food setup.

"Sorry, Grey is his father's son. There isn't a shy bone in his body. He tends to forget some people are nervous in new places." As much as she claimed her husband was outgoing, it was clear she was as well. "We're all glad you're here."

"I'm going to make sure everything is set on the field," Hannah said, taking a step away from us. "And deal with Jasper. I'll be back."

Over at the table, Greyson scooped up the bowl of strawberries. Then he disappeared under the tablecloth. A moment later, with one more look at me, Sam joined him.

My heart clenched. I'd love for him to find a friend. Although we'd never see these people again after today. Hannah had invited us for breakfast and mentioned a few photos on the grass with some of the players. She'd promised that the team would make a statement, and with any luck, it would deflect the wrath of Boston. Then my kids and I could live in peace again.

"We were fourteen minutes late today." Piper was focused on a nearby table, where three men stood. The only one I could name was Kyle Bosco. Baseball getup or not, I'd recognize him. He had broad shoulders and a perfect head of dirty blond hair with natural high-lights. His jaw was too chiseled for its own good, and he was impos-sibly good-looking. It was annoying. Piper had loved Streaks since she first discovered baseball, and in all that time, I'd secretly hoped she'd move on from him. Because the guy oozed southern boy charm, and no matter how much I pretended he didn't affect me, I couldn't help but get caught up in his good looks.

My mother had always warned me to be careful of the southern boys. She said they could charm a girl right into a broken heart. And she would know.

I forced my attention to another blond man who was a few inches taller than Kyle. He stood beside him, dressed in a gray shirt and jeans, rather than a Revs jersey and baseball pants. On Kyle's other side, a man with a 21 on the back of his pin-striped jersey stood.

"Yes, well…" Zara shrugged. "I hate to admit it, but I'm known for being late."

"So is Mom." Piper zeroed in on Zara's peach-colored shirt. Piper was only seven, but she came up to just below the tiny woman's shoul-der. "I don't like it."

"It drives Asher batty too."

"Asher Price. Number 5. Traded to the Revs from Los Angeles this season. Batting average .301 during the regular season. But in the play-offs, he averaged .420. Almost high enough to set a record."

"Aren't you a smarty pants?" Zara smiled.

Piper shook her head. "I have high-functioning ASD."

My heart clenched at her toneless words.

"That doesn't mean you're not smart."

The deep voice startled me, and when I looked up from my daugh-ter, I found a pair of warm brown eyes focused not on my girl, but on me. I hadn't seen him come our way, but now he stood just two steps away. And once again, meeting his eyes caused my stomach to flip. It was the same sensation that had hit me last night. I'd barely shaken it off in time to stop the ball from hitting Sam in the face.

I clenched my fists at my sides, almost successfully keeping myself from wincing at the pain in my hand as I did. Annoyance ran through me as I continued to assess this man. Why the hell did my body have such terrible taste in men? My only comfort was knowing, without a doubt, that my brain wasn't so dumb anymore. Jace had taught me that lesson.

Kyle shifted one step closer. "Hi. I'm—"

"Kyle Bosco," my daughter interrupted as she took two steps back. "Number 29. Right fielder for the Boston Revs, with a seasonal batting average of .225. One hundred sixty-five runs, twenty-eight home runs, fourteen assists. It was not your best."

Light brown eyes narrowing, he dropped to one knee. Adults did that a lot to help kids feel comfortable and on the same level. In Piper's case, it wouldn't encourage eye contact. In fact, she took another step back and turned her body slightly in response to the move.

Unfazed by her reaction, Kyle went on. "It also wasn't my worst season."

Piper nodded. "Your second season with the Revs was your worst."

My heart lurched at her comment, but Kyle just tossed his head back and laughed.

"Do you know everyone's stats, or am I just your favorite?"

"Yes." Piper focused on a spot on the other side of the room. "I like the whole team."

"You excited to go out onto the field and run bases?" Kyle asked.

Though Piper nodded, I doubted that she'd actually do it. She knew the infield was sand, but I wasn't sure she'd really thought about it. My daughter had aversions to several textures, sand being one of them. So as much as she might want to run the bases with her favorite athletes, I couldn't imagine her forcing herself to actually do it.

Braced for the meltdown that could very well cause—I always braced for the next meltdown—I said, "We'll see when the time comes."

I tried not to put any pressure on her. The poor girl already put too much on herself. I had no doubt she'd been in sensory overload before we left the stadium last night, and that was without coming into contact with sand.

Kyle glared at me. "Leaving early?"

"We are leaving at two o'clock," my daughter said.

Hannah had mentioned it to me, so I had told Piper to give her a

THE FOUL OUT   41

sense of security, and that absolutely locked us into a schedule in a way most people wouldn't understand. Leaving at 1:50 wouldn't do. Neither would 2:15.

I pulled my shoulders back. "We'll leave at two," I reassured Piper so she didn't get upset. "But the bases might not be her thing."

Kyle opened his mouth, as if to argue. But he quickly snapped it closed again. He pushed to his feet and angled in so Piper couldn't hear. "Give her a chance to do it." His gravelly voice felt like sandpaper. "She might surprise you."

As he stepped back, I fought the urge to slam my hands to hips. My hand ached enough as it was. Instead, I glowered at the bossy man. He didn't have the first clue what he was talking about. Before I could formulate a retort, a large hand came up and whacked him in the back of the head, making his hair fly.

Kyle whirled around, smoothing his blond locks to their former perfection. "What the heck, Cam?"

"Don't be an asshole," the man in the gray shirt replied.

"Bad word," Piper chided without looking at the new addition. "And you smell."

Kyle barked out a laugh, the sound so harsh that Piper and I startled.

"Piper." My face heated. She hated the smell of cologne or perfume, no matter what the scent. But her accusation made it seem so much worse. This man couldn't have known.

"She's not wrong," Kyle said when he finally stopped chuckling. "I always tell you to go lighter on the cologne."

With a sigh, the man turned to me. "I'm Cameron, Mr. Bosco's very patient assistant. And I'm sorry for my odor."

"You do not smell." I shot Piper a warning look.

She gave me a stink face before turning away.

I took Cameron's outstretched hand. "Harper Wallace."

"I know." He gave me a rueful smile. "You're all we've talked about today."

Irritation shot through me. "You and all of Boston."

Kyle chuckled again, but when Cameron and I shot him matching glares, he turned back to Piper. "Want to get away from the smell and come meet my friends? I promise they're less crabby than these two. You can give them details about their worst seasons too."

Piper tipped her chin up, her eyes tracking up to his face for an instant, then moving back to a spot on his chest, and nodded.

Warily, I kept my eye on her as Kyle Bosco led her over to where a few of his teammates were chatting. My heart pounded, urging me to chase them down and keep Piper close, in fear that they were still holding a grudge and would take it out on her.

"He was an idiot yesterday, but he's not a total jerk," Cam said, rocking back on his heels.

"My car tells a different story." I lowered my head and shook it. The strange fear turned into dread when I cataloged all the issues I had to deal with. Four tires, along with possible damage to the rims, and the paint. I groaned. I didn't have the time or money for that.

"That's actually on my to-do list."

Frowning, I assessed him. "My car is on your to-do list?"

Cam nodded. But that didn't make any sense.

"Where are the boys?" Zara asked, appearing at my side.

I waved a hand at the spread of food on the tables. "Under the blue tablecloth. With the bowl of berries."

"Keen eye." With a smirk, she strode over and lifted the cloth. Both boys looked up with very red smiles. "I think Grey found a new mate."

I swiped a napkin off the table and crouched in front of Sam. "Why is my car on your to-do list, Cameron?" I asked as I finished wiping the berry juice from my son's mouth.

"Oh, that's on me," Zara said. "I forgot to mention that Hannah, the lovely woman, gave me a job." Zara beamed as she straightened from cleaning Grey's mouth too. "Although I adore this little monster and his sister, I've recently realized how much I truly miss my work. I suppose I lost myself a bit over the years, and now I finally have the opportunity to rediscover my purpose."

That resonated a bit too well with me. The lost part, at least. At the moment, I had no time to even think about finding myself again. I hardly had time to keep up with day-to-day life, let alone rediscover my passions.

"I feel that." Only...what did my car have to do with Zara's job? "Are you a mechanic?"

A bubble of a laugh burst from her. "Oh, no, darling. I'm a fixer. Hannah hired me. So I'm going to take care of the damage done by Kyle's idiotic comment, and then..." She beamed at me. "Brace yourself, because it's my mission to ensure that, by the end of the week, Boston adores you."

I blinked. What the hell had I gotten into?

KYLE
6

"SINCE YOU ALREADY HAVE MY jersey, do you want the blue one? I could sign it."

I held up a blue jersey with the number 29 printed on the back. On the rack in front of us was the pin-striped version in a kids' size.

We'd been in the Revs store for about ten minutes, and Piper was struggling to decide what item she'd like. The boys were getting antsy, so Asher and Zara had taken them, along with their daughter, Clara, over to play with a bin of bouncy balls.

With every minute that passed, Piper was getting more agitated. Picking any item from the store could be fun, but for a kid like Piper, it was an overwhelming task. Especially in a bright space like this. The lighting was specifically set up to draw attention to multiple areas. For someone with sensory processing issues, this place was too bright, too loud, too overwhelming. If I'd asked Hannah what the plan was ahead of time, I could have made adjustments. But I had been pouting over a foul ball instead of focusing on what really mattered. Not that I'd known we'd have issues.

It wasn't until I looked across the room to see the little redhead with pigtail braids nervously blinking over and over that, with my background, I understood. My heart cracked as I took her in. And boy, had I wanted to give the poor kid a hug when she claimed she wasn't smart. An autism diagnosis didn't negate a child's intelligence. It didn't rule out anything completely. JJ had mentioned that Piper loved the Revs, so I'd expected an excited kid. He'd always said she had some issues, but he'd never elaborated, and I'd never asked.

Now, for someone like me, it was abundantly clear. And rushing her in this situation would only cause her to stress more. As long as Hannah didn't storm in, asking what was taking so long, I could be patient.

Hannah had a plan, though. She was geared up to take pictures and videos of us all laughing together while eating breakfast. She'd bribe the kids with Revs gear—that's what this stop in the store was about—then we'd head up to the field, where she'd take more pictures and videos of us dicking around. At the end of the day, I was to drive Harper and the kids home and get footage of me with Harper and the kids around their apartment. I'd post. The Revs would post. Then Zara would release the photos to her sources and change the narrative. That, supposedly, would make the world believe that rather than hating Harper, I'd befriended her. Stupid dumb shit.

Regardless, if Hannah rushed in here, it'd only cause more stress for Piper.

Normally, I'd send Cam to deal with the head of PR, but he'd bowed out before we finished breakfast in the team room so he could make it to a meeting.

"Mom says no signed clothes." Her slight pout reminded me of JJ. She looked so much like him. Sam too, especially in the eyes. They were the same brown color mixed with that mustardy yellow. "If it's signed, we can't wash it, and Mom has rules about washing clothes every day."

I was learning that Piper's mom had a lot of rules. The woman was so uptight. Though her constant state of clench might be why her ass looked so good in those black leggings. I shouldn't be noticing things like that, but each time she stormed away, my eyes were drawn to her perfect ass.

"If you're okay with never wearing the jersey, Mr. Bosco can sign it."

"Kyle," I corrected. Again.

Harper had a thing about the kids calling me "mister." It didn't seem right, given the situation. A situation I'd have to explain to Harper at some point. But that could wait. It was clear with every glare she shot my way that she disliked me. Telling her who I was, to her, to JJ wouldn't help that situation.

If my life wasn't consumed by baseball for ten months out of the year, and I hadn't been a selfish prick when JJ's life kinda imploded, there would be nothing to explain. I would know these people already. Hell, I should have known them long before everything went wrong. I *should* be Kyle to them.

In high school and college, when JJ and I played together, he'd easily been my best friend. When I was drafted and he wasn't, we'd drifted. Especially since I'd spent eight years in California. The space I'd created between my former life and the freedom I'd found since being drafted may have been a bit much, and I'd held on to it too hard. And definitely for too long. Even when he got married, I'd kept that distance. It had been in the middle of the season, and I'd missed the wedding.

When his dad died, it had hit me just how far we'd drifted. That's when I decided to make an effort with texts and phone calls. We'd seen each other more in the last year than in the ten before it, and I'd told myself I'd be even more involved once the season ended. That was why I'd promised to help with Harper and the kids.

"I'm not sure." Piper blinked rapidly as she worried her bottom lip.

I wanted to tell her she could have one of everything. That seemed fair. But crabby pants had been clear the kids could each choose *one* thing. I was doing my best to keep my promise to JJ, to be a good guy, but this damn woman was making it hard.

"How about we get Mom set up while you decide?" I suggested, hoping to take some pressure off Piper.

I shuffled over to the women's section and perused a rack. The kids had both shown up in Revs gear. Piper in my jersey and Sam in a gray Revs T-shirt. But Harper wasn't sporting the Revs blue. Just like last night, there was no outward indication that she was a fan of America's pastime. I swiped a medium jersey from the rack and undid the top two buttons.

"What are you doing?" Harper groused as I stalked toward her. Her lips were set in the same firm line they'd been in since she'd walked into the team room.

Between that and the perma-scowl, it was beyond clear that she was still upset with me. My job today was to fix that. If she'd only loosen up a bit and give me the chance.

As I approached her, I held the shirt up. She took a step back, but before she could get away, I yanked it over her head.

She sputtered and squirmed, clearly shocked, despite my obvious intention when I stepped up to her. What else could I have been doing with the jersey? I stepped back, and as I did, she struggled with the garment, fighting the fabric like it was on fire.

"If you put your arms through the holes, you'd be able to move," I said, choking back a laugh at her ridiculous need to free herself of her cotton confines.

"I'm not wearing *your* number." She stopped fighting then, snapping straight to glare at me.

I probably should have been offended, but it was hard to pull off when she looked so cute. Her auburn hair was falling out of the messy bun on the top of her head, and a scowl dusted with freckles adorned her face.

With a smirk, I pulled a pen from the center of one of the displays, pressed down on the end with a *click*, and closed in on her again.

"What are you doing?" she huffed as she wrestled with the sleeves of her jersey.

"Claiming what's mine," I teased as I pressed my pen against her shoulder. Years of practice meant I'd marked the back of the jersey with my name before she could balk.

I was stepping back when she went ramrod straight and fired visual daggers at me, her eyes sparking with anger. "I am not yours."

"But your shirt is, Crabby." Grinning, I clicked the pen again.

Her scowl deepened, and she spun, her arm brushing against my chest. An electric spark shot down my spine at the contact. For one second, I desperately wanted to touch her again. But looking into her amber eyes, I remembered exactly who she was. And I forced her back into the box labeled *not allowed*.

"Stop calling me that," she snapped.

"Then lighten up." I smirked.

"You don't understand anything," she huffed, fisting her hands at her sides. She tried to hide her pain, but she tamped down on the wince a moment too late. It was the third time I'd seen her do that.

"I want a sweatshirt," Piper announced.

Thankful for the distraction from the fiery woman giving me a run for my money, I turned to the little girl.

She pointed at a blue shirt with a circular Revs logo. "That one."

Dropping the pen back into its holder, I strode over to her. "This one?" I asked as I snagged the garment from where it hung high on a rack.

She nodded.

"Does it have a tag?" Harper, forgetting about my jersey, focused on Piper for a moment before scanning the store to check on her other child. Damn. This woman was more alert than any person I'd met, and that was saying a lot, since I played a professional sport. She was constantly waiting for one of her kids to explode. It must have been exhausting.

"No tag. No hood. It's soft inside," I assured Piper as I handed the shirt to her. She tilted her head and almost made eye contact, but rather than focusing on my face, she let her attention wander to the wall across the room. "Hey, guys," I said, turning. "We're done."

"Yes!" Asher called, slamming his fist into the air. "To the field." With that, he ran for the door.

"To infinity and beyond," Grey yelled, fist in the air as he chased after his dad.

"Yes!" Sam cheered, taking off too.

"They are so cringe." Clara, Asher's eight-year-old, rolled her eyes.

Laughing, Zara wrapped her arm around her daughter's shoulders and dragged her out of the store. Harper watched them until they disappeared, the look on her face one I could have sworn was longing. But when she turned to her daughter, her expression was neutral.

"Come on, Piper." She stepped up to the little girl, careful to keep several inches of space between them, and guided her from the room.

With a nod at the security guard who'd let us in, I followed them.

Although the group in front of us chattered as we moved through the stadium, voices high-pitched and echoing around the high ceilings and concrete walls, neither Harper nor Piper spoke a word. Each one was radiating anxiety so intense it thickened the air around us.

We'd hardly made it up to the dugout steps before Hannah was there.

She grinned, her eyes flashing. "I love that you're in his jersey."

Harper glanced down, eyes wide, like she was surprised to find that she still was sporting the pinstripes.

"Filming this is going to be perfect," Hannah said. "Couldn't have asked for a nicer fall day, either. Sixty and sunny? I'll take it. Everyone is here." She waved, pointing out Emerson and Gianna, who were standing with Mason, his girlfriend Rory, Avery, Christian, and Puff. The guys were all in uniform, and the girls were in street clothes—except Rory, who was wearing a Boston Bolts polo. She was probably headed over to the arena to work tonight's Bolts game.

Mason caught as many home games as he could over there. In fact, he'd purchased a box, and I joined him as often as I could.

"Oh my gosh. Puff's here." Clara's eyes lit up. She was too cool for most things lately, but she loved that bird.

Asher took off across the grass, headed straight for the puffin, with Clara and Grey on his heels. Sam glanced up at his mother, his lip caught between his teeth. When Harper gave him a small smile and nodded, he took off too. Piper, though, remained rooted to the spot as she took in the details of the field. I'd give her a minute to adjust.

I trotted out behind the others, giving my boys each a fist bump as I went, then bent down and held a hand out to Puff. With a squeak, he tapped his beak against my fist. It was still orange, though the color had begun to fade for winter.

"Want to dance, little man?" I asked, bobbing my head left and right.

Puff shook left and right and left again, making the three kids giggle.

With a finger in the air, I spun it, and Puff imitated the move, turning in a circle. When he stopped, he zeroed in on Avery and squawked.

In a way only someone who'd spent their days around animals could do, she dipped her bare hand into the small bucket and tossed a dead fish his way.

Puff caught it mid-leap.

Christian groaned. "Gloves, Blondie."

Avery pinched her fishy fingers together like she was going to launch into the chicken dance and moved toward her fiancé.

Chris shuddered and took a big step back. The dude was a total germophobe. "I say this with enormous amounts of love." He shook his head. "Don't touch me until you wash away the fish guts."

Laughing, Avery shuffled even closer.

I wasn't big on the whole lovey-dovey thing, but it was hard to deny that they were adorable. Barf.

With a grunt, Christian took off at a full sprint.

"No fair," Avery complained. "I'm nowhere close to as fast as you are."

"I'll get him for you, Av." Mason chuckled and took off after his friend.

"Traitor." Christian glared at him.

But now all three kids and Asher were running too.

Squawking, Puff fluttered into the air, then landed on the ground in front of Emerson and Gianna.

Emerson, our happy-go-lucky third baseman, bounced on his feet, a dopey smile pulling at his lips.

"Go." Gi rolled her eyes at her fiancé. "I'll watch the bird."

Emerson shot forward, tripping over his own feet. He righted himself quickly, and then he was off. It only took a moment for him to catch up to the group. The guy was the fastest of all the Revs. Hell, he was one of the fastest players in the league.

"They are ridiculous." Gianna shook her head as Puff pecked at the grass, inching closer to Rory.

Rory took a step away, her shoulders creeping up to her ears. For months, we'd been giving her crap about not liking Puff. So much so that she tried hard to hide her hesitation these days. I stepped between her and the bird, willing to be her shield. I had a favor to ask of her anyway. With my back to the chaos, I smiled.

"I swear he's adorable. Cutest thing ever," Rory promised, wide-eyed.

I chuckled. "We all know you like him better when he's wearing a harness. But I need a favor."

She pulled her long blond hair over her shoulder. "What's up?"

Exhaling, I glanced at Harper. Neither she nor Piper had moved from the grass by the dugout, and I had yet to figure out why. I scanned our surroundings. The bright, warm sun, the earthy scent of dirt and grass, the murmur of voices. It was all subtle to me, but Piper was probably far more affected by it all, and she likely picked up on things I couldn't even sense. I'd deal with her in a minute. Right now, her mother's issue was more pressing.

"See the redhead?"

"With Zara?"

I nodded. "Her left palm is injured. It's bruised pretty deeply, and she flinches when she moves her hand. Can you see if it needs an X-ray?"

She shrugged. "I'm not a hand expert." Her work with the Bolts focused on the head and neck. "But I'll look, and I can take her over to Langfield Corp if she needs one." She studied Harper, her expression thoughtful. "She's the one who caught the ball last night, right?"

I nodded.

"Does that mean she's being adopted into our Revs family like Puff was when Chris hit him with a ball?" she teased.

Considering the situation, that hit a bit too close to the truth. "Something like that."

Near the dugout, Piper pushed away from her mother, causing Harper to almost stumble. My heart lurched but settled quickly when Harper regained her balance. As the little girl took off down the third baseline just inside the grass, I strode over to Harper, leaving Rory without a word.

Hannah and Zara had stepped away, I assumed, to give Harper space to deal with Piper. I had no intention of doing the same. I stopped in front of her, blocking her view of her daughter and instantly earning a glare. She stepped to one side, as if to step around me, but I moved with her, keeping her in place.

"What do you want?" she demanded, peering around me at her daughter.

"What's her issue?" I asked the scowling woman.

She batted forcefully at a strand of hair that blew into her face. "Nothing that you could understand."

Jeez, what was her deal? Jaw locked, I fisted my hands at my sides. I was trying to help, and she'd been nothing but difficult since she'd arrived. If I was understanding correctly, Piper was out of sorts because of the grass or the sunlight. Maybe the dirt, the noise, or the bright colors of the stadium. Hell, maybe it was the way her sock felt against her ankle. If I could pinpoint the issue, I could help. Without the knowledge, I'd be left walking through a minefield.

Her only response was another glare.

Fine.

"Maybe ask about my background before you make assumptions about what I can and can't understand." With a huff, I stormed away from the damn woman.

Harper
7

KYLE FOLLOWED AFTER PIPER, bringing with him a chip on his shoulder the size of Texas. It was absurd. *He* was mad at *me*? I'd done nothing to him. We were only in this situation because he'd had a tantrum last night and had said some horrible things. From where I stood, there was no reason for me to learn anything about him. I knew enough.

"Harper?" I spun at the sound of my name, though I peered back at my daughter again.

She was standing in the grass just past third base, sneering at the sand in front of her. I knew the sand would be an issue.

Hannah, not knowing anything about Piper, had chirped about how she wanted the kids and the players to race around the bases while she recorded them.

Naturally, Piper had panicked and kicked me in the shin before running away.

Now, Kyle was squatted next to her, chatting. The two of them seemed good enough. Normally, I'd be mortified if she lashed out at anyone but me, but honestly, if she kicked Kyle, he deserved it.

In the outfield, Sam was in heaven. He and Grey were laughing as they picked grass and threw it at each other. My heart panged as I watched. Sam really needed more opportunity to be a carefree kid like that.

Knowing both kids were okay, I gave the blond woman in the blue shirt my attention.

"Yes?"

"I'm Rory. I'm a trainer. I work with the Bolts, but my boyfriend…" She surveyed the field, and when she stopped on the big guy lying on top of his friend, she huffed. "My boyfriend is Mason Dumpty, the center fielder. He's the one who is currently trying to…lick his teammate." She shook her head. "God, men never grow up, do they?"

I tried to fight it, but a chuckle rumbled out of me. "From my experience, no, they don't."

"Right?" She smirked. "Anyway, I heard you that have an injury." With her lips pressed together, she eyed my left hand. "I'd be happy to take a look."

Annoyance skittered through me. I did not want a favor. Plus, I didn't need the bill or the limitations a brace or a cast would create. It was sore. That was it. I didn't have time for more than that.

I waved her off with my good hand. "It's nothing."

"Can I look?"

Pulling my shoulders back, I racked my brain for a legitimate reason to say no.

"Please," she urged. "Just a look."

Begrudgingly, I held my hand out to her.

She was quiet as she inspected my palm and pressed on the area around the bruise. With a hum, she pressed against another spot, then asked me to move my fingers. Next, she had me make a fist. "Are you taking anything?"

Lowering my focus to my hand, I shook my head.

"How about this: take two Advil every six hours, ice it regularly, and rest it." She slipped a hand into her pocket and pulled out a white business card. "If it's not any better in a couple of days, call me."

Nodding, I tucked the card with the Boston Bolts logo into the side pocket of my leggings. I had no intention of making that call, but I'd entertain her for now.

When Rory released my hand, I checked on Piper again. Kyle had a hand cupped in front of him like he was holding something for Piper to inspect. My little girl held out a single finger, and with a grimace, she poked his palm. Quickly, she yanked her hand back and shuddered.

Rory cleared her throat, garnering my attention again. "Most people don't know this because Kyle is really private about it. But he and Mason run a foundation for kids diagnosed with autism. They award grants that help families pay for therapies they couldn't otherwise afford. They donate a lot of merch and tickets too, for fundraising."

My breath caught in my lungs as I looked from her to Kyle and back again.

"Like I said, he's really private about it." She watched the man in question, a small smile lifting one side of her mouth.

A woman with a camera stood a few feet away from him and Piper, snapping candid shots.

"He finished his master's degree in clinical psychology after he was drafted. He's super smart. Rumor is that when he retires, he's planning to practice ABA therapy."

That rocked me. No wonder Kyle had told me to ask about his background.

"Oh." I swallowed. Piper's school had recommended applied behavior analysis therapy. Though she received some during the day, she needed more.

The problem was that private therapy was expensive. We already did occupational therapy with a sensory focus and swim therapy. Those barely fit into my budget as it was. I'd applied for a few grants, but I hadn't heard back. Following up would be helpful, but between work, Piper's needs, and life in general, I didn't have the bandwidth.

Even so, therapy was important. And I had to make time for Sam. He deserved to have a life outside our little family unit. I had to start making these things happen.

"Yeah. Kyle…" She blew out a breath. "He comes across as an…" She cringed as she looked from him to me, but then she laughed. "An ass. There's no better way to say it."

I smirked. I couldn't disagree.

"But Mason and I got together while I worked for the Revs. Our relationship could have gotten me into a lot of trouble. Kyle found out, but he kept our secret like it was his own. And he's been a great friend to Mason. He's ridiculously competitive and has a temper, but he's got a lot of good qualities too. So don't write him off yet."

I didn't know what she wanted me to say. But before I could respond, a white and black flash in my periphery caught my attention.

"Oh shit." Rory screeched and jumped back, wide-eyed.

The world slowed around me as a flapping sound echoed in my ears. Rory took a step back, then another, her face a mask of terror.

The flapping got louder, and that's when it finally hit me.

Oh no. My stomach dropped.

The bird.

I spun toward the sound, but my movements were halted when I was thumped on the head. At the pressure that remained, my heart skipped, and a shiver raced down my spine. Frozen, I panicked, my heart taking off.

"Is there a bird on my head?"

She gave me a wide-eyed nod as she slowly backed down the dugout steps.

Internally, I was freaking out. Screaming and jumping around, smacking myself on the head, trying not to pee my pants as I darted away from the creature. Outwardly, though, I was frozen. I *wanted* to push the bird off, but my hand refused to move.

What if it bit me?

Did birds bite?

This one had a beak that looked like a huge orange lobster claw. I had no doubt it could take off my finger in a single chomp. And I needed my fingers.

My heart was pounding, and my lungs burned from a lack of oxygen. I was too afraid to inhale. But at the sharp poking sensation on my scalp, I sucked in a hard, whimpering breath. I had to be calm about this. If I freaked out, I'd scare Sam and Piper, who were probably watching me.

"You okay?" Kyle stepped in front of me.

When he'd crowded my space the first time, I wanted to push him away. But right now, I really wanted his help. Damn it. The last thing I wanted to do was ask him. I just needed to remain calm. Maybe the bird would fly away.

The weight on my head shifted, and an object floated in front of my face before coming to rest on my nose.

"There's a feather on my nose," I whispered, my voice tinny. "Because there's a bird on my head."

He chuckled as he gave me a once-over. "Uh-huh."

In that moment, terror won over pride and self-respect.

"Get. It. Off," I begged.

"The feather or the bird?"

"The bird," I hissed.

Smirking, he rubbed his hands together. "Afraid of our little Puff, huh, Crabby?"

The bird shifted on my head again, and a soft squeak slipped from between my lips.

Kyle chuckled again, and my blood pressure spiked. This was not funny.

I swallowed hard and closed my eyes for a moment. "My kids are watching, and I do not want to scare them by exposing them to my irrational fear of birds. So stop being a total asshole for one second and get it off."

Kyle's grin stayed firmly in place as he lifted his arm and tapped his wrist twice.

Instantly, the pressure disappeared, and in a flash of white and black, the bird was in front of me, happily resting on Kyle's forearm.

"I'm so sorry about that. We train them to fly to red." A blond with a sweet, high-pitched voice stepped up next to Kyle and held her arm out until the bird transferred to her hold. "I think the way the sun reflected off your hair got his attention."

"Pet it," Kyle demanded, his focus locked on me.

I took a step back. That was the last thing I wanted to do. "Wh—"

"Pet the bird now."

Behind me, Sam called my name. Not wanting him to sense my fear, I brushed my fingers along the bird's soft feathers. It took everything in me not to flinch as I did it. When the bird moved, I froze, holding my breath, my hand still raised.

Kyle eased my arm down as Sam came up next to us.

"Mom," he said. "You holded Puff. How cool."

I wanted to agree, but my throat had closed up. With a deep breath in through my nose, I swallowed and cleared my throat.

"So cool," Kyle said. "But she needs to wash her hands now." He gave Sam a soft smile, then stepped closer to me and murmured, "Go into the dugout. There's a bathroom down the hall. Take a minute to chill out. We're good here." Then he turned to Sam. "Want Avery to make him dance again? Let's move closer to the bucket of fish. She can show you some husbandry behaviors."

"What's that?" Sam scratched his head, his face tipped up as he looked from Kyle to the bird.

"That's what it's called when Puff mimics what we do." Kyle gently grasped my upper arm and spun me around. "Go wash your hands."

Robotically, I walked down the steps. When I made it to the hall and out of sight of my kids, I collapsed against the wall and let out a big breath. Thank God I hadn't freaked Sam out. I guessed I had Kyle to thank for that, regardless of how much it irked me.

I peeked back out at the field and found him bent over in the grass between my kids shaking his head back and forth. Beside him, Sam's shoulders shook with laughter. Even Piper was smiling.

I didn't know what to make of him.

"I'm so sorry I left you like that."

Startled, I turned and found a sheepish-looking Rory.

"I swear I'm the only person in the world who's scared of Puff."

"Not the only one," I promised wryly.

With a tilt of her head, she covered her mouth. "Oh my God. Now I feel even worse. You're afraid of him too?"

Between us, I held my forefinger and thumb an inch apart. "Little bit."

"I probably would have cried if he'd landed on me like that."

"I considered it. Along with jumping around and screaming."

She giggled. "Mason kissed me for the first time because of a bird."

She pressed her teeth into her bottom lip. "It's the only time I've ever been grateful for a feathered beast."

Allowing my shoulders to relax, I tipped my head, gesturing to my kids. "I'm going to go."

"I'm headed over to the Bolts Arena," she said. "But call me if you have any trouble with the hand."

I nodded, though I wouldn't call. Then I trotted up the stairs.

The group had congregated in the grass, and as I approached, Hannah was holding court. "How about a relay race around the bases? Each kid could be paired up with a baseball player. The kids could run from home to second, then they'd tag their Revs partner, and the guys would finish."

My stomach sank, and I searched for Piper in the group. Surprisingly, she wasn't blinking or fidgeting or showing any other sign of stress.

"Piper and I were talking about it," Kyle said, and Piper beamed up at him. "We thought maybe the kids could ride on our shoulders while we raced around the bases."

"Oh." Hannah paused for a moment, pursing her lips. Then she broke out in a smile. "That will be perfect. Let's set up the teams."

"I call Dad," Grey shouted, darting to Asher Price.

Sam ended up on Emerson Knight's shoulders while Kyle carried Piper and Mason carried Clara.

Sam and Emerson won the first race, no contest. They made it to home plate before anyone else could even round third.

I worried Piper would be upset, but before she could make a comment, Kyle demanded a do-over.

"He totally started early," he complained.

Mason tipped his head back, being careful to keep Clara on his shoulders. "Oh, here we go."

With a roll of his eyes, Emerson laughed.

But without argument, they all lined back up.

By the fourth race, it was clear that Emerson really was the fastest. Asher and Mason gave up then, but Kyle was still pumped to run again. Finally, during the seventh race, Kyle and Piper won. The smile on my daughter's face after they crossed over home plate was bigger than any I'd ever seen from her.

I couldn't help but feel grateful for Kyle. Even when he declared that he'd drop us off on his way home and wouldn't take no for an answer. It didn't take long to get our things loaded and to get the kids buckled, since Kyle insisted on keeping Piper on his shoulders and Emerson had carried Sam out. Having extra sets of hands like this was unusual and unfamiliar, but not something I'd complain about.

Kyle watched as I pulled out the kids' tablets and headphones. We had a twenty-five-minute drive ahead of us, and when my kids were stuck next to each other in the car like this, they could very quickly make a person want to stab their eardrums out.

Kyle eyed the kids, who were already homed in on their iPads in the third row of the Escalade. "So here's the thing—"

"If you're going to tell me screen time rots their brains, you can save your breath. I don't want to discuss it," I warned.

Frowning, he studied me. "I wasn't talking about screen time. They're your kids. You make those calls."

My chest tightened at the sentiment. Did he mean it, or was he pretending he agreed while silently judging my parenting?

"Plus, they've been running around for hours. They probably need some down time. Balance isn't a bad thing."

Oh. My cheeks heated. Dammit. Flicking at a piece of lint on my leggings, I focused on working up the nerve to apologize.

"Anyway," he said before I could formulate an appropriate statement. "I heard through the grapevine that you're having a day care crisis."

With a sharp intake of breath, I scrutinized him. How did he know that? I hadn't mentioned it to anyone on the team. "What?"

"Am I wrong?" He raised a brow, looking nothing like the guy who'd been laughing and running the bases with my kids. He'd quickly morphed into the cocky pain in the ass who spent a lot of time BSing with the reporters.

"No, but..." I regarded my kids. Neither was paying any attention. I'd been telling Piper since before the game yesterday that she wasn't going to the YMCA after school anymore. But I couldn't believe she'd opened up to Kyle about it.

"So like I was saying. You need a new day care. And I assume you need it by Monday."

I laughed. "Unless I'm somehow blessed with a fairy godmother in the next thirty-six hours, that isn't happening."

He rolled his eyes. "Langfield Corp has a day care. It's available to their employees and players. They can take Piper and Sam until you find a permanent spot for them."

"No, they can't." I shook my head.

He crossed his arms and leaned back in the seat. The move made the muscles of his forearms ripple against the sleeves of his fitted blue athletic shirt. He eyed the driver, a man wearing a black Langfield Corp polo, before shifting his attention back to me. "What do you mean?"

"There is no reason for that." Taking a few pictures together so that the whole city of Boston would no longer hate me was one thing. Even having a day of fun for the kids. But I wasn't taking anything else from him. "I don't work for the Revs or Langfield Corp, so there is no reason for my kids—"

"Look." He threw a hand up and huffed. "I get that I was a dick last night. I don't lose well." He shrugged the statement off like he was talking about a six-year-old rather than himself.

"Yeah," I agreed with a scoff. "That was clear when Emerson had to let you win a fun race around the bases."

Kyle sputtered. "*Let* me?"

"Kyle, he crushed you six races in a row," I explained, doing my best to keep my tone even despite the ridiculousness of this conversation. How could he not understand this? "And suddenly, on the seventh, you won." I cocked a brow. "Do you know why? He didn't want to have to go again, so he threw the race."

"No way." Kyle shook his head, his brow creased. "I'll prove it." He shifted to yank his phone out of his pocket and tapped out a message. Once he finished, he set it on his knee and glared at me. "I'm trying to apologize here, but you're being nothing but difficult."

"Me?" With a thumb, I pointed at my chest. Was he freaking kidding?

"Yes. *You*, Crabby. All glary and uptight and 'these are the rules. Oh wait, one more,'" he mocked.

With my lips pressed into a firm line, I clenched my fists on my lap, ignoring the pain. I didn't want to be this way, but Piper needed the structure. Plus, who was he to judge? "Better to be irresponsible and running my mouth like you?"

"Touché." He smirked, and his brown eyes danced. Almost like he enjoyed arguing with me. But almost as quickly as it came, the amusement vanished from his face. "So since I was running my mouth, let me fix it. The kids go to the Revs' day care for the time being. I've already cleared it with management. They'll email the onboarding paperwork tomorrow, so stop making it a thing."

I opened my mouth and shut it again. That might have been the worst apology I'd ever been given. And that was saying a lot after the half-assed apology I'd gotten from my ex-husband when he'd lied to me for over a year.

"I think the words you're looking for are *thank you*." Smirking, he sat back in his seat, his body relaxed, like he'd proven his point.

"Learn to read a room, dumbass. That's not even close." Seriously. And I'd almost apologized to this jerk?

"Listen." He huffed a deep breath out of his nose and angled over the space between the two bucket seats so he was a little too close. "I'm working on being patient with you. Everything the Langfields have is the best. So, Little Fingers? Best day care in Boston. And I've secured spots for your kids. But because of your own stubbornness, you're refusing?"

"That's not—"

"And," he said, drawing the word out, "finding one that can handle a child with ASD on short notice?" He snorted. "Good fuckin' luck."

Sighing, I let my shoulders fall. Damn, it stung to admit he was right.

So I wouldn't. Not out loud, at least. I wouldn't let this asshole win. I lifted my chin and narrowed my eyes at him. "They can come to work with me for a while."

With a snort, he dropped his head back against his headrest. "Bet you get a lot done that way."

I glared, only to find him staring right back, his eyes just as hard. He was waiting for me to cave. Waiting for me to admit he was right.

When I didn't, the ass sank even lower. "Greyson and Sam got along well today. Grey goes to Little Fingers. I'm sure Sam will be thrilled when I tell him that if you accept my offer, he'll get to play with his new buddy every day." He spun in his seat, one hand planted on the back of my seat, like he was going to call out to my son.

Eyes practically bugged out, I smacked his arm. "You wouldn't."

He lifted one shoulder, nonchalant. "When I want something, I don't play fair."

"And here I was, almost believing you weren't as terrible as your tantrum last night made you out to be," I huffed.

He glared. "How am I terrible? I'm helping you."

"No one asked you to," I snapped back.

He opened his mouth but slammed it shut again. With a long breath through his nose, he closed his eyes, and when he opened them again, he said, "Fill out the onboarding paperwork before Monday."

"We'll see." Crossing my arms, I glared out the damn window, wishing I had a better option for day care. Because I'd rather cut my tongue out than admit that I needed Kyle Bosco's help. And to think I'd almost let myself forget the cardinal rule.

Don't ever trust a southern boy.

KYLE
8

> Cam: She hasn't done the paperwork yet. But I'm almost to you.

STUBBORN WOMAN. Why was she so against sending her kids to Little Fingers? Dylan was incredible with kids. A little odd, but she knew her shit. They would be lucky to get to chill with her every day.

And Harper's fucking comment. *No one asked me to help?* Bullshit. JJ asked me to help.

I slammed the beer down on the ledge in front of me.

She didn't know that, of course. But that fact was neither here nor there. Why couldn't she just be grateful that I'd solved her childcare issue?

"What's got your panties in a knot?" Mason asked, his focus still fixed on the ice. The Bolts were up by one in the middle of the second period.

I took a pull of my beer and slammed it down again. "Nothing."

The crowd cheered, pulling my attention back to the game just as Brooks Langfield, goalie for the Bolts, stopped another shot. "The guy is on fire."

"I think he's showing off for his new girlfriend."

I tipped my chin up. "He's dating someone in the front office, right? You two paint each other's nails and chat about it?"

Mason turned my way, his lips tight. "Dick." He shook his head and focused on the game again, but not before I caught a hint of a smile on his face.

I loved to tease him about the way he and Rory had snuck around for weeks.

"Mock me all you want," he grumbled. "But while I'm snuggled up next to my girl every night, all you've got is cold sheets, your own hand, and Hannah on your back."

I flipped him off.

"Did you piss Hannah off too?" Jasper Quinn asked as he dropped into the seat beside me. "Because she ripped me a new one earlier."

"Stay out of the tabloids, and she'll leave you alone," Mason suggested, pointing at Jasper with the neck of his beer bottle.

"That shit lies." The first baseman held up his own drink, hiding a smirk behind it.

"Right." I kicked my feet up onto the ledge. "Sell that to someone who wasn't there. You deserve all the wrath for—"

He lurched forward and threw a hand out, but I dodged out of the way before he could touch my hair.

"Hands off."

"Don't touch the hair, man," Mason said in a low tone, mocking me. They all gave me shit about it, but my fans loved my hair, and I had no interest in being caught looking like I'd been electrocuted, then finding the photo circulating online. I was known for my perfect hair, and I wanted to keep it that way.

My phone buzzed in my pocket, so I tipped to one side and dug it out again.

> Bambi: It was for the greater good. Let it go, man.

I glared at the message. I still couldn't believe he'd thrown the race. The asshole really had let me win.

Me: Payback will be delivered.

Bambi: Meme of a guy dancing.

Me: That's a threat, not a promise. It shouldn't be exciting.

Bambi: But I love a good surprise. It gives me tingles.

A laugh worked its way up my chest, but I choked it back down. Because dammit, Harper was right. Not that I'd tell her that. Because she was wrong about the rest, and I didn't want to give her any ideas.

"Why'd everyone bail tonight?" Jasper asked with a frown.

"They want to hang with their girls." Mason shrugged, shifting in his seat. "After that long-ass playoff run, I can't blame them. If Aurora wasn't down there right now, I'd be at home with her too." He tipped his bottle to the Bolts' bench, where his girlfriend sat chatting with Fitz, the goalie coach. I didn't know the guy personally, but I'd heard he was tons of fun.

The door behind us opened, and Jasper whipped around.

"Yes," he cheered as Cam stepped inside the suite. "The fab four are together again."

Cam sauntered in and slapped four folders on the ledge in front of us. Then he dropped three bags of M&M's on top. Good man. I tore one open and tossed a handful into my mouth.

"Hope that excitement remains when you get a look at all that paperwork."

My shoulders sagged. When the M&M's appeared, I should have known that I'd be asked to deal with something I didn't want to do.

"Didn't Kayla narrow down the candidates?" Mason asked. "Wasn't that the point of your meeting today?"

With a shake of his head, he snagged a beer from the fridge at the back of the suite. He popped the cap off using the edge of the counter, then wandered our way again. "She narrowed it down to six candidates for the two grants, but I brought a few other things with me. The top folder is yours."

Mason picked it up, easing the remaining bags of candies to the folder beneath it before putting it on his lap. I'd let him go through them first, then I would weigh in. Though after four years, we rarely disagreed on our picks.

"First, though." Cam locked his gaze on me. "The repair bill for Harper's car."

"Repair bill?" What the hell was he talking about? I tossed another baseball candy into the air and caught it in my mouth. I loved the way it felt when they landed on my tongue. Almost as much as the crunch of the candy coating between my teeth.

"We had her car towed so we could fix the tires and the paint."

Frowning, I sat up straighter. "We did?"

"Yes, you wrecked her car."

Scoffing, I tossed another chocolate. After I'd chewed it up and swallowed, I added. "I didn't touch her car."

"Maybe not directly." Cam tipped his beer bottle at me. "But you opened your mouth and produced the words that caused the car's demise. So in turn, you wrecked it."

When he put it that way, I got it.

Jasper barked out a laugh. "Yes. That's like girl logic. I love it."

I frowned at the idiot.

Setting the candy down, I leaned forward in my seat. "She'll let me fix her car, but she won't let me help with the kids?"

Mason looked up from the document he was perusing, eyes wide. "You want to help with her kids? Aren't you allergic to things like girl-friends and little people?"

I waved him off with a sigh. "I'm not helping personally. I just talked Dylan into finding places for them at Little Fingers."

"Dude," he said, his brows practically in his hairline. "Does Cortney know?"

I shrugged. "Seems like those two communicate well, so I'd assume."

"Oh," he snickered, hiding his mouth behind a fist. "You are so dead."

My gut twisted at the warning. "Why?"

With a shake of his head, Mason went back to his papers.

Figuring it was best to leave that potential problem for later, I zeroed in on Cam again. "What's the deal with the car?"

"She let me have it towed to the shop, but she called and told them to send the bill to her." Cam dropped into the seat beside me and took a pull off his beer. "Apparently, they aren't allowed to work on it unless she's billed in full. She doesn't care what we told them."

Fuck. I ran a hand down my face. She was the most stubborn woman in the freaking world. "Where is this place? I'll stop by tomorrow. Sign autographs, take pictures, get them thinking my way."

"Two minutes ago, you didn't want to pay for it," Jasper piped in, "but now you're going to make her let you?"

"Two minutes ago, it wasn't a contest, Jazz," Cam said as he slid his phone out of his pocket.

That wasn't exactly true. I'd decided to pay for it before it was a contest. But I wasn't arguing.

Cam tapped the screen, and a moment later, mine buzzed with what must be the repair shop's info.

Jasper shook his head. "You've got to be the most competitive person ever."

That was not the point. The issue here was that I wouldn't allow Harper to boss me around. Her kids were going to Little Fingers. It made sense. And I would fix her damn car because I'm the one who put her in this situation. I'd fix it, but it'd be nice if she wouldn't make every step so difficult.

"Hold up." Mason raised a hand. "Is this real? Or a joke?" He held up the document he had laid out on his lap.

Cam shook his head. "It's a complete coincidence, I swear."

"What is?" I snagged the application from Mason's hand and scanned the list of services needed. Typical ASD list. Private ABA, sensory-focused OT, RDI, CBT. Low income. Single-parent household. But both mom and dad had Boston addresses. "What's the joke?" I asked, looking up at Mason.

"*Piper Wallace?*" He cocked a brow.

My breath stuttered as I scanned the page again. Oh shit. Harper had applied for assistance with Piper's therapies. They were expensive, so it made sense. But if she needed the financial help, then why the fuck was she so stubborn about the repairs and childcare?

As I reread the list of needs, it hit me. There was no way we could choose Piper. If we did, it could easily turn into a disaster. "She's not getting a grant, but don't worry. I'll take care of it."

Mason sighed and scratched at his jaw. "I don't know—"

"Veto." I spit the word out quick. We'd long ago agreed that we each had the power to veto a single candidate for any reason. No questions asked. And I did not want to explain Piper's connection to me.

The look on Mason's face as he shook his head was pure disappointment.

"Kyle," Cam warned, sitting forward and lacing his fingers together.

"I said I'll take care of it." I wasn't refusing to help her. I just couldn't offer her a grant.

The corners of Cam's mouth turned down in disapproval, but he didn't argue again. He knew why I was helping the Wallace family outside of the media issue, and he was fully on board with the idea. So the frown didn't make sense.

Behind us, the door flew open and slammed against the wall, startling all four of us.

"What the hell, Streaks?" Cortney Miller stood in the middle of the room with his arms crossed. He was a huge, hulking, pissed-off presence. He might be the GM of the Revs these days, but not all that long ago, he'd been my teammate. As intimidating as he could be, I knew him well. I knew how compassionate and caring he could be, and how *not* terrifying he really was.

I lifted my chin. "What?"

With a step closer, he narrowed his eyes. "Willow's eight months old."

Okay. I didn't know much about babies, but she wasn't walking yet, so I guessed that seemed right. But why had he stormed in here to announce that?

"Yeah?" I asked.

"Dylan doesn't need more. I was okay with getting the day care up and running. But we decided to limit the number of kids this year. Fewer employees, fewer kids. Because Dylan doesn't need more."

The man was ridiculously overprotective of his fiancée. And now I understood why Mason had said I was dead. Probably should have taken a step back and considered the reasons behind why the day care had so few kids enrolled.

"It's only two more. No big deal," I said, keeping my tone casual.

Cortney shook his head, making his blond hair brush over the tops of his shoulders. "Two more without the staff to handle them," he growled.

Boy, he was in a mood today.

"We can find someone to help out," I promised.

He huffed. "Not by Monday."

Well, that might be true.

"So you'll—"

The door opened again, this time not so violently, and in strode Beckett Langfield, owner of the Boston Revs and one of Cortney's best friends.

"Looks like this is turning into a party." Jasper chuckled.

"Man Bun," Beckett barked.

Cortney put his hands on his hips and glared at the newcomer. "How the hell did you know I was here?"

Beckett, who was dressed in an expensive suit, pulled out his phone and tapped a purple icon. He held his phone up, flashing the *Life 360* app.

The taller man dropped his head into his hand. "Are you tracking me now?"

Damn, it felt good to no longer be the source of Cortney's ire or the subject of his attention. I tossed another M&M into the air and caught it.

"No." Beckett huffed a laugh, the sound at odds with his usually stoic demeanor. "Shay set it up. She can track us all. That way she always knows where Kai is when he's with one of us. It's been a thing for a year."

Cortney crossed his arms.

"But also, I got a call from security when you got here. They assumed you were coming to see me. So imagine my extreme hurt when you never showed up."

"I love the vibe you two have." Jasper kicked his feet up. "It's like watching an eighty-year-old couple bicker."

Both men glared at him.

"Careful, Peter Pan, you're already on a short leash," Beckett warned.

"I do kinda look like him, don't I?" Jasper smiled. "It's the hair. But my thighs would look fucking spectacular in those tights."

I laughed.

"Don't encourage him," Cortney warned.

"Why are you hanging with the four stooges?" Beckett turned back to Cortney. "You fighting with Dippy Do?"

"No. Well..." Cortney glanced away and cleared his throat. "Bosco added two new kids to Little Fingers. They start on Monday. And Dylan doesn't need extra work added to her plate."

Beckett zeroed in on me, his face fixed in a glower. The guy could be fun, but no one fucked with his family without suffering his wrath. And after he married his wife, her four friends, one of whom was Cortney's fiancée and also the co-owner of Little Fingers, fell under the umbrella of Beckett's family. That meant I was on his shit list.

"It's the foul ball family," I rushed out, knowing Beckett wanted that situation fixed ASAP.

"The redhead? Huh. Wait..." Beckett rubbed his hands together, one brow lifted. "Back in the day, you made a pass at Dylan..."

Cortney growled.

"No I didn't." I did. But the last thing I wanted to do was remind my GM that before he and his fiancée were together, I had. Kinda.

"You have a thing for redheads." Beckett's green eyes sparkled under the can lights in the suite.

I opened my mouth to deny it, but before I could, Cam piped up.

"Don't bother. I've seen you with way too many to let you claim otherwise."

It was true, so I shrugged. No sense denying what was so obvious.

"Oh, oh, oh." Beckett laughed. "This is going to be so good. The kids are absolutely welcome at Little Fingers. It's the perfect way to get you and the redhead together."

My stomach sank at his suggestion. "Don't even start with the matchmaker shit. Harper isn't my type. Her kids are cute and all, but she's difficult." I frowned. "And stubborn." Peering out at the ice, I watched the play in progress. "And she's doesn't like Puff."

Although the face she'd made while trying to stay calm and be brave for her kids was adorable. Damn, I'd really wanted to hug her at that moment. The way her nose had creased, drawing attention to the freckles there—

What the fuck, Bosco?

Pushing away the thoughts of how pretty she was, I let out a groan. "The woman's making me crazy."

"*That's* what I'm talking about." Beckett clapped.

Beside him, Cortney ran his hands through his shoulder-length blond hair. "Normally, I'm opposed to his crazy ideas. But the words that just came out of your mouth could have come from any man who's finally met his match but doesn't have her yet."

Anxiety prickled across my skin. There was no way in hell I'd go there, even if I wanted to. I couldn't think about Harper that way. There were plenty of women out there I could think about naked. Available, single, adult women. Then there were women like Harper. Women I had to keep firmly in the *do not go there* zone. Because I didn't have a death wish, and I knew how JJ would react.

"But Bosco." Cortney pointed at me. "I was serious when I said that Dylan needs more hands. So you'll be there not only on Monday morning but every day for as long as Piper and Sam are at Little Fingers."

All the air was sucked from my lungs. Hold up… What? Unable to breathe, I couldn't formulate a response, and before I could force myself to inhale, Beckett nodded resolutely. Then the two men were gone.

Holy shit. What the hell had I gotten myself into? I couldn't work at a daycare.

Harper
9

"I SAID NO," Piper screamed. She pushed away while simultaneously landing the perfect kick to my shin.

I'd just finished braiding her hair to keep it from knotting throughout the day. That was normally the worst part of the morning routine. Apparently not today.

She kicked again, landing a hit to the same spot.

I winced at the pain. Another day, another bruise. It was exhausting, this relationship I had with my daughter. We'd come far over the last two years, but the road that led to a happily functioning adult felt miles long some days. More often than not, I felt like I was failing at this mom life. Every time I saw a mother give her daughter a hug, I was reminded of exactly how different our relationship was. I tried not to compare. This was about her, not anyone else. I had to remember that. But with each step forward, every time I thought things were getting better, a change or an adjustment would set us back again.

Knowing today had the potential to be awful had kept me up, tossing and turning, last night. Regardless of how badly I wanted today to go smoothly, the possibility of disaster made the acid burn of stress rumble more fiercely in my stomach and claw up my throat.

"We have to get dressed. You're going to Lang Field today. Remember? We talked about this." I pulled my Tums out of the pocket of my dress pants and popped two into my mouth. Once I'd put the roll away, I crouched down, holding Piper's shirt out. "Let's get dressed really quick."

"I want to be alone," she screamed. She lashed out and grasped my arm, her nails, desperately in need of a trim, biting into my flesh.

On instinct, I pulled back. As I did, it caused her nails to drag along my skin, leaving red scratches along the inside of my forearm.

"Piper," I scolded evenly as I stepped back and gave her space. "*Stop.*"

"I want to be alone," she repeated, this time without the aggression. That was something, at least.

"Mom," Sam called from the family room, where he was already dressed and ready to head over to day care. Although he was nervous about being in a new place, he was excited to see Grey.

Piper, on the other hand, couldn't wrap her head around the fact that it was Monday, since she didn't have school. Teacher in-service days and school holidays were the bane of my existence. Change didn't come easy in our house, so situations like this, where not only did the kids not have school, but they were starting at a new day care, were a struggle, no matter how much I prepared her.

The Tums had tempered the burn in my esophagus, but my stomach rumbled. I needed to eat before I left. I'd fed the kids, but while they were eating, I'd jumped into the shower and had gotten dressed.

"Mom, come here," Sam called again. He'd eaten, but he probably wanted another cup of almond milk. We'd been going through more than a gallon a week lately.

"I'll be right there," I hollered. Then I refocused on Piper. We had to get a move on, or I'd be late for work. "You have five minutes before it's time to pick one shirt and a pair of pants," I warned.

In response, she put her headphones over her ears and turned away from me.

Reining in my frustration, I set the alarm that would buzz when it was time for her to get dressed, then left her alone in the bedroom.

This method didn't always work, but I was crossing my fingers that it would do the trick today.

By the time I'd gotten home from Lang Field on Saturday, I'd had a welcome email from Little Fingers sitting in my inbox. After googling the program and looking into their New Jersey locations, I had to begrudging admit that I couldn't turn down their offer. So I had filled out the paperwork. Then I'd spoken with Dylan Machon last night. She had been lovely. Although the program was set up for employees of Langfield Corp, she had been understanding of my position and had agreed that I could pay the New Jersey rate for my two children. Once Dylan had assured me that transportation between their facility and Piper's school was available, I finally resigned myself to sending the kids to Little Fingers. At least for the time being.

Dylan had been so kind and helpful. The last thing I wanted to do was show up late on day one.

"Mom," Sam called again.

"I'm coming," I said as I hustled down the hall. When two men came into view, I pulled up short, and my heart took off at a run. It only took a moment to place them, and my fear was quickly replaced by annoyance. "Why are you here?"

Kyle smirked. "Glad to see you're in a better mood today, Crabby."

My doorbell had been broken for quite a while, and when I was in one of our bedrooms, it was impossible to hear visitor's knock. Even so, these guys hadn't just opened the door and walked in.

With my hands on my hips, I frowned at my son. "You are not allowed to let strange people in without me."

"They aren't that weird." He shrugged.

Both men chuckled, but I wasn't the least bit amused.

"Sorry to drop by unannounced," Cam said.

Kyle chuckled, his eyes dancing. "No we're not."

Cam and I huffed in unison.

Kyle just shook his head. His hair was damp, making his blond highlights stand out more than normal.

I surveyed the perfect streaks. They were even more annoying when they accompanied the "I didn't bother to shave" look he was sporting.

"I'm not sorry." Kyle's lips were pulled tight. "I came because I figured Piper would have a hard time this morning, knowing she was going to a new place. I thought it might be easier if her favorite baseball player was here to get her out the door."

That almost had me softening, but then he had to go and ruin it by opening his mouth again.

"Plus, I didn't want you to flake on Dylan."

Rage clouded my vision as I shot daggers at him. "I don't flake on anything." For all my flaws—and there were plenty—being a flake wasn't one of them. "And asking if I wanted help would have been the right way to handle things." Not that I wanted to admit that having his help could be a godsend.

"You would have said no." Kyle shrugged again. "And you don't have a car, so Cam will drop the kids and me at the stadium, and then he'll take you to work."

Cam shifted on his feet, grimacing.

With a sharp breath in, I crossed my arms. "We live in a city. Public transportation *and* Uber are *both* a thing."

Kyle tossed his arms in the air, the move displaying a script tattoo on the underside of his bicep. "This is exactly what I mean," he said, turning to Cam. "She's ridiculous. Most people would be thanking us for making their day easier. But Harper? She *wants* it to be hard. *Make it make sense.*"

Cam chuckled, though he still looked uncomfortable. "Like I said, you should have called."

"I don't have her number." He whipped around and motioned for me to step closer. "Which reminds me, give me your number."

My brow shot up, but I held firm. That was not happening. "No."

"No?" With a huff, he looked from me to Cam and back again, his eyes wide with disbelief. "*No?*" he repeated, as if the sentiment were a foreign concept to him.

Had anyone ever not given the great Kyle Bosco their number when he asked? Probably not.

"No." I straightened and pulled my shoulders back, then addressed Cam. "Thank you for coming. I'm sorry to have wasted your time, but I've got an Uber on the way, so we're all set."

"Mr. Kyle," Sam cut in before the man in front of me could argue. "We have your picture on our wall. Do you want to come see?"

"He doesn't want to—"

"Yes, I do," Kyle said, lifting his chin. The damn man. I swore he'd say yes to anything, just to spite me.

"Yes!" Sam lunged at him and grasped his arm. His little hand barely fit around Kyle's wrist as he pulled the very willing man down the hallway.

The gray Revs shirt Kyle wore pulled so tight against his muscular back, each ripple of muscle was visible from where I stood. He was too big, too broad, and too damn good-looking as he moved down our small hallway. I wished I hadn't noticed. Because, for as obvious as his looks were, it was just as clear that he didn't fit here in our apartment.

Like most professional athletes, Kyle was larger than life. And nothing about my life was more than average. Not my modest two-bedroom apartment or the basic Ikea furniture. Not the Legos scattered on top of the coffee table or the magnetic track that took up all the space between the couch and the wall. Even the dinosaurs that peppered the small four-person table in the dining room were average. Plastic and generic and inexpensive. The place was a mess.

I sighed as I took in the space, but with a shake of my head, I reminded myself that impressing Kyle Bosco was the last thing I should be worried about. I didn't care what he thought.

"Do you mind if I set this down?" Cam lifted a beverage holder I hadn't noticed. Three of the spots held white coffee cups.

"Not at all," I said, nodding at the tiny galley kitchen. "You can put it on the counter."

With an elbow, he switched the light on. Then set the cardboard carrier on the tan Formica and surveyed the organized space.

At least this room wasn't a mess.

"Do you take your coffee like a dessert?" He pointed to one white cup. "Or black?" He pointed to the other two, both sporting sleeves.

"Black."

"The right way." Laughing, he pulled out one cup with a sleeve and held it out to me.

I took a step back and raised a hand. "Oh, I couldn't."

"You can and you should." Cam moved closer, cup in hand. "In the two years I've worked for him, I've discovered that Kyle is a lot easier to deal with after a good dose of caffeine. And if I were you, I'd just choose your battles and cancel the Uber. He's not going to let it go until you and the kids are strapped into the car."

"Is that so?" I took the cup. "You know, you have my number. I'm surprised you didn't give it to bossy pants in there."

Cam and I had spoken on the phone and via texts a few times this weekend. Between his help with my car and his updates—along with Hannah's and Zara's—on their *fix Harper's standing with Boston* campaign, and details regarding Little Fingers, there had been plenty to talk about.

He propped himself up against the counter and pulled out the second cup of black coffee. "Collecting numbers from women for him isn't part of my job description."

I snorted. The idea that Kyle would want my number in that way was absurd. I was a single mom with two kids and no time. In fact, I was pretty sure I'd gotten toothpaste on my purple blouse this morning but had forgotten to change it. That was fitting.

I set my coffee on the counter and wet a paper towel. "He doesn't want my number. Not really. He's just being forced to fix the mess he made with that stupid comment."

Eyes narrowed, Cam sipped his coffee. "Yeah," he eventually said. "I'm just going to say it. That's the biggest lie I've heard this morning, and I heard Kyle swear that calling before showing up here wasn't necessary."

"Nice try." I snorted as I pulled at the satin fabric of my top, working on the toothpaste spot.

"Piper's getting dressed, and then we'll be ready." Kyle came trotting into the kitchen just as I dropped the paper towel onto the counter. "She and Sam are both excited for the day."

Head tilted, I assessed him. Day-old scruff on his strong jaw, lips turned up in a smile, and brown eyes sparkling like he'd just won a prize. "What did you do?"

"Nothing." He shook his head. "Piper and I went through our schedule for the day to make sure she was secure and understood it."

The acid was back and rising in my throat. "What do you mean 'our'?"

"I'm hanging out at Little Fingers today so I can help with the transition." He glanced at the remaining cup in the holder. "This one mine?"

Cam nodded.

"You're staying at the day care?" I straightened, crossing my arms. "Because if you say that to her, then you're committed." The meltdown she'd have if he didn't would be epic.

"Of course I'm staying," Kyle scoffed.

"Why?"

He shot an annoying grin my way. "Kid rearing is just one of my many skills."

Cam, who'd been taking a sip of his coffee, sputtered and choked. Coughing, he pounded a fist against his chest.

With a roll of his eyes, Kyle pulled the lid off the only cup without a sleeve and tossed it onto the counter. That wicked grin was back in an instant. "You drink your coffee black?"

How did he know that? Oh. That's right. Cam had given two options. "You like dessert coffee, I take it?"

He shuffled across the kitchen and stopped in front of me. "Black coffee is the worst. Don't knock this until you try it, Crabby. A little sugar might actually make you smile."

Lips pressed together, I shook my head.

"I dare you to try it. I bet you can't take a sip and not smile." He held the cup up and cocked a light brow.

Huffing, I took another sip of my plain black coffee, fighting the urge to roll my eyes at him over the top.

"What's the matter?" he teased. "Scared I'm right?" His eyes sparkled with the challenge.

"For Pete's sake." I yanked the cup from his hand and took a sip. The sweetness of marshmallow hit first, then creamy chocolate, followed by the familiar yum of coffee. Jeez, this really was dessert in a cup. And I'd love another sip.

"See? Good, isn't it?" Kyle took another step, boxing me in between his body and the counter.

He was so close I could feel the heat radiate off his massive chest. The sensation was almost foreign to me, since it had been over a year since I'd been this close to anyone but my kids.

"It's okay," I forced out. My mouth had gone dry, and without thinking, I took a second sip. We avoided sugar in this house, along with gluten, dairy, and red dye. It was better for Piper. But damn, this drink was really good.

Kyle's smile grew as he watched me take that second sip. "Don't lie to me. You love the dessert coffee."

I rolled my eyes but didn't respond.

He lifted a hand, but instead of taking his coffee cup from me, he brushed the rough pad of his thumb across the bow of my lip.

Despite my best efforts, I couldn't control the goose bumps that broke out across my entire body.

"You've got a little whipped cream right there," he mumbled as he pulled his hand away. For a moment, his thumb hovered between us, that dab of whipped cream a tease. His eyes were locked on me as he slowly moved it to his own mouth.

My heart pounded at the sight of his tongue peeking out between his lips, and when he licked the cream off his finger, my breath caught. How was it possible that I could feel his tongue on my skin, despite the distance between us?

"Delicious." The words were barely a whisper, but they sent a shiver down my spine, nonetheless.

He watched me for a moment, his eyes flashing with heat, before he blinked and spun away.

As he strode across the room, he cleared his throat. "See, Cam? Everyone loves a good morning dessert in a cup."

"Right," Cam said, though the way his lips pulled down belied the sentiment.

I set Kyle's cup on the counter and stepped away, feeling entirely too flustered. What had just happened? I didn't want to like Kyle, so what the heck was I doing? Kyle moved past me to the coffee on the counter. He fixed his cup with its lid again and took it with him as he exited the kitchen.

"I have decided that I am willing to go to Lang Field today." Piper appeared, wearing her pink T-shirt, silver leggings, and bright blue Crocs.

"Great," Kyle said from where he'd retreated into the living room. "We've got the car out front. No need for the Uber."

"Ubers smell," Piper agreed.

With a sigh, I hung my head. I gave up. This morning's debacles had been more than enough. Cam was right. I had to choose my battles. I'd ride with them to Little Fingers and I could Uber from there.

"Okay, everyone out," I called, grabbing my purse and coffee from the counter. As I stepped into the hall, I lifted my coffee to take a sip and was shocked at the burst of flavor that hit my tongue.

I froze.

"Everyone deserves some time to indulge," Kyle whispered. His warm hand covered my shoulder, giving it a quick squeeze. Then he followed the kids into the elevator, cup of coffee in hand.

Had he really switched our cups? But I thought he hated black coffee?

Harper
10

WHEN CAM DROPPED us off at Langfield Corp, a woman with curly red hair and a perma-grin met us at the door. "I'm Dylan," she said, extending her hand to me. "We spoke on the phone." Her smile grew almost impossibly wide when she crouched in front of my kids. "And I'm so excited to meet you both."

Sam eyed her warily, tightening his hold on my hand, and Piper stared straight ahead without acknowledging her. This morning could go one of many ways. There was a good chance Piper would have a complete meltdown and refuse to stay. Although it didn't happen as often as it had when she was younger, it was still a thing. The idea that she might take off running out the door, at any moment, into the road, made my stomach burn.

"I said we'd go through the turny door and then down a long hall-way. Remember?" Kyle said to Piper.

She didn't look at him, but she nodded and didn't put up a fight.

I was still annoyed with him for bullying his way into coming with us, but he knew where to go and had explained it to Piper. He'd also given her a heads-up about the length of the car ride. And amazingly produced a book with a story about the first day at a new day care and read it with her on the way over. As annoyed as I was with him, I couldn't deny that it made our morning go much more smoothly than it could have.

"Let's do that, just like we talked about," he said, turning toward the building.

"Sounds great," Dylan chirped, taking off. "Sam," she said over her shoulder, "I've heard so much about you from your friend."

"Friend?" He scratched his head with his free hand, his bright red hair flopping into his eyes. His other hand was still firmly locked around mine.

"Yeah. Grey's been talking about you all morning."

His little brown eyes widened, and his hold on me loosened. "Grey's here already?"

"Yes." Dylan beamed. "You two are going to have so much fun. I heard you love finger painting. I swear the universe is looking out for you, because today is finger painting day."

"Really?" He flashed a megawatt smile, though the expression quickly turned thoughtful as he peered up at Dylan. "What's the you-no-vas?"

"It's *everything*. The world. Outer space. The whole shebang." Dylan shrugged. "And you're a lucky kid, 'cause it's looking out for you today."

"Cool." Sam released my hand completely and moved closer to Dylan as we continued our hike down a long hallway.

On my other side, Piper almost seemed calm. She was keeping pace with us, and though she was blinking rapidly, her hands were mostly relaxed at her sides. That changed quickly, though, when we turned a corner, and the classroom came into view. Instantly, she pulled her hands up and pinched her arms. If I wasn't careful, she would hurt herself without meaning to. Especially with her nails as long as they were. Clipping them needed to happen soon, but that was another battle entirely.

The room was colorful and bright, and there were a good fifteen kids running around, along with three adults and even a baby. The place was pure chaos. There was no way she'd be okay with me leaving her here.

"Sorry about the madness. We don't normally have more than eight kids, but since there is no school today, the older kids are here," Dylan explained.

With a nod at her, I turned to my daughter. "Piper." I kept my tone calm and avoided touching her. As much as I wanted to stop her from pinching her forearms, I had to be strategic.

"I have an idea," Kyle said before I could gather my thoughts. He squatted next to her.

Instantly, she took a step away.

He ignored the move and instead dropped his backpack on the ground next to him and unzipped it. "I brought these noise-canceling headphones." Yanking a pair of blue headphones out, he showed them to Piper. They were blue, with a Revs logo on each ear.

She blinked rapidly, but her hands froze their pinching motion.

With a brow arched, he eased them a little closer to her. "Thought maybe you could borrow them."

"Don't—" I said. If he put them on her, there was a good chance she'd lose it. Piper didn't like having her shoulders, neck, ears, or hair touched.

To my relief, he just held them in his palm and made no other move.

Piper turned his way and carefully eyed the blue headphones.

"Mom, can I plays with Grey?" Sam tugged on my black dress pants, startling me.

"Come on," Dylan said, taking his hand. "I'll get you settled while Mom helps Piper."

To my absolute shock, he happily followed her to the classroom and didn't look back. The tension in my shoulders eased a fraction as I watched them disappear. At least he was happy.

Piper, however, stood stiff as a board, still blinking rapidly. Kyle hadn't moved, so he was still squatted beside her, holding the headphones out patiently.

Finally, she tentatively stretched an arm out and took them. After a careful inspection, she put them over her ears. It only took a second before her entire body sagged.

Kyle tapped his ear, and Piper, understanding the silent request, stretched the headphones away from her head.

"There is a quiet area." He pointed across the room to an area by the window with a single beanbag chair. A double-sided bookshelf sat three feet to its right, and just past that, there was a colorful rug with four more beanbags. "You can pick any of the beanbags to chill in while you get used to the place."

She nodded, and with that, the two of them walked off, leaving me on my own. Piper chose the chair away from the others and settled into it.

"Everyone seems good," Dylan said as she headed back my way. "We'll call you if we need you. Get to work."

"She might run away," I blurted out, wringing my hands.

Dylan smiled patiently. "If she tries, we're equipped to handle it." She smiled patiently. "We've got security set up at both exits, and they are aware of the possibility." She patted my arm. "I promise the universe wants this all to work out."

I wasn't sure I believed in that kind of thing, but I forced my body to relax and took one more peek at Sam, who was happily building a magnet tower with Grey. Then I sought out Piper, who was sitting in the beanbag chair with the blue headphones on. Kyle stood behind her, looking relaxed. It almost seemed too easy. But I wouldn't complain. Plus, I didn't have time to overthink the situation. I had to get to work. So I slipped out the front door and headed for work.

Boston Lights was thirty-five minutes from the Langfield Corp building, so even after the easy drop-off, I barely made it to my desk by eight thirty.

"You had quite a weekend?" Carolyn, our do-it-all assistant, popped into my office while I was getting settled.

"I guess."

"You guess," she scoffed, the sound full of excitement. "On Friday, you catch a foul ball and become Boston's enemy number one, and then on Saturday, you hang out with the Revs. By Sunday, Kyle Bosco is calling you and the kids his friends and swearing that his comments on Friday were all in good fun."

"Yeah. I'm hoping it all blows over." Bostonians were as

passionate as they come when it came to sports, but, thank God, they were great about moving on rather quickly. And with the Bolts' season beginning and football and basketball in full swing, the Revs and all the drama associated with them would fade away for the next few months.

Carolyn dropped her head back and cackled. "Sure. Blow over. That's why some British woman called first thing this morning with instructions to contact her if we have issues with reporters."

My heart dropped. *Issues with reporters?*

"Don't Worry," Carolyn said, stepping closer. "We haven't. But Mrs. Price requested an hour of your time at lunch."

Frowning, I straightened a stack of papers on my desk. "Zara wants to have lunch with me?"

Carolyn smirked. "On a first name basis with the Price family, now, are we?"

I supposed the Price family seemed like a big deal. They were both gorgeous and famous. The kind of people who walked the red carpet at the Met Gala. But though I *was* on a first-name basis with Zara, it wasn't because we were friends. "It's not like that."

The walkie on my desk beeped, and the tinny voice of the orderly working in the common area echoed around my office. "Ms. Sparrow hasn't made it to breakfast."

"Duty calls." I stood and clicked my radio to my belt, popped in the earpiece, and pressed the button to reply. "I'll check her room."

"This conversation isn't done," Carolyn assured as I breezed past her.

With a roll of my eyes, I waved over my shoulder and headed out.

In no time, I was approaching Eleanor Sparrow's room on the fifth floor.

"Ms. Sparrow." I rapped on the door. When she didn't answer, I pulled out my card and unlocked it. "Eleanor," I called as I stepped into the tidy space.

"In here, dear," she said from the bathroom.

I opened the door and peeked in tentatively. Inside, she was awkwardly sitting on the seat in her shower with a towel draped over her body.

"What happened?" I asked. I'd known the woman for years, since she had been friends with my late grandmother.

When I turned eighteen, my grandmother had moved from the apartment we, along with my mother, shared and into Boston Lights. In order to spend more time with her, and because I could use the money, I'd taken a job as an assistant in the office here.

After my mother passed away a year later, Boston Lights became more than just a job. I spent more time here than anywhere else, even through college. Over thirteen years, I worked my way from assistant to director. And even after my grandmother passed away two years ago, I didn't want to leave.

Eleanor smiled. "Just a little dizzy, that's all. Figured I'd best sit until it passed."

"Why didn't you hit your call button?" I glanced at her wrist, but the gray band was missing. Turning, I scanned the bathroom. "Where is it?"

"It's in the bedroom." Her tone was matter-of-fact.

"What?" The shower was one of the most dangerous places for the elderly. We always made it clear that they should wear the device at all times.

"I don't put it on until after my shower in the morning."

I blinked. "You shouldn't take it off. You know it's important to wear it at all times."

"Don't be ridiculous. I could never sleep in that thing." She waved me off. "And showering in it? Good lord, my wrist would chafe."

I shook my head. Falling out of bed was almost as common as falling in the shower, and this woman wasn't wearing her alert bracelet in either place.

"The rules—"

"You and the rules." She chuckled. "Always so uptight."

Irritation prickled through me. She was the second person who'd said that in the last couple of days. "My job is to make sure that you're safe and that everything runs smoothly."

"Just like Lucy." She shook her head. "Your grandmother worried herself into indigestion every day."

As if on cue, my esophagus burned. I knew that feeling. I lived on Tums. And coffee.

With one hand holding her towel in place, she patted my arm with the other. "I don't need a button. I have the good sense the lord gave me. And when I'm dizzy, I sit down."

I sighed. "The button is to help. It's there just in case. For situations like this one."

"If we're always thinking about the 'just in case,' we miss the good things in life," Eleanor said. "Lucy would want you to enjoy life sometimes, you know."

Shoulders slumping, I sighed. "I do."

"When was the last time you did something other than work or take care of your kids?" She raised a gray brow. "I haven't heard a single story from you about anything outside of parenting in years. Remember when you'd visit Lucy? You'd bring some newfangled coffee flavor to try and tell her about your week."

Yes. I did remember. That was back when I was twenty-one and fun. Back when I had stories to tell. About the ridiculous guy I'd met at a bar. Or the trip to California with my friends. Friends I drifted from after having Piper. Friends I drifted even farther from after separating from Jace almost two years ago. Now my friends consisted mostly of coworkers. And I only saw them at work.

That sounded a bit pathetic now that I thought about it.

"I had a s'mores coffee today," I admitted. "It's the new one from Dunkin."

Her lips turned up at the corners, and her eyes brightened. "The one with the marshmallow whipped cream?"

I nodded. "It's amazing. I should bring you one this week."

"I would like that."

"Good." I patted her arm. "How about you get dressed? Then I'll take you down to the nurse to see about the dizziness."

After we determined the cause—low blood sugar—and fed Eleanor, my day didn't slow down. I dealt with a housekeeping issue and then argued with a food supplier about the rise in prices. The morning went by so quickly that I didn't even have time to worry about the kids and how they were doing at Little Fingers.

"Knock, knock."

At the sound of a soft voice in the doorway, I looked up from the paperwork I'd been sorting through. Zara, dressed professionally and looking flawless, was holding a brown bag and smiling.

"I hope I'm not interrupting, but the young woman out front said I could come in. I can come back later if you need. I'm on your schedule." The Britishness of the word *schedule* had me smiling.

"Sure, come in." I rushed to my feet.

"Sit," she ordered, brow furrowed. "I brought lunch."

Obediently, I dropped back into my seat. "Oh, you didn't have to."

"Nonsense." She strode across the room and sat in the chair on the other side of my desk. "I wanted to," she said. "If our boys are going to be friends, we need to get on too. Plus, I wanted to check in to see how you're feeling about the social media stuff."

How I was feeling? I supposed I didn't have a lot of feelings about it. "No one is egging my door anymore, so that's good, right?"

"I would hope so." With a laugh, Zara passed me a container. "It's a cobb salad. No dairy, no gluten, no dressing, no peppers. The lovely woman I spoke with when I called this morning said that would be acceptable."

I winced. The order made me sound as uptight as both Eleanor and Kyle had claimed.

"I'm vegan, so if anyone understands a difficult food order, it's me." Zara pulled a second container from the bag and set it on the desk in front of her. "But back to the other thing. Have you had any issues since Saturday?"

I shook my head. "The Uber driver who picked me up from Langfield Corp and brought me to work this morning didn't drive away when he saw who I was, so that's progress."

"I'm shooting for a higher bar here, darling." She laughed. "What about on your socials? I don't have your handles, so I haven't tagged you, but that doesn't mean people won't find you."

"I don't have social media." I shrugged. Growing up, our budget had been tight, so as a teenager, I didn't have a cell phone or a home computer. When I started college, I was busy studying and working.

Not only did I not have the time, but I also didn't care to join the craze. And now, I had even less time. Dull was an apt way of describing me.

"Huh." Zara shook her head, looking amused rather than bored or judgmental. "I don't think I've ever met a person who didn't have any social media."

The trepidation that usually came when people commented on the topic swirled, though her kind expression lessened the severity.

"I don't have time."

"Makes sense. It's such a bloody time suck. This morning, I fell down a rabbit hole and spent an hour watching giant waves."

"Waves?"

"Yes." She chuckled. "I kept watching videos of huge waves hitting all over the world." She shrugged, the move causing the neckline of her gold sweater to slip off her shoulder. She yanked it up like the garment had personally offended her. "I think I'm entirely too bloody bored all the time."

She pulled out her phone and turned it toward me. On the screen was a video of a wave hitting the coast of Portugal.

"See why I was desperate to have lunch with you? I'm going insane."

I laughed. "I very much doubt that."

"Oh, trust me. Boredom is the worst kind of torture. Asher thinks finding help for me will fix it. But honestly, why is Grey in day care? So I can go to the gym? Play tennis? Or that god-awful pickle ball game? I feel like I'm doing a whole lot of nothing. And how is that fulfilling?" Zara stabbed at her salad, and as she held up her fork, she eyed me sheepishly. "I'm sorry. You're busy. The last thing you need is to listen to me whine."

Maybe I was busier than she was, but the honest frustration and sadness in the statement called to me. The grass always seemed greener for the person who wasn't cutting and watering it.

"Yes, I'm busy and exhausted, and some days, I swear my daughter is sucking the life out of me. But that doesn't mean you can't feel just as worn out. Or like your life is being sucked out of you too."

With a warm smile, Zara nodded. From there, she went on chatting about her kids and life in Boston. Apparently, it was vastly different from LA, where she'd lived for ten years.

She was mid-sentence when my desk phone rang.

Carolyn's name appeared on the screen, so with a grimace, I said, "Excuse me one second," and picked up the receiver.

"Sorry to interrupt your lunch, but Kayla from Hope Speaks is on line one. She said it's about a grant application for Piper. She tried your cell first, but you didn't pick up."

"Put her through." I pulled the phone away from my mouth and said, "I'm sorry, but it's about Piper."

Zara waved me off and stabbed another bite of her salad. "Take your time."

The phone clicked as Carolyn connected the call, and I greeted the person on the other end with a quick hello.

"Hi," she said, her voice bubbly. "Is this Harper Wallace? I'm calling about your daughter's grant application with Hope Speaks. I wanted to let you know that Piper was chosen for funding."

"Oh." All the air rushed from my lungs, leaving my chest aching. "That's great."

"Yes. She's eligible for ABA and RDI immediately. And then we will work in sensory and equestrian therapies as we find what works best for her. We'll compile a list of therapists this week, and ABA services will begin on Monday."

Wow, that was fast. "What will I need to do?"

"Not much," she chirped. "We'll set up meetings with Piper so she can meet her therapist. Make sure she's comfortable. Every professional we work with is thoroughly trained and vetted. You'll have the opportunity to meet the therapist, but all we need from you is some paperwork."

"That's great." And way too easy. These kinds of grants could be life-changing, sure, but I had been under the impression that though the organization would pay for services, I'd be the one doing the legwork to find therapists and schedule appointments. I'd applied to six or seven. I wasn't even sure anymore. Maybe this one was different. I jotted the name *Hope Speaks* on a sticky note so I could google it later and refresh my memory.

"You have her listed as attending West Side Elementary." She went on to list my address and her father's. "So I'll need information about childcare so we can schedule therapy for the hours after school. Or we can work with your parenting schedule and have it in your home."

With a deep breath in, I explained her current day care situation, but warned her that it was temporary.

"We'll worry about the change in your childcare situation later. For now, we'll get the ball rolling. It shouldn't be difficult. Langfield Corp is always great to work with. They even allow us access to their facilities for OT and things like that. So that makes it easy."

"Oh, good." I didn't know what else to say. Because how the hell did she know that off the top of her head? Dylan hadn't mentioned anything of the sort.

"I'll email you the forms and additional information. We can chat again later."

"Absolutely."

Unease crept through me as I hung up the phone. I could be jaded, and despite my best efforts, I was feeling that way now. Even as I wondered what kind of person looked a gift horse in the mouth like this.

"Good news?" Zara asked.

With a nod, I explained the situation with Piper with probably far more detail than Zara wanted. Though she listened attentively.

"That's amazing. Dylan is like magic. Everything about Little Fingers makes life easy." She rested her elbows on the desk and leaned in closer. "I have a request," she said. "This might seem crazy since we just met. But it's my birthday next Friday. Hitting the big three-oh." She rolled her bright blue eyes. "And Asher's throwing a party. Karaoke at some bar. It's more his thing than mine." She waved a hand. "My friends in Boston are few and far between, so the guest list consists of most of the team and WAGs."

"Wags?"

"Wives and girlfriends. They're lovely, but most are childless, and I have almost nothing in common with them." She sighed. "Would you come? Then I'd have someone to prattle on with."

"Oh." My heart thumped against my ribcage at the invitation. It had been a long time since I'd been invited to hang out like this. I wasn't the kind of person others wanted to go out with anymore. And I'd normally turn down invitations like this since the kids were with me the vast majority of the time. When they weren't, I was usually catching up on housework or sleep. But Sam and Grey had hit it off immediately, and I'd love to find a mom friend who wasn't intimidated by Piper. Zara had spent time around her, and so far, she hadn't been fazed. Maybe it was possible.

She sank back into her chair. Her smile remained, but it had gone brittle, forced. "If you think it's too much, or you don't want to—"

"No," I rushed out. "I'd love to come."

She perked up in her chair, her eyes brightening.

"But I haven't had the best luck with babysitters. My ex is supposed to have the kids that night, though. So as long as he doesn't cancel, I can make it work."

"Oh." She clapped quietly, grinning. "I'm so happy you're coming."

That wasn't anywhere near a guarantee, but I didn't correct her.

KYLE
11

"IF WE ADJUST the tube three-quarters of an inch to the right, then the ball will exit at the same angle as the next line," Collette explained to Piper as she bent down and used a ruler to adjust the tube, causing her blond braids to slip over her shoulder.

"Good." Phoebe, Collette's twin sister, nodded.

"We are so going to the crush them." I rubbed my hands together. I could taste our victory already. My girls were rocking this.

Across the room, Dylan's teenage son, Liam, and his team of six were setting up a piddly domino run. They didn't stand a chance against us. Grey had already knocked their line over twice in his excitement, and they hadn't even figured out how to get the last domino from the table to hit the first on the floor. Not to mention, ours went over a bookshelf, down the desk and across half the room. We had three twists and one Matchbox car run. Between the twins, who were smarter than most rocket scientists, and Piper, we were going to crush them.

Dylan coughed, garnering my attention, and when I eyed her, she gave me a frown.

"Right, right. Not a contest," I corrected, although I didn't mean it. "This is just for fun."

"Right." Collette's tone was just as placating as mine.

Piper surveyed the other group's setup. "I don't see a single category in which theirs would be better than ours."

"Exactly." A devilish cackle left Phoebe's lips as she held up a fist.

Piper looked at Phoebe's hand and blinked. Then she hesitantly tapped her knuckles against the older girl's. The twins were a few years older than she was, but they had taken her under their wing within an hour of our arrival.

My phone buzzed in my pocket, so without disturbing the girls or their dominoes, I shifted back and dug it out.

> Kayla: Got approval from the mom. She didn't ask too many questions, but I could hear them in her voice. Be ready for a bunch after she gets the email.

Of course Harper would make this hard. Because of their connection to me, it would be against guidelines and rules to award Piper a grant.

But I could get around that easily. Rather than give her the grant from Hope Speaks, I would pay for Piper's therapy outright. As long as I took care of the bills, I'd keep all communication running through Hope Speaks. Unless Harper became difficult. And already, the potential was looming.

> Me: Just keep the language in the email vague.

> Kayla: You're the boss. (But I'm telling you again that this is a bad idea. When it blows up, please don't fire me.)

> Me: You and Cam have made your opinions clear.

They had both given me the *just tell her the truth* speech. But that wouldn't get us anywhere. If she knew, then there was no way she'd accept any type of help from me. She was barely tolerating me as it was. Eventually I'd have to talk to her about my relationship with JJ, but I'd wait until she and I were on better terms.

"We are locking in this win," Phoebe called to a girl with dark hair on the other side of the room.

The girl, who was about her age, responded by sticking out her tongue.

"Winnie, Phoebe, don't fight," Dylan said, keeping her tone melodic, even as she reprimanded the kids. "Maybe it's time for a snack break."

"Is it cookie time, Auntie Dylan?" a boy with dark hair and wide eyes asked quietly.

A boy in jeans and a denim jacket buttoned up to his neck stepped up beside Kai. His curly hair was like a brown puffball on his head. "Can we all have cookies?"

Dylan smiled. "Sure, we can do a cookie break, Finn."

Piper whipped around, her pigtails smacking her cheeks. "It is *not* snack time. We had a snack at ten thirty. It's now 1:04." Her hands were balled into fists on either side of her and pressed into the carpet, and her body was rigid.

Bummer. A cookie sounded good. The gluten-free pretzels and juice boxes had been the bomb at snack time, even if Dylan's lanky teenager had given me a look when I sat down at the table with kids, patiently waiting for my serving. Apparently he thought he was too old for a juice box. I would never be too old, though.

But Piper thrived on a set schedule, and I didn't want her fight-or-flight instinct to kick in. For a kid like her, whose body wouldn't produce the dopamine reaction the ways others did, a small change like this could cause a panicked reaction, and it could be incredibly difficult for her to rein herself in.

I held a hand out to Dylan. "We don't have to have a snack." With a look that begged her to hold off for another few minutes before bringing out the cookies, I turned to Piper. "What time did I say I'd take you up to the batting cages?"

The question was simple, but it was a reassurance that we had a schedule and that we'd stick to it.

Piper blinked rapidly, her stress increasing. "*You said* we would leave here at 1:15 because *you said* we could bat at one thirty, since no one else would be there."

"Yes." I gave her a succinct nod. "That's exactly what we'll do."

With that, she let out a long breath, and her hands relaxed.

"So we can do this for another ten minutes. Okay?"

She surveyed the dominos, her focus moving over them quickly. "And Mom can see this when she comes because it will stay and she can see it?"

I nodded, glancing at Dylan for backup. Approval, really. I was taking a lot of liberties in her facility.

"We'll put up the play fence to protect it," she promised. Dylan was one of the most easy-going people I'd ever met, and her general calm seemed to help Piper. That was a relief, since I was only here until she found more help.

"We should take a video of the whole thing once it's set up," Phoebe suggested. "Then we should record it again when it's falling down."

Piper blinked, and then she smiled at the blond girl. She didn't make eye contact, but her focus was fixed somewhere around Phoebe's neck. Piper's smiles, I was learning, were few and far between.

"Yes," she said. "Then we will have it forever."

"Exactly," Collette agreed with a proud nod.

When the girls were finished, I used my phone to take a video of the entire run as it stood. Then Dylan got the toddler fence out of the closet and put it up around their creation to protect it. Once Piper was certain it was secure, she and I headed up to the cages.

The vibration of the metal bat against a ball was great sensory input. My hope was that the input, along with the pressure on her joints, would alleviate some of the stress that had built up inside Piper today. If it didn't help, then I'd take her to the training room and let her jump on the mini trampoline for a while.

"I know you love the Revs, but have you ever played baseball?"

"With Mom sometimes," she said, her eyes darting around, taking in the details of the space—the netting, the clean white walls with a blue Revs logo in the center of each one, the turf beneath our feet, and the sound-deadening pads hanging around us. "I tried once with Dad, but I don't like his mitt. It had bumps. He said I had to use it. Then he got frustrated and called Mom so we could go home."

I winced, and my heart ached for the kid and her dad. Parenting a child on the spectrum wasn't without its challenges. "How about hitting balls off a tee?"

She shrugged.

Taking that as a sign that she'd be up for trying, I pulled everything we'd need over and set it up. Ten minutes later, as she nailed another ball off the tee, it was clear this had been a great idea.

"Keep your swing level. You're pulling up after you make contact," I corrected.

She studied the tee, then the bat, and without looking at me, she nodded. I could see how people who didn't understand Piper would consider her difficult. She danced along the line of composure and being stressed out all day long. Though the closest thing I'd seen to a meltdown from her today was the aftermath of her argument with Harper this morning, I could imagine how easily these could happen.

But as we worked on hitting off the tee, she was eager to please. Just like with the domino run, she wanted to do it right. She liked the positive reinforcement. Craved it, really, but she was worried about making a mistake. Doing things wrong. Especially new things.

Her bat cracked against the ball and sent it flying hard and high.

"Awesome. That was it." I smiled, but I didn't offer her a fist bump or a high five. Although she might oblige, like she had with Phoebe, it was clear she preferred her space.

"How do you like Little Fingers so far?"

With a shrug, she picked up another ball and set it on the tee. "I like the girls with the dominos. They make sense."

I tried not to chuckle. Phoebe and Collette were definitely organizers. They didn't play. They created a group of children who could dominate whatever activity they were performing. I appreciated that they were intelligent enough to see potential in Piper.

"I'm going to hit some balls too, if that's okay."

She shrugged, her focus still fixed on the ball on the tee.

Since she was still relaxed, I forced out the big news and crossed my fingers that she'd take it well. "Some people are going to come in and talk to us. Hope that's all right with you."

Piper turned in my direction, her attention skating up so high her eyes almost met mine before she glanced away.

"Why?"

Because I knew better than to bullshit her, I stuck to the truth. "They want to meet you. And I want you to tell me which one you like the best."

She sent a ball sailing across the cage, then picked up another. "Do I have to stop playing?"

"No."

She nodded, then got into the position I'd shown her.

I fired off a message to Cam and then set up the pitching machine. I'd cracked off three good hits before the door opened and a tall brunette walked in. I ignored her. She wasn't here to talk to me. Thankfully, she headed straight to the fence. She chatted with Piper for about five minutes, and then she was gone. Two more women and a man popped in, one at a time, before I shut off my pitches.

"A bat weighs twenty-seven ounces."

Brows raised, I eyed Piper, who was surveying her bat seriously.

"But it feels like more after you swing a lot."

I chuckled. "Isn't that the truth. Do you have Jell-O arms?"

She assessed one arm, then the other, and with a frown, she zeroed in on a spot on my shirt. "My arms are made of bones and skin."

"I'm sorry." I bit back a laugh this time. A lot of kids with ASD were very literal. "Do they feel like wiggly bands?"

She gently dropped her bat, then stretched her arms out. As she dropped them, her lips turned up just a fraction. "Maybe."

"Means you worked them hard. Maybe you'll want to play baseball someday." I picked up her bat and headed for the rack. "Now we gotta get all the balls." I pointed to the end of the cage.

She strode toward them, on a mission, as I grabbed the bucket. Together, we picked the balls up off the turf and dropped them into the bucket.

"I can't play baseball," she finally said.

"Why not?"

"I tried T-ball last year, but my coach told Mom I wasn't normal enough to play."

The hot fury that rushed through me when her words registered was like nothing I'd experienced before. "Normal?" I tried not to grit my teeth as I spit out the word.

"It was raining, and I didn't want to get wet, so I ran back to the car." She snagged another ball from the ground. "But I heard the coach tell her that in order to be on his team, I had to be normal."

That was bullshit if I'd ever heard it. I wanted to wipe that idea from her head.

"Do you know Cortney Miller?"

Of course she did. Rather than just saying *yes*, she spouted his stats. She was fucking impressive.

"He can do some of the same things you do. List stats for anyone in the league. He's really good at it."

Straightening with another ball in her hand, she frowned down at the floor.

"But he worries a lot. Sometimes he would worry so much that he would have trouble playing the game. He couldn't focus if he was wearing the wrong socks or if a clip on his leg guard was the wrong color."

She blinked.

"And Christian Damiano? He's afraid of germs and dirty things. The entire league changed the resin rules for him."

Another blink.

"Emerson Knight? He has trouble focusing sometimes. He'll walk right into walls if he isn't careful." I squatted beside her, not the least bit surprised when she didn't look at me. I picked up a ball and held it out to her. "There is no set of rules that makes a person normal. Anyone can do anything they put their mind to."

She took the ball and swallowed audibly. "Are there players like them on other teams too?"

"You know Corey Matthews? The New York Metros' pitcher? He has dyslexia. He's struggled with reading his entire life. And Bennett King, the catcher on the Rose City Roasters, is deaf. And Asher Adler from Atlanta is diagnosed with ASD just like you."

She blinked twice and dropped the ball into the bucket. Then she was off, picking up another one. Rather than pressing her, I let the idea sink into her brain. Hopefully it resonated with her. Hopefully she'd recall it when she needed the reminder.

"Did you like any of the people who came in to talk to you today?" I asked as we finished up the ball collecting.

"Maybe the first one," she said. Her tone was emotionless, but she'd answered quickly.

Huh. She was Cam's favorite too. "Her name is Ashley. What did you like about her?"

"She didn't smell, and she didn't ask dumb questions. She does therapy like Ms. Temton does at school." She picked up the full bucket and waddled back toward the front of the cages. "It's three thirty. We are going back to the other room now, right?"

Once she'd set the bucket back exactly where we'd found it, I opened the gate and motioned for her to exit the cage. "Would you want to hang out with Ashley again?"

"When?" Without looking at me, she moved toward the door.

"After school most days. For an hour or so."

"Why?" She turned, her lips tugged down. "Are you not coming here anymore?"

"I can't come every day," I said honestly. "I'm still playing baseball. I have two years left on my contract. After that, I'll probably offer therapy like Ms. Temton and Ashley."

"When you do that," she said as we took the steps down to the underground tunnel that ran between the stadium and Langfield Corp, "will you do it with me?"

"I'd love that," I said. I really would. "But we'd have to see what Mom says before we made plans."

She was quiet as we moved through the hallways and when we stepped back into the Little Fingers rooms. Without a word, without needing reassurance, she shuffled over to the beanbag chair she'd been in earlier, put her headphones on, and just sat.

For a very out-of-the-ordinary day, Piper had been handling things exceptionally well. She hadn't had a fit or tantrum since we arrived this morning. There were a few moments when she was on the edge, but she remained in control. That was a testament to both her hard work and Harper's. After spending the day with Piper, I had to admit that Harper was raising an amazing little girl.

Dylan stepped up beside me. "You didn't agree to the twins' idea about posting the domino runs on your social media and having fans vote for the winner, right?"

A chuckle burst out of me. "Of course I did." I spun to the redhead. "I gotta show off my team's talent."

She sighed and fiddled with the pink stone pendant on the necklace she always wore. "But Kyle, the twins and Piper are clearly gifted. They created a…" She waved her hand at their masterpiece. It was truly amazing. It was rainbow-colored, starting with red and ending ten feet later with purple. Every part fit the color scheme, and the twists and turns were perfectly spaced. "A very clickable social media post." She frowned over at the other domino run. "And the other group tried really hard."

I wouldn't say it out loud, but it was borderline pathetic. It looked as if it had gotten knocked over again while I was gone, because it was only about three feet long at this point.

"You should have Cort post. Make sure the internet knows his son's team built it."

A deep growl sounded behind me. "Don't pick on Liam."

I turned, finding the giant man three steps behind me, holding his baby girl in the crook of one arm.

"You don't think you can out-post me? Come on, old man."

"Watch it, Streaks. We're almost the same age," he huffed.

"Nah, all those life points you've been collecting lately have added to your age." I pointed at him. "Retired. Plus ten life points. Practically married." I turned that finger to his fiancée. "Ten life points." I nodded at his daughter. "Kids. Twenty life points. So by my math, you're seventy-five."

He dropped his head and gave it a shake. "You're a moron."

"How about this? We'll deduct life points if you do this post-off against me and win."

"I have a feeling you'll be gaining 'life points'"—he lifted his free hand and made air quotes—"here soon."

Willow got a fistful of her dad's hair and yanked, but the move barely fazed him.

"I've got another two years before I even think about retiring." Chuckling, I crossed my arms over my chest.

He gently pried his daughter's fingers from his hair and straightened. "Not what I meant. More the practically married part."

Dylan's eyes widened, and she bounced on her toes. "Oh my God. Is this like what happened with Liv and Becks? Where he's all 'I'm not into her,' and they bicker all the time, but it's only because he doesn't have her yet?" Her voice was high-pitched as she finished the question.

My gut lurched. "No," I assured her quickly and curtly.

But Cortney just raised a brow and smirked.

"I love that." Dylan laced her fingers under her chin and tipped her head.

With a sharp breath in, I gathered my thoughts, ready to explain again that Harper wasn't my type. But I was stopped by the sound of a grating voice behind me.

"You co-own Hope Speaks?"

Wincing, I slowly turned around, finding myself trapped in Harper's glare.

"Ooh." Dylan shook her head. "Let's get that orangy-red passion out in the hall."

I didn't know what the orangy-red shit she was talking about was, but I nodded anyway and led a glaring Harper out the door.

"You're Hope Speaks, and you picked Piper for a grant." With her mouth pressed in a firm line like that, the small bow of her upper lip became more pronounced.

I tried not to think about how that lip had felt against my finger this morning. It was no use. The memory of the warm satin flesh was a taunt. And the slow puff of air that rushed across my skin when she'd released her breath?

Damn. Those simple thoughts had a wave of need rolling through me.

Her eyes sparked with fire like they had this morning. "Are you going to even bother responding?"

Fuck. With a thick swallow, I forced myself to focus. "I do run Hope Speaks, but I didn't pick the grant recipients this year."

That was the truth. Kayla had narrowed them down, and Mason had picked the two recipients, neither of whom was Piper. But that nugget of information wasn't going to help me win this argument.

She huffed. "I don't like being bulldozed."

"Bulldozed." I repeated the word to give myself a moment to come up with an answer because, shit, I knew exactly what she meant.

"Yes, Kyle. I googled Hope Speaks. It's definitely you. You can't come into our lives and start trying to take control. I don't understand your motives here. And—"

That was fair. What I was doing only made sense to me, and I was doing it because I'd made a promise to my best friend. A promise that definitely didn't include tasting whipped cream off this woman's lip. But fucking hell, I'd seen that flash of pleasure in her eyes as she sipped my coffee, and instinct had taken over.

But that wouldn't happen again. I knew better. Harper needed help, and unfortunately, that kind of help didn't include orgasms. I shook my head. Harper and orgasms should be two very separate topics in my mind. Harper went with things like *stay away*. And *you know better than to even think about her that way.*

"Why are you shaking your head? I'm dead serious."

I believed it, but I had been too in my head for the last few minutes to hear what she'd said.

"I know."

"Good. So we agree that Boston seems pretty much over the whole foul ball thing. And you've more than made up for your tirade. And you agree that it's time to move on?" Harper cocked her head to the side, and a stray piece of hair swept across her cheek.

My hand twitched with the urge to brush it back, but I restrained myself by locking my arm against my side. "Piper needs the therapy that Hope Speaks can offer. Don't stop her from getting it because you're annoyed with me."

Her shoulders tightened and her jaw locked. "I'm not saying she can't accept the grant."

The grimace she was sporting made it clear it hurt to say those words. Fuck. If she knew I was personally paying for the services? She'd probably combust. It was a good thing I didn't plan to tell her that.

"Good. You can run it all through Hope Speaks. She met a therapist she liked today. Ashley is qualified to do ABA and RDI."

She opened her mouth, but before she could respond, I kept going.

"Kayla will set up a meeting so you can meet Ashley before she starts. I won't be there, so no worries."

Some of the wind left her sails. "Good."

"Yup. So we're good. No more bulldozing. Just the kids getting what they need."

She sighed, her shoulders lowering. "Yes. Great. Thank you." It still pained her to say it, but her grimace wasn't quite so pronounced this time.

"You're welcome."

With her chin lifted, she stepped around me and into the classroom. That could have gone worse.

KYLE
12

Me: Hey, clicky-clicky and vote for my team.

Dragon: Why am I voting on dominos falling down?

Bambi: Look how cute the little one is it's like that book. What's it called the little train that could

Angel Boy: Engine.

Bambi: GIF of I think I can, I think I can

Me: Why is my lead shrinking? Did any of you vote?

Bambi: I voted for the little one

Me: That's the wrong one.

Angel Boy: Grey made that one. I voted for it too.

New guy: Sorry Beckett and Cortney already cornered me and told me I had to vote and share their kids' dominos thing.

Me: Team loyalty man

New guy: They're the ones who pay me.

Bambi: Yeah don't bite the fork that feeds you.

Dragon: It's about a hand not a fork

New guy: Who the fuck eats people's hands?

Me: You all suck. But I'm still winning.

Me: GIF of a hell yeah!

Me: GIF of victory

DRAGON LEFT THE CHAT

Mama: I voted just like you asked. And walked Ryan and Bill through voting too.

Me: You're the best Mom. Did you ask your friends from the club?

Mama: Of course, darling. I always ask the girls to vote. Now what do you think of black granite?

Mama: Pic of sample of granite sitting on half-finished cabinets

Mama: Or soapstone?

Mama: Pic of sample of soapstone

Me: Are you remodeling your kitchen?

Mama: Bill and I got inspired when Joan did hers.

Me: You didn't tell me?

Mama: You talk as if you tell me everything you do.

Me: I will.

Mama: No thank you. Some things are better for mothers to never know.

Harper
13

"YOU'RE the worst mom in the world," Piper shouted as she clutched the headrest of my driver's seat and held on for dear life. From my position outside her door, I couldn't easily get her out.

My heart pounded and my stomach burned. That was exactly what I was trying *not* to be—the worst parent in the world. Keeping a tight hold on my patience was getting harder by the second. After almost ten minutes of this, I wanted to yank my daughter out of the car and tell her to suck it up.

But I couldn't. She wasn't trying to be difficult. Her anxiety was just so high that her body was experiencing real fear. From my perspective, we were sitting safely in the drop-off line. But Piper might as well have been fleeing from a bear for the amount of adrenaline and fear flowing through her system. So the only option was to work through this.

At least I'd gotten my car back from the repair shop last night. If we had been having this fight in an Uber or a cab, I might have cried.

But I wasn't crying. It would all be okay. I had already let Little Fingers know Sam would be late, and I'd texted Carolyn, asking her to push my morning meeting back to ten. See? I had my life under control.

"It's Thursday, Piper. It's a school day." I kept my tone calm, reassuring. Although she'd been off on Monday, she'd gone to school without a fight on Tuesday and Wednesday. "So we are going to school today."

"I. Am. Not."

She threw a leg out, and I dodged her sneaker-clad foot. Barely.

"You are mean. I need a break."

You and me both, kid. What I'd give to say *you know what, Pipe? I need a break too. Let's stay home.* Especially since she'd been up four times throughout the night. Neither of us was at our best after that. Staying home meant we wouldn't have had to fight about the dirty purple shirt she'd wanted to wear. Not going to school would have meant not having to braid her hair, which would have kept my arm free of teeth marks. Staying home would have been easy, but I had a job, and she had school. We didn't have the luxury of staying home.

"Piper." I swallowed. Then, with a deep breath in, I forced the next words out of my mouth. It was a challenge, because more than anything, I wanted to say *yes baby, we can have a break.* "It's a school day and I have work."

"I don't care," she screeched. When she kicked again, I did my best to dodge it, but a woman appeared at my side, startling me, and Piper's sneaker caught my hip.

I winced at the instant throb. This was exhausting. Most days, I could pretend I wasn't alone. Like I didn't feel like I was treading water in the middle of a lake while strangers and even people I knew stood at the shoreline and threw rocks at me. But as I dodged her foot again, I couldn't get the metaphor out of my brain.

"Ma'am. I'm telling you again," this stranger said, "you can't park here. This is a drop-off area."

If she knew what was good for her, she'd walk away and leave us to our chaos. But this was the third time she'd asked me to move, and she didn't understand that if I climbed back in and moved this car even a foot, Piper would see it as a win, and she'd only double down when I tried to coax her out again.

I hadn't planned on participating in World War III when I pulled up this morning. Most of the time, Piper got out of the car without a problem and walked inside. To encourage that, I pulled up this way every day, even on the bad ones, acting as if I was certain she'd get out. And sometimes it was all she needed to snap out of it and feel ready to face the day. That semblance of normalcy, of routine.

"I know," I replied to the woman I'd never seen before, though I was still looking at my daughter.

The woman huffed. "You need to move."

I wanted to lose it on this crossing guard with an overly inflated ego. Could she not see what I was dealing with? Couldn't she wait until I'd gotten Piper out of the car before she harassed me?

From his car seat, Sam set his worried brown eyes on me. They were full of apprehension, but also embarrassment. He hated days like this. I had to remain cool and collected for him as well as Piper, because next year, this would be his school, and the last thing I wanted was for him to dread being here.

"No school. You can't make me." Piper grasped the armrest of her booster seat and tugged.

Before I remembered not to use my left hand, I locked it around the other armrest and held it in place. Although the injury was improving and the bruise had started to fade, pain still radiated up my arm.

"Put it down."

She kicked again. This time landing a blow to my ribs.

My eyes burned. Between my hand and my hip, I was done. I grabbed the seat with my good hand and let my injured one dangle at my side. "Put it down," I pleaded, my voice cracking.

"Excuse me," a deep voice called from behind me.

I ignored it. Having a bigger audience would do me no good. When Piper was in a mood as bad as this one, it was a struggle to get her back in control. Dealing with people we didn't know hovering nearby only made it worse.

My hand was still locked onto the car seat, my eyes on her face, although she wouldn't look at me. "Let go of the seat."

The newcomer stood so close, his heat soaked into my back. An arm brushed against my shoulder, and then there was a set of blue Revs headphones dangling between my daughter and me.

With a blink, Piper stopped yanking on the seat she had been trying to throw at me.

I didn't have to turn to know who had joined us. The headphones were identical to the noise-canceling kind Kyle had given her at Little Fingers.

On Monday, we'd come to an agreement about keeping our distance, and so far, we'd stuck to it. Though Sam and Piper talked about seeing him each day, I hadn't. So why was he here now?

Piper blinked again, then she finally released the booster seat so she could snag the headphones. Once she'd pulled them over her ears, she shut her eyes and slumped against the front seat.

I should have been relieved. The fight was over, at least for the moment, and I was no longer drowning. But now I was wallowing in the guilt and defeat that came with feeling as if I'd failed my child. I'd fought with her for almost fifteen minutes, yet Kyle had calmed her in a matter of seconds.

I dropped the booster seat and spun to the man behind me.

"Why are you here?" I asked, my tone harsher than I meant it to be.

He held both hands up and took a step back. "Dylan said you were running late because Piper didn't want to go to school. I'm just trying to help."

"Why?"

It didn't make sense. Days like today were emotionally exhausting. I loved my daughter fiercely, but even I didn't want to be here right now, so why the hell did this man keep showing up?

He took another step back, his palms still in the air. "I just wanted to help."

I glanced down at the kids. Piper's eyes were shut, and Sam was watching us. Though his expression had evened out a bit. Lightly, I pushed the car door shut. And then I took a deep breath.

"I'm not trying to be rude, but Kyle, I barely have enough band-width to get through good days, let alone days like this, without your commentary."

His deep brown eyes met mine. The lines around them softened slightly.

"I don't have anything left, and even if I did, I literally don't have time. Not for games, not for criticism, not for anything." My voice cracked, and I cleared my throat. "So whatever you want from me, whatever you're looking for, I can assure you, I don't have it."

The last thing I expected when I poured it all out like that was for him to pull me into his chest. Though that wasn't true, I supposed, because what was even more surprising was the way my body melted into him like a hug was exactly what I needed.

The second I was encircled in his strong arms, I sagged. Like I'd let out a breath I hadn't realized I was holding. The wall of his chest was the solid support I needed to keep me upright, and my head rested perfectly below his shoulder. It was odd, the way a simple hug made me feel like I wasn't carrying the weight of the world on my shoulders anymore. My eyes welled, but I blinked hard, staving off the tears. I was not going to cry over a hug. That was ridiculous.

I forced in a deep breath. Despite my efforts, it was shaky. But there was nothing I could do to hide that detail.

After my second breath, Kyle finally spoke. "I don't want anything from you, Crabby," he whispered against the top of my head. "I promise I'm asking for nothing. Just let me be the rope you can grab on to when you need me. Because, trust me, I know what it is to feel like you're drowning."

With another breath, this one steadier, I pulled back and tipped my head back.

He watched me with an expression so earnest I couldn't help but take him at his word. I was too tired to question him, anyway. Too worn out from treading water alone.

Slowly, I nodded.

One corner of his mouth quirked up. "Cam's over there. Take Sam and go." He released me and tipped his head toward the black Escalade parked in a spot designated for guests. Right where it was supposed to be.

"I can't—"

"You have a meeting. I have a free day." The small smile turned into the kind of smirk he often wore when he was photographed by the media. A playboy expression that said *I always get what I want.* "All I have is a lot of time on my hands and a competitive streak that just won't die, so if Piper wants to try to beat me in a battle of wills about school, then I say good fucking luck."

I snorted, but my mouth unwillingly pulled up in a smile.

"Seriously, you have a busy day. I've got this." He held his hand out, palm up.

It took me a moment to realize he wanted my keys, and when I did, I was tempted to say no. Because this was my job as a parent. But the truth was that I did have a meeting. And I was mentally drained, which meant I was at risk of giving in to Piper. And if I did that, I could guarantee tomorrow would be impossible. Once Piper knew she could win, she would fight that much harder. So instead of arguing, I passed him my keys.

"And don't worry. I got Medusa handled."

"Medusa?" I paused with my hand on the door handle.

He pointed to the woman who was standing on the steps leading to the school's entrance, her face set in a firm scowl. "You can't tell me you didn't notice the way she tries to turn people to stone with that glare."

With a laugh, I shook my head. Then I opened the back door. "Come on, Sam. We're going to ride with Mr. Cam."

Sam climbed out, hauling his booster seat with him, and took my hand, his expression one of relief.

We'd only taken two steps when I turned back. "Kyle."

He looked my way.

"Thank you."

His smile was surprisingly humble when he gave me a quick nod. As Sam and I headed across the lot, Kyle climbed into the car with my daughter and quietly shut the door.

"Next stop, Little Fingers," Cam called as I buckled Sam into his booster. "That," he said as I climbed into the passenger seat, "is for you." He pointed to the cup in the console between us. "Kyle seems to think you like his kind of coffee. Whipped cream and all."

I rolled my eyes but picked up the cup and brought it to my lips. The truth of it was, I kinda did. There were a lot of things I was starting to like about Kyle Bosco, and that meant I needed to be really careful.

KYLE
14

Unknown: Did you get her inside? Or are you still sitting in my car?

Me: Who dis?

Crabby: More than one person handed over a set of car keys to the great Kyle Bosco today?

Me: Good to see you got your sass back Crabby.

Me: But yes, she's inside the school building and your car is in your parking spot at Boston Lights with the key on the back wheel.

Crabby: You've got the magic touch today huh?

Kyle: I am always magic baby.

Crabby: 😶

Me: I think what you're trying to say is thank you.

Crabby: Yes. It actually is. Thank you Kyle.

Me: Careful if you're too nice I might think this is a prank text and not really Harper Wallace.

Crabby: Selfie of Harper at her desk frowning

Me: Selfie of Kyle and Sam, both grinning, in front of a Lego tower

KYLE
15

JJ: Harper says Hope Speaks is helping with Piper's therapies?

Me: Are you asking for the details, or are you asking what we told Harper?

JJ: Motherfucker. I know we agreed that you staying neutral would be better, all things considered, but lying is what got me into this situation to begin with.

Me: No one has lied. Some things are just being left vague.

JJ: GIF of a man beating his head against a desk.

Me: Look she seems less uptight and stressed right?

JJ: I guess...

Me: And I guarantee the kids are happier. I see them every day.

JJ: Rub it in man. You said you'd help me get more time with them and fix this fucking mess of a family.

Me: I am. I swear. Trust me.

Mama: You'll be home for Thanksgiving?

Me: Of course. I need some of my favorite chocolate cream pie.

Mama: JJ had just mentioned a trip to Tahiti with some other ball players.

Me: Yeah I ended up canceling that.

Mama: Oh really? That doesn't sound like my boy.

Me: Just got some stuff here.

Mama: Would stuff happen to be a girl?

Me: Don't start again Mama.

KYLE
16

"THIRTY-FOUR?" Dylan scrutinized the massive pile of colored boxes, a frown tugging at her lips.

"Sam wanted more Lego sets. It didn't seem fair to get him a new set only, so I got a few for everyone." I shrugged.

"Our facility isn't big enough for all the stuff you keep bringing in."

The place looked plenty big to me. There were huge areas of play space, and there was room for more shelves under the far windows.

"It's not that much stuff."

She pursed her lips as she dragged the pink crystal on her neck along its silver chain. "First it was more dominos so you and Piper could beat the other team."

"It's not my fault your fiancé cheated." I shrugged. Cortney had gone out of his way to get just about all of my teammates here, as well as his former teammates from the New York Metros, to vote for his domino run. "I had the lead almost all day, but then he pulled ahead." I roughed a hand over my jaw. Still couldn't get over how close I'd come to losing. "Piper and I needed some extra material for the final push."

"And you won." Dylan sighed. "Then you got the full Playmobil

set. Do you know how many pieces came with it? I still don't understand why you thought we needed it." She put her hands on her hips
and scanned the colorful space.

"Grey and Sam asked for a pirate ship, so I did a little research.
Once I started looking, I couldn't pick just one. There were so many
awesome options." I'd never put much thought into kids' toys. At least
not since I was little. So I'd never realized how cool they could be.
These, especially, had so many details. The cannons on the ships even
had little balls that shot out of them. "So I bought a few."

She pointed across the room. "A few? Try a few *dozen*. And then
you figured we needed more finger paint colors?"

"You only had three..."

"Yeah. The primary colors. So I can teach kids how to mix them to
make their own shades." She turned and pointed. "Now I have a new
shelf and every color ever made."

I nodded. "So Sam has options. I'll get a table and some more
shelving for the Legos too."

Her shoulders slumped. "Kyle Bosco, you have a big heart. And
apparently way too much time and money." She patted my arm. "So
later this week, we're going to have to start thinking about what we're
donating to The Greater Boston Family Crisis Network. Delia has put a
lot of time and effort into it, and they're always in need of items or
monetary donations for the moms and kids they support. It'd do a
whole lot more good there than here. No one here needs any more
stuff."

I wasn't sure that was true, but it was a battle for another day.

"Okay." That didn't mean I had to stop buying things for Sam and
Grey.

The door opened, and Piper slipped inside. Ashley, her therapist,
came in behind her. The two had started ABA therapy on Monday, and
they'd had their third session today. I was tempted to pull Ashley
aside and pick her brain. Ask how it was going. Find out what Piper
needed to work on. But that wasn't my place. Harper was right. I'd
been bulldozing like crazy. So I was trying to help while keeping
myself removed.

When I showed up last at Piper's school on Thursday, I expected

Harper to send me away with a glare. But it had been clear before I even stepped out of the Escalade that between her daughter's fit and the awful woman running drop-off, she was on the verge of breaking down.

The sight of those glassy, exhausted, amber eyes mixed with the iron will she possessed to get her daughter to school had yanked hard at my soul. The woman was tough as nails, but she needed support, a friend to lean on. And dammit if I didn't wish I could be that friend.

Even if JJ didn't entirely trust my plan, a friendship between Harper and me would be a good thing. For all of us.

"Hey, Pipe," I called.

She turned, her eyes lifting to my face for a second before she looked away.

"Want to build something with Legos?"

With a succinct nod, she shuffled to the tower of boxes and chose one. Although Sam needed help to follow the step-by-step instructions and find the right pieces, Piper was the Lego queen. She'd have at least one of the sets finished before her mother picked her up at five thirty.

It was just after five when my phone vibrated. I yanked it out of my pocket, and when *Crabby* flashed across the screen, I couldn't help but smile.

She'd been insistent that she wouldn't give me her number when I asked, so I'd been shocked when she texted me last week. But now that I had her contact information, I had this weird desire to text her multiple times a day, just to check in. Make her laugh about something. Send her an annoying meme or a picture that would have her sending me a photo of her glaring.

I didn't understand it. Yet I didn't hate it either.

> Crabby: Head's up. There is an accident on Storrow Drive, and I'm stuck in bumper-to-bumper traffic. I'm not going to make it by five thirty. Piper will be upset.

Across the room, Piper was almost finished with her Lego set. She'd start watching the clock any minute, like she had at this time every day since she started here.

Me: Want me to take them home?

Crabby: No. You don't have to do that.

That was her go-to answer. She acted like any help I offered was some big inconvenience to me. I was still working on how to make her see it differently.

Me: I leave here when they do. I might as well drop them off. Your place isn't that far out of the way.

That second part was a lie. It was in the opposite direction from my apartment, but honestly, I didn't mind.

Crabby: It might be easier on Piper.

Me: I agree.

Tucking the phone back into my pocket, I strode across the open space. Across the tiny table from Piper, I dropped into a child-size chair. It had been awkward squishing my body into such small furniture at first, but I had mastered the art of pretzeling my legs by now.

I tapped the table next to her Legos to get her attention.

With a sigh, she looked up. Her eyes almost met mine before she glanced over my shoulder and focused on something behind me. Slowly, she was getting more comfortable with me.

"I was thinking maybe Cam and I would take you home today. What do you think?"

She zeroed in on the clock over the door, her hands fisting so tightly on the table her knuckles went white. "At five thirty?"

"Yes."

Her shoulders and hands relaxed in unison, and with a nod, she went back to her project, clicking a pink brick into a larger piece that looked to be taking the shape of a tree.

I stood, pulled my phone out, shot Harper a text to confirm that Piper was okay with the change of plan, then headed to Sam. "Hey, dude. Ten-minute warning. We need to start getting packed up. Mom's stuck in traffic, so I'm going to take you home."

"Ooh, do we get M&M's in the car again?"

Harper was strict about what the kids ate. It made sense for Piper, but it was harder for Sam. I was very aware of how difficult it was to live by rules that were created because they were what was best for someone else.

"How about I give you a few to have after dinner?"

His brows disappeared behind his shaggy red hair, and his eyes went wide. "Mom is going to let you stay for dinner?"

"I'm not sure." The answer should have been no. We hadn't talked about it. But now that Sam mentioned it, maybe it wasn't such a bad idea.

Harper
17

"LET ME HELP." Trevor snagged one of the bags I was juggling as I headed into the apartment building.

"Thanks," I said as he took a second plastic bag. Since I didn't have to go across town to get the kids from Langfield Corp, I had time to stop at the grocery. It had gone by so quickly. So smoothly. Instead of being this awful chore, it had been a quick pit stop. I couldn't remember the last time I'd gone into a store alone. Without a kid begging or throwing a temper tantrum. I didn't have to worry about them wandering off or getting in the way of other shoppers.

"Where are the kids?" Trevor asked.

"A friend is bringing them home for me." We stepped onto the elevator, and with his free hand, he hit number four.

"Marissa called me today and asked if I'd trade weekends. She wants to have the kids Friday and Saturday."

"Really?"

His ex-wife tended to be rigid about the custody schedule, so it was almost shocking that she'd called on Monday to switch for the coming weekend.

He smirked. "She's going to a family wedding. And since I'm not the asshole that she is, I agreed without a fight, so we swapped."

"Good for you, being the bigger person." Last year his kids had missed his sister's wedding because it had fallen on his ex's weekend. While most people would be tempted to get payback, it spoke volumes that he wasn't.

"You know what that means?"

"What?" I asked as we stepped out of the elevator.

"You and I are kid-free on the same weekend."

I froze outside my door, my stomach sinking. That was...something that had never happened before. I wasn't sure what to say, so I focused on digging through my purse for my keys while I considered a response. I took my time pretending I couldn't find them in the pocket where my keys always lived and continued my fake search until I hoped enough time had passed that I could move on from the implication that we would both be kid-free this weekend.

When I'd played the game for as long as I thought I could get away with it, I unlocked the door and headed into the kitchen to set the bags down.

"I'm sure you can guess what I'm going to ask now." He stepped up behind me and set the white plastic bags beside mine.

My chest tightened. Shit. I really hoped I couldn't.

He smiled, the expression only filling me with dread. "Drinks Friday?"

Cringing, I searched for an excuse. A reason I wasn't available. Then a lightbulb went off. *Perfect.* "Actually," I said, "I can't." The urge to beam was strong, but I schooled my expression into a sympathetic grin. "My friend's having a birthday party on Friday night."

"Really?" He arched a skeptical brow. I couldn't blame him. I never went out, and we'd been neighbors long enough for him to know that.

"Yeah, it's at the karaoke bar, by Lang Field. The big one. Do you know it?" What was the name? It was on the tip of my tongue. Zara had texted me about it this afternoon.

Mic dropping? Mic Dropper?

"Drop the Mic?"

That was the one. Nodding, I pulled out the almond milk from the bag and quickly tucked it into the fridge so Piper wouldn't walk in and see it. They were out of her normal brand, and if she saw it before I could pour it into the almost empty carton, it would be a long night.

"Love that place." He leaned back against my counter, settling in as I shut the fridge.

"I think it'll be fun." I hoped. As long as Zara didn't leave me alone when I knew literally no one else.

"What's going to be fun?" Piper asked from the doorway.

I tilted to one side so I could see around Trevor. There, in the entrance to the kitchen, stood Piper and Sam. They were still wearing their backpacks. Kyle was behind them, his arms crossed over his chest and his attention fixed on Trevor.

"Did you ask Mom out again?" Sam stepped close and tipped his head back to assess the neighbor.

I winced. It happened so regularly that even the kids expected it.

With a laugh, Trevor mussed Sam's hair. "The *again* should make me feel pathetic. But this is the first time I really have hope."

That was ironic, because I'd said no.

"I'll see you later." With a wave, he turned toward the entryway, only to freeze when he caught sight of the large man in my foyer. "Who are you?"

Without responding, Kyle removed his baseball cap, turned it around, and slipped it on backward. Then he settled his hands on his hips.

"Holy shit," Trevor muttered.

"Bad word," Piper announced.

"Kyle Bosco." Trevor's eyes widened as he looked from Kyle to me and back again. "How?"

I was surprised he recognized Kyle like this. Nothing about the man in the tight black T-shirt and jeans who was standing in my entryway and glaring looked like the Boston Revs' fun-loving Kyle Bosco.

"You and Streaks are friends?"

"Another person who doesn't do social media?" Kyle had been more stunned than Zara when he'd discovered that I didn't have Instagram or TikTok or any of the other apps I couldn't name.

I cleared my throat. "I think he does."

Trevor was usually in the know when it came to local sports and other media gossip, so I'd have guessed he probably wasted hours a week scrolling.

"Didn't see any of my posts this week, man?" His attention was on Trevor.

"Huh?" I asked, arms falling slack at my sides. I was thoroughly confused about where this conversation was going.

With a smirk, Kyle lifted his chin. "Your kids are all over my social media, Crabby."

I had signed social media waivers, but I'd assumed Hannah would be the one posting, I guess, since she ran the Revs' official social media pages. And I supposed I figured there would be a post or two, but not much more. If that wasn't the case, then I was surprised I hadn't heard from Jace. He was a huge Revs fan.

"Did you see that we won the domino run poll?" The expectation in Piper's voice made it clear that everyone should know what that meant. She had been very proud of their massive toy creation, so I couldn't blame her. Though I couldn't imagine all that many people really cared about a silly competition between kids.

"But the...the foul ball thing," Trevor stuttered.

"Mom should never have done that." Piper scowled. "Just looking at the stats, the Revs were the better team. And the Revs would have crushed the Metros going head-to-head. Especially if Asher Price's and Kyle's batting averages stayed over .300."

"That's my girl." Kyle smiled down at my daughter.

Trevor stared with his mouth open.

It baffled me, the way so many people fawned over celebrities and athletes. Trevor had been completely capable of conversation, almost too capable, but when Kyle appeared, the man had turned into a stammering mess. People were just people, no matter how well-known they were.

Kyle chuckled. "But I'm an ass. That's well established. And my jokes, like the foul ball one, miss sometimes. We've cleared it up. Harper's been patient with me, even though she thinks I'm her cross to bear."

"What kind of a bear?" Sam asked, his hands on his hips like Kyle's.

I shook my head. Kyle had made a lot of statements like that over the last two weeks. Revs' representatives too. It was ridiculous that people actually believed that Kyle and I had been friends for a long time. But they did.

"He means a pain in my neck," I said to my son.

"Oh." Sam turned to Kyle and nodded vigorously. "She does say that."

Kyle laughed, the move catching my attention. I couldn't help but notice the hard line of his jaw, the sparkle in his brown eyes, or the way his hair peeked out from under his hat.

I forced my attention away and focused on my kids. "Okay, shoes off, backpacks away. Let's go."

They groaned in unison but didn't put up any more of a fight as they moved out of the kitchen.

"I'll get out of the way," Trevor said, stepping around Kyle. "Have fun on Friday. Maybe I'll see you."

Kyle kicked the door shut behind him. "You like that tool bag?" he asked, the question laced with an intensity I didn't understand.

"He's nice," I assured him. "He helped carry in my groceries."

"I would have too."

I scoffed and sent him a side eye. "You would have had Cam help me carry in the bags." I hadn't known Kyle long, but I had his number.

"Oh please." He lifted both arms and flexed his biceps. "I'm perfectly capable of doing the heavy lifting."

Holy moly, he was. A wave of heat washed through me as the muscle bulged, pulling at the sleeve of his fitted T-shirt. Jeez. That simple move was more of a turn-on than anything I'd experienced in years. I gave myself one second to stare before I went back to unpacking the groceries.

"Put the biceps away, Bosco. There aren't any ball bunnies to impress here."

He stepped up next to me and pulled a box of granola bars from another bag. "It might be hard to believe, but it's been a few years since I've had any interest in the ball bunnies."

I narrowed my eyes at him. "That's not the glowing character state-ment you think it is."

"You are fiery tonight, Crabby."

Head tilted, I smirked. "Am I not normally?"

"You always are." He chuckled. "It's one of my favorite things about you."

"Mom." Sam stepped back into the galley kitchen. "I put my stuff away. Can Kyle eat wiff us?"

My stomach twisted at the thought. With a shake of my head, I gave my son a sympathetic smile. "I'm sure Kyle has other plans."

"Nah, I don't," Kyle said.

I shot him a quick glare. *Thanks for the help.* "We're having gluten-free chicken nuggets and lima beans."

"My favorite." He smiled.

"There is no world in which that isn't a lie." I laughed at the absur-dity of the idea. He probably ate gourmet meals seven nights a week, either out at four-star restaurants or sent in by a personal chef. Lima beans surely wouldn't make his list of favorites.

Kyle waved his arms wide in an arc over his head. "A stretch of the truth."

"Seriously? It's like I say no, and you say—"

"World Series."

I blinked. What the hell?

Kyle held a hand up. "You were going with unicorn there, weren't you? But honestly, the World Series is my unicorn, so it fits."

"You know how some people get each other so completely that they can finish each other's sentences?"

He nodded, his brows lifted and his eyes dancing.

"That's not our thing," I deadpanned.

Head tossed back, he barked out a laugh.

"So is he staying for dinner?"

"No."

"Yes."

"Awesome." With a pump of his fist, Sam ran out of the kitchen.

I sighed.

"Am I making the lima beans or the nuggets?" Kyle asked, holding up two white bags.

I rolled my eyes.

"So both? Cool."

Despite my annoyance, a laugh escaped me.

He dropped the bags to the counter and pulled open the fridge. "Can I get you a drink?"

"Isn't that my line?" I asked.

He shrugged. "It looks like you've got Citizen's Cider or Knocked Out IPA. Which do you want?"

"Cider."

Kyle pulled out one of each and passed me the cider.

"Are you really cooking?"

"Sure." He flipped the bag of nuggets over and studied the cooking instructions. "How hard can air frying these things be?"

I leaned against the counter and took a slow sip of my cider, settling in to watch the show.

After a silent moment, he spun and zeroed in on me. "I'm really serious. How hard is this?"

Shaking my head, I pointed at the air fryer. "See that black thing? Hit the power button. I'll walk you through it."

Once the chicken was going and I'd given the kids a ten-minute warning for dinner, I turned and asked the question that had been haunting me for almost a week.

"Why did you start Hope Speaks?"

Kyle froze, his beer halfway to his lips. "I guess you don't want the token answer." He smirked, but it was forced.

I shook my head. Since that moment last week when he'd told me he knew what it was like to be drowning, I'd been thinking that maybe his life hadn't been what I thought it was.

He set his bottle down and rested the heels of his hands on the edge of the counter on either side of his hips. "I have an older brother, Ryan, who was diagnosed back when they called it Asperger syndrome."

I stepped up beside him, a hip propped against the cabinets and a palm flat on the Formica.

His hand was just two inches from mine, I realized, as he looked down at it and I followed his gaze.

"My dad left when I was two," he said, focusing on my face again. "I don't remember him. I guess we saw him here and there during those early years." He shrugged.

Instinctively, my hand twitched with the need to reach out and offer him comfort. But as he swallowed and glanced away, focusing on his beer, I choked back the urge.

"But by the time I was five, he didn't come around anymore. So it was just Mom and Ryan and me."

He tucked his chin to his chest and let out a slow breath. Then he turned so he was facing me and covered my hand with his. The rough skin encased mine in a warmth that soaked into me, deep down in my bones. His deep brown eyes locked on mine.

"I see so much of myself in Sam. And so much of my mom in you. I started Hope Speaks not only to help families financially, but because my mom walked a lonely road for a lot of years, and I never want anyone to have to follow that same path."

The words wound through me, snaking their way to my heart and ensnaring it. I blinked hard and swallowed the lump in my throat.

"Don't give me too much credit, Crabby. For the most part, I'm still a selfish good-time guy."

There was vulnerability in that statement. Like he wouldn't allow himself to believe he was more than just the fun baseball guy.

I shook my head. "You might do a pretty good job of hiding it, but you're so much more than that."

Angling close, I pressed my lips against his cheek.

His breath hitched, and his body tensed. The hand on top of mine tightened. I hesitated for a moment, letting his five o'clock shadow tickle my lips.

His eyes met mine. Questions floating in his deep brown irises. His teeth pressed into his lower lip. And my heart skipped.

"*Mom!* You said ten minutes, but it's already been eleven."

Harper
18

I JUMPED BACK from Kyle just as Piper came barreling into the kitchen. "It's been eleven minutes," she repeated. "And I want milk."

Kyle's eyes were wide for a moment. Then he blinked away the expression and swallowed, shaking his head like he was shaking something off. Without a word, he turned back to the air fryer and got to work pulling out the nuggets.

"Milk." Clearing my throat, I tried to focus on my daughter. But I was haunted by what had almost happened. I didn't know whether I was relieved that we were interrupted or disappointed. Not that it mattered, because when it came to Kyle, I didn't have time for anything more than a very low-maintenance friendship.

"Yes. Milk," she gritted out, her jaw tight.

"Sure." I glanced at Kyle again, but he was taking chicken nuggets out of the fryer with so much focus one would think he was defusing a bomb rather than making dinner. With a shake of my head, I pulled Piper's favorite cup from the cabinet and took it to the fridge.

"What is that?" she asked, her tone full of accusation.

As I turned around, I glanced at my hand, and my heart sank. Oh no. In my distraction, I'd totally forgotten to hide the incorrect almond milk from my eagle-eyed child.

"Almond milk."

"No." She blinked. "That's not my milk."

With a calming breath in and back out, I set the milk on the counter. Then I turned back to her. "The carton is different, but it tastes the same."

Piper shook her head. "I want *my* milk."

"It's the same, Pipe," I repeated, holding tight to my patience so I didn't betray the tension that was running through me. If she could sense it, then it'd only make the situation worse.

Piper blinked three times, and then a fourth, her anxiety starting to climb. "No." She lifted a hand, but before she could smack the milk out of my grasp, I caught her wrist.

"Piper. Deep breath, please."

"No," she bit out, the volume of her voice raising. "I want the normal milk."

Any minute, Kyle would probably jump in. That had become his MO. But the best way for Piper to work through this was to work to calm herself down. Refocus her aggression into something else. Slowly, I stepped forward, still holding her wrist, and she stepped back, saying *no* once again. I eased the almond milk onto the counter and took another step out of the room. We took it one step at a time all the way down the hallway to my room.

There, I said, "I want you to jump fifty times."

She glared at me, then at the mini trampoline, but she obeyed. And with every bounce, the tension eased from shoulders.

"Fifty more," I said when she finished the first set and was still frowning.

Time-out could be successful for many kids who needed to chill out. But Piper needed the outlet of expending energy. Sitting on a step or chair wouldn't settle her. The anxiety and adrenaline flowing through her needed to be burned off. Her OT had suggested jumping instead. And it had been a lifesaver for me.

After the second set, when she was winded and her expression was neutral, I asked, "Can we talk about what you want to drink now?"

Piper sighed. "Water. And I want to watch my show while I eat."

"Okay," I agreed, guiding her back into the kitchen.

When we entered the room, expecting to find the dinner mess, I discovered the place had been organized. There were two plates on the counter, and Kyle and Sam were eating at the table. Normally, when Piper had a meltdown, Sam would have to wait it out. Sometimes, while she threw a fit and I talked her down, dinner burned, and I'd have to throw the whole thing away.

This sight and the vast difference in what happened today versus what dinnertime often looked like, made my chest constrict. I had to remind myself not to get used to this.

I didn't want to be jaded, but I knew that the only person I could trust in life was me.

Once I got Piper settled with her dinner at the small table by the television, I grabbed my plate and moved to sit with the boys.

"How come she bees bad and then gets a special treat? She's watching the Revs. Can I watch *Bluey*? I wasn't bad," Sam complained, his little lips turned down.

Part of me wanted to say no, to insist he sit at the table, because I expected that behavior from him. But he was right. It was unfair, regardless of their differences. He was the one who behaved, and in his mind, he was being punished for it.

"I thought you wanted to eat with Kyle?" I'd given up on the battle to call him Mr. Bosco since Kyle was so opposed. He was so offended by the idea of being a mister that I wondered if he had an issue with getting older.

Sam narrowed his eyes at Kyle, then surveyed the television across the room. As he focused on his plate again, his mouth lifted at the corner. "I ate my nuggies with Kyle already. Now I eat my lima beans with *Bluey*."

Kyle chuckled, though he covered it up by coughing.

Hiding a smirk, I shook my head. "Fine. This time. But you know the rules. We eat together."

Sam frowned but grabbed his plate and shuffled to the coffee table.

"It's nice that you give him some grace." Kyle watched Sam as he settled in. "I used to get so upset when I had to follow my own set of rules and expectations, rules that Ryan didn't have to follow, then also have to follow the rules set in place for him too. We never got to have chocolate or sugar, and we didn't go out to eat. We never went on vacation because Ryan's therapies took every penny Mom made. Even if they hadn't, Ryan couldn't handle being away from home and his routines like that."

I tried to be conscious of those issues, and I worked to make life as normal as I could for Sam, but it took a lot of juggling.

"I try." With my fork, I moved the lima beans around my plate, head lowered.

For a moment, we sat in an awkward silence heavy with all that lingered between us.

I didn't have the first clue what to talk about next, but anything would be better than the silence, so I went for it. "Thanks for not jumping in with Piper."

Kyle set his fork down and studied me. "You had that handled. You didn't need me getting in the way."

I tracked his face, taking in the lines around his eyes and his tight lips, waiting for the moment he explained how I should have done it.

"I'm not trying to overstep or bulldoze." He didn't break eye contact. "You're fully capable of dealing with Piper's outburst and fits. She's an incredible little girl, and that's because of you." He shrugged, his expression nothing but genuine.

But no one had ever described Piper that way before. She was difficult and trying and frustrating. And some days I felt like I was the only one who saw the good in her.

And here he was, telling me he saw it all. That made my heart swell and my eyes burn.

"I just want to help when you need it. When you could use another set of hands. Because it doesn't seem like you have that."

"Their dad has them for a night every other weekend." The response was lame, but it was the truth. That was all the help I had these days.

"Can I overstep and ask what happened with you two?" The question was delivered with the charming smirk I was getting used to.

A year ago, the story had embarrassed me. It had made me feel somehow lacking. But I didn't have the energy to be upset by it anymore.

"We struggled with Piper's diagnosis." I tried to keep my thoughts on Jace neutral for my kids' sake, but also because he was only part of the issue. "It's hard accepting a diagnosis that is going to make your child's life different from what you expected. More challenging too. He and I handled things differently. I dove in full force, researching all I could to help her. He wanted the diagnosis to be wrong."

"That's not uncommon."

"I was hyper-focused on her, and Sam too. He was only a few months old. And I was still working. He felt ignored. Insignificant." He never helped, and I was exhausted, which only exacerbated our issues. But I could admit that I was overwhelmed and didn't make the time for us the way I should have. "I thought if we could make it through a year or two, things would get better. But he got more distant and more obstinate. He became dead set on reducing the number of therapies she was doing. Then he got furious about the diet I had the kids on. It was so strange how uptight he became about money."

Kyle rested his forearms on the table, his eyes narrowing.

The things I missed or ignored should have been glaring red flags. "When he filed for an extension rather than submitting our income taxes, I should have been concerned. But I had too many other things on my mind." I shook my head. "I was juggling so much, and the one thing he handled without needing my input or guidance was our finances. God." My stomach knotted at the memories. "I was dumb. Because it took fifteen months for me to discover that he'd lost his job and had been lying to me about going to work."

"What?" Kyle's jaw ticked, and a vein pulsed in his temple.

I had been so furious when I found out. Not only about the lies, but because, for more than a year, I had been juggling work and almost every one of our kids' needs, and he had been spending his days sitting at a bar. Or going for walks in the park. The jealousy I'd felt about his free time was almost overwhelming.

I cleared my throat. "By the time I found out, we'd chewed through most of our savings, and…" I shook my head. That time had been awful. The betrayal and lies were bad enough, but then there was the lingering doubt I hadn't been able to shake. And his audacity, to tell me I was being unreasonable when I questioned his actions and his motives. "He wasn't as sorry as I thought he should have been. And I couldn't bring myself to trust him. So we separated. He found out pretty quickly that he couldn't handle Piper on his own, so he decided he didn't want them for more than one night at a time. That part, I was okay with, because she would come back all out of sorts. It was easier to just keep her with me. But that meant his child support payments were higher, and he couldn't afford them."

Eyes closed, I blew out a hard breath, willing myself to keep the emotions where they belonged—in the past. Because getting upset didn't help anyone.

"So," I said, forcing my shoulders back, "after an expensive divorce, I ended up with a three-year alimony obligation."

"*You* pay *him*?" Kyle asked through gritted teeth.

I nodded. "I had always made more money than he did, and for the last two years of our marriage, he was unemployed."

He balled his hands into fists on top of the table. "That's fucking ridiculous."

"At first I was upset about it too, but I didn't want my kids to see me as this bitter, angry person." I shrugged. "So it is what it is."

"What does your family say?"

I swallowed. "My mom and grandmother raised me, and they're both gone now." I took a bite of a nugget, giving myself time to put my thoughts in order. "My family stuff is…" I took a breath. "It's a bunch of soap opera drama that no one wants to hear about."

He reached out and put his hand over mine. "I do." His warmth soaked into me and radiated up my arm, soothing me. At the same time, the intensity of his stare threatened to make me shiver. There was anger simmering in his eyes, but also an emotion that I swore looked like genuine care. It wasn't a look directed my way often.

I took another breath and let it all spill out. "For most of my life, I thought my father was dead. He wasn't. Another one of the many times in my life that someone lied to me."

His hand tightened over mine, and his eyes flared with anger.

"As an adult, I discovered that I was the product of an affair. My mom worked for Southwest's corporate office. She traveled a lot for work, and she fell in love with a married man in a position much higher up the ladder. She got pregnant, and he didn't want to leave his family. That broke her heart, and she never got over it. So she spent the rest of her life drinking away the pain. Or trying to, I guess."

He rolled his lips in on themselves and huffed out a breath through his nose before he spoke. "Which is why you don't want your kids to view you as a bitter, angry person."

I dipped my chin and nodded.

He straightened in his seat, wearing a concerned frown. "How did you find out about your dad?"

I wanted to laugh. The story was that ridiculous. "When she died, she left behind a letter. She spelled it all out for me. But I never contacted him. Figured that if he didn't want to leave his family, then he probably wouldn't appreciate his illegitimate child showing up, looking for a relationship. But four years later, his estate attorney called. I guess he had a lot of money, and he left some to me."

He cocked his head, one brow lifted.

"But it doesn't matter. His wife is contesting the will."

"That's…" He sputtered, choking on the words, his eyes bulging. "That's…awful."

I sighed. "Honestly, I don't care. Let them have the money. I haven't had the best experience with his family." Hurt and frustration bubbled inside me, so I blew out a breath. I would not let any of it seep out. "I met my half brother, James, almost two years ago. He came into Boston Lights under the guise of moving his father in."

Kyle leaned back in his chair and crossed his arms over his chest, his throat working. "What did he say? 'Surprise, we're related'?"

I held back a sardonic laugh. That would have been better.

"He never mentioned our connection. He spent the whole time acting as if he needed information about our facilities and options for long-term care." Head lowered, I shook it. "After wasting hours upon hours of my time, following me around for two tours of the facility, communicating over the phone probably a dozen times, and what felt like a million emails, the guy ghosted me. It wasn't until last year, when I walked into the reading of the will—"

Kyle lunged forward in his chair. "You went to the reading of the will?"

Another moment of naïvety on my part. "My father's attorney told me I had to. I had no idea that they weren't expecting me or that I wouldn't be welcome." I used my fork to push a single lima bean back and forth on my plate. "When I saw James, I was confused. Turns out, his mother didn't know he'd been in contact with me. That he'd met me. His sister didn't even know I existed." Emotion pricked at the backs of my eyes, but I blinked it away. It had been a total shit show. "After a bunch of screaming and some name-calling—"

"Name-calling?" Kyle gritted out, his brows pulled low in anger.

I cleared my throat. "Yeah. James's mother made a comment along the lines of 'who invited the slut's daughter?'"

I remembered her comment word for word, but I had nowhere near the energy to rehash the confrontation. My mother was far from perfect —I knew that—but that woman had acted as if I was somehow to blame for her husband's infidelity.

"It was a disaster. She and I both said things we shouldn't have." I glanced over at the kids, who were still locked into their show. "After she lost her shit on me, I basically told them all to F-off and stormed out."

Kyle's jaw was tight again, the tendons in his neck strained. "Seems fair to me."

"James chased me down in the parking lot and apologized." I tightened my hold on my fork, trying not to frown at the memory that played in my head. "He wanted a chance to get to know the kids and me." He'd begged, and after I left, saying I'd think about it, he got my number from the attorney. Which seriously pissed me off at first. "Since we don't have any other family, I'm trying to give him a chance. For the kids' sake."

Kyle studied me, a swirl of emotion in his eyes I couldn't interpret.

"Maybe it's dumb." I shrugged, swallowing back my apprehension. Because maybe I shouldn't have shared any of this.

"It's not dumb." His eyes blazed now, this time with an aggressive protectiveness that made no sense to me. "It's a testament to how forgiving you are."

I shook my head. "I'm not that nice to him. Trust me. If you asked him, he'd probably tell you I'm difficult."

He reached out and covered my hand with his once more, warming me in a way I shouldn't like. Long fingers wrapped around my hand, and the tips pressed into my palm.

"You're different. Not difficult." His deep voice vibrated through my bones. Our gazes stay locked, and this odd antsy energy rushed through me. "There's something about you..." He shook his head, lowering it.

The sincerity in his tone, in his demeanor, made my breath catch. Dammit. I could not let myself like this man.

"Every day, you impress me more." With a small smile, he gave my hand another squeeze.

"I finished all my food," Sam hollered, his voice jarring me out of the moment. He scurried toward the table, carrying his empty plate, dropping his fork to the floor halfway to us. "Can we play and sneak M&M's now?" he asked Kyle.

Kyle released my hand and stood up.

"*Sneak* M&M's?" I cocked a brow at my child, then at our guest.

"Kyle has the best baseball M&M's. They're so yummy. He gaves me some at school every day." Sam beamed up at his buddy.

Lips pursed, I fought the smile that was pulling at me as I looked between the two of them again.

"No ratting me out to Mom, kiddo." Kyle chuckled. "Let's play clean-up, and then we'll do the Lego set you brought home." He picked up my plate.

I stood and held a hand out, ready to take it back. "You don't need to."

"But I want to." His focus was set on my face, his eyes warm, his words nothing but sincere. "I want to be someone you can count on."

My stomach flipped as I took in the open honesty in his expression. And for the first time in a long time, I felt like maybe I *could* trust someone.

KYLE
19

Me: WTF, man?

JJ: Huh?

Me: Seems like you gave me a lot of half stories with Harper.

JJ: What did she say?

Me: Not a lot but I can't believe you're taking her money.

Me: GIF of a dog shaking his head.

JJ: It's not that simple.

Me: Seems pretty fucking simple.

JJ: Not answering my calls anymore?

Me: Picture of Sam building a Lego set.

JJ: You're hanging out at her place now????

Me: Sam asked me to stay for dinner.

JJ: I wish he'd ask me to stay. I'll explain everything next week when you're here.

Me: Damn, how is it almost Thanksgiving already?

BAMBI ADDED DRAGON TO BASEBALL BROS

Bambi: I have a plan for Zara's party

New Guy: I'm scared.

Me: You're not even here.

New Guy: Yeah, unlike you, I didn't bail on our Tahiti trip.

Me: Like Miller would let me leave Little Fingers

Dumpty: GIF of a crowd chanting bullshit

Angel Boy: Yeah, sure, blame Miller. You're so oblivious to your own obsession.

New Guy: Wait. What did I miss?

Dumpty: Our own little Streaks has his first crush.

Me: Photo of me flipping off the camera

Me: I'm helping out Harper and her kids. Nothing more.

Angel Boy: Replied to GIF of Crowd chanting bullshit THIS

Dragon: Stop adding me to this nonsense

DRAGON LEFT BASEBALL BROS

Bambi added Dragon to Baseball Bros

Bambi: This is a karaoke idea, not nonsense.

Dragon: And in what world do you think I'm doing karaoke?

DRAGON LEFT BASEBALL BROS

Me: Did you really think he'd sing or dance with you?

Bambi: He did when I proposed.

Dumpty: Dude you can't see a difference?

Me: I'm in for any karaoke plan.

Angel Boy: Going to sing a love song?

YOU REMOVED ANGEL BOY FROM BASEBALL BROS

Dumpty: 😂😂😂😂 dead

Harper
20

"ID," the giant standing at the door barked.

"Oh." I should probably have expected that, but it had been so long since I'd gone out like this that it hadn't even crossed my mind. As I was digging my wallet out of my bag, my phone buzzed.

> Jace: What's the name of the pizza place the kids like?

For the love of God, it was almost eight thirty, and he was only now thinking about feeding them? I guessed I shouldn't be so surprised. He had been almost an hour late, so why wouldn't dinner be late too? I knew better than to bring it up, though. If I did, it would lead to a fight and delay dinner further, so I just fired off the answer and then got my driver's license out.

An exasperated sigh sounded behind me, garnering my attention. The group of women behind me were all dressed in ridiculously short dresses and sky-high heels. My own leggings and boots screamed *mom* suddenly. But it was November in Boston. I was wearing double the clothing these girls were, and I was still freezing. The one closest to me scrutinized my sweater, then turned her nose up like it offended her. Tough shit. So I wasn't wearing a sparkling cropped tank top like her and every other Gen Zer in the line. Even if I had the first clue what was in style these days, it wouldn't matter. The last time I'd purchased new clothing was probably shortly after Sam was born.

I'd had lunch with Zara three times over the last couple of weeks, and I'd never felt dowdy or frumpy. But beside these women, I felt very out of place.

"You're good." The bouncer tipped his head like I should go in.

But I wasn't sure where to go. Zara had said they would check the list and send me the right way. I'd waited almost forty minutes already, and I still didn't have the first clue.

"I think I'm supposed to tell you that I'm here for Zara Price's party?"

He lifted one dark brow and peered down at me. "Why didn't you go to the VIP line?" He pointed to the other side of the door, where two people stood at a podium and there wasn't a single person in line.

Why? Because I had no idea what I was doing. There was a line here, so I got in it.

"Harper."

At the sound of my name, I turned. A blond in ripped jeans and a gorgeous brunette in a crop top and black leggings very similar to mine—although with her curves, she wore them much better—approached. I'd met them at the stadium. The blond had pulled the bird off me.

"Hi." I half waved to the two women who were now standing by the VIP check-in. Although I wasn't positive of their names, they were definitely part of the Revs' wives and girlfriends group. The realization that neither of them was dressed like the women in line behind me made me feel a million times better.

"Are they giving you a hard time, Avery?" Christian—I thought he was the pitcher for team—came up beside the blond and scowled.

"Damiano!"

"Dragon!"

The calls echoed from the line I was holding up, but Christian ignored the noise like he hadn't heard it, remaining completely focused on Avery.

"No." She shook her head and pointed my way. "We were grabbing Harper."

"Oh." The corner of his mouth tipped up almost imperceptibly at the sight of me, making him look slightly less pissed off. "Wrong line. Come this way." He waved my way, and the bouncer let me out through the red rope.

"Wait, Dragon," a man called.

This time Christian turned, as if suddenly the outside world existed to him. Though when I recognized the man as another Revs player, it made more sense.

"I said no." Christian glared.

"Need me to scare them off?" The curvy brunette's glare rivaled Christian's as she turned to the line of mostly women.

"Not them. It's kids, Mariposa." Emerson, that was his name, shrugged sheepishly.

"Kids at a bar?" Christian huffed, a brow cocked.

Emerson shook his head. "They were coming out of the restaurant next door."

"Gi, watch these two," Christian barked at the brunette.

In response, she crossed her arms under her chest and cocked a brow that looked eerily like Christian's. She stared the man down, as if silently saying *who do you think you are to boss me around?*

Unfazed by her death look, Christian squeezed Avery's shoulder. Then he pulled a rose-gold Sharpie out of his pocket and followed Emerson down the street, where he squatted to pose for a photo with two boys who looked about ten.

"That was nice of them," I said.

"They always make time for kids." The brunette—Gianna, I remembered—watched them with an expression that could almost be considered soft.

A minute later, the guys came back and hustled us past the two security guards and up to the second floor. The space was much bigger than I expected, since Zara had insisted she didn't know many people in Boston and that it was a small party. But there had to be at least twenty high-top tables, and each was surrounded, meaning there were a good hundred people here. It took a moment, but eventually, I found her. She was dressed in a silver tank top and black skirt, like a classier, trendier version of every woman in the line outside.

"Harper," she called when she spotted me. Beaming, she beckoned me over with a wave. "I'm so glad you came." After receiving two air kisses from her, I turned to greet the rest of the table.

Kyle, who was dressed in a white button-down, stood next to Cam. Our eyes locked, and a bolt of electricity buzzed through me. His irises darkened as he took me in from head to toe and back up again. The top button of his shirt was open, showing off the thick column of his neck. His perpetual five-o'clock shadow was gone, and in its place was a smooth, hard jaw line. Though it softened as he lit up, grinning, and angled toward me. His exhale brushed across my skin before full lips pressed to my cheek. He pulled in a slow breath, making a shiver race down my spine. My skin broke out in goose bumps, and for a second, I forgot to breathe. Frozen, I swallowed harshly, willing my racing heart to steady.

When he was this close, the rest of the room faded away.

"You smell delicious, Crabby." His lips brushed my ear as the almost silent words registered, and a fire ignited low in my belly. He pulled back, but not far enough to deprive me of his body heat.

I wet my lips, and his eyes locked on to my mouth, cranking up the heat in my core.

Cam cleared his throat and elbowed his friend, pulling us back to the present.

Kyle frowned at him before turning back to me, his expression turning light. "It's like you're whipped-cream scented." He smirked.

I never wore perfume, knowing it bothered Piper, so it had to be my lotion.

"We all know you love sugar," I teased, holding tight to the charged moment.

He laughed, and above his white collar, his pronounced Adam's apple bobbed, snagging my attention. From there, I couldn't help but survey his jaw, then his lips.

"Hey."

Kyle jerked back, his head snapping to one side, where Emerson was watching him with his brows arched.

"I need my backup, Streaks."

With a nod, Kyle eyed me once more. "I'll be back." The words were laced with a promise that bubbled with anticipation in my belly.

The moment they disappeared, Avery leaned in. "Is there something going on between you two?"

With my heart lodged in my throat, I shook my head.

"Are you sure?" Gianna asked. "Because that looked like something."

"See how easy it is to recognize from the outside?" Avery giggled.

Gianna rolled her eyes. "Shut up."

"We all knew something was going on between her and Emerson long before he finally came to Chris and copped to it."

Christian grunted.

Confused, I glanced at the man in question. "To you?"

Christian frowned but didn't respond.

"He's my brother, and Emerson is his best friend." Gianna shrugged, her expression unimpressed. "Emerson was worried he'd have an opinion on the matter."

Our conversation was cut short when music blared from the stage nearby. Emerson stood front and center, with Asher, Kyle, and Mason behind him. It took three beats before I recognized the Katy Perry song.

"Eyes on me, Mariposa," Emerson said into the mic, and Gianna flushed, a small smile tipping her lips.

"Oh, for fuck's sake. He thought I would do this with them?" Christian shook his head, and when his best friend sang the first line of the song about two octaves too high, he stepped back from the table. "I'm getting a drink."

But Gianna and Avery giggled at the guys who were dancing to "Teenage Dream," heart hands, chest tapping, choreographed spins, and all.

"They practiced for like two hours last night. Emerson wanted it to be perfect for her." Zara sighed, her head tilting to one side.

"Did Asher plan one for you too?" I asked.

She scrunched her nose up and shook her head. "That nonsense stopped years ago for us." Though she was trying to play it off, acting as if she wouldn't care for a gesture like this, there was just a hint of longing in her voice.

I looked up, intending to study Asher, because here and there, she made comments about their relationship that surprised me. As if it wasn't as picture perfect as it seemed. But the second my attention shifted to the stage, Kyle stole my focus. Although Emerson couldn't look away from Gianna as he danced and sang, there was no reason for Kyle to be looking our way. Especially not with the number of beautiful women around. On all sides, there were cheers and catcalls.

Still, Kyle's focus was fixed on our table. Our eyes met, and his smile grew. It became more teasing as he formed a heart with his hands, then lifted it to circle his head. Just before he turned, he winked. And somehow, that tiny gesture felt as intimate as a kiss. It warmed me from the inside out.

Stomach dropping, I gaped at him. Holy shit. Somehow, I had let myself start crushing on Kyle freaking Bosco. Internally, I cringed. Was I seriously dumb enough to fall for the playboy man-child of the Boston Revs?

Apparently. Except…

The Kyle I knew, the man who had been showing up for both me and my kids, was the farthest thing from a man-child or a playboy. Yeah, maybe he was obsessed with M&M's and whipped cream. Maybe he was unable to lose gracefully. But he was always eager to help. And the way he looked at me said he cared.

"You okay? You look utterly gobsmacked." Zara pushed her black hair behind her ear as she studied me.

With a shake of my head, I worked to dislodge the ridiculous thoughts from my mind. Kyle Bosco was gorgeous, rich, famous, and, it turned out, a decent guy.

But he had hordes of women throwing themselves at him. Tonight alone. At this very moment, there were two tables full of women trying to get his attention, calling his name, holding up their phones to record his moves, whispering to one another. We might have had a few deep moments, but to think he was interested in me, and my very momish clothes, was absurd.

"Just out of my element," I admitted.

"Rubbish." She frowned. "Let's—"

"Zara!"

She turned. "Wren."

She greeted the taller woman with two air kisses.

"Do you know Harper?" She waved my way. "Harper, Wren is Avery's best friend."

I waved, and Wren sent me a smile.

"I adore the shoes." Zara pulled back as she glanced down at the strappy designer pumps with red soles.

Wren tipped her head, and the front of her reverse bob brushed her bare shoulders. "The newest addition to my overflowing closet." She laughed. "And they go perfectly with this dress."

"Are you not freezing?" The deep voice from behind me had me jumping.

As I turned, I saw the coach of the Revs standing, frowning at Wren's long, bare legs. The short sleeveless dress, although stunning on Wren, was much more Miami than November in Boston.

Wren batted her eyes. "Don't you know the expression *beauty knows no pain*, Daddy Wilson?"

His frown deepened as his eyes lifted to hers. "Mr. Wilson," he corrected, but I could have sworn something flashed in his eyes before he schooled his features.

She rolled her eyes. "Okay, Mr. Wilson. You can buy me a drink for trying to kill my vibe." She latched on to his arm and tugged him toward the bar, leaving me wondering what exactly was going on between the young, stunning woman and the much older coach.

"Let's go grab a drink for you too," Zara insisted.

It sounded like a fantastic idea. But before we could move, my phone vibrated in the pocket of my leggings. I pulled it out, and when I caught sight of Jace's name on the screen, my stomach sank. Crap. There was a good chance that the night was already over. I held a finger up, and when Zara nodded, I slid my thumb across my phone's screen and held it to my ear.

"Hello?" Instantly, I realized there was no way I'd be able to hear anything he said, so I stepped away from the stage. "Jace?"

I walked toward the edge of the room, but between the music, the singing, and the chatter, I couldn't make out his words.

"Hold on." I slipped down the stairs and into a quieter hallway with black walls and dim lighting. "Hello?" I tried again.

"Where the hell are you?"

"Jace." I sighed. He no longer had the right to ask that kind of question, but I wasn't interested in arguing at the moment. "I told you I was going to Zara's birthday party tonight."

"That's right. Friends with Revs royalty now," he sneered. "I bet Bosco is there too. The kids haven't stopped talking about him, by the way."

"Great. Something you have in common, since you're a fan. Piper would love to chat all about the Revs with you."

He grunted.

Irritation flared inside me, but I tamped it down and kept my tone even as I asked, "So, is there a problem?"

A woman in a short dress slipped past me and sashayed toward a black door. Only then did I realize this small, dark hallway led to the bathrooms.

"Yeah, can you tell Piper that I ordered the right pizza? I'm putting you on speaker." There was a rustle down the line, a little fumbling, and the sound of *Bluey* on the television in the background.

"Hey, Pipe. Daddy checked with me about the pizza. He ordered it from Gio's."

"Are you sure?" The nervousness in her voice made my heart squeeze. God, why couldn't Jace figure his shit out and work on his relationship with her? If he did, then he'd know how to calm her.

"I am," I promised. After a quick good-night to her and one to Sam, I ended the call and blew out a breath. He had things at least partially under control tonight. With any luck, it would be enough to keep them content until he dropped them off at ten tomorrow morning. That wasn't always the case. Some nights they didn't even get out the door of my apartment.

I slipped out of the hallway and turned for the stairs, but I had just planted my foot on the first step when I heard the familiar voice.

"Harper?"

Turning, I pasted a smile to my lips, even as unease tugged at my gut. "Trevor."

He looked good in his dress shirt and fitted jeans, his baby blues sparkling and a big smile on his lips. But I wasn't interested, and he wasn't taking the hint.

"I wasn't sure you'd really be here." He smirked, shoving his hands into his pockets.

"Yeah." I pointed awkwardly over my shoulder. "My friend's party is upstairs."

"You know Zara Price?" A guy I'd never seen before butted into the conversation.

"Mitch." Trevor frowned.

"Sorry, sorry," the guy said. "Mitchell Houton." He held out his hand, and, hesitantly, I shook it. "You know Zara Price?" he repeated.

I nodded. "Our kids are friends."

"Harper," Zara called from halfway up the steps, catching the attention of half the patrons downstairs. "Where did you get off to?"

People all over the bar edged toward the stairs, realizing she was just a few feet away.

"We're hogging her. Sorry about that." Trevor smiled past the two big men who had taken up residence at the bottom of the stairs to stop unwelcome guests from coming toward Zara.

"No worries." She waved dismissively.

A man in a suit a step behind her whispered in her ear, snagging her attention.

With a nod at him, she turned back to me. "Bring your friends up, Harper," she called. Then she turned and jogged back up the stairs.

I held back a wince, wishing I could uninvite the guys. But good manners took over, so with a tight smile, I moved up the steps past the two men, with Trevor and Mitch on my heels.

When I hit the top, I headed straight for Zara, who was only a few feet away, as if she was waiting for me. "This is my neighbor Trevor, and his friend Mitch."

Trevor held out his hand. "Happy birthday," he said to Zara. "Thanks for letting us up."

"Any mate of Harper's is a mate of mine." She snaked her arm through mine. "You must come. Asher just went for drinks, and Kyle is singing."

That was Kyle? I'd recognized the Billy Joel song from the stairs, though I hadn't recognized the voice. As we stepped through the opening in the curtain and into the big room, there he was, mic in hand. The lyrics for "Only the Good Die Young," one of my favorite songs, poured easily from his lips. He wasn't even off key.

As if he could sense my presence, he found me immediately, and a smirk lifted his lips. Instantly, butterflies flitted through my stomach, and once again, something that felt like anticipation settled in my chest. But his smirk fell as his gaze moved past me, and he didn't look back my way.

"He always sings this one. But it still took me forever to work out the meaning of his tattoo." She led me back to the high-top.

"Tattoo?" I asked, my focus locked on Kyle. He'd rolled the sleeves of his white button-down to his elbows, showing off the tan skin of his forearms.

"I have a feeling you'll become acquainted with it very soon," Zara said, her voice full of innuendo.

Before I could refute, Trevor edged in closer and interrupted. "Love your accent."

"Flirting with my girl?" Asher set two martini glasses filled with some sort of pink drink in front of us, then pushed one my way and hooked the other to his wife.

"Thanks," I said, giving him a small smile.

He nodded, then shifted his attention to Zara. "Trying to make me jealous, wife?"

"Like you'd ever be jealous." Zara rolled her eyes, though the expression was full of affection.

Asher cozied up behind her and wrapped his large arm around her tiny waist. "You're gorgeous, and tonight, everyone sees it. I don't think I'll be able to let you out of my arms."

"That would be a pleasant change." She smiled, and as he crowded even closer and kissed her bare shoulder, I swore she shuddered.

I had thought they were having issues, but clearly, I was wrong. It was easy to see that Asher was smitten with his wife. And when I looked back to the stage, I found I'd been wrong about Kyle too. His song had ended, and he hadn't come our way. No, he'd found another group to hang out with. One full of scantily dressed women. The instant the scene registered, all the anticipation bubbling in my system dissipated, leaving a sour taste in my mouth.

I reminded myself again that single moms in their thirties didn't end up with baseball stars. I was entirely too old to believe in fairy tales.

KYLE
21

AFTER THE SONG ENDED, it had taken everything in me to not slam the mic into the stand and storm across the room so I could chase away Harper's annoying neighbor. But Asher had been giving me shit about her for two weeks, and that would never end if he had any inkling that I was jealous of some douche bag.

Not that I was jealous. I wasn't. But Harper deserved someone better than the wannabe surf boy who lived next door.

"Are you even listening to me?" I didn't know her name, but her voice was too nasally and her perfume was practically choking me. And fuck, if she rubbed against me one more time, scraping my forearm with that damn sequined dress, I might have to walk away.

"Streaks isn't known for his conversational skills. You know that, Amber," said the brunette tucked under Cam's arm. "And we aren't here to talk."

Silently I glared at my friend, hoping he could read the *what the fuck?* in my expression. Because this woman wasn't his normal type.

He dropped his arm from around the chick and stepped back. "Excuse us, ladies. We're going to grab refills."

I fell into step with him as we headed toward the bar in the corner.

"What's up with you tonight?" I asked when we were out of earshot of the women.

"I asked Ashley to come, but she blew me off." With a sigh, he ran a hand through his hair.

"Ashley?" I stopped short. "Like Piper's Ashley?"

He grabbed my upper arm and pulled me along with him.

"Yes," he hissed. "And keep it down."

"But I hired her to work with Piper."

"And you hired me to pick up your dry cleaning. I didn't realize either position required a vow of celibacy," he snapped.

I frowned at his reaction, totally confused by the un-Cam-like behavior. "It doesn't, man. I just didn't realize."

"It doesn't matter." He waved me off and ordered a whiskey.

"Seems like it does." I eyed the drink as the bartender set it down and Cam immediately picked it up and tossed it back. "You're upset. So what happened?" I asked as the bartender set a beer in front of me.

Frowning, Cam spun his now empty glass in a small circle. "She apparently just got out of a relationship, and I'm not the type of guy you get under in order to get over someone else."

I scoffed. "Ashley did not say that." I may have been ignorant of the way my friend was pining over her, but I'd been around this girl enough to know she didn't talk that way.

"Close enough." He shook his head and held up a hand, signaling for another glass of whiskey. "Basically, I'm a nice guy, not someone she'd want to rebound with, and she's not ready for more than that."

"Sounds like all you need is a little patience." I patted his back and took a sip of my beer.

Grunting, he peered over his shoulder. I set my beer on the bar and turned too. Instantly, I zeroed in on the red hair across the room. Harper's hair was always up in a bun or a braid or a twist. I'd never seen it down before tonight. She'd done that thing women do when they make their hair have waves without the curl. And between that and the hunter-green sweater that kept slipping off her right shoulder, I had struggled to take my eyes off her since she walked in.

There were a lot of sexy women in this room. Any direction I looked, I'd find another tight dress, another set of high heels, another pair of long lashes, many of which were being batted at me. But not one of them could compete. Harper wasn't even looking for attention, yet she was the *I could spend forever watching her* type of beautiful.

I frowned. Because currently, she was glowing as she smiled at the neighbor.

"It seems like Harper is long over her ex," Cam said beside me, picking up his second glass of whiskey. "Definitely a single and ready to mingle situation. So maybe don't dick around and let someone else get into those tight-ass leggings."

I reared back, and in doing so, I slammed into the bar behind me.

Cam gave me a concerned once-over. I stared at him in return, slack jawed. Because once again, that didn't sound like Cam. For weeks, he'd been telling me to stay away from her. Every time he'd witnessed me dancing a line with her, he'd been loud in his opinion.

I balled my hands into fists at my sides when the implication of what he'd said finally registered.

"Sorry," he added, quickly holding up a palm. "Not trying to be disrespectful to her. I adore Harper. She has grit and personality. I'm just in a mood."

Still annoyed by his comment, I crossed my arms over my chest. "And smarts. And she would probably verbally eviscerate you for talking about her."

He dropped his head back and guffawed. "But man, you like her. For the first time since I met you, I can see that you genuinely like a woman."

I brought my beer to my lips and took a slow sip, giving myself a second to collect my thoughts. Was he right? Was that what this sensation was?

She was hot, and I was attracted to her, but I'd known that the instant I saw her. But I'd forced her into the *not allowed* box. Or I'd tried. Across the room, she was worrying her lip. The move had my gut tightening. What if I stopped fighting it…?

I shook that thought off. That wasn't what Cam meant. He was talking about other types of feelings.

Like the desperate need to help her. But that was easy to justify.

Because she was an incredible person, and she deserved someone on her side. And she didn't have many people. So I wanted to be one.

Understanding that *I wanted* to see her smile at me, wanted to see her name pop up on my phone screen, and wanted to hear her voice wasn't the same as understanding *why* I wanted those things. And the burning need to punch people on her behalf, on her kids' behalf, was new. I rarely felt that kind of anger unless I was losing a competition.

Did that all mean I liked her?

I sighed at my own ridiculousness as I set my bottle back on the bar. Of course I did. She was cool. And riling her up was the highlight of my day. But he was implying a deeper feeling. A stronger one.

"It's why you keep glaring at the beach bum over there." Chuckling darkly, he turned back to the bar and lifted his drink.

I took another swig from my bottle. "Total tool, right?"

Cam shrugged. "I've never met him. But he looks like he should be out riding waves."

"I met him. He was trying to get her to go out with him when I brought the kids home last week," I growled.

"And you were jealous." He spun his drink on the lacquered surface of the bar. "Ever feel that way before?"

I scoffed. "I wasn't jealous, I was annoyed."

He lifted his whiskey and held it toward me. "Let's toast. To all of us having your level of self-awareness."

Fucker. Biting back a curse, I flipped him off.

"Look," he said, laughing, "I'm giving you shit, but…" Head tilted, he cocked a brow. "She's watching you in the same way you watch her when you think no one is looking. Don't be dumb. Go after that."

I studied her, found she was watching me too, then scanned the group she was with. Maybe Cam was right. Maybe I should stop holding back, have some fun, and see what happened.

"Can I get five chilled vodka shots?" I asked the man behind the bar.

"Just remember," Cam said, patting my shoulder, "before you cross lines, she and JJ need some honesty from you. Make sure you balance out the fun with the truth."

Right. Of course. Only there was a damn good chance that would ruin everything.

Harper
22

"ONCE WE TOAST the birthday girl, this party can officially start." Kyle sidled up next to me and set a tray of shots on the table. As he did, he lingered there, the heat of his arm soaking through my sweater.

For the last twenty minutes, I'd been attempting not to watch him chat with Cam across the room. I'd failed miserably.

"Ooh, fun." Zara clapped as Kyle handed her a small glass. "As long as it's not that bloody tequila."

"Vodka?" Asher asked, a brow quirked.

Kyle nodded as he passed one to him. Then he continued around the table, holding glasses out to Trevor, Mitch, and Cam, who slipped in beside Asher, making the table a bit crowded. Then he dropped taller, skinnier shot glasses in front of the two of us.

"Wait, why do I get the huge one?" I hadn't had a shot in years, and vodka burned.

Kyle smirked. "Because bigger is always better."

He wanted to be childish? I'd play along. I leaned closer and tapped him on the nose. "Funny, Kyle, I always found it wasn't the size of the boat, but the motion of the ocean."

With his lip caught between his teeth, he waggled his brows. "Spicy tonight. My favorite." He stepped closer, if that was possible, and gave my hip a squeeze.

That small move sent a shock of electricity through me. As the heat of his palm burned through the thin material of my leggings, I tried to remember that, only twenty minutes ago, he had been hanging out with a table full of women.

It was a challenge in this moment, though, because he was watching me like I was the only person in the room.

"Is it?" I whispered.

"Hell yeah." His hold on me tightened, his fingers biting into my flesh. Clearing his throat, he lowered his gaze to my tall, skinny shot glass and released me. Instantly, I missed his touch. "You're a light-weight, aren't you? Need me to take some off the top?"

A scoff escaped me. Annoyed, I glowered up at him. I might not be a regular at the bar scene, but I could do a shot. "Why are you like this?"

Across the table, Cam laughed.

Kyle frowned, his brows pulled low. "Like what? A man who doesn't force alcohol on women?"

"You didn't offer to take some off Zara's, so don't steal mine." I carefully grasped my drink and slid it toward me.

"She loves her vodka, right, Z?" He reached past me and held his fist out to the birthday girl.

Smiling, she pounded it. "You know me."

Focused on me again, Kyle said, "And I know you don't normally hang out at bars."

I bristled again. Everything he'd said was true, but they were coming off like insults.

"Whatever. I can do a shot." Grumbling, I lifted the cold glass from the table. "What are we drinking to?"

I expected some kind of birthday wish. Instead, Zara said, "Sinners," her smile devilish.

On her other side, Asher chuckled.

"Why?" I scanned the table.

Zara and Asher were smiling at one another. Cam was watching

Kyle, and Trevor and his friend looked lost. So I zeroed in on Kyle, who was watching me.

"Because." He hovered closer, smirking, the look sending a shiver down my spine. "Sinners are much more fun." He tapped my glass with his, then downed his vodka, the thick collum of his throat bobbing as he swallowed.

"To Sinners." Asher chuckled and held his glass aloft. As everyone lifted their drinks to their lips, I did too. I braced for the burn of pure vodka. Instead, I was pleasantly surprised by the sweetness that hit my tongue. The slight burn of the liquor as it coated my throat was far smoother than I anticipated.

Kyle leaned close again, his words dancing across my ear. "You can always trust me to keep it sweet with just enough heat."

I swallowed back the apprehension and desire hitting me. Then I swiped the last bit of alcohol from my top lip.

He zeroed in on my mouth, his dark brown irises almost black. The heat there made my breath hitch. I didn't understand this visceral chemistry we had. Every time he was near me, my body came alive. It was like nothing I'd ever felt before.

Trevor coughed, breaking the moment.

"Too strong for you?" Kyle shifted his attention across the table to the guys, but he didn't move from my side. He had angled himself so that if either of us shifted, I'd be standing between his legs. I had this deep longing to do it. To feel his hand on my hip again.

"No," Trevor croaked. "Gotta love the burn."

"I need a chaser," Mitch announced.

Trevor nodded at his friend, then the two of them headed to the bar.

"You owe me a dance, wife." Asher pulled Zara away from the table, his arm wrapped around her waist.

"Remember to balance out the sinning." Smirking, Cam tilted his rocks glass at Kyle and walked away.

"What does that mean?" I asked when we were alone.

"Do you know 'Only the good die young'?" He leaned his forearm on the table and spun to face me completely.

I rested my chin on my fist. "I love Billy Joel."

"My stepdad got me into Billy. He and his brother were super fans. Anytime we road-tripped, his greatest hits were all we listened to."

I smiled. "Funny, my mom too. She always had one of his albums in the CD player of her car."

"CD." He chuckled, his dark eyes lightening. "You're dating yourself."

I shook my head. "More like dating her car."

"If you say so," he teased.

Playfully, I smacked the hard plane of his tight abs with the back of my hand. "Hey! I have not hit the midpoint between thirty and forty yet," I said, flicking a finger between the two of us. "Unlike one of us at this table."

"Someday I'll explain my life points theory about age." Then the thief snagged my martini glass from the table and took a sip.

"Does this theory explain drink thievery?" I tilted my head, and a wisp of hair fell across my eye.

Without hesitation, he lifted his hand and brushed it back, causing my breath to catch. He ran the rough pads of his fingers along my temple before caressing my cheek with the back of his hand.

I swore my heart skipped as he watched me, wearing the most sincere expression. We remained locked like that for a breath or two. Then he finally lowered his arm, but my eyes tracked it the entire way.

"Nah," he said softly, wearing a small smile. "You're just good at sharing. I could never order a pink drink in a glass like that. I'd get shit for months. I have to order whiskey or vodka. No passion fruit martinis." He lifted my drink to his lips, settling on the thin rim as he took another large sip.

"Are you trying to distract me from the sinner question?" I cocked a brow.

He set the drink down and pulled up the sleeve of his white dress shirt, where the word *sinners* in ink was barely visible. "The rest of the line is there too. I was a pain in the ass as a teenager, and I used to believe it was my motto."

"That sentence is full of past tense that doesn't belong," I teased.

"Someone's got the jokes tonight." He smirked. "But my mother has always told me to keep it balanced out. So"—he lifted the arm with the tattoo—"fun is on my left arm, and"—he lifted his right arm—"baseball, the arm that does that work, the throwing and hitting, is my right. It's all about balance." With both forearms on the table now, he had to cock his head to the side to look at me.

I had to admit that was kind of adorable. I was working on a way to tease him about it when he looked over my shoulder and frowned.

"What?" I asked, afraid to look.

"Looks like your neighbor is headed back this way," Kyle muttered as he shifted so he faced me again.

A sigh escaped me. I had no interest in looking for the two men. For the last hour, I had been polite. I'd worked to engage in conversation with Trevor when he chatted me up earlier, but there was no chemistry between us. Yet he wouldn't give up.

"Is there an easy way to let a guy know you're not just feeling it?" I pressed my lips together in a small pout, studying the tabletop. I didn't want to hurt his feelings, but honestly, I wished he'd just go.

After a somewhat pregnant pause, Kyle finally asked, "Trevor?"

Tipping my chin up, I nodded. "Yeah. I—"

Kyle cupped my cheek, stealing all words, along with rational thought, and pressed his full lips to mine. A spark jolted through me as his warm mouth touched my own. I might have gasped, or maybe not. It all happened so quickly, it was hard to tell. The kiss was more than a peck, but all too soon, he eased back.

Dumbstruck, I blinked up at him.

"Done," Kyle announced casually, then licked his lower lip.

"Done?" I whispered.

He couldn't mean what he was implying. Swallowing thickly, I opened my mouth and searched for the words to ask for clarification. None came.

"They made a quick turn to another table. Surf boy got the message," Kyle said with an easy shrug.

Was he kidding? The man had just kissed me, and now he stood there, twirling the stem of my glass between his long fingers like none of this was a big deal. But it had been over two years since I'd been kissed, so it was a big deal to me.

I choked out a scoff. It was the only sound I could create at the moment.

Brows pulling together, he examined me, clearly confused by the noise.

With my jaw locked, I inhaled through my nose, finally clearing my head. "You did not just kiss me to get Trevor to go away." It was a statement and a question and an accusation all rolled into one.

The smile Kyle gave me was the one he wore any time he won. He nodded, still so damn nonchalant. He was so unbothered, and that made anger pulse through me. "You're right. I did not kiss you *just* to get Trevor to go away."

I froze, my breath catching in my lungs. Wait. Was he agreeing with me or not?

Laughing, Kyle cupped the back of my neck and pulled my mouth to his once more. It was another quick press of our lips, but it made my heart skip all the same.

"You kissed me again," I mumbled as he pulled back.

"Is this like when the bird landed on your head? When you were so flustered you kept stating obvious things?" he teased, wiping at my lip with his thumb this time.

Uck. I whacked him in the stomach again. "I hate you."

He flashed that toothy, shiny-eyed smile. "That's okay. I like you enough for both of us, Crabby."

Jutting my chin up, I clenched my fists at my sides. More often than not, I deserved the term of not-so-endearment because I had cranky tendencies. But tonight, I was smiling, even laughing. I'd just taken a massive shot, for goodness' sake. "I'm not cranky tonight."

"I didn't say cranky," he corrected, one brow arched.

I cocked a brow too.

He smirked. "I think you got the idea wrong. You're like the uh…" He waved his hand. "That crab, from the mermaid movie."

"Sebastian?"

"Yeah, the red little guy with all the schedules and rules. Can't do this, can't do that." His voice dropped as he mimicked the little crab. "We must have a plan." With a sigh, he scratched at his jaw. "He never would have had fun if not for Ariel coming along and making him nuts."

I really tried to scowl at him, but my lips pulled up instead, and a giggle burst from between my lips. "Are you implying that I need a redheaded mermaid to save me?"

"Nah." He smirked, dropping one forearm to the table again, and angling in so his lips ghosted over my ear when he said, "Personally, I'm rooting for the blond baseball god."

That caused me to laugh so hard I snorted. Instantly horrified, I smacked my hand over my mouth to stop the sound and to hide the blush that heated my cheeks.

"You're adorable." He shook his head and pushed my half-drunk martini toward me. "Have some liquid courage."

"Why?" I asked.

"We're going to sing."

"Sing?" My heart stopped in my chest, and, breath held, I scanned the crowded room.

He waved a hand. "Karaoke party at a karaoke bar. There are expectations."

"Have you lost your mind?" I croaked. "I can't sing." There were like a hundred people here. There was no way I'd make a fool of myself in front of this many people.

"Can't do this, can't do that," he chanted, lowering his voice teasingly again, and then leaned back into me. "Come on. You can't tell me you've never done karaoke before."

I had. Years ago. I used to love it. When I was twenty-two and pretty, and I stupidly believed I could do anything. But here, in this moment, in this room full of people, I was none of those things.

"That's what I thought. Come on." He had moved in so close that our noses almost brushed. "I dare you."

"I…"

He pushed the drink closer. "I'll be right beside you the whole time. Trust me."

And for some unknown reason, I did. If there was one thing Kyle had earned over the last few weeks, it was a little trust.

I huffed out a sigh. "Fine." I tossed my drink back and turned to the stage. "Come on. Let's get this over with."

"That's the spirit, Crabby." With an arm wrapped around my shoulders, he guided me to the stage. "I've got the perfect song."

When it was our turn and the DJ cued up "You may be right," I laughed.

"You're right. This is the perfect song for you," I teased as I took one of the mics from the man running things. "You seriously might be crazy."

Kyle shook his head, making his highlights pop under the bright stage lighting. "Or." He smirked. "Maybe I'm just the lunatic you've been looking for."

A thrill coursed through me as he grasped my arm and pulled me onto the stage. Because I was starting to believe that could be true.

KYLE
23

THREE HOURS, four dances, two drinks, and one Disney song later, we pulled up in front of her building. All the uncertainty that had plagued me a few hours earlier had disappeared. A switch had flipped tonight. And it had happened even before my lips touched hers.

For one long second, when Harper had casually asked about letting a guy down easy, my heart plummeted. My first thought was that she had been referring to me. It was in that moment that it became abundantly clear: I never wanted to be friend-zoned by this woman.

Elation rushed through me like a tidal wave when I realized she was talking about her douchey neighbor. The sensation was only slightly cooled by the reality of the situation I'd found myself in. But it was too late to fight it. It might be wrong, but I wanted her anyway.

I never walked away from a challenge, and this had the potential to be the biggest one of my life.

I needed to kiss her again. To hold her in my arms. To call her mine.

I was going to have to talk to JJ. And my parents. My entire family would have a lot to say about this. There would be heated opinions about a relationship between Harper and me. But that problem wasn't insurmountable. It was a topic I'd broach when I was home for

Thanksgiving next week. Emotions might run high at first, but they'd all settle in time. Once I handled that, I could talk to Harper.

"Well." She glanced at me, then out the window, clearly nervous, as the driver stopped at the curb. "This is me."

Like I didn't know where she lived.

A flustered Harper might give baby kittens a run for their money in the cuteness department.

"Yeah." I opened the door and climbed out, then turned and held out a hand to her.

"Y-you're coming in?" She blinked in a way that reminded me so much of Piper. Her eyes were filled with a mix of uncertainty and concern, emotions her daughter, unfortunately, experienced too often.

"I grew up in Texas, and where I come from, walking a woman to her door is nonnegotiable."

With a light sigh, she took my hand and stepped down.

"What happens after we get to her door," I murmured, pulling her close, "is in her hands."

She froze for a beat, letting me hold her there. But when she finally rebooted and brushed past me, I got another whiff of the whipped-cream scent. It had faded as the night went on, but like a moth to a flame, I had to lean in as she passed.

"Did you just sniff me?" She spun, her lips pursed with displeasure as she assessed me.

I shrugged.

"Do I smell?" she asked, her tone laced with worry.

Chuckling, I tucked her into my side. "Like the best kind of dessert, Crabby." I pressed my lips to the crown of her head.

She pulled out her key fob, but before we made it to the front door, I took it, along with her door key.

"Hey!" She pouted.

"You're drunk. I don't want you dropping them."

For that comment, she rewarded me with the cute little line between her brows that came only when she glared. Pissing her off should not light me up the way it did, but I'd developed this obsession with getting her riled up, then working to make her smile again.

Clearly, there was something wrong with me.

"You're doing it on purpose. Aren't you?" she accused as I held the fob up to the sensor.

"Of course," I said, grasping the door handle. "We want to go inside, so obviously, opening the door is required."

"No." She stomped straight for the elevator, leaving me behind. "I meant making me nuts."

"Oh," I said, feigning ignorance. "We should watch that mermaid movie together. I'm telling you, the entire point of it was that the mermaid made the crab nuts."

At the elevator bank, she crossed her arms, the move forcing her breasts up and together. There was no stopping the way I homed in on her tits. They were full and round, and they pushed against the tight knit fabric of her sweater in a way that made my body temperature spike. More than once tonight, I'd imagined cupping them in my palms. Running my tongue from one to the other. I could picture them, pale and covered in freckles, just like her shoulder. And I could imagine the way her nipple would tighten to a firm bud I could pull between my lips.

"Kyle."

I blinked and silently chastised myself for getting lost in my fantasies. "Should I sing 'Under the Sea' again?"

With a groan, she shook her head. "That once-in-a-lifetime experience has already happened tonight."

And we'd crushed that. I'd started out alone, but Asher had jumped in—the guy knew the words, thanks to his kids. Emerson was next, because the guy always had to be in on the fun. Even Mason and Eddie Martinez hopped up to finish us off. The best part of it all was Harper's smile as she laughed at us. In that moment, I understood why Emerson was so willing to act like a lovesick puppy for Gianna. Even grumpy-ass Chris would pretzel himself for a smile from Avery. Getting a smile from the right woman could feel like the biggest win.

She leaned into the wall, and her sweater slipped down her arm again. The red mark it uncovered looked angry in the bright light of the lobby.

"What happened?"

She tucked her chin and inspected it, catching on to what I was referring to quickly. "Oh." Looking up, but not at me, she swallowed. "Cutting Piper's nails is like going into battle, so I put it off. But she got upset last night, and I paid the price for not taking care of them when I should have."

The outbursts. Ryan had them too. They got better as he got older, but for years, my mom worked to teach him how to manage his anger and frustration. It was a long, bumpy road. That was for sure.

The elevator dinged, and the doors slid open.

"Harper," I murmured as I followed her off.

She peered up at me, her lips pressed into a straight line, probably bracing for a comment about Piper.

"Tonight was one of my favorite nights in years." I brushed a strand of her silky red hair back from her face. "I really like hanging out with you."

She pressed her teeth into her bottom lip, but the smile that spread across her face pulled it free. "Me too." She blinked at me, her expression full of apprehension and hope, then lowered her eyes, trying to hide it all from me.

I brushed the back of my hand over her satin skin as I tipped her chin up.

"I'd really like to do it again."

"I would too. But…" She shook her head, pain flashing across her face. "I have Piper and Sam."

"I'm well aware." I chuckled. "I spend eight hours a day with one of them."

She rolled her amber-colored eyes, though she was still more subdued than I was used to.

"But I wouldn't mind if we hung out here. With them."

When the elevator doors opened, I followed her into her hall. She was two doors down on the right side, the door with the Revs sticker at the bottom.

When we reached her apartment, she spun with her back to it and took a breath. "I might be willing to give that a try."

This answer was all coy. The shyness from moments ago had completely evaporated.

"Might, huh?" I stepped between her legs and rested my palm on the warm bare skin of her shoulder. "How might I get a firmer yes?"

Smiling, she shrugged, but she didn't respond.

I ran my hand up to her neck and held it there, brushing my thumb over her jawline.

She tilted her chin up to mine, and I dropped my face closer to hers. Her breath skated against my lips.

"I lied." I swallowed, pulling back a little and blinking.

She inhaled a little sharply, her eyes narrowing on me.

"In fairness," I said, rushing the words, out, "when I said it, it was true."

"I don't understand," she said, frowning, each word pressing against me.

"I said I didn't want anything from you. But lately, I have this want—this need—and I can't stop it," I admitted, resting my forehead against hers.

"What is it you want from me?" she whispered, closing her eyes.

"The ability to call you mine."

Her eyes flew open, and her lips parted in a shocked breath.

Without second-guessing myself, I stole my chance and dropped my mouth to hers.

As I cupped the sides of her face, keeping her close, she melted into me. I swept my tongue along her bottom lip, then into her mouth, dominating, dancing with hers, every move full of desire, of need. The tastes of her flooded my mouth, made me desperate for more.

She looped her arms around my neck, pressing every soft curve of her body against me.

My heart pounded, causing blood to rush in my ears and to my cock, as I savored each moment her soft lips touched mine. It was a perfect kiss—sweet, warm, and wet. But as a soft moan left her lips, I remembered exactly what I needed to say.

I pulled back and rested my forehead against hers. Our ragged breaths mingled, and her soft, sweet scent surrounded me, making my cock throb. I wanted her. More than I'd ever wanted anything.

"Harper," I panted, "before this goes any farther, I need to tell you some things."

Slowly, she blinked once, twice, and focused on me, her eyes swimming with need. "Kyle, I know a kiss isn't a promise of forever."

I frowned, my heart sinking. That wasn't at all what I meant. I'd probably said those exact words more than once, but that was the furthest thing from my mind right now. With Harper, there was no need to seek reassurance that she was good with just one night, because *I* wanted more than that.

That little line appeared between her eyes again, and for the first time tonight, I didn't enjoy the sight of it.

"I'm not going to cry or freak out if you don't call me tomorrow."

I wanted to call her tomorrow. What was she talking about?

"Don't worry," she said, her tone far too even, unaffected.

"No. Call me any time you want. Hearing from you is the highlight of my day." I shook my head and pulled back a bit more. "I'm not walking through this door if you're thinking this is just a one-off."

"Oh." Her lips parted, her eyes going wide.

I traced her plush bottom lip with my thumb. She shivered in response, the unintentional move making my gut tighten. I angled in, ready to claim her mouth once more, but before my lips could touch hers, I forced myself to stop. Words. Dumbass.

"I...just." I sighed, straightening again. Start with the easy part. "You need to know that I'm the one paying for Piper's therapy."

In an instant, she went from chocolate syrup, warm and gooey, to solid ice, rigid and cold and sharp.

"What?" she hissed, yanking her arms from around my neck and taking a step back. "You, as in Hope Speaks, you mean."

The desperate hope in that sentence made me feel like a jerk.

I shook my head. "No, me. Kyle Bosco."

She reared back, stumbling into the door in her haste. And when I reached out to steady her, she flinched away. A sharp piece of that ice pierced my heart. Dammit. I hadn't intended to hurt her. I wanted to help.

"Why didn't you tell me?"

I pressed a palm to my chest and rubbed a small circle. But the betrayal in her eyes only made the pain flare. "I'm telling you now," I said. Now. Before it went any farther. Before our relationship shifted, and details like that would matter.

Hands balled into fists, she lifted her chin, those golden eyes hard. "Why. Not. Before?" The tone reminded me so much of Piper. Each angry word was like a peck to the pain in my chest.

This wasn't the kind of mad I liked. The kind of exasperation I worked to pull out of her. No, this was something else.

I didn't want to lie to her. I could live with not giving her every detail, but I would never lie.

"Because Piper needed it. And if not for our connection, she would have easily been chosen for a grant."

Understanding flashed across her face, and for a moment, I thought maybe we would get through this. Either way, I wouldn't go down without a fight.

"That connection, which ultimately meant we couldn't consider her, wasn't her fault. And it wasn't your fault. It was mine." I reached across the two feet of space between us, a small distance that felt more like the length of I-95. But the second my thumb brushed her cheek, she jerked back so hard her head hit the door.

"Don't," she snapped.

"I wanted to help," I whispered. "I want Piper to have what she needs." I could lie, sugarcoat the truth, but I wouldn't, even though it wouldn't go over well. "And I was worried you would throw a fit and refuse to accept my help."

She scoffed and crossed her arms, her nails digging into her sweater. "I am not so proud that I would throw a fit when offered help for my daughter."

Now probably wasn't the time to point out the argument we'd had about Little Fingers.

"I would have worked something out. I would have figured out a payment plan or called it a loan or, I don't know, pawned jewelry if I needed to." She ran her hands over her face. "But it was wrong of you not to tell me."

"*I'm sorry.*" I hoped like hell she could see my honest remorse, because I never meant to hurt her. "I was trying to take some stress off you."

She snapped her head up, her eyes slits. "This was the exact type of bulldozing I told you I wasn't okay with."

"Technically," I argued, though she was so fucking right, "that conversation was after I'd done this." I flashed her my most adorable smile.

Rather than crack a smile like I hoped—clearly, being my cute-ass self wasn't going to help me right now—she glowered. "Go home, Kyle."

"Harper, please. I was kidding."

"Go home," she repeated, holding her hand out.

Deflating, I dropped the keys into her palm. Then I watched as she opened the door and disappeared inside without looking back. The door clicked shut, and at the metallic sound of the lock turning, I splayed my hand on the solid wood painted white and leaned close.

"I'm sorry, Harper. I just want to take care of you and the kids. Make all your lives better." I waited, resting my forehead against the door, and when she didn't respond after several heartbeats, I turned back to the elevator. I'd only taken a step or two when the stainless-steel doors slid open and Trevor stepped off. Twenty minutes ago, I might have made a smug remark. Now? I couldn't bring myself to even speak. So I gave him a quick chin tilt and walked past.

"Hey, Bosco," he called as I stepped onto the elevator. "Harper is great," he said when I met his eye. "Just be good to her, okay?"

With a nod, I swallowed the lump in my throat. Harper was amazing. And I was trying to be good to her, but I was apparently terrible at it. Even so, I was the kind of guy who always went down swinging. I just had to figure out how to fix this. Because if anything was worth my effort, it was Harper.

Harper
24

Sunday

Harper I'm apologizing again. Paying for Piper's therapy wasn't meant to upset you or make you feel badly. Although I can see now how it could. Especially since I didn't tell you I was doing it. Just talk to me.

-Kyle

Monday

So, it gives me hope to see you finally read my messages. Maybe by tomorrow you'll reply to them?

-Kyle

Flew to Texas yesterday. My mom made me a chocolate cream pie. Made me think of you. I almost couldn't eat it. But then I realized its best to drown my sorrow in chocolate so I ate three pieces. I hope you weren't attached to my abs because if you don't talk to me soon they might be gone.   -Kyle

Wednesday

Dear Diary,

Tomorrow is Thanksgiving, this year I'm most thankful for a fiery redhead reaching out and stealing a foul ball from me. I hate losing but losing the game was worth it because I got to know her and her amazing kids. Too bad I'm an idiot and messed it up.

-Kyle

I'm sad. I need advice on what to do to get my little crabby worrier talking to me again. I miss her.

-Kyle

KYLE
25

I TUCKED my phone into my pocket, knowing that Harper wouldn't answer. I hoped she'd smile at the messages, at least, and know that I was thinking about her.

"What's got my boy so blue this week?" My mom rested her forearms on her new soapstone counters. That had been the perfect choice against the white cabinets.

I forced my lips to lift into a facsimile of a smile. "How could I be sad when I'm home with my mama?"

She rolled her eyes and shook her head, making her blondish-gray hair brush her shoulders. "Don't try to be cute. Doesn't work on me anymore."

Apparently it didn't work on Harper either.

"I'm good, Mom. Just stuff going on at home."

She tapped her deep burgundy nails on the counter, the sound snagging my attention.

"Are those turkeys on your nails?" I swore they had been burnt orange with white polka dots yesterday.

"Yes. Aren't they adorable?" She held out her hand so I could inspect each perfect little bird. "I found this company called Color Street. They make the cutest designs."

"How long do your nail appointments take? I didn't even see you leave today."

"Oh, I do them myself. And it's way cheaper than a salon, so I'm saving money," she said proudly. "Let me show you the new sets I ordered." She hurried around the counter and out of the room. Less than a minute later, she was back with a full plastic bin.

"Whoa. How many of those did you buy, ma?"

"Don't start with me. I get enough crap from Bill. There are too many cute designs to choose from. Look at these." She held up a set that looked like paper-wrapped gifts, and another that were supposed to be parts of a snowman. "They're flat polish. You stick them on your nail like a sticker, then file off the extra length. It's so easy."

She kept digging, showing me one set after another—some with glitter, some with flowers, and some with rainbows. She had every design known to man.

"Very cute." If it made her happy, then it made me happy.

"Here they are!" She pushed a flat pack of blue nail-shaped stickers my way. "I got five sets of them."

"Is that the Revs Logo?" I grasped the package and squinted, studying the design. It was pretty impressive.

"Yes." My mom beamed, clutching the bin to her chest.

As I held the slim package, an idea struck. "Could I have two of these, Mama?"

She pursed her lips and hummed, confused or maybe disbelieving. Like she thought I planned to apply them to my own nails.

"Not for me," I assured her. "For the little girl I work with."

Face softening, my mother pushed a second set across the bar to me. "How is she doing?"

Wincing, I tucked them into my back pocket. I'd only told my mom that, during the offseason, I was working with a little girl who had been diagnosed with high-functioning ASD. My mother had seen pictures of the kids on my Instagram page, but because I was careful not to post any shots of their faces, it was unlikely that she'd recognize them. And JJ certainly wasn't telling any of them that he'd asked me to help.

At this point, it may not even matter anymore. Four days ago, I'd been ready to sit them all down and admit that I had feelings for Harper. Now, with where she and I stood, the drama seemed unnecessary. What was I going to say? *Hey, all, I have an announcement. I have a massive crush on Harper Wallace. But don't worry, she won't talk to me.* Yeah, that would be a waste of emotional outbursts all around.

"I hope I can see her again when I get home, but I'm not sure her mom will let me keep working with her."

She frowned. "What did you do?" she asked, knowing right away that whatever it was, I was likely to blame for the rift. If she hadn't been 100 percent right, I might have been offended.

Clasping my hands on the countertop, forearms resting on the cool stone, I sighed. "You know me. I overstep."

She straightened and arched a brow. "Like going behind my back and paying the contractor to add every bell and whistle to my kitchen remodel?"

"Hey, now." I frowned, dropping my head between my shoulders with a huff. "I offered to pay to upgrade this kitchen last year, but you two told me it was perfect. Then you went and did it without telling me. I *wanted* to pay for it. That way you and Bill can use your money for fun stuff."

Mom leaned across the counter and patted my biceps. "Big heart and no boundaries. How did you turn out this way?"

"Probably because you have no boundaries either, love." Bill stepped inside the house and dropped his keys on the counter. He'd barely made it off the doormat when he was eyeing the bin of nail paint like he was worried it might have cost him more money today.

"Hey, now." My mother frowned.

Bill's expression morphed into a warm smile as he approached her. He kissed her cheek, sidled up behind her and rested his chin on the crown of her head, like one puzzle piece clicking into another perfectly. So many times over the years, I'd seen Bill come home and immediately find my mom. Maybe I'd ignored it, or maybe I'd written it off as something every couple does, but now I knew that wasn't the case.

Their teasing sprinkled with genuine affection and unwavering support was exactly what I wanted in a relationship.

Mom smiled over her shoulder at him. "Don't start with me already."

"But he is right. You do not have boundaries." Ryan walked straight to the fridge and took out the dairy-free smoothie my mother always left him. My brother's habits hadn't changed even now that he was an adult.

"How was your day?" Mom asked.

"See? You are nosy." He smirked at her as he took a sip of his smoothie.

I chuckled. It was fun to see him teasing and joking.

"Even Kyle sees it."

Reeling back, I held both hands up. "No way, Mama's perfect." Bill and Ryan could get on her bad side all they wanted, but I liked being the forever favorite.

Both groaned at me.

"Sucking up so you can have more chocolate cream pie," Ryan accused.

I beamed at my mom. Of course I was. Her pie was the best. We'd gone through two already this week.

"Did you program code thingies that do fun stuff today?" she asked Ryan, her expression bright.

"I don't think you understand my job." He took a sip of his smoothie.

"I don't." She shook her head. "But I'm so proud of you anyway."

That was Mom. Always proud, unless we pissed her off. Then she chewed our ears off.

I leaned back on the bar stool. "You should become a professional game player like me, then she'd get it."

He narrowed his eyes, although he didn't look directly at me. "I develop code to help increase firewall strength and cyber security. Why would I want to play games?"

The kitchen door opened, diverting everyone's attention and saving me from having to explain my joke.

"Hey, Aunt Viv," JJ said as he walked in.

Behind him, his mother appeared. Not only was Aunt Susan my mother's best friend, but when my mother married Bill, the women became sisters-in-law.

"It's been forever since you and Kyle were both in Texas," my mom gushed, hugging JJ.

I hugged him next, then he held out a fist to Ryan for a bump. My brother wasn't big on people invading his personal space.

Mom was right. It had been years since JJ and I had been home at the same time. He had been living on the East Coast since college, so for as little time as I'd spent in Texas since going pro, he spent less.

"Right? For once, the entire family will be here." Aunt Susan smiled as we all settled around the kitchen island again.

"Not the entire family," JJ muttered from next to me, his head hanging.

I froze, my heart sinking. I may not have been around much in recent years, but I knew exactly where this was going.

"We are not calling her family." Aunt Susan scowled.

"She is *my* family," JJ bit out. "So if she's not here, if the kids aren't here, then no, the entire family is *not* here."

She clicked her tongue, and the harsh sound echoed down my spine like a shot of adrenaline. "We're all glad that horrible woman isn't here. Moving on from that terrible mistake, that's what we are doing."

Every atom in my being was now primed and ready for a fight. Knowing how my aunt felt about Harper and hearing it were two very different things. I glanced at JJ, who'd slumped back against the barstool, jaw locked and clearly not planning to stick up for a woman who wasn't here to do it for herself.

"Harper has done nothing to you, Aunt Susan," I forced out. "You're a better person than this, and I won't sit here and listen to you throw out that kind of nastiness." I pushed away from the island and stood.

The room was full of shocked faces, and every wide eye was fixed on me. All but Ryan's, which were still wide, but locked on the floor.

There was no way I could stay in the room, so I spun and stormed out. Without looking back, I called out, "Be better."

I was out the back door and into the yard before anyone could respond. It probably wasn't my place to defend Harper, but no one else was going to, and she deserved to have an ally. A person who would defend her. Be there for her. And I had promised her that I could be that person.

I pulled my phone out, determined to keep another promise.

> Me: I promised Piper that I would send her some video messages while I was gone. I know we aren't in a great spot, but would you mind if I kept my promise?

My heart skipped when the three dots appeared on my screen. They disappeared quickly, but a moment later, they were back. I waited, holding my breath, until finally, the dots disappeared again. But no message came.

My stomach sank.

The mild November air did little to cool my mood, and I was still on edge, staring at my phone, when JJ walked out the back door.

He came to stand next to me. "Thanks for sticking up for her."

"Someone should, and it didn't seem like you were going to." I had the phone tucked halfway into my pocket when it buzzed, so I yanked it back out, bumbling it in my excitement. And when I saw that *Crabby* had appeared on the screen, my heart soared.

It was only one word, and probably one she felt compelled to send, but still she had responded.

The dots appeared again, making my pulse take off.

Crabby

Me: I promised Piper I would send her some video messages while I was gone. I know we aren't in a great spot but would you mind if I kept my promise?

Crabby: Yes.

Me: YOU'RE TALKING TO ME!!

Me:

Crabby: No I am not. But you can come over and we'll talk when you get home.

Beside me, JJ sighed. "Are you listening to me?"

"Yes." I glanced back up and assessed him. Guilt clawed up my throat because, despite my assurance, I hadn't been listening.

"So you get why it's complicated." He blew out a breath, shoulders slumping. The extreme exhaustion with the situation was wearing on him.

But I had no sympathy for him. My situation with Harper was complicated too. Not only was the truth going to put a massive strain on my oldest friendship, but it had the potential to ruin my relationships with my family. Though none of it really mattered in comparison to how I felt about Harper.

"That's where you're wrong," I corrected. "If you really want her in your life, it should be fucking simple."

My phone buzzed, snagging my attention again.

> Crabby: No I'm not. But you can come over when you get home, and we'll talk.

That didn't sound great. But if it meant seeing her, then I could work with it. If I could see her face to face, then maybe I'd get her talking to me again. Maybe I hadn't fucked it all up.

> Me: GIF of a man waving his hands by his face in excitement.

I tucked my phone into my pocket, head bowed, and when I straightened, he was staring at me.

He crossed his arms and rocked back on his heels. "I wasn't expecting you to be so intense about this."

Silently, I blinked at him.

"You're right." He sighed, his shoulders slumping. "Mom is unreasonable. It's part of the reason I was hoping you would help with Harper. Because if I'm not the only one doing the talking, then maybe Mom will listen."

"I'm happy to defend her." That was as natural as breathing. "But the narrative in that house is fucked up. So first things first, you need to fix that."

"I know." He ran a hand over his face. "I'll explain what really happened."

Arms crossed, I planted my feet wide on the grass. "Good."

"And Kyle." JJ looked down, his expression sheepish. "Thank you for helping me with this."

I nodded and left it at that. Because if he knew exactly how I felt about Harper, I wasn't sure he would still be thanking me.

Harper
26

ON THE SOFA, Piper wore her headphones, her focus fixed on her tablet, and giggled. On the floor in front of her, Grey and Sam played happily.

"What is she watching?" Zara asked from across the table.

"Videos of Kyle. He sent them from Texas."

For the first few days after he had left, Piper hadn't stopped obsessing over his promise to record videos and send them to her. After I'd yelled at him, I assumed he wouldn't do it—and why would he?—so I had put her off, making excuses and biding my time.

When he finally did send them, my heart twisted in a way that was much more violent than it had when he'd sent his silly diary messages.

There were moments this week when I truly wanted to punch him. But his dramatic messages were also making me smile.

"You're allowing him to talk to her?" Zara cocked a brow and lifted her tea to her lips.

She'd come over an hour ago with Grey and Starbucks, because apparently Kyle had told Asher that I was upset, and Asher had told her.

"I told you—I am not making this a thing." I fidgeted with my hair and ended up redoing the messy bun on my head simply to keep myself busy so that I wouldn't admit to watching a few of the videos after Piper had gone to bed. Kyle and his brother Ryan were hysterical, so it wasn't shocking that Piper was laughing.

"I cannot believe you didn't call me the morning after and tell me about it. When you left my party with Kyle, I was sure I'd hear all about a happy ending. I daydreamed about it all week while we were at Asher's awful mother's house."

"You are dreaming if you think my happy ending is Kyle Bosco." I tried to force a chuckle past my lips, because the truth of it was, I still found myself thinking about the annoying man. And his adorable smirk. And the kisses. Though I wasn't happy about any of it. And I hated that he had been paying for Piper's therapies.

Something I'd fixed.

"Why? I adore Kyle," she pouted.

I cocked a brow. She couldn't be serious.

"Okay. Okay. But he only hid one tiny thing." She held her thumb and pointer finger an inch apart.

I loved that she called over a thousand dollars a month a tiny thing. A sigh escaped me at the thought. It wasn't just the ABA and RDI that Piper was doing with Ashley either. Her equestrian and sensory therapy were starting next week, and that would add significantly to the cost.

"His heart was in the right place. You have to see that. And he told you before anything happened between the two of you."

"Well, yes…" That's what I'd been arguing with myself about. He should have told me from the start, but I could respect him for informing me before we crossed the line of being just friends. Even so… "But I can't imagine Kyle Bosco settling down. Let alone with someone like me."

She crossed her arms over her chest. "I don't like when people put down my friends."

I blew out a breath. "I know Kyle is great…I just…" I backpedaled a little. I hadn't meant to insult her friend. I just couldn't see myself being enough for him.

"Kyle would be lucky to end up with a smart, caring, beautiful woman like you. Someone who challenges him and makes him smile."

Oh. I blinked. She was upset that I'd put *myself* down? Was it possible for a heart to sink and lift at the same time?

"Exactly." She nodded, one corner of her lips tipping up when the realization hit me. Angling forward, she put a hand on mine on the table. "I'm also upset that you didn't come to me for Piper's therapy stuff. I would have helped."

I shook my head, my stomach twisting. "Don't be ridiculous. I'm not asking you for money."

"What are friends for if not to help?" She frowned, her brow creasing.

Yes, we were friends, but we'd only just met. And even if we'd been friends for years, I couldn't see myself ever asking for financial help.

"Asher just hired a personal shopper and spent a disgusting amount of money so I don't have to worry about shopping on my own. She just brings things to our house," she scoffed. "Heaven forbid I pick out my own clothes or the kids' stuff. I have no idea what the idiot was thinking."

Asher did tend to spoil her. But although I was pretty certain it came from a good place, it was obvious that Zara was bored. Rather than ask her what she wanted, he just kept doing these things, thinking that by making her life easier, he would make her happy. But what she really wanted wasn't more free time or more *stuff*. She just wanted his attention. His time. The man was always busy.

"Our money would be better spent helping Piper," she huffed.

I swallowed past the lump in my throat. "I told you I took care of it."

"By pawning your great grandmother's engagement ring," she chided, wearing a frown that etched lines on either side of her mouth and her forehead.

It was the only thing I owned that had any value, and it would pay for a few months of therapies. I hadn't wanted to do it, of course. I'd always planned to give it to Piper when she was grown. Jace had wanted to buy his own ring when he proposed, so I hadn't ever worn it. And my mom never married, so she hadn't either. But it was a gorgeous antique, the platinum snaking between the small diamonds on either side of a big square stone in the center. But in the end, therapies were more important to Piper than a ring. So I went to the jewelry shop two blocks from Boston Lights and sold it for enough to pay for the next eight months of Piper's therapy. In the meantime, I'd work on finding another grant for her. I had to.

"It had been sitting in a jewelry box for years, collecting dust." I shrugged and shifted in my chair, sighing. "It means so much that you would offer to help. But I would feel like I was taking advantage of you or Asher or even Kyle if I let you pay for her therapy."

Her shoulders slumped, but understanding shone in her eyes.

"So yeah, it was sad to sell the ring, but it's metal and rocks. And what wouldn't you do for your kids?"

"I get it. I just don't like it." She picked up her cup and took another sip just as a knock echoed through the small space.

"I'll get it," Sam yelled.

"No. I'll get it," I called. "We've had this talk about the door." I pushed back and hustled to the door just as my son pulled it open. And then I was face to face with deep brown eyes and blond hair full of natural highlights.

"Kyle." I swallowed. What was he doing here? Because of his dear diary messages, I knew his plans were to fly home on Sunday.

"You're back." Sam jumped up and down and then flung himself at the tall man without pause.

Chuckling, Kyle caught him. As he lifted him, he adjusted the small bag he was carrying. "Miss me, little man?"

"Lots. Miss Dylan says she can't play Legos and playdough and Playmobil and Trouble with me all days."

He snorted a laugh. "She has to take care of the other kids too, buddy."

"You play with me all the times until Piper gets there."

He shrugged. "I can't argue with that. But it's only because Miss Dylan is there making sure everybody is safe and having fun."

"Sam, are you coming back?" Grey popped up from behind the couch. "Uncle Kyle? I didn't know you were coming over too."

A chair scraped along the floor, and then Zara peeked around the corner.

"Oh." Kyle winced. "I didn't realize you had company. Sorry to interrupt."

"No." Zara shook her head. "I was getting ready to take the boys to the park down the block."

Frowning, I shook my head. That had not been the plan.

"Oh, yay! I need my shoes." Like a cartoon character, Sam took off at a run, heading for his room.

With her brows raised, Zara looked from me to the door, where Kyle rocked back on his heels, still half in and half out, then back again.

Exhaling loudly, I said, "Come in."

Zara beamed. "Grey, get your shoes."

In less than a minute, she was herding both boys into the hall. "Cheers!" she called as she pulled the door shut behind her.

As it clicked shut, I turned, finding Kyle watching me, his eyes full of uncertainty.

"I thought you were coming home tomorrow."

With his teeth pressed into his full bottom lip, he shrugged. "I got a call from Kayla, and I couldn't wait any longer to talk to you."

He glanced over at Piper, who was still on the sofa. She hadn't noticed him come in. Her ability to hyper-focus amazed me sometimes. Fireworks could go off in the room, and with her headphones on, she wouldn't even notice.

"I brought something for Piper and me to do. We've had a deal for a while, and it's time for her to pay up. But can we talk first, since she's content for now?"

Swallowing past the boulder that had formed in my throat and kept growing, I waved him to the table. "Let's sit." On my way, I snagged the envelope with his name on it from my purse.

"I'm sorry," he said as he eased into a chair.

I held a hand up. "You've apologized probably twenty times at this point. No more. Please. I understand what you did and why you did it."

Lips parting in shock, he blinked at me.

"I don't love it. But I can appreciate that it came from a good place, and I accept your apology."

He leaned slightly forward, and his expression eased. For the first time since he'd walked in, some of his confidence was back.

Exhaling, bracing myself, I slid the white envelope across the dark wood table. "However, I can't let you pay for my daughter."

"Harper—"

I put that hand up again. "Let me finish."

He nodded.

"If you talked to Kayla already, then you know that, going forward, she will be billing me for Piper's therapies. Your foundation's connections are amazing." I shook my head. "And I'd like to be able to schedule things through her."

He reared back, his shoulders slamming into the seat back. "One hundred percent. I would *never* say no to that. To anyone. Not just you and Piper."

"Good." I swallowed. "So she will set things up, and then she'll bill *me* for them. This"—I tapped the envelope—"is the amount you've already paid."

He frowned at it like it smelled like a decomposing body and pushed it back toward me. "Why would I take your money?"

This was the part that had worried me for days. Because if I was wrong about what Kyle wanted, then I was about to embarrass myself.

But I gathered all my courage, pulled my shoulders back, and laid it out. "I'm getting the impression that you'd like to start something between us."

He snagged my hand with athletic speed, his warmth encapsulating me and filling me with a flush of comfort. "Hell yes, I do. If I haven't made that clear, then I've fucked up more than I thought I had."

The intensity of the statement flipped my stomach. But I pulled my hand away and pushed the envelope with the check closer again.

"Then I need you to cash the check."

His lips parted, and his focus narrowed, like he was ready to argue. But I kept going before he could.

"We can't see where this goes if I feel indebted to you. I don't want you to pay for my life. That's not what this should be."

His eyes swam with mixed emotions. With frustration and determination, but also with acceptance. He knew I wouldn't give in.

"You've done more than enough," I continued. "I can't let you pay for Piper's therapies too."

"You are a very annoying woman," he gritted out as he snatched up the envelope and shoved it into his pocket.

"And you are an exceedingly frustrating man." But for the first time in days, my shoulders relaxed, and I slumped in my chair.

Harper
27

"HOW LONG WILL the boys be gone?" Kyle asked.

"Probably not too long." Although I couldn't be sure because Zara had gone rogue by taking them to the park. "Jace is supposed to pick up the kids at six, which probably means six thirty. And then they won't eat until—" I snapped my mouth shut. No one liked to hear a person rant about their ex. "Sorry."

"You have nothing to be sorry about." Lips pursed, he took my hand between his. As he rubbed his thumb in a circle on my palm, an electric warmth eased into my stomach. Our eyes met for a beat before his gaze dropped to my lips.

The memory of his kiss swamped me. The way his mouth had pressed into mine desperately. Like he'd been trying to devour me. Like he needed me.

Heart skipping, I shifted closer. With my hand still locked in one of his, he pushed a piece of hair back from my face with the other. The brush of his thumb felt like fire on my cheek. Our eyes met, and he leaned toward me, cupping my cheek. The warmth of his palm flooded my system.

My breath picked up. My body throbbed. I was desperate to close the inches of space between us. Press my lips to his. Let him pull me onto his lap so I could feel his hard body against mine.

But a noise from Piper across the room had my heart lurching and had us both jerking back. Away from each other. Away from that magnetic connection that lingered just below the surface.

He lowered his hand from my face but didn't break eye contact. "How about I go out and pick up dinner while you get them off with their dad, and then we can hang out?"

"Oh, I..." Wanted that. I thought. My heart was still racing, and my cheeks were hot. My whole body was flushed, really. My body wanted him. And he'd come clean. He'd taken the money like I asked, and I'd told him I had forgiven him. Now I had to actually do it.

What had put that last nail in the coffin of my marriage was my inability to move on from Jace's lies. And Kyle didn't deserve that. So then and there, I resigned myself to doing whatever it took to let it go.

He smirked, though it was a bit forced, and leaned farther back against his chair, releasing his hold on my hand. "We have two hours before their dad will be here, and Piper owes me a manicure. So you think about what you want for dinner while she and I do that."

"Yeah." I blinked at his hands, already missing the feel of his rough, warm palms. Shaking my head, I forced myself out of the haze I'd fallen into. "Wait, did you say manicure?"

"Girl needs her nails clipped, and I have a plan." He reached down to the floor beside his chair and picked up the bag he'd brought with him.

He couldn't mean that. When it came to clipping her nails, Piper was impossible. It always led to a complete meltdown where I had to all but physically restrain her so I could get it done. It was easier to just let her claw me when she was upset than to cut them. If Kyle thought she would happily let him do her nails, he had no idea what he was in for.

"What kind of plan?" I leaned forward and reached for the bag, but he yanked it away with a sparkle in his eyes.

"Don't be nosy."

"Nosy?" I balked, straightening.

THE FOUL OUT 213

"Yes, Crabby. This is my plan." With a laugh, he stood, then strode over to Piper in four steps.

At the movement, she glanced up from her tablet, her eyes going wide. And then she did something I never would have expected. She dropped the tablet and jumped off the couch, wrapping her arms around his waist. Piper was not a hugger. She wasn't normally comfortable enough to initiate physical contact. Once in a while, she hugged me, but even that was so rare that I soaked up each occasion, knowing it wouldn't happen again for some time.

He looked as shocked as I felt. That didn't stop him from carefully patting her back, though he was sure to avoid her head and neck, knowing touching either might trigger her. But the smile that split his face as he sank into her embrace wasn't at all careful.

The way the two of them responded to each other made my heart swell.

"You said you'd come home Monday," Piper practically yelled as she pulled back.

Kyle tapped his ears, always so patient, and smiled.

Yanking off the headphones, Piper repeated her statement at a normal volume.

"I missed you all, so I came home early."

"Does that mean I get to do your nails with the baseballs and Revs stuff?" She surveyed him from head to toe, then scanned the room. When her gaze landed on the bag, she rushed over.

He didn't even bother to stop her.

"Oh, so she can look?" I teased, cocking a brow.

"Feeling jealous, Crabby?" His blond hair flopped forward a bit, messier than usual. God, he looked so damn sexy in that moment. Brown eyes sparkling, lips pulled up in a grin.

Chuckling, I shook my head, then I watched Piper pull out two flat white pieces of cardboard.

"Look." She flashed them my way, showing me the blue shapes behind plastic. "They have baseballs and the Revs logo. Kyle promised I could put them on his nails."

"He did?" I turned back to the man in question.

He tipped his head, cocking a brow at my daughter. "As long as I get to do yours too, Pipe. You know the deal."

She nodded, her pigtail braids bobbing.

For the next hour, I sat on the sofa with my heart in my throat as Piper turned all the baseball star's nails blue and he didn't bat an eye. He showed her how to use the clippers and then the file. Then he helped her make sure the sticker was straight on each of his large nails.

He was known for being a man obsessed with his image, and yet he was painting his nails for my daughter. Talking about her week, asking about therapy. He was content with her one-word answers, though he didn't once give up his unaggressive attempt to engage her.

"What do you mean you wouldn't try turkey?" Kyle feigned shock, splaying a hand against his chest, making the blue stickers that had yet to be trimmed flap against his T-shirt. "It's the best."

"It made the entire room smell yucky." Piper kept her focus fixed on lining up the last blue sticker on his pinky nail.

"Yeah, it can sometimes have a strong smell, but it tastes so good. Maybe next time, you'll try some with me."

She froze. From where I sat on the sofa, I braced for her response. Instead of panicking like I expected, she simply lifted her head and almost looked at him before refocusing on his fingers.

"*Maybe*," she said. "But that's not a promise deal, like doing my nails."

Warmth blossomed in my chest at her reaction, and I couldn't help but smile at her.

Kyle, though, kept his expression very serious. "Oh, of course not." He wiggled his fingers, the blue color hanging off each nail. "Now we file them."

Piper typically couldn't stand the sound of a nail file, but she made not one peep as she filed off the extra color. When she finished, Kyle held up his hands and wiggled his fingers.

"What do you think?" he asked, his brows arched expectantly.

Piper nodded and almost smiled.

"Good. Now we do you?" Though it was a question, Kyle had been clear about their deal. If she did his nails, then he got to do hers.

I was still relatively certain his plan would fail. But Piper solemnly nodded and held her hands out.

She flinched multiple times and definitely wore a pained expression through most of the process, but she didn't cry, and she didn't fight him. She just let him clip her nails nice and short and then make hers match his.

Eventually, she held them up and looked into the living room. "Look, Mom."

"They look beautiful." My eyes welled, and my chest ached. For most kids, clipping their nails was a simple task. But it was such a struggle for us. For years, I'd dreaded it almost as much as she did. Now I didn't have to have the fight. I blinked hard, fighting the tears pooling in my eyes, and once they were under control, I took a deep breath and turned to Kyle. "Thank you," I mouthed.

Piper rubbed her fingers together, cringing. "Can I wash this dust off?"

"Yes." I gave her a smile. Once she was shuffling down the hallway, I approached Kyle, who was standing next to the table, cleaning up, and lifted onto my toes and pressed my lips against his cheek.

His breath hitched at the small gesture, surprising a smile from me.

"Thank you," I repeated.

He wrapped his arm around me and held me tight to his solid chest, the connection flooding me with a weird mix of warm comfort and antsy desire. "Anything," he whispered into my hair.

"Knock, knock," Zara called as she pushed the door open.

Kyle and I flinched apart. We had nothing to hide, especially not from Zara, who was smirking like she'd seen our embrace. But it felt strange. Like the bond between us was too new for other people's eyes yet. Like it was just ours. And I kind of wanted it to stay that way for a bit.

"I'm dropping Sam and heading out," Zara said. "I know—" Her eyes went wide, and she took a step toward Kyle. "Are you wearing nail polish?"

I expected Kyle to try to hide it or play it off. Instead, he proudly held them up just as Piper came back into the room.

"I am. Piper did a good job, didn't she?"

"Is that a Revs logo?" Zara stepped closer, head tilted, inspecting his hand.

"Yeah. Very talented girl." He pointed to Piper.

"They match," Piper said, her cheeks pink, as she tentatively lifted her hand next to his.

"Quite lovely." Zara nodded. "I'm going to dash."

"Remind Asher that I'm picking him up Monday at six for the hockey game."

"What?" Zara's eyes narrowed.

"The Bolts game."

"Oh." She frowned. "Right," she said, though it was clear by her confusion, then by her disappointment, that she hadn't known. Pasting a fake smile on, she waved to me and herded Grey out the door.

"I'm going to head out too." Kyle studied me, his jaw tight and his eyes swimming with uncertainty once again. "Unless—"

Before I could second guess myself, I said, "I'd love if you picked up dinner."

"Cool." The lines around his eyes disappeared, and a relieved grin spread across his face. "I'll text you a few options and see you later." Then he turned to the kids and held a fist to Sam first. "I'll see you Monday, little man. Have fun with Dad." Then he wiggled his fingers at Piper. "Thanks again, Pipe."

She nodded.

As soon as the door closed, she said, "Dad said six o'clock, right? Because it is 5:53."

Dropping onto the sofa, I sighed and patted the seat next to me, signaling for her to sit. "He'll be here *around* six."

"Who got me this?" Sam asked from where he was on his knees at the table. He held up a package of M&M's decorated like baseballs and two cans of whipped cream.

"Were they in Kyle's bag?" I eyed the brown bag still sitting by the table where they'd done nails.

Without responding, Sam picked up one can and flipped it in the air. It spun, and as it fell, he grasped for it but missed. When it hit the ground, he scooped it up and popped off the red top. Then, with a burst of aerosol, he squirted it into his mouth.

"Where did you learn that?"

"At Little Fingers. Kyle showed me."

I rolled my eyes, though I couldn't help but smile. Of course.

"No more whipped cream." I grabbed the cans and the candy and put them back on the table. "Let's get ready to go to Dad's."

A half hour later, the kids were gone. They'd left with Jace, and the transaction had gone pretty easily.

"I got tacos," Kyle said when he showed up a few minutes later. He brought the bag to the table and set it down. "Since you don't normally do gluten, dairy, sugar, or dyes, one set is free of all that. It's also taste-free. The other set is full of it all. That one, you might actually enjoy."

Oh, we were back to the jokes, huh?

"What happened to the nice guy who wasn't giving me crap?" I braced my hands on my hips and gave him a mock glare.

He rocked back on his heels and crossed his arms over his broad chest. "He got some confidence back because you invited him to dinner." He grinned.

I rolled my eyes.

"I see Sam found my treat." He snagged the whipped cream from the table and flipped it into the air. Then he caught it with all the grace that Sam hadn't managed.

"Yeah, and he showed me how you taught him to squirt it straight into his mouth."

"I would never." He smirked, popping the cap off with his thumb, sending it shooting toward me.

I swiped it out of the air.

"Nice, Crabby." He squirted a dollop of cream onto his finger.

"Do you actually want that, or are you just messing around?"

"I definitely want it." He brought his finger to his lips and hummed as the cream disappeared.

Suddenly hotter than I'd been only a moment before, I zeroed in on his mouth and watched as he released his finger.

"Not bad, but…"

He clutched my wrist, and the second his rough fingers locked around it, goose bumps broke out across my skin. Watching my face, he tilted the whipped cream can, each move slow and steady. There was no part of me that questioned what he was doing. I knew. And I wanted it.

The burst of condensed air echoed off the walls as the cold cream landed on my finger. With his eyes locked on mine, he lifted my hand. My heart pounded loud in my ears when, without breaking eye contact, he wrapped his warm lips around my finger, and when he sucked, my body throbbed.

I didn't need this complication. I didn't have time to devote to another person. But damn, I wanted him.

"Mmm." The sound vibrated through me, from my finger straight to my core. He slipped my finger from between his lips and rasped, "Maybe one more taste." He pulled on my wrist, and I let him tuck me against him.

This time the cold cream hit my skin at the crook of my neck. Before I could even process the sensation, his mouth was on me. Something between a whimper and a gasp escaped me as the rough stubble of his jaw brushed my skin.

"Kyle." That single syllable was so full of wanting, it was almost embarrassing.

The warmth deep in my core blazed hotter as he moved up the column of my neck, nipping and sucking.

"You're sweeter than any dessert, Crabby," he said, skimming up along my jaw until his lips brushed my ear, forcing a moan from deep within me. "You're driving me insane." He pulled in a deep breath through his nose, inhaling me. "That sound. God, I want to hear it over and over as I taste every inch of skin." He peppered kisses along my cheek. "I want to know whether your pussy is as sweet as the rest of you."

My thighs clenched, searching for friction to ease the throb.

"I need you to moan my name while you coat my tongue with your pleasure." He tipped my chin back and captured my mouth with his.

Just like last time, my body came alive with the brush of his lips. Weeks of tension melted instantly and was replaced with waves of desire as he toyed and coaxed my mouth open. The second my lips parted, he swept his tongue between them, invading, and he locked his arms around me, pulling me to him.

A deep groan echoed up his chest.

He spun to press me against the table, his thigh between mine and a hand on my ass. One squeeze, and he lifted, sliding me up his thigh. I rocked into him, seeking the pressure, something to ease the throbbing.

With a ragged breath, he broke our kiss and shook his head. Cupping my cheek, he blinked, as if trying to come back to reality. "Sorry." Pupils blown, his eyes blazing with desire, he swallowed hard and slid me down his thigh.

I leaned into the slow friction, needing more.

He grunted as he steadied me on my feet. "You make me forget every one of my good intentions."

The statement made my chest swell with affection and pride. The idea that I could drive this gorgeous man to forget his control was a boost to my ego. It made me feel like more than a tired mom who was past her prime. It made me feel attractive and wanted.

And I desperately missed that feeling.

So why was I fighting it?

This didn't need to be love or forever. It could be selfish desire. A blip in time where I felt incredible.

"Oh, a smirk." He tickled my side, making me squirm.

As I brushed against him, his thick erection startled me, and when I'd righted myself and I did it again, this time on purpose, his dick jumped, and he hissed out a breath. Encouraged by his reaction, I dropped my hand to rub along the swell of his cock.

"Fuck, baby." He pressed the long, thick length into my hand. "You like torturing me a bit too much."

"Oh, but it'll be so worth it when you finally moan my name as you're coming."

His eyes popped wide.

My heart lurched at his reaction. Letting up on my hold of his dick, I stepped back. "Is that not where this was heading?"

"If you want that." He pulled me into him again, his eyes dropping from mine to my mouth. "You have no idea the fantasies I've had..."

"Show me," I dared.

"Challenge accepted." With that, he hoisted me up and I wrapped my legs around his waist.

KYLE
28

THIS MORNING, there was no way I would have guessed I'd finally have my hands on Harper again. My arms around her waist, her lips pressed to mine, her need matching my own. Wished, yes, but it seemed more like a fantasy.

So even though I wasn't happy about having to swallow my pride and cash her check, I would do it. Because I wanted her. Wanted us.

In the back of my mind, my conscience itched. I hadn't told her about JJ yet, but that was an issue we could work through in time.

Heart racing, I laid her out on the sofa and hovered above her. "You're sure about this?"

"Don't expect me to beg." With a smirk, she pulled my head down and brought her lips to mine again. The way her kiss ignited a fire inside me was unfamiliar but so damn incredible. The electric desire that coursed through my extremities and went straight to my cock every time her lips met mine was unlike any sensation I'd ever experienced. But I needed more of it.

I skimmed a hand down her neck and over the mound of her breast, fucking finally getting to feel her soft tits. I was a boob guy. I loved the weight in my palm, the soft skin against my lips, the pebbling of a nipple on my tongue. Hers were a perfect handful. I squeezed, and her answering moan had my cock throbbing against my zipper, begging to be released.

I toyed with the edge of her T-shirt, teasing the warm skin underneath, and ran my hand up farther, flattening my palm along her soft skin as my tongue tangled with hers. The soft whimper that reverberated up her throat had my heart pounding.

With a grunt, I broke the kiss and yanked the T-shirt over her head. Then I pulled back. Her breasts were covered in a simple white bra, but above the cups, her pale skin was peppered by freckles. I wanted to lick each one. Run my thumbs beneath them and make her quiver. Tease the nipples just barely visible through the white fabric. I'd do it all until she was begging and needy.

Lowering my gaze, I took in her soft stomach and the swell of her hips. Unable to resist, I let my finger dance just above the line of her leggings.

Her muscles clenched. "I know I'm not like the models…"

Instantly, I zeroed in on her face, cupping her cheeks, and took in the crease of worry on her brow I didn't quite understand.

"What?" I searched her expression, finding apprehension and a little fear where, only moments ago, I'd seen nothing but confidence.

"You date models with perfect bodies, and I have stretch marks and loose skin. I don't have time to even think about the gym or a sit-up." She glanced away from me, her chin lowered.

Had she somehow mistaken my adoration for disappointment?

"Harper," I said, that word catching in my throat. "Look at me."

It took a moment, but eventually, she focused those amber eyes on me. They were glassy and wide.

"Is there something in the way I can't catch my breath, in the way I can't think beyond getting to touch you, getting to give you pleasure, that makes it seem like I'm not blown the fuck away by you?"

Her lips parted, but she didn't respond.

"Crabby, in my eyes, every stretch mark, every soft curve, every freckle, every part of you, is perfection."

She lifted a hand and raked her fingers through my hair. I leaned into her touch, craving more of it.

As I shifted, my cock pressed into her thigh, and a deep groan worked up my chest. "My body is literally begging for you. Don't mistake my complete adoration for anything else."

"The feeling is pretty mutual." She lifted to press her lips to mine once more, sending another tingle through me.

I slid my hand around her ribcage and unclasped the bra keeping her tits from me. The second they were free, I pulled my mouth from hers and yanked the straps off her arms. At the sight of her perfect light pink nipples, I dropped my head and lapped at one slowly.

In response, she hissed a breath and scraped her nails along my scalp.

"You like that?"

"Yes," she moaned, dropping her head back.

"Good, because I fucking love it." I nipped and lapped and sucked one nipple until she was squirming, then switched to the other and back again.

"Kyle, please," she begged.

"Please, what?" I pulled back and fisted my green henley at the back of my neck, then yanked it off. On my knees before her, I moved in closer, and she spread her legs wider for me. I rocked against her, and even through our clothes, I felt the heat of her pussy. I groaned as her wet nipples pressed into my chest. "Do you need me to make you come, Crabby?"

She clawed at my back, pulling herself even closer. "I need to feel you inside me."

"We'll get there." With that promise, I slid down her body, pulling her leggings off as I went. "But first, I want a taste, because I fully intend to make this your best orgasm ever."

Brow cocked, she pushed up onto her elbows. "Even sex is a competition?"

"Oh baby, there won't be a competition. I'll blow everyone else out of the water." Grinning, I ran my hands up her smooth, creamy thighs and parted her legs. Her pussy was pink and glistening for me, begging for my tongue.

Unable to resist for another second, I lowered and gave her one long, teasing stroke. She fell back on the sofa with a moan, clutching the back of my head. Holding me against her. The taste of her exploded on my tongue, salty and sweeter than I could have imagined. She was my favorite flavor. And I wanted more of it.

As I lapped against her clit, she tightened her thighs around me, holding me in place. "Again," she croaked out.

Gladly. I licked and sucked and feasted until she was shaking, crying, begging me. With my lips clamped around her clit, I sank two fingers inside her.

"Yes," she called.

With her hands tangled in my hair, she rode my face and my fingers while I devoured her. Her body tightened, and she shuddered, calling my name as she came in my mouth. Eager and so fucking turned on, I worked her through her release, not relenting until her body slumped back against the cushions.

"Holy shit," she mumbled, still spread out on the sofa, and damn if I didn't have the perfect view. Harper, flushed and dazed from the orgasm I'd given her, her pussy wet and ready for me.

My cock leaked in my pants. Begging for attention. Begging for her.

I scrambled to my feet and yanked out my wallet for a condom. Then I dropped my jeans and boxer briefs in one swipe, leaving my needy dick jutting toward her.

With her eyes locked on my length, she sat up and took the condom out of my hands. "Can I?"

Could she touch me?

"Ab-so-fucking-lutely. I'd be thrilled to have your hands on my dick anytime, anywhere."

Chuckling, the sound breathy, she rolled her eyes and tore open the wrapper. Instead of rolling the latex over me, she grasped my cock, her fingers brushing against the sensitive flesh there.

"Fuck. Squeeze it, baby."

"Say please?" she teased, giving me shit, as always.

"Please," I croaked.

She didn't hesitate, thank fuck, to brush her thumb across the tip, spreading the precum. Then she wrapped her fingers around me, just like I'd requested. God damn. I had to lock my knees to stop myself from falling. She pumped once and then again. My gut tightened and my toes tingled. No fucking way. I yanked out of her hand. I wasn't coming until I was deep inside her.

"God damn, Harper. Put the condom on. I need you to ride me. Fast and hard," I ordered. "While you do that, I'm gonna play with the best tits I've ever seen."

Though she smirked at the demand, she slipped the condom over my tip and then ran her fist down me, taking the latex with her. When I was fully sheathed, her fingers brushed my balls, sending a zap of electricity through me.

Hissing at the sensation, I grasped her, lifting her off the sofa so I could settle in her place, and brought her down on my lap.

Still flooded with need, I pinched her nipples, teasing, rolling, flicking until she was squirming.

"Damn, you do that so well. It's the perfect pressure. I need—" She gasps.

"Me too, baby," I promised.

She pressed her knees into the cushion on either side of me and lined herself up with my dick. Slowly, she sank against me until I was enveloped in hot, wet heaven.

"Fuck. You're tight." I groaned when I was fully seated. She was tighter than anything I'd felt in forever. Like her pussy was made to grip every inch of my cock.

With her hands on my shoulders, she slowly lifted herself up and dropped down once more, back arching. "It's been a while."

I ran my thumbs across her nipples, and she clenched around me in response. Damn, I fucking loved how sensitive her tits were, how responsive she was to every small touch. "Then we better make it worth the wait."

She lifted and dropped down once more, then circled her hips, grinding against me.

Yeah, this was heaven. Engulfed in the feel and the scent of the woman who not only turned me on but challenged me and made me laugh. I'd never known that kind of connection existed.

Her eyes drifted closed as she rocked against me, going even deeper.

"Don't you dare," I gritted out, pinching her nipples hard.

Her eyes snapped open, meeting mine.

"Yes," I rasped. "Look at me. Watch the man making your body ignite."

I continued teasing her, circling the sensitive flesh around her nipples, flicking the buds into sharp points, all while meeting every motion of her hips again and again. Her tits bounced with every thrust. And in her eyes, her pleasure matched my own.

With each movement, with every roll of our hips, we were building into something more. The connection was unlike anything I'd ever experienced. The desire, the emotion reflecting back at me, was so new, yet also familiar, because the same feelings were coursing through me. An animalistic need snapped inside me, and I pistoned up hard and faster, brutal in my need to fuck her, claim her, own her.

Her legs quivered as her pussy gripped me like a vise, and her breaths came in pants until finally she exploded around me.

"Kyle." She dug her nails into my shoulders, no doubt leaving marks. "Oh my God."

"Fuck, Harper." I came like a bomb had detonated, sending pleasure rocketing through my body. Desperate to hold on to this moment, I rocked up into her again and again until after what seemed like forever and yet not long enough. Finally, I collapsed against the sofa, pulling her with me, as the last pulses of pleasure rocked me.

She rested her head against my shoulder, her body melting against mine despite how fast her breaths still came. I wasn't in the best position for cuddling, but in this moment, I just wanted to hold her. Keep her in my arms and feel her heart pound against my chest. After-care wasn't my thing. I'd never understood it. Until now. Because with her, I was hit with a sense of security I'd never known. Like this, with her tucked into my body, skin to skin, I'd never been more content. I dipped and lightly kissed her forehead.

She squirmed like she was ready to stand, but I locked her in place with one arm banded around her torso. Typically, this was when I'd bolt. That was what I did. Sex and then head out in search of food.

Instead, I hugged her closer. "Want some tacos?" I asked against her forehead.

"Food?" She pulled back, studying me, that small line forming between her brows again.

Might as well fill her in on one of my quirks because I had plans to do this a few more times.

"Sex makes me ravenous. I always need food right away. Especially after I come so hard I can't feel my legs."

She rolled her eyes like I was messing with her. But I wasn't. About either thing.

"That must be awkward at two a.m."

I shrugged. I didn't really want to fight about my somewhat colorful past, but I wanted to be honest with her. "Not really. I'd make a quick escape and then grab something on the way home."

"What if you bring a woman to your place?" She shook her head. "Do you just sneak out of bed and leave her while you go out for food?"

"No one comes back to my place." I fought the urge to wince. That comment made me sound like an asshole, but I was determined not to lie or skirt around the truth. What we had was so different from anything I'd ever experienced with another woman, but that didn't change the past.

"So." She pulled back, and this time, I begrudgingly allowed her to stand. "Do you want to leave?"

"Nope," I said simply, heaving myself up. I snagged my shirt and boxer briefs but didn't bother to put them on. "I want to get rid of this condom and eat tacos with my girl."

Her eyes popped wide as I headed toward the hall. I didn't stop. I didn't want to talk about this anymore. She knew what I used to be like. Now I was showing her what I was with her. With a glance back, I tossed her my shirt. "Be right back."

I was worried she might bring the topic back up when I emerged from the bathroom. Instead, to my relief, I found her sitting at the table, wearing my shirt, with the bags of tacos I'd brought.

"So." I reached into the bag and pulled out the tacos I'd gotten for her. The ones that didn't follow her daughter's diet. "I respect that when you're with Piper, you have restrictions."

She huffed, her eyes turning to slits.

"Because," I said before she could argue, "her diet is very important. It helps her."

The tightness in her shoulder and jaw eased slightly.

"However. I do think that when you're not with her, you could work on balance. Live a little."

I opened the container that housed the tacos with the cheese and sour cream drizzle.

"It's your call," I said. "Always. I'm just pointing out that you're allowed to enjoy stuff."

She surveyed one taco container, then the other, then picked one of each for her plate. Progress.

I took the seat next to her and picked up my taco. But I paused with it halfway to my mouth, watching her as she pulled her hair into a messy side braid. The buttons of my green henley were open, the garment hanging on her like a tent and the sleeves way too long. Yet she stole the breath from my chest.

"What?" she asked. "I'm doing the balance thing."

I smiled. "You are." And she had no idea how gorgeous she was. That was just one of a thousand things that drew me to her.

"Then eat your tacos. You were the one who insisted you needed food." With a roll of her eyes, she took a bite.

The moment the flavors hit her taste buds, her eyes softened, and something like joy hit her face. Yeah, she needed more of that feeling. In all aspects of her life. I enjoyed watching her savor every bite of the taco, even while finishing all of mine in a few mouthfuls.

"Wait." She tipped her head, holding half of her second taco aloft. "That's my phone." Dropping the taco onto her plate, she hopped up. Then she ran from the room.

"Hello?" she said, her voice already laced with stress. "Yup, coming." She flew back into the room with her phone in her hand. "Sorry. Piper is melting down. I have to go." She scanned the room, stopping when she caught sight of her leggings. If she hadn't been rushing around like her hair was on fire, I might have enjoyed the view as she bent to step into the damn things. Her Uggs were on, and she was moving for her purse when I stood and caught her arm.

"Wait."

"I really have to go." She yanked her arm back, but I held tight.

"Not like this."

Her brows slammed together, that defiance that lived within her flaring to the surface, along with true panic for her child.

"Crabby." I pulled her into my arms and hugged her. It took a second for her to relax against me. "I get that Piper is upset. But taking two minutes to get yourself together won't hurt her," I mumbled against the crown of her head. "So slow down, put on a bra, and"—I hated these next words because I really loved her in my clothes—"put on your own shirt. Maybe a coat too, since it's below freezing."

Swallowing audibly, she glanced down at herself and then at me. "It's not like he's—"

I put my hand over her mouth. "Turns out I'm not as evolved as you are, and I'm not chill about the fact that other people ever have gotten to touch you. So let's not go there," I growled.

My hand still covered her mouth, but those amber eyes danced, like maybe she was smiling. She pulled on my arm, and I lowered my hand, settling it just above the curve of her ass.

"Are you jealous, Kyle Bosco?" Her tone was exponentially lighter. Damn, I loved it, even if it was at my expense.

I dropped my hand lower and gave her ass a squeeze. "Apparently, I've become somewhat possessive, but it's your fault. This was never an issue for me until I met you."

Her smile grew.

"So, for my peace of mind, will you put on a damn bra?"

She pulled away and headed across the room, and when she found her bra and shirt, she turned back to me and pulled my henley over her head.

My mouth watered at the sight of her pale breasts dusted with freckles. In response to the cool air, or maybe to my attention, her nipples pebbled. But before I could cross the room and run my tongue over them again, she slipped her arms into the straps of her bra. Dammit. And when she clasped it, then tossed her shirt over her head, I wanted to cry.

"Happier?" she asked.

"Not at all. But Piper needs you, so you can take a raincheck on the rest of the night." I opened her coat closet and found her black coat. Once she was in front of me, I held it up and let her slip her arms in. "I'll clean up and lock the door behind me."

"Thanks." Expression soft and full of gratitude, she lifted onto the balls of her feet. She gave me one more all too quick kiss, and then she was gone.

After a sigh, I pulled out my phone.

> Me: Need a ride home.

> Cam: That bad, huh?

> Me: No, everything is perfect. Pipe just needed her, so she had to leave.

> Cam: Did you talk about JJ?

> Me: No. I'll get there eventually.

> Cam: Not smart.

I frowned at my phone, swallowing back my unease. I needed some time to talk to JJ first. Then I'd work up to talking to Harper too. I knew what I was doing. At least I thought I did.

KYLE
29

Dear Diary,

Last night, I finally got to call the most amazing woman mine. I'm hoping it's official. Like I get to call her my girlfriend and do one of those growly things and glare at any other idiots who come near her. I've hinted that to her, but she hasn't confirmed, so wish me luck.

-Kyle

BOSCO
29

Crabby: You could just ask me this like a normal person...

Me: GIF of Jimmy Fallon saying he is shocked

Me: Are you saying you don't love my daily messages?

Crabby: I just figured you would stop now that you're home.

Me: Do they make you smile or laugh?

Crabby: Well yeah.

Me: Then I will do them every day until the end of time.

Angel Boy: So what's the deal with Harper?

Me: Mine.

Me: She's mine.

Angel Boy: Okay caveman. I'm married. Not looking. Chill the fuck out.

Me: Why ask that way?

Angel Boy: I know something, and I feel like if I were you, I'd want to know. So I think I should tell you.

Me: ...

Me: You said that ten fucking minutes ago.

Me: WTF? It's been an hour?

Angel Boy: Sorry got distracted.

Angel Boy: Zara is ranting about something Harper did.

Me: Angel Boy I swear my patience is about to run out.

Angel Boy: I'm trying to tell you. Chill out.

Me: What did Harper do?

Angel Boy: Would you give me ten fucking seconds to type a reply?

Angel Boy: Harper sold a family heirloom to pay for Piper's therapies. Zara thinks we need to track it down.

Me: Answer my call.

Angel Boy: Give me five minutes to get away from the wife. She's got a short fuse lately and she'll freak out if she knows I told you. Plus she's pissed about the game tomorrow. She and I were supposed to have a date night and I forgot.

Me: Dude skip the game. Go out with your girl.

Angel Boy: Who are you? For months you've given us all shit for skipping boys' night.

Me: I'm reformed. I get it now.

Angel Boy: But I'm coming to the game. Zara said forget it. So if I force the issue it will make us both miserable.

Me: I have a job for us.

Me: It's going to suck.

Cam: What else is new?

Me: GIF of a man rolling his eyes

Me: You have the best job and the best boss.

Cam: ...

Me: How am I not the best?

Cam: Is this really the job you want me to do?
Tell you how you're not the best?

Me: GIF of a dude flipping off the camera

Me: Call me.

Crabby: You're going to be crushed but I have an IEP meeting so Zara is bringing Sam today.

Me: Photo of Kyle in a green shirt making a pouting face.

Crabby: With a smile and wink that shirt would melt anyone into a puddle.

Me: Video of Kyle winking at the camera.

DUMPTY ADDED DRAGON TO BASEBALL BROS

Dumpty: Sorry man but you gotta see this.

Dumpty: Pic of a man's hands decorated in Revs blue polish

Bambi: Whoa! How did you get that done

Dumpty: Not me. That's Streaks.

New Guy: nail polish??

Me: Piper did them for me. I dare any of you assholes to make a comment.

Angel Boy: She did a great job.

Dumpty: Yeah no I wasn't mocking them.

Bambi: Can she do mine?

Dragon: Piper is cute. She's got talent. Glad you're happy.

Dragon left Baseball Bros

Bambi: I think that was Avery. That was too many words for Dragon.

Dumpty: Dude I just said that.

Angel Boy: He did.

New Guy: Wait...did you guys not invite me to the hockey game tonight?

Me: Pic of Dumpty, Angel Boy, and Bambi at the Bolts game.

New Guy: You all suck.

Crabby: You are so weird about people touching your hair.

Me: Not you. I love when your hands are in my hair when you're riding my cock. The little moan that you whisper in my ear while I suck on your perfect tits.

Crabby: Breakfast with the kids is not sexing time.

Me: But I miss you. I haven't seen you in days.

Harper
30

"SO SAM IS WRONG?"

The sound of Piper's voice echoing across the gym brought me up short. I shuffled closer to the door so she couldn't see me. She was jumping on a mini trampoline, her red ponytail bobbing up and down.

"It's not fair that just 'cause you're old and you're a boy, you can't be my best friend."

I fought back a laugh at the comment about Kyle's age. He hated being called old. But at the same time, my heart squeezed. Piper really didn't have friends, so it wasn't strange for her to think that Kyle was her best friend. She was closer to him than just about anyone.

Like I knew he would, Kyle handled the question with grace. "A best friend is a person you like hanging out with and talking to. A person who gets you." His deep voice echoed off all the hard services. "And I think that's true of us."

I could see him from my hiding spot, dressed in a tight white shirt and black gym shorts, holding a jump rope in his hand. His nails were still painted blue. I thought he'd have taken it off the instant he got home so the guys wouldn't give him a hard time. Instead, he wore it proudly and grinned each time Piper wanted to show off their matching manicures.

"Does that mean Grey can be Sam's best friend and I'm your best friend?" She was getting shorter on breath as she jumped, but even still, the tone of her voice was more questioning than hopeful.

"You're definitely one of my favorite people, so I'd say you're one of them."

"Who are your other favorite people?"

He glanced around and froze when our eyes met in the mirror. A smile tipped his lips, and he turned back to Piper "Don't tell her I said so, but your mom is definitely one of my favorite people."

I pressed a hand to my mouth to hold in my laugh.

"Me too. She's pretty okay." Piper stopped jumping. "That's two hundred. Your turn."

He shifted the rope so he held one end in each hand and swung it over his head so it hit the floor behind him with a *thwack*. "You going to count for me?"

She nodded. "Five hundred this time?"

He scoffed. "You're going to kill me kid."

Chin tipped up, she said, "Perseverance. You can do it."

"Oh, you're using my own words against me now." He pursed his lips and sent her a playful glare.

"Perseverance," she repeated.

With a grin at me, he said, "Okay, count, girlie."

Piper nodded, and he started to jump. Holy hell. I wasn't prepared. Maybe I hadn't paid enough attention to jump-roping in the past, because damn, each hop sent another wave of liquid fire through my veins. His calves and thighs tightened each time he launched himself off the ground, and his shoulders bunched, along with his abs, in a rhythmic way that was hypnotizing. It was a perfect showcase of how amazing his entire body was.

Not that this was news to me. I pulled my bottom lip between my teeth and watched. Good God, was it hard to believe that he'd had that body pressed against mine just a few days ago. That every one of his muscles had tightened in pleasure when he pulsed inside me.

Sex with Kyle had been like nothing else. It shouldn't have

surprised me. Everything with Kyle was new and challenging and exhilarating. I snorted, thinking about his Dear Diary message from this morning. I was sure he'd drop the silliness now that we'd talked, but I should have known better. Because when he said something, he followed through.

"Three hundred," Piper announced.

Each flick of his wrists made the corded muscle of his forearms bunch, and his brow was slicked with sweat, causing his hair to stick to his skin. His face was tightening in effort. And although I knew he wouldn't quit before five hundred, he was getting tired.

At 450, I announced myself by stepping all the way into the room.

"Shh, Mommy. I'm counting. Four-fifty-seven. Four-fifty-eight." Piper focused on each smack of the rope against the ground.

I leaned against a machine nearby, one I didn't recognize and would never figure out how to work. The gym wasn't my thing. But Kyle had made it clear he liked my soft thighs and stretch marks. So I just waited, enjoying the view.

"Five hundred," Piper announced.

Kyle stopped the rope and bent in half with a huff.

"Why are you here?" Piper asked me. "It is only 5:05."

"Work was slow, so I thought I'd pick you and Sam up early." I stopped myself from brushing a hair off her forehead. "Look at you working up a sweat."

"That's 'cause I did six hundred jumps." She nodded. "But I'm done now."

"Me too," Kyle announced, straightening but still breathing heavy.

"Yes, you did three hundred plus four hundred plus five hundred." Her little nose scrunched up as she did the mental math. "You did 1200 jumps."

Whoa, no wonder he was sweaty.

"That means I deserve a good-job hug." He moved toward me, dropping the rope and holding his arms out.

"Wait, what?" I stepped back, but I wasn't fast enough. From behind, he looped his arms around me and pressed his sweaty chest into my back. "Oh God, you're gross."

"Not what you said the other night," he murmured, the vibration of each word sending a chill down my spine. "I even turn you on when I'm sweaty."

I turned in his arms, and he loosened his hold so he could give me a quick peck.

"Yuck," Piper complained. "You kissed my mom."

My breath caught in my lungs, and my body flushed. Shit. What was I supposed to say to that?

Kyle stepped away carefully, like he understood that this could be a minefield. "I like kissing her. Is that okay with you?" he asked, his voice soft and even.

"If she doesn't care." Piper stepped off the trampoline. "It's 5:10. We go back to the room now."

"Yeah, we can."

She hopped off the trampoline and led us out of the gym. She stayed five steps ahead of us the whole way, surrounded by an air of assurance that showed without words how comfortable she was here at Langfield Corp. She even waved to a security guard.

And when I smiled at the guy, Kyle dropped a sweaty arm over my shoulder.

I pushed him off. "No," I warned. "You really are gross."

He pouted, sticking his lower lip out. "Does that mean I can't come for dinner like you promised?"

I rolled my eyes. "Well, I, uh." I glanced at Piper, who was still charging forward, and swallowed. "I got my period this morning."

He grasped my upper arm and pulled me to a stop. "Just because" —he glanced at Piper too, noting that she was still continuing down the hall—"we have a physical relationship now, doesn't mean that's the only thing I want to do. I'm not coming over for that." He smirked. "I'm never going to turn that down. But that's not the only thing I want from you."

My heart tripped over itself at the sincerity in his expression. Wow, this man was way sweeter than the world at large realized.

"So you're after my chicken and broccoli, then, huh?" I teased.

He chuckled. "That and your smiles and your laughs. I like hanging out with you and the kids."

"In that case, you can come over. But…" I waved a hand in front of my nose. "Shower first, yeah?"

He laughed. "Yeah." Then he was dragging me along down the hall again.

And I wondered if what we had could really be this easy. Trust and laughter and support. Because that sounded almost too good to be true.

KYLE
31

I KNOCKED, though from the sound of the muffled voices, I wasn't sure they could hear me.

Before I could try the knob, the door swung open, and Sam beamed up at me. "Hi."

"Didn't Mommy tell you that you shouldn't be opening the door?" I crouched so we were eye to eye and gave him a warning frown.

He sighed. "Yes. But it was you, so it was fine," he chirped and smiled, feigning innocence.

Head tilted, I hummed. "But what if it wasn't me?"

"Then Mommy would be mad at me." He glanced over his shoulder at the sound of raised voices.

"I understand that you don't like the way broccoli smells when it's cooking, but slamming your door and then hanging on the doorknob so I couldn't turn it caused it to break."

"I don't care. I didn't want you to cook broccoli."

"I care that the doorknob is broken, and you should care that I'm upset."

Sam winced. "It's not going good here."

Poor kid. My heart hurt for him. I remembered those nights. When

I stayed out of the way because my mother was overwhelmed with Ryan.

"Give me a second, and then you and I can go on a mission." I pushed to my feet and headed down the short hall, pulling out my phone and shooting off a text as I went.

> Me: Come back.

Harper turned at the sound of my footsteps, and with a sigh, she held up the broken doorknob.

I peeked past her, eyeing Piper, who was sitting on her bed, arms crossed, frowning. She looked my way but glanced away again without making eye contact.

"Did you break Mommy's door?"

Her shoulders sank slightly, and she curled in on herself. Piper didn't like to be called out for her wrongdoings. It embarrassed her. So I had to be very careful with my reaction, otherwise the situation would only escalate.

"I thought Ashley gave you a Metros stuffed baseball to hit when you were mad." One of the tenets of ABA therapy was replacement. Piper's extreme anxiety in situations where she was melting down caused her actual fear, and often her fight response kicked in. So instead of fighting people and breaking things, a therapist would redirect her fight to something safer. And I had to give Ashley credit. A pillow emblazoned with the logo of one of our team's biggest rivals was perfect for that.

Piper growled, but she didn't lash out. Her eyes landed on the white pillow with the Metros' logo. I could step in and mediate, but Harper had this, and it was important to show her that I supported her in that. But that didn't mean I couldn't help in other ways.

I turned back to Harper and tipped her chin up. "You're a good mom. You've got this." I gave her a quick kiss. "Give me the door handle. Sam and I will go pick up a new one."

For a moment, she just looked at me. I braced for a *you don't have to*, but she surprised me by dropping the brass knob into my palm, then turning back to Piper.

It might be dumb, but that felt like progress. Like trust. And I couldn't help but smile as I put the knob in my coat pocket and headed back to get Sam.

"Shoes and coat, bud. We're going out."

My phone buzzed.

> Cam: You fucked up already? I'm not even out of the neighborhood.

> Me: No I did not. Sam and I are running an errand.

> Cam: It better not be to a jewelry store again. We've been to sixty this week.

That had sucked. But it had paid off eventually, and we'd found the place where Harper had pawned her grandmother's ring. Just an hour ago, I'd swung by and bought it. We located it a couple of days ago, but I had to wait for the seven-day waiting period to end.

> Me: Don't be dramatic. We just need a hardware store.

> Cam: Any hardware store or a specific one?

Clearly, I'd traumatized Cam with my last errand.

> Me: Whichever is closest.

> Cam: I'm sure I can find a Lowes.

> Cam: Side note, our life has gotten so weird.

I rolled my eyes.

"Ready?" I asked Sam as I zipped up his coat.

"Yup. What's our mission?" he asked as we headed down the hall to the elevator.

I pulled the metal ball out of my pocket and held it out. "To replace this and install it so Mom isn't stressed."

"Do you know how to fix that thing?" As he stared at it, he frowned in a way that made his brow furrow just like his mother's.

"Nope. Not a clue. But I'll figure it out. Plus, we'll have Cam's help."

"Mommy says I can't call him Cam." He pushed the down button and stepped back while we waited for the elevator.

"How about Uncle Cam, then?"

"Is he my family?" Sam fixed his golden eyes on my face.

There was a chance I'd screw this up, but I went with my gut.

"Family can be a lot of things. Sometimes it's blood relatives, and sometimes it's a group of people who love you and who can be counted on when you need them. And Cam falls into that category." That was the thing about having great friends like I had. My friends loved me as much as I loved them, and they cared about what I cared about. And the Wallace family currently topped my list.

"Then I think it's okay to call him uncle."

"Yeah, I think so too."

Cam was at the curb when we stepped out onto the sidewalk.

"Hey, Uncle Cam." Sam climbed in and plopped into the booster seat I kept in my car constantly now.

Cam turned, and though his brows were arched in surprised, the smile on his face said he didn't mind the title. "Hey, man. I heard we need to make a Lowes run."

"Yeah, I guess. We need to make Mommy happy." Sam clicked his seat belt.

"I figured that was the case." Cam reached out a hand toward me, and I flinched away.

"Give me a hard time, but don't touch the hair, dude," I warned, leaning toward the window. He thought it was funny as hell that I hated for my hair to look shitty. But my hair was a thing for the entire world. And if someone got a shitty picture of me, it would end up everywhere for days on end. And I didn't need that hassle.

He laughed but turned his attention back to the road as he pulled off the curb. I dropped the doorknob onto the console beside him. "This."

A deep chuckle started in his chest, then rumbled up his throat. "Good luck."

With a grin, I shrugged. I'd figure it out.

And I did. It only took twenty minutes and the help of a guy in blue to find the right knob and get a rundown of how to install it. As luck would have it, Piper had broken something that was easy to fix, so we were headed to the register in record time. But just as we approached, Sam yanked on my arm.

"Look." He pointed to a display of boxes. "Gingerbread houses!"

Well, fuck me. I clearly understood the longing in the three-year-old's tone. But those boxes were loaded full of sugar and all the red dye numbers that were forbidden. Harper would kill me if I brought them home. But I was a sucker, and I couldn't say no to Sam.

"Mom always says no." He looked up at me, those golden eyes round and sad.

Shit.

"Kyle," Cam warned behind me.

"Wouldn't it be fun?" Sam asked.

Hell yeah, it would be. If we could make it work. If I could find alternatives to all the junk Piper couldn't have. My brain started to puzzle out ideas.

"Let's do it," I announced.

"Yes!" Sam cheered, jumping a foot in the air, one fist pumping.

Cam groaned.

"We're going to have to stop at Trader Joes and Whole Foods on our way home."

Building gingerbread houses at Christmastime was a tradition every kid should take part in. And I could make that happen. Both for Sam, who could have some of the sugar, and for Piper, who shouldn't.

It took another forty-five minutes, so I had to text Harper while we were in the middle of Whole Foods to let her know we were going to be late.

She hadn't even started the chicken yet, so that gave me hope that she wasn't too mad. Although the look in her eye when we walked in with four grocery bags didn't give me warm fuzzies.

"I can explain," I promised.

"We got gingerbread houses." Sam announced.

"And I modified them," I promised before Harper could say no. "Look." I pulled out the gluten-free graham crackers, gluten-free sugar-free granola balls, green grapes, golden berries, dye-free gluten-free sugar-free fruit O's, no-sugar-added blueberry ropes, tiny broccoli florets, dairy-free cream cheese and yogurt, gluten-free pretzel rounds, and tiny tree crackers.

"Piper can do this. We can do this." I beamed.

"Wow." Harper gaped at all the shit I put on the counter. "You deserve a medal or something."

"I can think of a prize." I leaned in and kissed the side of her neck, barely getting a peck in before she pushed me off with a chuckle.

After we were done building the houses, after an hour of smiles and laughter and fun while the kids decorated their gingerbread houses—and after I fixed the doorknob so Harper didn't have to stress —I didn't feel like I needed a prize. It felt like I'd already gotten one.

KYLE
32

Dear Diary,
Today is the start of a new tradition and I'm here for it. I can't wait to learn how to put together and fluff a Christmas tree.

-Kyle

BOSCO
29

Crabby: You are 36. I can't believe you have never done that before.

Me: Excited you get to pop my cherry?

Crabby: GIF of an eye roll

Me: What do we want for tonight?

Crabby: Probably a string or two of colored lights and some hooks. I never keep the extras and then we are always short.

Me: I meant food-wise. Since you're getting the tree boxes up from storage, I figured I can handle dinner.

Me: But I'll get that other shit too.

Crabby: Oh oops. Can we do Gio's pizza?

Me: Can Sam have pepperoni with regular cheese?

Crabby: Yeah, just do the gluten-free dairy-free for Pipe and me.

Me: you got it.

Dumpty: Who's in for the game tonight?

Angel Boy: I'm in, but I'm bringing Grey.

New guy: I'm in.

Bambi: I'm in but Gi wants to come and we're bringing Dragon and Avery

Dumpty: Wow, grumpy and his princess are coming out of their wedding-planning cave?

Bambi: Yeah can you believe it's only five weeks away

Angel Boy: No shit? That's crazy.

Dumpty: Streaks, you in?

Me: I'm out. Decorating the tree.

New Guy: You're no fun anymore. Today it's the tree. Last weekend it was movie night and baking cookies. And the weekend before it was gingerbread houses.

Me: I'll send Cam if you want me to but unless I can bring Harper and the kids I'm probably out for a while.

Dumpty: You mocked me for so long about Rory. I love seeing you finally getting it.

Me: GIF of a big group hug

KYLE
33

I STARED at the massive windows of my penthouse, studying the way the lights of the tree reflected in the glass.

I frowned.

It was perfect. The green, black, and gold ornaments were evenly spaced and fit the vibe of my apartment. Which was all sleek, dark wood and black furniture. Modern, masculine, and expensive while also being comfortable and homey. I'd paid someone to make sure it was perfect. But to be honest, the tree sucked. Some designer had come and put it up for me. Cam had arranged it. I had nothing to do with it.

The one at Harper's was strung haphazardly with lights. The ornaments were heavy on the lower half, and the entire tree tilted just a little to the left.

But I loved it. I loved everything about Harper's apartment. Including how small and chaotic the space was.

My mood was in the gutter tonight. I was stuck at home rather than over at my new favorite place, waiting to see how many times I could make the snowman sing Feliz Navidad before Harper lost it. Usually it was twelve times. But every once in a while, she made it to play number thirteen before her eyes twitched and she whacked me in the stomach.

She was out with Zara at the WAGS holiday bar hop, and the kids were with their dad. I was thrilled that Zara and Gianna had thought to include her, but I was less than pleased that they hadn't included me too. I wasn't a wife or girlfriend. That was true. So I told them their party was sexist, hoping to guilt them into opening it up to us guys, but Zara just laughed and called me ridiculous. Apparently, the issue wasn't that I was a guy. It was that I played for the Revs, and this was a significant others' bonding thing.

Whatever. I could entertain myself for a night. Although I was currently doing a shit job of it, because I was sitting home, pouting.

My phone buzzed on the kitchen counter, so I hustled to it, hoping it was Harper, ready to be picked up for the night. Or maybe the guys would want to hang out.

Instead, Piper's name flashed across the screen. My stomach sank. Shit. She'd never called, which meant this couldn't be good. But I swallowed my panic and answered the FaceTime request.

"Hey, Pipe. What's up?"

Her eyes were red, and her cheeks were tearstained. My initial reaction was to freak the fuck out. But I curbed the urge. It was possible that Piper was crying because the TV was one tick too loud or something as easy to fix.

"You said if I needed you, I could call." She sniffed.

"Always," I agreed.

"My headphones broke. I need them to stop the noise from up above us. They're banging around up there, and it's too loud."

I had four extra pairs of the blue Boston Revs noise-canceling headphones in a cabinet here, one pair in my Escalade, and one in my backpack, just in case Piper ever needed them.

"Okay, we can fix this. Just take a deep breath."

"So you will bring me some?" She sniffed again, but it was followed but a long inhale.

"Sure."

Before I could say anything else, she hung up. Her faith in my ability to fix this situation without any more information was remarkable. But luckily, I knew where her father lived. Sighing, I ran a hand over my face. I couldn't imagine this would go well, but I'd do anything for Piper. So with a set of headphones tucked under my arm, I ordered an Uber. Cam was off tonight, and I didn't want to take the time to schedule a car using the Revs car service.

Twenty minutes later, the car was pulling up in front of the building. I had no issues getting past the doorman, and it only took a minute to find the correct apartment. With a knock, I inhaled deeply and waited. This could go a lot of ways, so I'd be prepared for all of them.

When the door swung open, I held up the box.

He stood in the doorway, taking me in from head to toe. "She said it was okay to let her call you."

I nodded. "Always."

"Come in." He stepped back and waved me into the apartment.

As I stepped into the entryway, I tried really hard not to be irritated, because his apartment was bigger than Harper's, yet she was paying him alimony.

But that wasn't my business or my fight.

Instead, I went to the reason I was here. It took me five minutes to get Piper settled and happy with her headphones. Then I spent another five helping Sam with a section of the Lego set he was working on. Finally, I moved back to address their dad.

"I'll get out of your way and let you enjoy your time."

"Actually." He swallowed. "I could use some more help."

I froze.

"Clearly, you get this, and I don't. So I'm asking, man to man, can you help me figure out how to help her feel comfortable here?"

A small part of me wanted to leave him to fend for himself. But the bigger part of me remembered being a kid and desperately wanting my dad to be there, to show up, to show interest. To care. "Absolutely, man."

He opened his fridge and pulled out two bottles. "Want a beer while we talk?"

I nodded, because now that he'd asked for help with Piper, I had so much to say.

Harper
34

Kyle: You make it home safe?

Me: On my way now.

Kyle: Have fun?

Me: So much. The guys have such great women.

Kyle: They really do.

Kyle: But listen, I need to tell you something.

Me: That sounds ominous.

Kyle: It's not that deep. But Pipe called me tonight and asked me to come over. So I did and I talked to Jace some. I'm sure you'll hear about it from the kids.

Me: Was she okay? Why didn't she call me?

Kyle: She was fine. She just needed a set of headphones.

Me: So was that weird?

Kyle: No. That wasn't what I meant. I just wanted you to know. I brought her the headphones. Jace and I talked. It was fine. No issues. I just wanted you to hear it from me.

Me: Thanks 💜💜💜

Kyle: Right back at you. Onto another topic... Is there really nothing I can do to get you to come to my place instead of yours?

Me: Well the guy at the front desk is really wrecking this surprise.

Kyle: What????

Me: If you really want me to come to your place can you come get me from the lobby?

Harper
35

THE ELEVATOR DOORS OPENED, and Kyle stepped off, dressed in a white T-shirt and gray sweats. He hadn't even bothered with shoes.

His eyes lit as he saw me. "Damn, Crabby, you look hot."

I was wearing a simple black wrap dress and heels. It wasn't an elaborate outfit by any stretch of the imagination. But the way he ate up every inch of me as he approached made me feel like a goddess.

When he stopped in front of me, he dipped low and pressed his lips to mine in a breath-stealing kiss.

"Happy to see me?" I teased when he pulled back.

"Always." He turned to the man behind the desk who had been giving me a hard time. "Wesley, meet Harper." He tugged me into his side. "And remember this face, because anytime she's here, she's allowed up, got it?"

"Sorry, man. Didn't know you'd wifed up." The man's dark eyes shifted to me. "If you need anything, let me know. A big part of my job is keeping the fans out. Now that I know you, I promise I'm helpful."

"Wes really is."

I turned at the sound of a familiar voice and found Rory and Mason standing behind us.

"I thought you were staying home with that book you've been obsessed with," Kyle said to his teammate, who was dressed in dark-wash jeans and an overcoat.

"Yeah." He lifted a white kindle. "Aurora got me hooked on *ACOTAR*, so I read while I rode with the car service to pick her up."

Rory shrugged. "Our schedules keep us apart a lot, so Mason insists on picking me up and dropping me off so we at least get the car rides together."

Mason wrapped his arm around his girlfriend and tucked her close. "I can't help but miss you when you're not with me, Aurora."

"I had fun tonight." Rory smiled at me. "I hope you come out with us again. And I swear Wren isn't usually so cagey."

Kyle took my hand and led me to the elevators. "What did Wren do?"

"Nothing," I assured him. Avery's friend really wasn't a problem. "It was my fault. I was trying to put together who went with who, because I'm still getting to know everyone, and I was running out of players."

"She guessed that Wren was dating Coach Wilson." Rory chuckled as the stainless-steel doors slid open.

"And that bothered Wren?" Kyle cocked a brow and pulled me onto the elevator.

"I know, right?" Rory laughed.

"Weird. She usually jokes about that herself. So much so that Avery gets annoyed." Frowning, Mason swiped his key fob and then pushed the buttons for the top two floors.

"She got flustered and then ended up leaving early. I felt bad," I said, shrugging. "But Avery promised that she'd just gotten home from a business trip and was jet-lagged."

"I'll ask Dragon about it." Kyle reached into his pants pocket.

"No." I grabbed his hand through his sweats to stop him. And as I did, I accidentally brushed my pinky against his cock. My breath caught in my lungs, and I froze.

He simply chuckled. "You can grab me all you want when we get upstairs. Trust me, I'm as eager as you, baby."

Jeez. I yanked my hand back as my face flamed.

Kyle wrapped his arm around me and tucked me against him.

"Sorry," I muttered, although I wasn't sure to whom.

"No need to apologize," Rory said with a casual wave. "Mason loves making people uncomfortable as much as Kyle does."

Beside her, Mason chuckled. A moment later, the elevator doors slid open, and he stepped off, guiding Rory into what looked like a foyer.

"He lives right below you?" I asked once the doors had closed again.

"Yeah. He used to live a few floors down, but when Rory moved in, they upgraded to the lower penthouse."

The lower penthouse. And if Kyle lived above him, that had to mean he also lived in a penthouse. Why didn't that surprise me? The man had been playing major league baseball for fourteen years. He had to make good money, and that was before his endorsement deals. Even though I was expecting it, I still wasn't prepared when the doors to opened to his massive space.

"Whoa," I whispered as I took it all in.

In the center of the foyer sat a circular table, where Kyle tossed his key fob and phone as he walked by. On either side of the space was an office, and straight ahead was a huge living area and kitchen. The back wall was nothing but two-story floor-to-ceiling windows and french doors that opened to a patio with a pool, hot tub, and a 180-degree view of the Boston Harbor.

I spun and assessed him, my eyes wide. "Why the heck do you come to my tiny apartment?"

"All my favorite people live there." He shrugged, clearly unimpressed by his own incredible home. "Cam's not here now, but he might be later. He lives in what would be the nanny quarters at the end of the hall." He pointed behind us. "My room and the guest rooms are this way," he said, pointing to the hall on the right side of the main space. "You probably won't notice that Cam's even here until morning. Can I interest you in a cider or a White Out?" he asked as he headed for the kitchen.

"You have my favorites?" I was still focused on the details of his home. One corner was set up like a reading nook, with two comfortable-looking chairs and a wall of bookshelves. In another spot was a row of shelves lined with toys. In the middle of the room was a sectional situated in front a huge TV that was mounted above the mantel of a massive marble fireplace.

"Of course I have what you like. So which do you want?"

He rounded an enormous black island and moved straight for what looked like dark cherry cabinets but turned out to be a fridge. I stepped toward the island, still in shock. Even the way the black granite seemed to waterfall off the edge to the floor was gorgeous. This place was amazing.

"You are so out of my league." With a shake of my head, I rested my hands on the cool stone.

Kyle set both drinks on the counter and took my hand in his. "No," he said, giving it an assuring squeeze. "I'm lucky enough to get paid a lot of money to play a game nine months a year."

I frowned, feeling defensive for him. Making light of his abilities is something I'd never seen him do.

"Don't look at me like that. Professional baseball is hard work, but it's also a lot of luck. If my stepdad hadn't come into the picture when he did and taken me to practices, then worked with me after for hours, I would never be playing now." He pulled me closer and rested his chin on my head. "Before him, my mom skipped dinner quite a bit to ensure that my brother and I would have enough to eat. She is one of the best people I know." He tipped my chin up, his eyes blazing into mine. "And you're the other."

My heart skipped, and though my instinct was to deny it, I couldn't form a coherent sentence to save my life.

"So don't you ever dare say I'm out of your league, because in every way that matters, you're out of my league."

He dipped his head and kissed me softly. A warmth rushed through me at the connection, urging me to part my lips and give him access. As his tongue stroked mine, that warmth ignited into a low flame in my belly. His arms tightened around my waist, pressing me into the solid plane of his body.

Although his kiss always made my stomach jump and my blood pump faster, his touch also brought with it a sense of safety that was hard to explain. Being in his arms like this lowered my defenses and allowed me to relax, because I knew he had me.

He pulled back. "Let's hang out in my room. It's less intimidating." Then he was tugging on my hand, snagging the beer and cider off the island nimbly, and guiding me down the hallway on the right.

The second we stepped into the room, I frowned. "It's bigger than my entire apartment." This was his idea of less intimidating?

"I'll happily buy you a bigger place if you want."

I whacked his stomach with the back of my hand.

"I do not want that."

"I figured." He smirked. He held up both drinks, silently reminding me that I hadn't chosen yet.

With a sigh, I took the White Out from him. The winter lager was one of my favorites.

"Do you want to sit?" He motioned to the sofa in front of a smaller fireplace with another television above it. Opposite that was a king-size platform bed. On another wall were two solid-wood doors with a rich mahogany dresser between. And the last wall had a...

"You have a trifold mirror?"

He laughed. "I told you that. Remember, in order to keep my ego this big, I have to look in it every morning and tell myself I'm pretty three times." He stepped up to it and looked at his reflection with a big smirk. "You look so pretty. You're going to own it today."

I snorted. "I thought you were making that up."

With a roll of his eyes, he spun around and slipped his hands into the pocket of his sweats. "No, everything I tell you is 100 percent the truth."

Nodding, I took a swig of my beer. It was incredible, knowing I didn't have to question his honesty. Because although he was way too good-looking and had enough money to purchase a small county—and those things were intimidating as hell—at least I never doubted whether I could trust him.

"But right now, I'd much rather look at your reflection than mine." He took the bottle from me and set it on the dresser before taking my hand and leading me to stand directly in front of the mirror.

With the way each panel was angled, it looked like there were twenty of us. He towered over me, one hand on my shoulder and the other brushing my hair out of the way. Leaning down, he kissed his way up my neck.

"I have this fantasy with you and this mirror," he whispered against my ear, making me shiver. "I want to show you, but I have a condition."

I turned to look at him, but he grasped my hips and forced me to face the mirror again.

When I met his gaze there, he continued.

"You can only watch me in the mirror."

Anticipation at the idea bubbled through me. And I slowly nodded.

His smile turned sinister as he grasped the tie holding my dress together and slowly pulled the string.

The panels of black fabric separated, showing off just a strip of pale skin.

He pushed the material aside, revealing one side of my black lace bra. "Fuck, Crabby," he said, zeroing in on the transparent fabric. "That's sexy. I fucking love your boobs." With a thumb, he caressed the swell of one breast. "This is one of my favorite spots." His voice was a low rumble that reverberated through me, sending a shot of desire down my spine. "The tease of perfection. Of the treasure below. The silky skin dusted with patterns of freckles."

"I hate the freckles," I admitted.

"No." He shook his head, making eye contact with me in the mirror. "I love them. Every spot, every cluster. They're all so uniquely you. One of a kind." He dipped his thumb below the lace.

Watching his large rough hands move against me in the mirror made my heart pound and blood rush in my ears. I was desperate for him to dip lower. To tease my nipple with the callused pad of his thumb.

But he didn't.

"Right here? This is my perfect circle of freckles. I love tracing the dots with my tongue, torturing you as I do because I'm so close to where you want me to be, but not close enough."

With his free hand, he brushed my hair back and to the side. Then he pressed his lips to the bare skin where my neck and shoulder met. Seeing the image in front of me while simultaneously feeling each move had the fire burning low in my belly flaring, like Kyle had just thrown gasoline onto it.

"Right here." He dipped a finger between my breasts. "I swear there is a perfect heart. See?" The front clasp of my bra popped open, and my breasts fell free.

Although I couldn't see my freckles clearly from this distance, I believed him. He used that same finger to draw a heart on my skin. As his other hand brushed the underside of my breast, I clenched. His ability to tease me, to slowly feed the burning need in my system, was thrilling.

He pushed my bra and dress off my shoulders and let them fall to the floor, leaving me standing in just a lace pair of boy shirts and heels in front of a very well-lit mirror. I wasn't a perky twenty-three-year-old. I was a woman who'd given birth to two children. My body was soft and had years of wear and tear.

With my heart in my throat and a wave of not-so-wanted heat washing through me, I dropped my focus to the floor.

"Hey." He slid his palm down my ribs, creating sparks in his wake, then over my soft stomach to my hip. From there, he pulled me back against his erection. "Do you feel that?"

I nodded.

"You look away because you think you're lacking. But I can't tear my eyes from you. I couldn't look away if someone paid me. Because getting to touch you, getting to see you on display for me, is worth any price."

He reached up and tipped my chin, forcing me to look at our reflection again.

"Your full breasts." With both tan hands, he cupped them. Then he brushed my nipples with his thumbs, sending heat rushing through me. "That flare in your eyes when you're turned on. Damn, that's hot. I love the curve of your hips and your soft thighs."

He continued to toy with my nipples, creating a heavy thrumming between my legs.

"Watch me pleasure you," he whispered against my ear. "Watch us pleasure each other." He ghosted his lips along my neck, peppering my skin with kisses as he continued teasing my breasts until I was squirming and my panties were soaked and my body was burning.

Whimpering, I dropped my head back against his chest.

"You ready to watch me make your body come alive?" he murmured against my skin as he ran his hands down my sides. "You ready to watch us both come apart?"

"Yes," I moaned.

With his fingers hooked into my lace boy shorts, he slowly dragged them down my legs, torturing me the whole way, letting hot fingers trail lightly against my skin as he lowered, his eyes still locked on mine in the mirror. He disappeared from sight, and a moment later, he pressed his lips to my right ass cheek.

"Step," he commanded. And when I complied, he pressed his lips to my other cheek. "Again."

I shivered, and he chuckled darkly, which only sent a more violent shudder through me.

"I never would have guessed you'd like to be told what to do." He ran his tongue over his lower lip and leaned into my hip, inhaling deeply. "Oh, baby. You're so wet for me."

I was. Wet, desperate, and ready. I rubbed my thighs together to ease the ache.

He clicked his tongue. "No you don't." He brought his arms around me and ran his palms up the inside of my legs separating them. Then he inched closer to the apex of my thighs, closer to the place I so desperately needed his touch. But just as the tips of his thumb brushed my pussy, he pulled away and pushed to his feet.

"Do not move," he whispered against my ear. Then his heat was gone, and he was stepping away.

I started to turn, so I could catalog his every move, guess as to what he would do next.

"Stop," he commanded. "Remember my rule. You can only watch me in the mirror."

With a groan, I straightened, obeying, and a moment later, he disappeared from sight. He was still in the room, but I couldn't find him in the mirror. I could, however, hear him sliding a heavy object across the carpet.

Finally, he stepped back into view, fully naked.

My breath hitched as I drank him in. He was utter perfection. Broad shoulders, high, tight pecs dusted with a small amount of hair. His six-pack abs twitched with each inhale. Narrow hips. And his dick. Thick and long and jutting toward me. A statue should be erected in his honor. Every inch of his body was more beautiful than any work of art on display in any museum.

"You're much more comfortable looking at me." He smirked.

I met his eyes in the mirror, still finding it hard to breathe. "You're perfect."

"That's how I feel about you, Crabby. Every inch of you makes me want to fall to my knees and worship your body." He moved toward me and dropped a kiss to the bare skin of my shoulder. "Hold this." The vibration of his words echoed through me.

He grasped my hip with one hand and held out a condom.

I pinched it between my fingers, surveyed it. The sight of it was wrong. This moment was too intimate for barriers.

"I'm on the Depo shot," I whispered, focus fixed on his face in the mirror.

His brows shot up to his hairline as his eyes snapped back to mine. "Are you sure?"

Heart pounding, I nodded. "I'm good if you are."

"My end-of-season physical." He swallowed audibly. "Everything was negative. And it's only been you since then."

Not letting my eyes leave his, I dropped the condom, letting it fall to the floor. "Then I want to feel you. Just you."

His fingers at my hip bit into my skin as he shuddered. "Fuck, I need that too."

He tipped to one side, the top of his body moving just outside the view of the mirror, and yanked a chair toward us. Ah, the dragging sound made sense now.

He settled it behind me and then dropped into it. "Sit," he commanded, grabbing my hips and pulling me back to him.

I complied, letting him manipulate my body and drape my legs over his. My heels brushed along his calves, my knees positioned on the outside of his. Once he had me where he wanted me, he pushed his thighs apart, separating mine.

"Mmm." He groaned, his eyes locked on my pussy in the mirror. "Look at you glisten for me." Sliding a hand down my hip and along the apex of thigh, he tortured me with the softest of touches before finally making contact where I needed him most.

I moaned when he ran those long, tan fingers along my pink flesh. Seeing him, watching this, only made every touch more intense.

For a moment, he stroked me, growling with pleasure as he did. And when his fingers were drenched in my arousal, he sank one deep inside me. His jaw locked in restraint, his dick rock hard against me. But he continued teasing me, prolonging this moment.

"Fuck, you're going to feel like liquid fire against my cock, baby. I can't wait to watch those tits bounce while you ride me." He curled his finger deep inside me as he brushed my clit with his thumb.

"Kyle." My legs quivered. "I need you."

"Tell me exactly what you need," he ordered.

I met his eyes in the mirror. And the burn of desire painted on his face melted any hesitation away. "I need your cock inside me, fucking me deep, while you play with my tits."

He sucked in a breath, his heart pounding against my back.

"Lean forward," he commanded, splaying a hand over my abdomen and tipping me just a bit. "Rest your hands above my knees."

Obediently, I steadied myself with my palms on his thighs. His rock-hard quads pushed back against my palms, the coarse hair tickling. He shifted, slowly removing his finger. Then he lined up his long cock.

I rocked back, transfixed by the image of him sinking into me.

"Harper," he groaned. "See how we fit? See how good your pussy looks swallowing my cock? It's like it was made for me." He slid his hand lower, teasing my clit, letting his fingers brush his dick. "Mine."

And it was. I was.

As a wave of heat engulfed me, I rocked against him. He met my movements, thrusting up and hitting a spot so deep it felt like he was becoming part of me.

"That's it, Crabby. Ride me. Use me to make yourself feel good. I need you to come all over my dick."

When he pinched my nipples, heat flared in my lower stomach, pushing me closer to the edge. The filthy sounds of our bodies slapping, compounded with the sight of our reflection, every damn angle, were all too much.

"I'm so close," I cried, dropping my head forward.

He pumped faster as he pinched, pulled, and twisted my breast with the perfect pressure. The sensation had my legs quivering. I spiraled higher and higher. Rocking faster. My heart pounding and an inferno blazing. Until finally, in a burst of hot pleasure, I came, pulsing around his cock over and over.

"Yes. That's it," he moaned. "Fuck, Harper. You're like a vise. Holy shit." He pumped faster, his breaths becoming more ragged. Until he gripped my hips, held me tight to him, and moaned out my name as he came.

He collapsed back in the chair, pulling me with him, breaths sawing in and out of him. His arms wrapped around my waist and his lips pressed to my bare shoulder.

"That was so much better than anything I could have imagined," he mumbled against my skin.

"Yeah." I twisted in his arms. The move caused him to slip from me, but I needed to be closer. I tucked my head against his shoulder, letting my nose rest against his neck.

He dropped a hand and pulled one heel from my foot, then the other, letting them fall to the floor in a *thunk*.

"Come on. Let's get you cleaned up."

Before I could pull back, he lifted and kept me pressed to his body, then strode into the massive bathroom. He set me on what had to be a heated tile floor while he started the shower. In the large space on the other side of the glass, water sprayed from the ceiling and two walls.

Once the steam started to billow out into the rest of the room, he tugged my arm and pulled me in.

He grabbed a familiar-looking bottle and squirted a dollop of liquid into his palm.

"You have my shampoo?"

"I was hoping you'd change your mind and spend the night." He set the bottle on the ledge again and rubbed his hands together. Then he stepped closer and massaged the soapy bubbles over my scalp and through my hair. "I wanted to get this right so you'd come back."

I opened my eyes and looked up at his face. "You know you don't have to be perfect to make me want to spend time with you, right?" He was already too good. Too perfect. It was almost hard to keep up with.

"I know." He rinsed the soap out of my hair, every move gentle. And then leaned forward, pressing his lips against my forehead. "But I want to try. You deserve it."

My heart stuttered, and when it went back to its normal beat, it felt different.

And it was, because Kyle Bosco had wormed his way into my heart in a way that was irreversible. I was head-over-heels in love with him. And I had no idea what to do with that.

KYLE
36

DECEMBER 23

Crabby: You're cute but I wouldn't quit the day job for a writing career.

Me: Aww I thought that was a good one.

Crabby: I'm not sure drabby is even a word.

Me: Screenshot of Google definition of drabby.

Crabby: Okay I stand corrected.

December 24

Dear Diary,

All I want for Christmas is my girl spread out next to me, moaning my name as I play with her tits. I want to feel her nipple hardened against my tongue and hear the hitch in her breathing as pleasure burns through her system. I want to run my thumbs under the lower swell of her breast, the spot that makes her back arch and press her tit deeper into my mouth. To know her panties are soaked and that I'm the one making her body turn to liquid desire. Making her burn hotter and hotter until she's squirming and moaning my name. If my Christmas wish came true, then I'd kiss my way down her ribs and over her hips, then lap at my favorite dessert. Lick her wet pussy until she came in a clenching burst of pleasure.

Crabby: Okay I take it back. Your writing might not be that bad.

Me: That was not sexy...

Crabby: I'm eating breakfast with the kids. It feels wrong to sext with you right now.

Me: Rain check?

Crabby: Maybe...

December 25

Me: Merry Christmas. I hope you guys have a fun morning.

Crabby: Pictures of the kids opening presents.

Crabby: You got them new jerseys and plane tickets to Florida to watch you play?

Me: I need you guys there for our first spring game. The fourth ticket is so you can bring someone along to help with Piper. Maybe Ashley.

Crabby: Kyle...

Crabby: Selfie of Harper hugging a note to her heart smiling with watery eyes.

Me: You said all you wanted was time. So Instacart is dropping off groceries this week, and your car is scheduled for an oil change and tire rotation. They'll pick it up from the parking lot of your apartment and bring it back with a full tank of gas. Cam is taking Piper to therapy tomorrow and Thursday (trust me this is as much a present for him as it is for you. He'll never pass up an opportunity to see Ashley) and Zara is picking up Sam for playdates both mornings. I offered Jacki a bonus if she'd work tomorrow and Thursday for you. And my cleaning service will be at your place on Friday. This way, you should have two days of time to do whatever you want.

Crabby: You are amazing.

Crabby: And all I got you was lingerie and vodka-infused whipped cream.

Me: 😳

Me: Do I get a picture at least?

Crabby: Pic of black lace one-piece and red lace bralette and thong.

Me: Damn what I wouldn't give to see those on your body right now.

Crabby: As soon as you get home baby. I promise.

Me: Aww you called me baby!

Me: GIF of a man jumping up and down

December 26

Crabby: How does the world not know you are like this?

December 27

Crabby: Your imagination is the best kind of picture.

December 28

Crabby: You're relentless.

Crabby: Photo of her breasts.

Me: You just made my day. I'm so jacking off to this.

December 29

Crabby: Is painted nails going to be your thing next season?

Me: As long as my manicurist doesn't quit on me.

December 30

Crabby: We miss you too baby.

Harper
37

Dear Diary,
New Year's is not the
same without my girl.
                    -Kyle

> Me: It's not even midnight yet. This came early.

> Kyle: I know but I'm extra blue so I need the moral support.

I WAS BLUE TOO. It was an hour before midnight, and for the first time in I don't know how long, instead of overwhelmed and exhausted, I was lonely. Even with all the texting and phone calls, I missed Kyle, and so did the kids. Spring training, when he'd be gone for weeks, was going to suck. For all of us.

The kids had been asleep for a couple of hours. We'd celebrated New Year's a little before eight, with Kyle joining in on FaceTime. After that, he was headed out, and I put the kids to bed at eight thirty. I'd be asleep now if Kyle hadn't made me promise to FaceTime with him when the ball dropped. He'd still be out, I was sure, but knowing that he wanted to see me at midnight made the idea of him having fun without me sting less.

I had *Ryan Seacrest's New Year's Rockin' Eve* on the TV, and I was just starting to doze when a knock startled me.

My heart raced as I straightened on the couch. Who the hell was here? Maybe Trevor? The girls were with him tonight, so maybe he needed help with them? I heaved myself up and shuffled to the door, straightening my pajamas as I went.

As I pulled the door open, my heart stuttered and my eyes popped wide open. "Kyle?"

"Happy New Year, Crabby." He stepped inside and dropped his suitcase and bag on the floor. Then he wrapped me in a tight hug. With his lips on mine, he kicked the door shut with his foot and pressed me up against the wall. Leaning his entire body into mine as his tongue dominated my mouth.

When we were both breathless, he pulled back and rested his forehead against mine. "I couldn't start the new year without you."

"I'm really glad you're here," I mumbled against the rough skin of his jaw.

With both hands on my ass, he lifted me. Then he guided my legs around his hips. "Can we take this to your room so we can try out that black lace? I really want to ring in the new year with my dick inside you."

I giggled as he carried me down the short hall. "You'll have to be quiet, though."

"Oh, Crabby." He shook his head and grinned. "You're the one who's always moaning and yelling my name."

"Shut up." I whacked his shoulder.

Inside my bedroom, he set me on my feet and locked the door behind us. "God, I missed you," he said, and then dropped his lips to mine.

I was so distracted by the fact that he was here that I forgot I had an entire plan for when he returned. He peppered kissed down my neck as his hand slipped under my tank top.

"Kyle, wait."

"Hmm?" he mumbled against my skin, the vibration sending shivers through me.

"Kyle?"

He pulled back, his brow crinkling with concern.

"Can you get the whipped cream from the fridge?"

His lips pulled up in a smirk that flipped my stomach. "Whipped cream. My girl's feeling kinky tonight?"

"Maybe." Coyly, I ran a finger down his chest and over his abs. He grabbed my arm just as I reached the button of his jeans. He lifted it, bringing my wrist to his mouth. He nipped once before pressing a soft kiss against my skin.

"I'll be quick," he promised.

As soon as he slipped out the door. I rushed to the dresser and pulled out the black lingerie I'd bought. I had just slipped the second strap over my shoulder when the bedroom door opened.

"Fuck." He groaned, immediately adjusting himself in his jeans.

"You like it?" I asked as his eyes ate up every inch of the mesh and lace covering me. The way he responded to me gave me a confidence I didn't know I could have.

"You are the sexiest woman I've ever seen." He shook the can in his hand and popped the white cap off.

"Not so fast. That is for me." I grinned as I took the can from him.

"Ooh, feisty tonight." He rocked back on his heels. "You going to be the one issuing commands?"

"Yes." For about five minutes before Kyle's naturally assertive personality took over, I was sure. "Take your shirt off."

Grinning, he swiped it over his head. At the sight of him, my breath hitched. It never got old. For a moment, I just drank him in, tracking over every swell and dip of muscle on his chest. My teeth pressed into my bottom lip as his pecs tightened.

Show off.

I glanced up to find him full-on glowing.

"Love that I turn you on, Crabby."

"Who said I was turned on?" I teased.

He snaked a hand out, catching the hem of my one piece. "Should I check?" His finger barely slipped underneath, but it was enough to make me shudder. His eyes flashed wickedly. "You were saying?"

I never would have believed that cockiness could be so adorable.

"I was saying that I'm in charge."

As I shook the can, he zeroed in on it, and his eyes went wide when I pressed the white top and a dollop of white cream burst out, painting his pec. A breath hissed from between his teeth.

Heart racing, I leaned forward to lightly lick it off his chest, being sure to let my teeth graze his nipple.

Before I could even swallow, he'd locked a hand around my throat, making a thrill shoot down my spine. He forced my mouth to his and thrust his tongue between my lips, licking the whipped cream from mine.

"My two favorite flavors," he growled as he backed me toward my bed.

Before he could lay me down, I spun. "I'm in charge, remember?"

Looming over me, he chuckled.

"Pants off and lay down." With one brow arched, I shook the can.

He made a show of slowly unbuttoning his jeans before shucking them off. Then he lay on the bed in just his boxer briefs, locking his wrists together over his head.

For a moment I just stood above him, enjoying the view. Every curve and swell of muscle on what could only be described as a perfect body. The way his tan skin popped against the white comforter. The bulge that pressed hard and long against the black material of his boxers. A slow burn built deep in my core as I longed to feel him inside me.

"Do your worst, baby."

The challenge in his voice pulled me out of my stupor. Shaking the can again, I climbed onto his hips. Then I settled my legs on either side of his so his cock lined up with the apex of my thighs. I rocked slowly, feeling his dick jump against me. He groaned and his eyes flitted shut. I rocked one more time, and this time, I sent a line of whipped cream down the center of his chest.

"Shit. That's cold," he hissed, his eyes popping wide.

"Aw, poor baby. I'll get it." Slowly, starting at the top, I licked my way down, teasing every line of muscles with my tongue. With every swipe, his abs tightened further. I shifted down as I worked my way closer to the waistband of his underwear.

I toyed with the edge. Then dropped my head to place a kiss on the swell of his erection through the fabric.

"Please." He groaned, his hips jumping. "Please tell me I get that hot mouth around me."

I smiled up at him. "Patience, Mr. Bosco."

His eyes flashed in response to that command.

Feeling damn proud of myself, I turned back to the black waistband. He lifted his hips so I could tug them down, and the second it was free of the material, his cock jutted up.

I traced the vein down the back with my thumb. "Mmm." Angling forward, I teased him, keeping my mouth only inches from his length. When my breath brushed his dick, his breath caught.

I pulled back. "Oh, wait, I forgot."

He let out a curse, but he snapped his mouth shut quickly when he caught sight of the whipped cream I'd picked up.

I sprayed the white cream along the underside of his cock, pulling a sharp hiss from him. Then, in one lick, I ran my tongue from root to tip. Fisting him, I circled the head twice and finally took him into my mouth.

"Holy fuck." His body locked. "The cold and your hot mouth." He groaned. "Fuck, baby." He grabbed a fistful of my hair and held me in place. "Yeah, just like that." His dick hit the back of my throat, making me gag. "The sound of you gagging on my cock is so fucking hot."

With his hand guiding me, I worked him over, teasing his tip and then taking him deep again. I dropped the can and reached up to toy with his balls.

"Yes, tug on them." His hips shot off the bed. "Shit, that feels so damn good."

I did it again, and he groaned.

"Stop."

My scalp tingled as he pulled my hair. But I ignored him. I slipped my hands under his ass, locking myself against him. Peeking up, I continue to work him over. He panted, looking down at me with wild eyes. And I took him deep.

"Crabby." He groaned, his grip on my hair shifting from pulling me away to holding me tight. His hips thrust off the bed and the tip of his cock hit my throat. "Shit." His hand tightened on my hair and his legs tightened under me. "I'm going to come." The words had hardly left his mouth before his dick began to pulse, and with a deep groan the hot liquid hit my mouth. Swallowing, I continued my motion until his entire body relaxed. The second I released him, he pulled me up and pressed his mouth to mine.

"Damn, your mouth is perfection," he mumbled against my lips, sounding relaxed and blissed out.

"Did I wear you out?" I teased.

He scoffed. "That was amazing but it's been a week, I need to feel that pussy contract around me."

With an arm locked around my waist, he spun so I was flat on my back and he hovered over me. Hooking his fingers into the straps of my lingerie, he slid them down my arms, letting my breasts fall free.

"But first..." He grabbed the can with a teasing smile. "I think I should get a turn."

I pursed my lips. "Only because you were such a good boy."

"I'll always be a good boy for you."

The burst of cold hit my nipple, and I squeaked.

His deep chuckle echoed its way down my spine. "I'll warm you up, baby." He dipped and latched on to my nipple, teasing and toying with his tongue, switching between his hot mouth and the cold whipped cream until I was shaking, begging.

"Kyle," I whimpered.

He slipped the black lace over my hips and off, then slipped a hand between my thighs and slid two fingers into me.

He groaned. "You're so ready for me, Crabby."

With a thumb, he teased my clit, rubbing small circles around it, sending bursts of pleasure shooting up my spine.

"Yes." I arched into him. He shifted and my eyes drifted closed. "That feels so"—a burst of cold cream hit my flesh—"cold." I coughed the words out.

"Just wanted some whipped cream on my dessert." He chuckled as another squirt of whipped cream hit the apex of my thighs. "Now to clean up this mess."

He toyed, licking at the whipped cream. Teasing me before he finally flattened his tongue against me, and a moan worked its way out of my chest and echoed around us. With each swirl of his tongue, I spun closer to release, and when he sucked my clit and slid one finger inside me, then two, I moaned.

I never wanted him to stop. The throbbing built so deep inside me I was panting and shaking. My legs quivered. His tongue flicked two more times, and I broke. Pleasure rocketed through me so fast it took my breath away. He stayed with me the entire time, lapping up every last drop of pleasure. My body sagged against the bed as he slowly kissed his way up my stomach and over my chest until he pressed his lips to mine.

"Glad I'm back, baby?" He smirked and slipped his hand between my thighs again.

I groaned, my body already heated again for him. "Yes, and I need you to fuck me."

"Your wish is my command."

When he pulled his hand back, I groaned, but before I could complain about the loss of his touch, he hooked my leg over his hip, lined himself up, and with his lips pressed to mine, he pushed into me. He moved with slow, even strokes as his tongue mimicked the motion. Claiming all of me. We moved like that, skin to skin, using each other, our breaths mingling and our bodies sticky with whipped cream.

"Harder, baby," I begged.

"You're in charge." He grasped my arms and locked them over my head. "And you are mine." He thrust hard, pounding fast, hitting that spot that caused such a wave of pleasure to pulse through me that it was impossible for my eyes to focus. "Mine," he gritted again. "Say it."

"I'm yours," I panted. "Yes." My back bowed off the bed, thrusting toward him. "Yes, right there," I cried.

The sound was cut off when he covered my mouth with his and swallowed the moan that left my lips.

He thrust deep, causing the echo of our bodies colliding to flood the room.

"I need you to come," he grunted against my lips.

He shifted so he could toy and pinch my nipple until I couldn't take it anymore. A wave of euphoria rocked through me. And when I cried his name and came in a violent explosion, he swallowed the sound.

"Fuck." He groaned as he lost his own control, rutting into me frantically. "Fuck, Harper," he repeated as his cock jumped and pulsed inside me. Finally he collapsed on me, and for two breaths, his weight pressed into me before he spun us.

He pulled me close and kissed the top of my head, holding me as our hearts slowed and our breathing evened out.

"Come on, let's get you cleaned up." After a quick shower, Kyle swiped his boxer briefs off the floor and stepped into them, followed by his jeans.

My stomach sank. He'd told me that he always left after sex, but stupidly, I thought he'd stay with me.

"I'm going to grab a gluten-free muffin or fruit or whatever you have, and I'll be back." He slipped out the door.

The sinking feeling was replaced by a chuckle. He hadn't been kidding about eating after sex. I climbed into bed and braced for his goodbye.

But the second he was back in the room, holding two bananas, he stepped out of his jeans.

"Are you staying?"

"Of course. There's nowhere else I'd want to be, Crabby."

As he slipped in next to me, my heart squeezed hard in my chest. I didn't even know why I had doubted him. A warmth spread through me as I drank him in, knowing with certainty that for once, I could trust someone.

Harper
38

"KYLE LIVES HERE?" Sam asked as we moved through the spinning doors and into the lobby of his high-rise.

"Yes, and we need to be on our best behavior, okay?" I said as I led him and Piper toward the elevator bank.

Wesley stood and rounded the big desk, headed our way. I braced to be told, like last time, that I needed to leave.

Instead, he gave me a warm smile. "Harper."

"H-hi," I stammered, shocked that he'd remember me. I'd only met him once, and that was weeks ago.

"You must be Piper and Sam," he said, nodding at the kids. With his lips pressed together, he focused on me again. "Did you have trouble with parking?"

"Uh." The whole encounter was the opposite of what I'd expected, so I was having trouble finding my bearings. "Cam dropped us off before he went to pick up dinner."

"Ah. Okay. If you do drive over, buzz me at the garage entrance and let me know you're here. You can park in the reserved spaces below. Makes it much easier, especially with the kids."

"Thanks?" I said, though the word came out more like a question.

"I promise." He pressed his hands together in a prayer pose. "I am at your service. We got off on the wrong foot. As I said, Kyle left out some important details. But now I know." He beamed.

That sounded like Kyle. He didn't always focus on specifics that, to others, mattered. Other times, he pushed his way into a person's business until blatantly told he was crossing a line. But he'd been great about Piper's therapy. He'd given me zero pushback about paying for it. In fact, he'd never brought it up again, which showed me he cared about my feelings.

"Come on. I'll get you in the elevator." Wesley led us over, and when the stainless-steel doors opened, he stepped inside too and flashed a key fob. Then he hit the button for the top floor and stepped out again. "Enjoy your night."

"He smells," Piper announced as soon as the door closed.

My heart sank. At least she'd waited until he was gone to make that statement.

"Not everyone thinks cologne smells bad," I reminded her for the ten thousandth time.

When the elevator opened on the top floor, Kyle was in the foyer, waiting for us. "Hey, guys. Welcome to my house."

"Why don't you smell?" Piper asked, frowning.

He glanced at me for help with context.

"Cologne," I mouthed.

"Oh." He kneeled in front of Piper. "You know my brother? Ryan? He doesn't like smells. Just like you."

My daughter looked directly at him for one beat before she looked away.

"My mom always made sure everything was unscented," Kyle continued. "I got used to not wearing it. So I still don't."

"I would like you to never smell," Piper said, matter-of-fact, and walked past him. Don't smell, end of conversation. If only she could always express her feelings that easily.

With a smile, I held out my hand to Kyle.

He took it and stood, then gave me a quick kiss before hurrying after the kids. Clearly, he was nervous about having them over for the first time. It would set a precedent for Piper. We'd talked about it, but if we were going to keep dating, then she had to get used to being here too. He'd been at our place enough.

"Since this is your first time here, I'll give you a tour." Kyle caught up to them as they gawked at his living room.

I stepped into the room too, and right away, the changes jumped out at me. Two of the barstools had been replaced with the kid-friendly climber stools that wouldn't tip or flip easily. A pair of beanbag chairs with backs, like the kids had at home, sat in front of the television, and there was a small table and chair set in one corner. And that wasn't it.

"This stuff over here." Kyle waved at the area of the room with chairs and bookshelves. "Some of it's breakable, so let's try to avoid it. But this area." He pointed at the shelves that last month had only housed a few Lego sets but was now stuffed full of toys. There was a huge rug designed like a city, with roads to drive cars on spread out in front of it, and to one side, a Lego table had been set up. "This area is where you can go wild."

"This is so cool." Sam darted for the red candy dispenser. It looked just like the kind of machines lined up at a grocery store.

"You bought that for them?" I asked, frowning.

Kyle was pretty careful with sweets. Although he indulged Sam a little, he kept to Piper's diet strictly, so it seemed so odd.

Stuffing his hands into his pockets, he chuckled uncomfortably. "Actually, I already had those. I just had them moved."

I shook my head. I should have guessed. The man did have a sweet tooth, and clearly, he had too much money to spend on frivolous things.

"One is filled with baseball M&M's, but I swear it's not all candy." He tapped one compartment. "This one is gumballs." He tapped a second. "And this one is full of those cool sticky hands that always get stuck on the ceiling."

"I love those," Sam announced, peeking through the machine's glass. "Look. A blue one. Blue's my favorite."

"Me too," Kyle agreed, his lips quirking up on one side. "And this one is light-up bouncy balls. When I did my practicum," he said, "the, uh, internship before I got my master's degree"—he ducked his head when he caught me watching him—"the woman I trained under had one for the kids she saw. She'd give them quarters on good days, and they could use them for prizes. They loved it, so I thought I'd get one when I open up my practice."

"But rather than wait until then, you bought it right away," I teased.

That sounded like Kyle. One hundred percent in on an idea once he decided he wanted to do it. It was one of many traits that made him so reliable.

"Where do I get quarters?" Sam asked, jumping up and down.

Kyle was watching Piper, who was rapidly blinking in the unfamiliar space, his hands still in his pockets, his face a mask of apprehension.

"We can grab some in a minute," he said, making a point to focus solely on Sam for a moment. "I want to show you guys the rest of my place first." Then he took a step closer to Piper. "Hey, Pipe, let me show you this area." He walked down the hallway toward his room, but instead of going to the end, where the master was, he stopped at the first door. "Sam, you can check out the room across from this one."

He opened the door and flipped on the light.

When the sight registered, I gasped. One quarter of the room was a replica of Piper's bedroom at home. The bins at the end of her bed. The dresser with the flower drawer pulls. Even the white headboard with his poster above it, the baseball sheets, and the Boston Revs weighted blanket. The beanbag chair she loved was next to a bookshelf and a table.

"You set up a room here for her?" I asked, my chest so tight the words were barely audible.

Unlike me, Piper wasn't shocked. No, she happily shuffled to her big beanbag and plopped onto it. Then she reached for the blue headphones that sat on the small table beside it. Once they were over her ears, she closed her eyes, and I swore she almost smiled. The rest of the space was set up like an occupational therapy room. A ball pit, a mini trampoline, mats in a variety of shapes, a big exercise ball, a marble wall, and some kind of rollers big enough for a child to crawl between. As well as a table and chairs that sat in the far corner.

"I want her to feel comfortable here." He sighed. "I knew the differ-

ences between your place and mine would overwhelm her. This way."
He pointed to her in her beanbag chair. "She can ease her way into
being at my house."

I pressed my hand over my heart. "You're—"

"The lunatic you've been waiting for?" he asked with a hopeful lift
to his lips.

Giggling, I kissed his cheek. "Something like that."

"Mom, this is so cool," Sam shouted. "Come here."

Swallowing back my emotion, I stepped across the hall, where Sam
was rushing down a slide from a bunked fort. This room was every
boy's dream. A full-on jungle gym, including a swing mounted to one
wall. And the fort with the slide was actually a bed. He had a gaming
area with chairs and another play zone with a rock-climbing wall.

"Jeez, Kyle. They'll never want to leave now."

He came up behind me and pulled me against his chest. "That's
what I'm hoping for. I want you all here as often as I can have you.
Hell, if you moved in, I'd be thrilled."

"Stop messing around." Head lowered, I gave it a shake. "You can't
mean that."

The main door slammed, interrupting our conversation. "I got
food," Cam called.

"Uncle Cam," Sam shouted. "You gots to come see this."

Cam appeared in the hall and peered around us.

"Did you know this was here?" Sam asked.

"In fact," Cam said, grinning, "I helped Kyle build it."

"Don't worry," Kyle assured me. "There were only a handful of
extra pieces."

I groaned. "You're not funny." I slipped out of his arms. "But I'm
going to get the kids' plates ready."

"Hey, Kyle, can I have quarters to make the machine goes?" Sam
asked.

"No candy until after dinner," Kyle responded as I wandered to the
kitchen. I'd only been here twice, and I'd yet to learn where he kept
things, so it took some searching, but eventually, I found plates and
cutlery, then got to work cutting up the grilled chicken for the kids.
We'd never tried this Italian restaurant, but they offered plain gluten-

free pasta and grilled chicken, so we were giving it a try. Hopefully Piper wouldn't melt down over it. But if she did. Kyle had prepared for it.

Sam ran by, holding a quarter aloft, and a moment later, he darted back down the hall toward his room. Probably to climb or jump on something. But Kyle was watching.

Knowing he was always paying attention and thinking ahead took a ton of weight off my shoulders. And though his comment about moving in had been a joke, who knew what the future held. I stopped cutting for a moment and surveyed the space. I wasn't sure I could picture making this my home. But it was easy to see a future that included Kyle.

Cam stepped up to the counter. "I'm going to grab my food and head to my room."

"You don't have to," I assured him, a sliver of guilt working its way through me.

The smile he gave me was genuine and patient. "Honestly, I'm a lot like your daughter in that I need time to adjust to change. Kyle jumps in and expects everyone to ride the wave with him. And you'd think that after working for him for so many years, I'd be used to his chaos, but—"

He was interrupted by a loud crash, followed by a shout. But no crying ensued, so I decided to let Kyle handle it.

Cam cleared his throat. "But I promise that in time, I'll be used to it."

I cringed. "Sorry. We are a lot."

"But you're the exact *a lot* that he needs." With that, Cam pulled a takeout container from the bag and wandered away.

When another shout rang out, followed by the slamming of a door, I put the knife down, ready to investigate.

Before I made it to the hallway, Piper came flying out, with Kyle on her heels.

Her fists were by her face, and she was shaking. "You can't. You can't. You can't," she chanted.

"Hey, hey. Deep breath," I reminded her.

"Sam got gum in her hair," Kyle said sheepishly, his cheeks pink and his eyes wide. "I guess I wasn't clear that gum is candy. They were in the ball pit. And somehow it got out of his mouth and into her hair."

Stepping closer to Piper, yet careful not to touch her, I searched her red hair. It only took a moment to locate the sticky blue wad. I winced.

"This is on me," Kyle said. "Why don't you check on Sam? He feels awful. While you do that, I'll try to handle the gum."

My instinct was to tell him no. He was giving me the easier of the two tasks. But before I could get the word out, he grasped me by the upper arms and turned me so I was facing the hallway.

Resigned, I exhaled and headed off to find Sam. When I did, he was hiding in the corner of Piper's room, his face wet with tears.

"Hey, bud." I sat on the floor next to him. "So gum, huh?"

"It's not allowed," he whispered.

I shook my head. "Do you understand why now?"

He nodded, wrapping his arms around his knees and squeezing. "I'm sorry. I just wanted to try it. I got a blue one, and it was so big. And I got to chew and chew it."

"Then it got stuck in Piper's hair. And it probably hurts."

He frowned, and another tear tracked down his cheek. "I'm sorry."

"I know you are. You should probably apologize to Piper, though."

"I tried." He sniffed and pointed at a blue bin lying on its side on the floor. "She threw that at me. It hit my arm and gave me a red mark." He pulled up his sleeve, his little lip quivering.

"Need me to kiss it?"

He nodded and held his arm out.

Leaning forward, I gave him a quick kiss.

"All better." He smiled. "Can I go play again?"

"Will you apologize to Kyle for not listening and to Piper for getting gum in her hair once they get it out?"

Wiping at his face with the back of one hand, he nodded.

My heart squeezed at the sincerity in his expression. "Then okay."

Without a word, he jumped up and raced back to his room. For a moment, I sat on the floor, taking in the room, marveling at Kyle's thoughtfulness. But I didn't stay long, knowing he may need my help.

In the living room, he and Piper sat calmly in the middle of the floor with a pair of scissors between them.

"So it will be just like cutting my nails?" Piper asked.

Kyle nodded, his face solemn.

"Okay." She swallowed audibly and picked up the scissors.

My heart lurched. He was going to let her cut it out herself? Instantly, I wanted to intervene. To stop this. But I trusted him, and he'd yet to get things wrong with her. So I stayed where I was, though I couldn't help but cringe.

Instead of cutting her own hair, though, something so much worse happened. Piper shifted forward on her knees and snipped a chunk of Kyle's hair. Then she did it again.

I was frozen, heart in my throat, unable to breathe, as she went for a third snip.

And Kyle didn't move. He didn't even flinch.

No. No, no, no, no, no.

Kyle was incredibly weird about his hair. He didn't even let most people touch it. And the fact that it now had two uneven chunks out of the right side and one on the left made me feel sick. It looked like he'd gotten into a fight with garden clippers.

"Omygod," I whispered, my stomach bottoming out.

"My turn," Kyle said calmly, holding out a hand.

Piper passed the scissors to him without argument, though her little body was rigid and her shoulders were practically at her ears as he lifted them.

But in two clips, the gum was out.

"All done," he announced.

"Just like my nails," she repeated.

"Yup," he agreed with a nod and an encouraging smile.

"I want my room."

"Ten minutes, and then we have to eat," he warned with a cocked brow.

Nodding, she scrambled to her feet, and then she took off for her room.

"Kyle." I finally forced his name out through my tight throat.

He turned to look at me, and all the blood drained from my face. Oh my God. It was so bad. So bad. He would never forgive us.

KYLE
39

"WHAT'S WRONG?" I spun to Harper.

She was white as a sheet. "Your hair."

Yeah, based on the pile of clippings in front of me, I could imagine it was awful. At least until I got to my hairdresser, and hopefully that could be tomorrow.

"You don't like it?" I joked.

Instead of laughing, she sniffled, and her eyes welled with tears.

"Aww, Crabby, come here." I pushed to my feet and ate up the distance between us. "Don't cry. I promise it will grow back."

"I don't care about your hair," she stuttered. "You do. You're going to hate us. We're wrecking your life. We're difficult. We're loud. We're messy."

Taking half a step back, I tilted her chin so she was forced to look at me.

"Harper Wallace. You're right."

A tear crested her lashes and streaked down her cheek.

With my thumb, I wiped away the moisture. "You're inconvenient. Everything I never wanted. Everything I avoided. And yet now I can't stand the idea of you not being part of every tomorrow."

She went rigid, blinking in a way that was so much like Piper. "What?"

I cupped her cheek. "My hair will grow back. The kids will grow up and become easier. They will break shit and ruin stuff. And we will get through it. Because the only thing that matters is us."

Her shoulders slumped, and she sniffed twice. "How are you so perfect?"

A wry chuckle escaped me. "Oh, I am not at all perfect. Look at my hair, Crabby."

She snorted a very wet laugh, leaning into me. "I can't imagine you not being in my tomorrows either."

That statement yanked hard at my heart. It was all I wanted to hear.

"So this is what we're going to do," I said, choking back the stinging sensation behind my eyes. "You're going to finish filling the kids' plates, then get them to the table. I'll sweep up the hair. Then I'll get rid of the gum from the machine for at least a few years."

Thankfully, the rest of the night went off without a hitch. Piper ate without complaint, and by eight, the three of them were loaded into the Revs' car service and headed back to their place.

I was putting the last of the Legos away when Cam walked out and froze in the middle of the room.

"Holy fucking shit."

"That bad, huh?" I asked as he gaped at me. I hadn't looked in the mirror yet because I really didn't want to know.

"Yeah, that bad." Blinking, he ran a hand over his mouth. "You're going to need to get a buzz cut."

"I think it will suit me." Not really. They suited no one. I ran my hand through my hair, wincing when I hit the short spots. There wasn't much I could do but wait for it to grow back.

"What the fuck did you do?" He was still staring.

"Pipe cut my hair."

Eyes wide, he opened his mouth, then slammed it shut again. "You love her."

It wasn't a question. And he wasn't talking about Piper.

I shrugged. "Yeah, man. I love all of them." There was no doubt in my mind about that.

He shook his head and ran his hand over his face again. "I'm avoiding her because I'm afraid I'll say something that tips her off. I'm not answering any of your family's calls or even JJ's. Everyone thinks I'm in a funk," he said, huffing out a breath. "Really, though, I'm terrified of accidentally unraveling your web of lies." Barefoot, he paced across the hardwood floor.

I frowned, my chest tightening. "That seems dramatic. I've never lied to Harper."

Freezing in the middle of the room, he scoffed.

"I haven't told her about my connection to JJ. That's it. Just that one little thing."

"It is a big fucking thing."

I winced. Was it? Maybe he was right. But hopefully the relationship Harper and I were building was strong enough, stable enough, to get through that.

"You have to talk to them both."

Swallowing back a wave of nerves that suddenly overtook me, I nodded. "I plan to text JJ. Find a time to meet up before I leave for spring training. After that, I'll talk to Harper too. You're right. It's past time."

"Thank God. I'm exhausted from stressing about it."

"It's going to be fine," I assured him.

I guessed it was a good thing Harper thought I was perfect at the moment. Because when she found out, I'd need all the built-up points I had in my favor to get us through it.

KYLE
40

Me: picture of new haircut

Crabby: Oh wow. It's so much better than I thought it would be.

Me: Thanks Crabby. Way to build a guy up. You know I have insecurity issues.

Crabby: You know you are the sexiest man I have ever met. You literally have been the sexiest man in baseball two years in a row. How could you possibly worry that I don't think you are hot as hell?

Me: GIF of a very sad kitten

Me: Because my hair is different.

Crabby: I'm sorry baby. You look hot with the haircut. I can't wait to run my hands through it.

Me: So much better.

BAMBI ADDED DRAGON TO BASEBALL BROS

Bambi: He asked me to do it this time

Dumpty: He asked you?

Dragon: Yeah I need a favor. Any chance we can get all the girls and hang out at the Langfields' bar tonight?

Angel Boy: Everything okay?

Dragon: Avery just needs a fun relaxing night.

Me: Wedding stress?

Dragon: Family drama but I don't want to talk about it. And I don't want any of you to talk about it. I just want to make tonight fun for her.

Me: If Ashley can babysit, then Harper and I will be there.

Angel Boy: Zara and I will be there.

New guy: I'm in.

Bambi: You know Gi and I will be there.

Dumpty: Aurora's off so we'll be there.

Dragon: Thanks, guys.

Bambi: No need to thank us that's what family is for.

Me: Quick thing before we meet up so we can get all the shit out of the way now.

Me: Pic of new haircut

Dumpty: Holy Fuck. You cut your hair.

New guy: Did hell freeze over, and I didn't know about it?

Angel Boy: Whoa.

Bambi: I think it looks good

DRAGON LEFT THE CHAT

Me: Okay it's been a week. Are you avoiding me?

JJ: Sorry I haven't responded. Life has been hectic. What's up?

Me: I want to talk.

JJ: I can call you tonight.

Me: No like meet for dinner or a drink and really talk.

JJ: Next Saturday?

Me: I have a wedding Saturday night. How about Sunday afternoon?

JJ: Sure I'll come to your place. Noonish?

Me: Noon works. Let's meet at O'Hannigan's instead.

JJ: Sounds good.

KYLE
41

"THINK IT WENT OKAY?" Harper asked, grabbing the skirt of her green dress so she could climb out of the car in front of my building. I grasped her waist and lifted her out, then held on to her as she found her balance.

If Avery was still dealing with family drama, it didn't show. She had glowed during the wedding ceremony and seemed to enjoy herself at the reception. The only person who had seemed anything but wonderfully happy today was Avery's best friend, Wren. Which was strange, since she was in the wedding party and was close to both the bride and the groom. But she'd been quiet, like she wished the floor would open up and swallow her.

"Seemed great. Did you see Dragon?" I shook my head, remembering the look on his face when Avery walked down the aisle toward him. "I've never seen him so happy."

"The wedding was gorgeous. I was there too, you know." She whacked my stomach as we headed through my lobby. "I meant the babysitting." Harper sighed.

Oh. "You know how good Ashley is with Piper. And Cam stayed home in case she needed an extra set of hands." When he heard the kids were staying at my place with Ashley, he insisted he stay rather than attend the wedding with us. "I'm sure it all went smoothly."

When we got off the elevator, I was proven right. It was quiet, apart from the TV, which was playing a movie I didn't recognize.

"How were the kids?" Harper asked, stepping toward the couch.

"Shh." Cam pointed to his shoulder, where Ashley was out cold. "Kids were great. No issues. Asleep by eight thirty."

So he'd gotten four hours with his girl. I bet he was happy.

"You taking her home?" I asked, being sure to hit him with a smirk.

He shook his head. "I told her she could stay."

I cocked a brow. "And she was good with that?"

Lips pressed together, he nodded. "Nothing's going to happen."

"*Right.*" Scratching at my jaw, I took a step back. "Have a good night."

While he dealt with his girl, I ushered mine down our hall with an arm around her shoulders.

Harper stopped at both kids' rooms and peeked in. Although they'd been here a few times, this was the first time they'd spent the night, so to have them in bed and asleep on time was a feat.

Having them all under my roof was a relief. It kept me from having to worry about whether Piper was having a bad night or whether Harper could use my help. A feeling of complete peace washed over me as we made our way down to the end of the hall. We needed to do this more often.

I shut the door behind us and clicked the lock before turning to my girl. "Did I tell how stunning you look tonight?"

She giggled. "At least ten times."

My heart thumped out a steady rhythm against my ribs as I drank her in once again. "Good."

She reached along her side for the zipper of the fitted hunter-green dress, but I covered her hands with mine.

"Let me." Slowly, I pulled the zipper down, exposing her freckled skin, and let the fabric puddle around her feet.

Once she stepped out, she swiped the dress off the floor and hung it up. Then she moved into the bathroom, probably to let her hair out of its twist and remove her makeup.

As I undressed, I watched her every move, relishing the normalcy of the moment. The comfort of just being together.

When she came back into the bedroom and began digging through her bag, I shucked off my dress pants. "Don't bother with clothes. I'm just going to take them off," I teased as I slipped into bed in my boxer briefs.

She didn't listen, of course. Instead, she shook her head, chuckling, then exchanged her bra and panties for a satin night dress before she slid beneath the sheet beside me.

She turned my way, and I pulled her closer to kiss her, wrapping her up, my bare skin pressed to hers. Our bodies moved together as I slipped into her.

After we both came, we fell asleep in each other's arms. As I dozed, it hit me. I finally had everything I needed. Harper was tucked under my right arm. The one I told her months ago represented what was important to me. And here I was, with that arm literally cradling the most important thing in my life, and it had nothing to do with baseball. So much had changed in one offseason, even the fact that I'd rather keep holding her than get up and find myself something to eat.

Waking up with her was even better. And even though it was only six when a knock sounded on the bedroom door, I didn't mind in the slightest. Making breakfast for the kids and drinking coffee with Harper was the best way to start a day.

It was the picture of what I hoped our future would look like.

"You have plans at noon, right? Let me jump in the shower, then we'll get out of your hair," Harper said once the kids had eaten and were both happily playing. Piper in her room, Sam at the Lego table in the living room.

As much as I wanted to join her in the shower, that wouldn't happen while the kids were here.

So I took my coffee over to my chair and watched Sam work on his newest Lego dino. At about ten thirty, Ashley and Cam slipped out of his room.

"I'm going to drive her home," Cam announced, keys in hand.

I held my mug aloft and nodded. "Thanks for watching the kids, Ashley."

"Anytime." She dipped her chin in acknowledgment, then wiggled her fingers at Sam. Then she and Cam were gone.

Shaking my head, I grinned at the empty space where they'd been a moment ago. I couldn't wait to hear how that had gone. When the elevator dinged ten minutes later, I stood, expecting to see Cam.

"What did you forget?" I asked as I shuffled into the entryway.

But it wasn't Cam.

"JJ." My heart stopped in my chest. Oh shit.

"Traffic was light coming up from New York, so I figured I'd come here rather than kill time wandering the city." He tossed his keys onto the round table where I kept mine and moved into the main room.

Normally, I'd be cool with him showing up like this. He was always welcome, and he knew that. But with Harper and the kids still here...

I opened my mouth, but before I could form a single word, Harper called.

"Kyle, I can't get the—" She appeared at the mouth of the hallway, her wet hair dripping onto my T-shirt, the only thing she currently wore. My stomach dropped.

"Harper?" JJ whispered, his eyes going wide.

Fuck.

"James?" she asked, just as shocked to see him here.

No one called him James, so it was odd coming from her. His father, my uncle, was James. But his son, James Junior, had always gone by JJ.

Blinking, she zeroed in on me, then a line of confusion appeared between her brows. "Do you know James?"

I sucked in a breath, then tried to clear the lump in my throat.

"We're cousins," JJ said, beating me to the punch. "What's going on?" This he directed at me while wearing a look that could definitely kill.

All the color drained from Harper's face, and I swore she swayed on her feet.

Shit.

"No." With my heart in my throat, I darted to her side. "Not like that." I rushed the words out. "Look at me." I cupped her cheek, forcing her panicked eyes to mine. "My stepfather is his biological uncle. You and I *aren't* related."

The air rushed out of her lungs, and her shoulders sagged. For one second, I thought this might be okay. But then her spine went ramrod straight, and she yanked away from me.

"Wait," she murmured, her eyes going hard and turning to slits. "You knew James was my brother." She turned her attention to James, then focused on me again. "That means your aunt and uncle." She swallowed. "Wait, your stepfather."

I winced. Yes. Every one of them had been awful to her.

"Yeah," I breathed, gripping the back of my neck. "I know."

"You knew." Her lips parted. Her eyes flicked between us again. "You both knew."

"I asked him to help me with our situation, but I had no idea that he was fuc—"

"Don't." I cut him off with a warning glare.

"Uncle James?" Sam stood two feet behind him.

JJ cringed. Yeah, dumbass, exactly.

"Hi, Sam." He spun around and crouched in front of his nephew. "You know Kyle."

"Uh-huh," he said, keeping his tone even. "He's been my best friend since we were seven." He glowered at me over his shoulder.

That comment twisted the knife that had lodged itself in my chest the moment he stepped off the elevator.

Beside me, Harper's breath came faster, and I worried she might hyperventilate.

"Sam, bud. Can you do me a favor?" I forced a smile his way.

He tipped his head, angling closer to his uncle. Their red hair was almost the same shade. I'd known they looked alike, the hair and the golden eyes, but I hadn't realized just how many other features they shared until this moment.

I swallowed, determined to focus on the issue at hand for now. "Can you go play in your room for a bit?"

Nodding, he skipped across the room and darted past his mom, oblivious to the tension thickening the air.

"His room?" JJ asked through clenched teeth. "You don't even let the women you fuck into your house, and yet you moved her and the kids in?"

I took a deep breath, garnering all the control I possessed. "JJ. Don't say something you can't take back," I warned. "We are all aware of how easily that can ruin things."

That might have been a cheap shot, but it hit the mark. His mouth snapped shut, and he simply grunted.

"Give Harper and me a few minutes, and I'll meet you at the restaurant at noon like we planned."

He scoffed, his face reddening. "Are you kidding me?"

I shook my head. Maybe fixing a decades-long friendship should have been my priority, but the only thing I cared about was the silent woman who'd gone ghostly white beside me.

"Fuck it," JJ mumbled. "We don't need to talk. The reason you invited me is pretty damn obvious." Sneering, he spun on his heel and stormed to the elevator. "Thanks for your help, bro."

Nausea rolled in my gut. That definitely could have gone better. But as I turned back to my girl, it was clear the bigger problem was in front of me. Because the shock was gone, and in its place was pure anger.

"Harper?" I grasped her upper arm gently.

"Don't touch me." Shaking free of my hold, she stepped back. "You knew. How long did you know that your family—" She swallowed, her bottom lip wobbling, but she held it together. "God, I can't believe it."

I wouldn't lie to her. Especially not now.

"The whole time."

"What?" she screeched.

I tried not to wince, though I knew how bad this sounded without context.

"I knew who you were to JJ, who you were to my family, the moment I met you at Lang Field."

She blinked back a sheen of moisture and crossed her arms over her chest. "Vivianne," she said, lifting her chin. "That's your mom?"

Stuffing my hands into my pockets, I nodded.

"She was actually the nicest. All she did was ask me to please leave."

With a scoff, she took another step back.

"Bill is your stepfather?"

I nodded again.

"He straight-up asked me if I was using my father's apparent dementia, dementia I wasn't even aware of, to steal his money. And Susan, your aunt?"

I nodded, despite how badly I hated admitting that I belonged to a family who'd treated her so poorly.

"She called me a money-grubbing slut *just like my mother.*"

I balled my hands into fists in my pockets and gritted my teeth. I loved my aunt, but at the moment, I really wanted to have words with her.

Harper swallowed, and this time when she spoke, her voice was barely a whisper. "My kids were with me. They heard it."

I flinched.

"Danielle, your cousin? She came to see me here in Boston. She told me to stay away from her brother. Told me to stop trying to trick him into giving away the family money. Because I'd never be family." Lips pursed, she shook her head. "She didn't care that he was the one who'd sought me out."

I swallowed. "I am aware of the full story." Now.

"How nice that one of us was."

"Harper." I reached for her, and once again, she flinched away.

The move caused a sharp pain in my chest. Rubbing at it, I assessed her. I understood the anger, but I didn't do any of this to hurt her. There were reasons. If she'd hear me out, maybe she'd understand them.

"If I'd told you who I was at the start, would you have had anything to do with me?"

She didn't hesitate. Chin lifted again and voice strong, she said, "No."

Exactly. It was a punch to the gut to hear it, but I wasn't surprised. "I wanted to help you. To help JJ. And I couldn't have done any of that if you knew who I was. So can you understand why I didn't tell you?"

"No."

"Harper. Please. I get why you're mad."

"Then you get that there is nothing you can say." The response was so chilly I almost couldn't believe it had come from my fiery girl.

My heart dropped. "You don't mean that."

"I do." She snapped her mouth shut, and her anger morphed into a mixture of pain and defeat right in front of me. Eyes welling with tears, she said, "I don't know why everyone I love lies to me." Her voice cracked, and she blinked furiously. "But I do know you can't come back from it."

"I never lied." The words were loud, full of frustration, causing her to step back. But I pressed on. "Everything I told you was 100 percent true. Not telling you about my family wasn't a lie."

"It was." Her voice cracked. "I need to go."

Panicked, I moved closer. "Please."

She held out a hand, stopping me, and shook her head. "I need time to think. The kids and I will be out of here in five minutes. Please don't make a scene in front of them."

That request was what made my heart crack in two. Fuck. "You know I wouldn't."

With a nod, she turned away.

"Harper. Please."

She froze, but she didn't turn back around. "There is nothing left to say." Her shoulders shook for a moment, but then she took a deep breath, steadied herself, and walked out of the room. She didn't appear again until she had the kids and their stuff.

Throat tight, I stood from where I'd been doubled over with my head in my hands. "Can I help with the bags?"

"No thank you." Her voice was formal. "Wes called a car."

Of course he did. I'd made it very clear that her wish was his command. Boy, had that come back to bite me in the ass.

"Say goodbye to Kyle." She swallowed, and her eyes flitted shut. Subtly, her breathing hitched, but then she pulled her shoulders back and lifted her chin.

She was the woman from months ago. The one with a bird on her head, barely keeping it together in front of her kids. I desperately wanted to hug her, to hold her. And for a moment, I convinced myself that was exactly what I'd do. But before I could, she opened her eyes and inhaled deeply.

"He's going to spring training and won't be back for a very long time."

Sam ran over and jumped into my arms. "I'll miss you," he said, squeezing my neck. "You'll FaceTime Piper, right?"

I glanced over his head at his mom, who shrugged.

"Yes. Help Mom with stuff, okay?" I told him as I set him down.

Piper stepped up next and threw her arms around my waist. My heart squeezed and my eyes burned. I couldn't lose these three. I couldn't lose my family.

"You'll message me, right?" she asked, her head tipped back but her focus roaming.

"Every—"

"Don't say something you don't mean," Harper said, her words hitting me like a slap.

My entire body tightened, and when I answered Piper's question, I made sure I was looking straight at her mother. "I will message you and your mother every day." It was a promise I intended to keep.

Harper's jaw locked, and she looked away.

In front of me, Piper nodded and stepped away.

"Wait," I said, darting to the cabinet. I pulled out several extra sets of headphones and held them out to her. "Take these, girlie. Just in case."

"Thanks."

I nodded.

"Come on, Piper," Harper called as she herded Sam toward the door.

And as soon as the elevator doors shut. I collapsed into a chair in the living room and dropped my head in my hands, letting the sob I'd been holding back break free.

I. Could. Not. Lose. Them.

Harper

42

Dear Diary,

I messed up big time and hurt my girl. That was never my intention and I'll do anything to fix it. I love her more than she can imagine and I just need a chance to make it right again.

-Kyle

Me: Kyle stop. Don't keep doing this.

Kyle: I said yesterday that I would message every day. And I will message every day.

Me: Cute won't fix this. You lied to me for months.

Kyle: I never lied to you. Yeah I didn't tell you something. But that's not the same thing as lying.

Me: Funny Jace said the same thing about not working for eighteen months.

Kyle: Don't compare me to your ex-husband.

Me: I wish I didn't have to

Kyle: That's not fair. What was I supposed to do, tell you right off the bat that I was part of the family that hated you and was ridiculously dead set on blaming you for something that you had nothing to do with? Because like I said yesterday you wouldn't have ever talked to me if that was the case.

Me: Stop. Just stop Kyle. This can't be fixed.

Kyle: I'm leaving tomorrow for seven weeks. You're really not going to talk to me before that?

Me: No. I have nothing to say.

Dear Diary,

What do you do when you're so sorry about something but you have no idea how to fix it? How to make it right? When even the solution of going back in time and doing something different wouldn't get the result you need as badly as the air you breathe? What do you then? I need to know.

—Kyle

Dear Diary,

Spring training is usually
my favorite time of the
year. It's a new beginning.
A start to the thing I love
most. But baseball isn't the
love of my life anymore.
And for the first time
ever I wish I wasn't going.

-Kyle

Dear Diary,

I'm just going to start making a list of the things I love about Harper Wallace.

-I love her strength.
-The fierce ability to do anything that she puts her mind to.
-I want to be more like her.

-Kyle

Dear Diary,

I love her smart mouth.
She's always quick with a
comeback or snappy
response to put me in my
place.

-Kyle

Dear Diary,

I love her ability to figure it out. Whatever it is, Harper Wallace has never met a problem she can't solve.

-Kyle

KYLE
43

FIVE DAYS, six hours, and ten minutes. It felt like longer. It felt like a part of me had died. I had come to spring training. I worked out. I practiced batting. I did sprints. I did the work. Because my team depended on me, and because I didn't lose. My right side, the responsible side, was here, working hard. But the left side, the fun side of me, had disappeared when Harper left.

I studied the bottle of beer I wasn't drinking while I sat at the table on the patio. I'd rented a house down in Clearwater, just like I'd done every year. And I let the guys come over and hang at the pool, like always. But I hardly talked.

A chair scraped against the cement, and then Asher dropped into the seat next to me.

"You okay?"

"No."

"I feel that." He sighed. For a long moment, he didn't say anything else, and when he did, it was the last thing I expected. "I'm not telling anyone else, but it seems like maybe your misery needs some company, so I'm going to lay it out. Zara asked for a separation."

That penetrated my haze. Heart dropping, I snapped my head around and assessed him. "Fuck."

He nodded, his eyes downcast.

"You okay?"

"Not at all. I'm just trying to get through these next few weeks so I can get home and fix this shit."

I felt that. I didn't have the first clue how to fix things with Harper, but that didn't mean I was giving up. No, it meant that I'd have to try harder, figure out a new plan. Because other than that first text conversation after she left, she hadn't responded to a single message.

"What happened with you and Harper?"

I lowered my head and closed my eyes. "I was hiding something."

Beside me, he choked on his beer. "Like another chick?" he asked, eyes wide, when he recovered.

"No." I spat the word out. "It's about my family. She found out and feels like I was lying. That's a hot button for her, so she won't talk to me."

With a thoughtful nod, he took a long swig of his beer.

"What happened with Zara?"

Huffing, he set his bottle down on the glass tabletop a bit too forcefully. "I don't have any idea, man. She thinks I don't act like I want to be married anymore and that a separation will make me happy or some bullshit like that." He scowled. "Didn't seem to care that the only thing I want is her."

"I feel that." Sighing, I picked at the label on my bottle. "I know I'm miserable company, but if you need to talk…"

He lifted his chin and surveyed the guys horsing around in the pool. "Thanks."

My phone buzzed on the table, and when my mother's name flashed on the screen, my stomach sank. I'd ignored her calls for days, but I couldn't keep it up forever. Honestly, I was surprised she hadn't flown out to yank on my ear and yell at me already.

"I gotta get this."

Standing, I picked up the device. Then I headed inside so I could talk to her in private.

"Hey, Mama," I said when I'd pulled the sliding door shut behind me.

"About damn time."

Sighing, I leaned onto the white marble counters. "I'm going to start this out simple. If you say one bad word about Harper Wallace, I will hang up, and I won't answer again. Ever." It wasn't a statement I made or took lightly. But I meant it. Cutting my family off, especially my mother, would suck, but I wouldn't stand by and let them utter even a single bad word about the woman I loved.

"I have nothing negative to say about your girlfriend."

I coughed out a humorless laugh. "I'd love it if she'd accept that title, but she broke up with me, Mama."

"That situation has been nothing but drama for decades." She sighed, making the line between us crackle.

Surprise had me straightening. That wasn't exactly the response I expected from her.

"Secrets, all of them, cause nothing but problems. And like I promised Bill, I'm done with them." The click of her nails tapping, probably on her kitchen countertop, echoed through the phone. "Susan told me about James's affair before I even started dating Bill. Maybe this is a PSA about falling in love with your best friend's family member. Clearly, you and I have that in common."

She and Aunt Susan had been friends since JJ and I were in second grade, but my mom hadn't married Bill until I was twelve.

"Little late, Mama."

"I was pretty sure of that by Christmas."

My breath caught, and I spun and leaned against the cabinets for support. "What?"

"I know my son. You were moony after someone at Christmas. Always on your phone, pouting like you wanted to be somewhere else. And I don't know how Aunt Susan didn't recognize those kids on your Instagram. Even though you didn't show their faces, the resemblance to JJ, Danielle, and the grandkids was obvious."

I swallowed. Guess I wasn't as clever as I thought.

"However, telling us might have helped."

My heart clenched. "There is an annoying echo in my life," I muttered, bringing a hand to my hair. Before I could rake my fingers through it, though, I pulled back. I'd adjusted to the short cut, and so had fans. But every time I touched it, I was reminded of what I'd lost.

"I didn't call to lecture," my mom went on. "Actually, the opposite. I thought I'd share a little with you. Some things you may not know." She sighed. "When Bill found out that I knew about Harper and hadn't told him, he was upset. Things weren't great between us for a while after that."

"You knew about Harper." I scowled, not that my mom could see me. I thought she'd found out at the reading of the will, just like my stepfather had.

She sighed. "I found out about Harper when you and JJ were nine or ten. Harper's mother had asked for money. Susan and James had fought about it. And she came to my door, crying. But it wasn't my secret to tell. Even to Bill. However, when everything blew up at the meeting last March, I assured Bill that Harper Wallace was, in fact, James's daughter and that James had been well aware of her existence."

That took a second to process. "Oh."

"Bill thought Harper had to be making the story up, because he couldn't imagine his brother keeping something like that from him. He was crushed that your uncle never confided in him. The idea that I didn't either was a betrayal, and it took a bit for us to get past."

"But you did?" I asked, filled with a little flicker of hope for the first time in days.

"The thing about commitment is that you're choosing to get past it. Whatever the *it* is. Relationships are full of good times and bad." She took a deep breath. "Trust me, there are tons of bad ones. Fights, misunderstandings, hurt feelings. Times when it seems like she's choosing other priorities over you. It's not all roses, son. But," she said, her tone going softer, "when you choose to stay, choose to work through the bad moments, that's when it lasts. Bill has shown me that over the years."

I glanced down at the tattoo on my left arm. Balance. The good and the bad. That was what she was talking about. Along with the amazing part of loving someone came the hard parts too. The hurt. The arguments. But the couples that made it did so because they chose balance. They chose to enjoy the good times and work through the bad. Because, in the end, they did it all together. I could keep showing Harper that I'd choose her. That wasn't a problem. But I didn't know how to make her want to choose me.

Harper
44

Dear Diary,

My girl once told me that I don't have to be perfect. Which is good because I'm not. I mess up often. She and I met because I was a dick about her hurting herself to stop a ball from breaking her son's nose. I think about what a jerk I was that day a lot. I'm sure I'll make a million more mistakes in my lifetime. So the comfort in her statement about not needing perfect? It was huge. Loving someone is about taking the good and the bad, and then trying to be better for them every day. And that's what I want with her.   —Kyle

I'D READ that damn message seventeen times today. Every time, I felt like a complete asshole. No, I didn't expect him to be perfect, but I expected him to be honest. And how did that make me wrong?

I didn't believe I was wrong. Yet I still felt like an ass. I'd read every torturous message he'd sent for the last ten days. And I missed him. The gut-wrenching hurt that had hit me when I realized he'd been hiding something so big from me didn't invalidate the love I had for him. A heaviness had settled over me since he left. One I'd shed months ago and had forgotten about. It was the weight of carrying it all. The stress of every tomorrow. But he'd lied. And now I'd always wonder if he'd do it again.

An alarm sounded, startling me out of my stupor. Dammit. A resident's panic button was going off.

"Oh shit." I popped to my feet and scanned the notification. Eleanor Sparrow, room 567. She wasn't one to hit her button for the TV or because she needed more ice water. No, she was the opposite. She hardly wore the damn thing.

I flew out of my office.

Carolyn glanced up from her screen as I darted past her. "It's—"

"I know." I ran straight to the stairs, bypassing the elevator, and took them two at a time, all the while praying she was okay. My heart pounded as I hit floor five and burst into the hall. The elevator doors opened as I passed them, and a young male nurse on duty today fell into step behind me.

"I've got the key," I announced as I approached Eleanor's quarters. I flashed the card, and once the door beeped, I flung it open.

"Eleanor," I called, running inside. I'd only made it a couple of steps in before the sight registered. I halted and slapped a hand over my face. "Oh my God!"

Old man ass. Old man ass. The image was burned into my brain so that even though my eyes were pinched shut and my hand was covering them, all I could see was the hairy white ass.

"Henry, did you hit my button?" Eleanor huffed.

"I told you to take the damn thing off, sweet stuff."

I cringed.

"Are you standing with your eyes closed too?" the nurse behind me asked.

Of course I was. I spun, and when I was facing him, I forced my eyes open. Now I was staring at the twenty-five-year-old whose face was scrunched up in horror.

"Just spin around," I muttered. But even as I studied the door, I still couldn't shake the image of Eleanor's hands pinned over her head while Henry's pale body slammed her into the sofa.

"You should have knocked," she declared.

"You hit your button!" I cried. "We were under the impression that it was an emergency."

She sighed. "This is why I keep telling you, Harper, that at times, it's okay to take it off and live a little. If I'm always afraid of the what-ifs, I'll miss all the good things. Or in this case, the good stuff gets interrupted by nosy young people."

Annoyance flashed through me, but it was quickly followed by shame. She'd told me the same thing dozens of times, but today, the message hit me differently.

Was that what I was doing with Kyle? Was I missing out on the good moments because I was scared? Scared of trusting, scared of getting hurt.

"I don't mean to be rude," Henry grumped, "but I'd appreciate it if you two left. We were in the middle of something."

I cringed. I did not want to think about that.

"Oh, I think we're finished," Eleanor groused.

"Like hell we are," Henry said. "I took two of those blue pills. We have a good few hours left."

Tempted to cover my ears, I pushed the man in front of me out into the hall and let the door slam shut behind us.

"Pretty sure I'll be traumatized for life after that…"

I stared at him. No shit. But I reined in my composure. "Our residents deserve privacy and respect, so let's just forget it happened."

His face screwed up as he regarded me, as if I'd grown horns right in front of him.

Yeah, kid, I know. There's no way I'll forget it either.

"Maybe just go home tonight and get drunk. Come on." I headed back for the elevator.

My coms beeped in my ear. "Do we need a bus?" Carolyn asked.

"No. False alarm. I'm coming down." I hit the button to call the elevator.

"Good," she said. "By the way, you have company waiting in your office."

Company? Zara was the only one who visited me, but we hadn't made plans to have lunch today. Though I supposed it wasn't totally out of character for her to show up like this. Especially this last week and a half.

I cringed twice on the way down when flashes of the scene upstairs hit me and got sympathetic smiles from the nurse with me.

"Zara's here?" I asked as I approached Carolyn's desk.

"No," she said. "It's your ex-husband."

Jace?

I stopped just inside the door and found him sitting in the chair in front of my desk.

"Hi, Harp."

"Hi." Without moving closer, I put my hands into my pockets and waited.

"Can we talk?" He waved at my desk chair.

Sighing, I pushed the door shut. A conversation with my ex was nowhere remotely close to enjoyable, but maybe it would cleanse my mind of the vision of my resident's ass. Jace was good at pissing me off, and that would likely keep me thinking about whatever the hell he was going to say.

I moved around my desk and sank down into my chair. "What do you want to talk about?"

He set a check on the surface between us and pushed it my way. A check made out to me. For $10,710.

"That's the last seven months of alimony." He sighed. "I've got a job, and I'm doing well now. I was saving it to take the kids on a trip. Disney or something." He lifted one shoulder, sheepish.

I bit back a frown. Piper would absolutely hate Disney at this point in her life.

"I'm working on being a better dad." He ducked his head and cleared his throat. "And a big part of that is understanding my daughter. I realize now that though maybe a lot of girls her age would love to meet princesses, she probably wouldn't do well with that kind of stimulation."

The awareness he displayed in that statement blew me away.

"I know." He sighed, probably reading into my expression. "I'd like you to put it toward activities for them or things they need. Maybe swim lessons for Sam and some therapies for Piper. Whatever you think. And I'm meeting with my attorney next week. I'll have him draw something up to end alimony effective seven months ago."

My heart pounded hard against my breastbone, and my hands shook. "Are you serious?" I wasn't complaining, an extra fifteen hundred dollars a month would go a long way.

"Yeah. Your boyfriend—"

"Kyle?"

Jace nodded. "I didn't know what to make of it at first. You dating some rich athlete. But the guy's solid. He's been a huge help."

"To you?" My mind spun. Kyle had gone over that day, and I knew that Jace had texted him a few times, but Kyle hadn't said much about it.

"Yeah." He clasped his hands on the desktop. "He's given me great suggestions and helped me plan out some ways to make my place more comfortable for Piper. And he got me in touch with a therapist through his organization. Somebody I can talk to about parenting Piper, and even Sam."

Wow. I was blown away by all of it. By Jace's total one-eighty and his dealings with Kyle. Though maybe I shouldn't have been surprised by that last part. It was all totally on point for Kyle.

"The other thing I've realized…" He sighed and shifted in his chair. "I owe you a sincere apology. For all the lies."

I blinked. This couldn't be real. I must have passed out from the shock of witnessing eighty-year-old sex, and now I was dreaming.

"Harp," he said, his tone concerned and his light brown brows pulled together.

"I think I misheard you," I choked out.

He chuckled. "No, you didn't."

"For two years, you swore you hadn't lied."

He frowned. "I never lied about being fired. But I told you ten lies a day to cover it up. I lied about where I was. I lied about how my day had gone. I lied about what money I was using to pay for things." He shook his head. "I wish I could say that I had a good reason. That I did it to protect you or take care of you. But I did it for myself. Plain and simple. That made me an utter ass, and you deserve better."

"I...I—" I was in shock. The words wouldn't come.

"I don't expect you to accept my apology. But I wanted you to hear it." He frowned again, a look full of self-reproach. "And I'd like to try to be a better co-parent."

I should forgive him, and I should be grateful for the changes he'd been making. But I couldn't wrap my head around it all. "How are you going to do that?"

"Listen more when you talk about the kids. Remind myself that Piper is going to respond to things in ways I wouldn't. I'd love your help with it, but you owe me nothing."

He was right. But I owed my kids the opportunity to have a better relationship with their dad. I'd grown up without a father, and the last thing I wanted for Piper and Sam was to experience the same thing.

I sighed, letting my shoulders relax. "Want to come to dinner on Wednesday? You can see Piper at home, and we can talk more. If it works out, then maybe we can make it a regular thing."

"I would appreciate that." He gave me a genuine smile. "And if your boyfriend wants to come, that's cool too."

"Kyle and I aren't..." I fidgeted with the pen on my desk, doing my best to ignore the way my chest pinched. "We ended things."

"I didn't see that coming. The guy seemed perfect." With a sympathetic frown, he stood. "See you Wednesday?"

I nodded, and when he was gone, I unlocked my phone and read Kyle's last text again.

I'd thought he was perfect too. But he'd lied, just like Jace had.

My brain chirped at that last thought. Because unlike Jace, Kyle had lied for a reason. The issue was that I didn't know if I could get past it.

KYLE
45

AS THE BALL hurtled toward me, I focused on it, and when the time was right, I swung. The bat connected with the leather, sending vibrations up my arms. Then the ball was flying out to left field, just past third base, before it once again tipped foul.

"Still pulling up at the end. Keep the swing even, Bosco," Coach Wilson barked from behind the fence. "I know the bicep is sore, but you can't pull up."

Fuck. Coach had been a pitcher in his day, and during preseason, he ran batting practice himself. There was nothing like having a perfectionist as both judge and jury.

"Got it, Coach."

"Ten more," he barked.

Groaning, I shook my right arm a few times. Then I stepped back to the plate. After ten pitches and five even swings, he called it.

"I need you focused for the game on Friday," he said as we headed to the locker room.

"Absolutely. We will win," I assured him, forcing the competitive smirk I was known for to my face.

"And you're good for the press conference tomorrow?"

I nodded. "Best behavior. Scout's honor." I held up two fingers.

"That's not the fucking Scouts' sign." He shook his head. "Dumb-ass," he muttered as he headed into his office.

"Isn't it fun to be back, getting called dumbasses?" Emerson dropped an arm over my shoulder when I shuffled up to my locker.

I grunted.

"Want to come out tonight before the girls get here tomorrow?" Emerson asked.

I eyed Asher, who shrugged noncommittally. He and I had spent most of the last two weeks sitting on my couch, watching bad TV. Until yesterday, he'd had hope that Zara and the kids were coming to the first game. But when he'd FaceTimed with Clara last night, she'd confirmed that they weren't, and his mood had been in the toilet since then. I'd mentioned the idea of reaching out to Zara directly, but he refused. He thought he was giving her what she wanted. At this point, I wasn't sure Zara even knew he was talking to the kids regularly, because he didn't want her to know. I felt like he was handling the separation the wrong way, but what the hell did I know? I reached out every day, and Harper still wasn't talking to me.

"Yes, no, maybe so?" Emerson sang the words, pulling my attention back to him and the question of going out tonight.

"I guess."

Emerson clapped and broke into a wide grin. "The gang will all be there. Like old times." He pumped his fist. "We should find karaoke."

Turning to his locker space, Dragon groaned. "No."

My phone vibrated on the shelf in my locker, and my heart picked up speed. I knew it wouldn't be Harper, but a guy could hope.

Though I was right, and she was still no-contact, the name on the screen did lift my spirits.

I slid my thumb to answer, and Piper's face appeared.

"Hey, girlie." My chest warmed with affection at the sight of her.

"I ran the bases today," she said, her tone matter-of-fact, like usual, but there was a hint of pride there too.

There was no stopping my grin. "No way!"

"Yes." She nodded. "With Ashley. And the sand got on me, but I finished before I changed my shoes."

"Well done," I praised.

"I knew you would get it. When I told Daddy, he just wanted to know why I changed my shoes."

A weird pang resonated through my chest. Her father was trying, and I was thrilled for both her and Sam. But I hated that she'd told him about this feat before me. Fuck, was it petty, but I hadn't been at my best lately.

"When are you coming home? I like your house." Piper wasn't looking at the screen, but I could see her lips pull down. "It feels safe there."

That yanked hard at my heart. That was my hope when I set up her space. To give her somewhere she could feel safe. Somewhere she would want to come back to. But at this point, I didn't even know if she'd ever be allowed back.

"Oh, I've got a few more weeks in Florida," I hedged. "Tell me about the rest of your day," I said as I settled in the chair by my locker.

As she dove into the first of her stories, she tilted her iPad, and the view changed.

She was on the sofa, like normal. But behind her, at the small table where I'd sat so many times, Harper and Jace were sitting across from each other. Their plates were still in front of them, and Harper was sipping from a bottle of White Out.

I was dying to ask what was going on. Especially when Harper laughed at something he said. I thought the pang in my chest was bad before, but at the sound, it felt like a gaping hole.

The tablet shifted again, and Piper's little face was back. "We worked on subtraction for too long. It was boring."

She continued to tell me all the stories, and I half listened. Because half my brain was still stuck on Jace's presence at their dining table. As soon as Piper ended the FaceTime call—abruptly, as always—I pocketed my phone and opted against the locker room shower so I could head home sooner.

Outside the locker room, I headed down the hall to my car. I never drove in Boston, but Cam usually stayed home while I was at spring training, so for a few weeks every year, I got behind the wheel.

"Kyle."

The voice resonated deep in my bones. The familiar sound of my name as I left the locker room seeped into my every cell. I'd heard it thousands of time. Mostly in high school.

Holding my breath, I spun around. "Bill."

My stepdad was leaning against the wall with a small duffel in one hand and a backpack on his back.

"I didn't know you were coming," I croaked

"Well." He pushed off the wall and headed toward the parking lot, clearly expecting me to follow. "Your mother and Aunt Susan are galli-vanting around the country for the next week, so I figured I'd come watch you play."

Falling into step with him, I said, "I didn't realize Mom was traveling."

He nodded as we continued down the tunnel.

"I was pretty upset when I found out about Harper."

Jaw clenched, I bit back a curse. Because his next words had the potential to forever change our relationship. But I had to ask. "Why?"

"I struggled, still do, with the idea of my brother hiding the exis-tence of a child from me. And worse, walking away from her. I can't imagine being so heartless. I carry a lot of guilt surrounding the way I accused her of lying about being his daughter when we met, but I truly couldn't imagine James just walking away from her. Hell, if I'd known about Harper, I'd have done everything I could to have a relationship with my niece."

My breath had been knocked from my lungs like I'd just taken a fastball to the gut. That admission wasn't anything like what I'd been expecting.

"You and I don't share any DNA, and yet from the moment I fell in love with your mom, you and Ryan each owned a piece of my heart." He tapped his chest. "I'd never have been able to give either of you up."

Images of Piper and Sam flashed in my mind, making my throat go tight and my eyes get hot. "I know that feeling all too well."

"So the idea that my brother could just walk away from his daugh-ter?" Lowering his head, he shook it. "I struggle with it." He sighed. "But I do think he'd love seeing you with Harper."

Stomach lurching, I pulled up short and fisted my hands. "What?"

"JJ said that James was very worried about her being alone. He wanted her to have someone she could depend on. Someone who'd be there for her through life. In a way he never got to be."

"Chose not to be."

Bill sighed. "Now that he's gone, that's something Harper and Susan will hopefully work through."

That stung. I wanted to be part of every aspect of Harper's life. Though with every day that went by, that idea felt more like a dream than a real possibility.

"But I think it would make James happy to know you're with Harper," he said as he took off again. "I know it would make me happy to see you two together."

I jogged to catch up. "Even if it causes drama with Aunt Susan and Danielle?"

He nodded. "In the end, I think they'll find themselves on the right side of this situation. Even if it takes them a little while to get there."

"Maybe. Although I'm not sure it matters, since Harper won't speak to me."

He shifted the duffel in his hand. "Can I give you some advice?"

I nodded. "You might be oddly suited to offer it."

"I'm not talking about your mother keeping Harper's existence a secret. This is about relationships." He inhaled deeply, like he was ready to lay it on me. "When you fall in love with someone who has been hurt, they might try to throw you back a few times. Whether they know it or not, they want to know you'll stick around. Fight for them."

"What?"

"I'm saying Harper is probably afraid of getting hurt. You might have to hold on tight enough for the both of you for a little while. Especially since she's protecting two other little hearts."

The grief that had been plaguing me for weeks flared. If only it were a matter of holding on. I could do that forever. I never wanted to let go.

Defeated yet thankful for his compassion and advice, I pulled my key fob from my pocket. "Thanks, Bill. Need a ride?"

"Sure."

Once I'd unlocked the Ram I'd rented for my time here, he dropped his bag in the back seat and then climbed in.

I pressed the ignition button and shifted into reverse. "Where to?"

"Any hotel will work."

Scoffing, I slowly backed out. "That ridiculous. If you haven't already set something up, just stay with me. I could use the company."

"You sure?"

Slowly, I headed for the exit. "Maybe you can help me come up with a grand gesture that Harper won't be able to refuse."

He pointed to my arm. "Wasn't that the grand gesture?"

"Nah." My arm was for me. To remind me to choose them every day. Because if I ever have doubts, it would remind me of exactly what it was like to lose them. And if I somehow managed to get them back, I never wanted to put myself through that again.

Harper
46

Dear Diary,

Hope is a hard thing to hold on to. Especially after twenty-one days. But the fact that she reads my messages every day that within five minutes of sending them, the read notification appears gives me hope.

         -Kyle

. . .

"ARE WE REALLY WATCHING THIS?"

In response, Zara gave me a clipped nod.

My kids were in bed. Hers were home with the nanny. And instead of having fun, we were watching the playback of today's Boston Revs press conference.

"Why?" I sank deeper into the couch cushions.

"I want to see what Asher said." Zara picked up her glass of wine and took a sip, her eyes locked on the screen.

That was code for *I want to see if Asher mentioned me.*

"You could call him," I suggested.

She scrunched up her nose and finally turned to me. "He hasn't reached out at all. He doesn't even call the kids. He just waits for them to call him."

My heart hurt for her. Every day, I expected a call from her. One where she'd giddily tell me that Asher had finally called and told her this break idea she'd come up with was ridiculous. But he hadn't. And the more time that went on, the more I started to wonder if maybe Zara was right. Maybe he didn't mind the break.

For the first fifteen minutes of the press conference, Coach Wilson droned on about game plans and stats that made little sense to me.

"I thought the players would get to talk." Zara pouted, bringing her glass to her lips again.

"I think they do eventually." Piper lived for this stuff, so I'd caught enough of these over the years to have some idea. It was another five minutes, though, before I was proven right.

"Now I'll open the floor to the guys." Coach Wilson flashed a smile at the camera. It was hard to believe the guy was Avery's father. He hardly looked forty. And when his dimples popped, I could see why he was so popular.

"Bosco," a man in the sea of reporters called out.

The camera zoomed in on Kyle as he rested his left forearm on the table in front of him and raised his brows in expectation.

My heart clenched as I drank him in. My worries about his hair were so silly. The short cut only made his deep brown eyes more fathomless. If possible, he looked sexier this way.

"Is it true your new tat is messing with your swing?"

He chuckled, and I swore the sound vibrated through my chest. "Wow, talk about the gossip mill working overtime." He glanced at a person on one side of the room, just off camera, and rolled his eyes. "I will firmly deny that I have any issue with my swing."

"But you don't deny the new tat?"

"Nosy much?" Kyle teased, making the reporters and his teammates laugh. "But sure, I'll tell you about it. My life is split into two parts. There's the fun side." He held up his left arm, showing off the words inked on his arm. "Then there's the shit that matters." He held up his right.

The camera zoomed in, and when it focused on Kyle's new tattoo, I sucked in a hard breath. There, on the underside of his bicep, in matching script, were the words *Harper, Piper*, and *Sam*. "This year, I just added some people to my life that really matter to me."

We were broken up. We were over. Lacking a future. And yet he cared so much about us that he'd had our names permanently inked on his skin. And then he announced to the world that we were people who mattered to him.

I swallowed back a mixture of awe and heartbreak.

"Bloody hell." Huffing, Zara shifted on the couch and hit me with a look. "How many gestures do you need?"

"I could ask you the same thing. Asher would literally buy you the world."

"Buying things I haven't asked for is not a gesture," she argued. "Asher doesn't do stuff. He throws money at it. To him, the kids and I…" Wearing an expression of pure misery, she sniffed and shook her head, as if shaking off the hurt. "We're convenient when we're convenient. And when we're not, we don't exist." Slumping against the couch, she closed her eyes. "I told him I wanted a break, and he didn't even put up a fight. He just left for spring training. He hasn't called or texted to check in. He's out living his baseball dreams. That's what matters to him. That's what he'd tattoo on his arm. Not our names."

Heart aching, I sighed and slumped back too. I hoped she was wrong. Asher must have cared. Maybe he just didn't know how to show it.

"Kyle is different. He sends you a message every day. And you don't even answer." She gulped her wine this time. "What would you have done if he'd told you he was your..." She frowned. "Your cousin?"

With my head dropped back against the cushion, I groaned. "We are *not* related."

"The King doesn't have a problem with cousins marrying, and I'm certainly not going to judge." She shrugged.

I chuckled. Zara was something. I couldn't deny her humor made me feel a modicum lighter.

"If he'd told me..." I hedged, wishing I could say I would have given him a chance. That we would have had the same beginning, just without the horrible end. But that would be a lie. "I would have asked him to leave us alone. And I would have shut him out, just like I have with James."

"So he wasn't wrong to keep it from you?"

Irritation flickered through me. "He should have told me."

"When, though?" She cocked one thin brow. "At what point could he have admitted his aunt was the shrew suing you without the threat of having the door slammed in his face?"

"She's not suing me," I said for what had to be the zillionth time. She hired an attorney so she could sue the estate. It had very little to do with me.

Zara only lifted that brow higher.

I sighed. "Lying isn't the answer."

"So you said, 'Hey, are we cousins?' and he denied it?"

Scoffing, I picked up my drink. "Of course not. Can you imagine if I'd said, 'Hey, Kyle, do you happen to know if were related?' How would that even go?"

She shrugged. "My father and uncle are lords. In some circles, asking is a necessity."

Her life was so odd.

"Not telling me is still a lie."

"Not telling you was a god-awful decision. But." She held up a single finger. "Tell me about one time he actually lied."

I tipped my chin up and inhaled deeply, then let it out slowly. This was something I'd thought about over and over since the day Jace apologized. I'd tried to pinpoint small lies Kyle must have told me to cover up the truth. But I couldn't find one.

"Like I said, it was a bloody awful decision. But he didn't lie." She scooted closer and grasped my hand. "His omission doesn't negate all the good things. Because there were bucketloads of those. If you expect perfection from everyone, you'll only be disappointed."

"I don't expect him to be perfect," I snapped, lurching forward and slamming my beer onto the coffee table. "I'm the issue here."

"What?" She cocked her head, her brow creasing.

"You're right. He may have withheld information, but he didn't lie. I've replayed every interaction we've had, and I can't come up with one time he lied to me. I get it. But still, this awful feeling lingers inside me." My voice cracked as I pressed a hand over the ache in my chest. "What if I can't trust him? What if I drive him away with my need to constantly question things? What if I'll never be good enough for his family? What if I'm the problem?" Now that I'd said the words aloud, the fear crept farther up my throat.

This was exactly what Eleanor had warned against. This was why I couldn't forgive Jace. It was why I didn't trust my half brother enough to let him in. This was what I did. I pushed people away. So it was only a matter of time before I did it to Kyle.

"Darling." She wrapped her arm around my shoulder and pulled me in. "Self-sabotage is such an easy trap to fall into."

Reeling back, I glared at her.

"But nothing in life is certain. It's all a risk. And I don't think Kyle expects you to be perfect either."

I slumped against her.

"Is someone knocking?" Zara tilted her head, frowning. "Blimey, Harper, you need to fix the doorbell." She released me and shuffled to the door, and a moment later, tone accusatory, she asked, "Who are you?"

I straightened and turned toward the door, my stomach dropping.

James stood at the threshold. Behind him, his mother and his aunt hovered.

"James." I jumped to my feet.

"Oh." Zara, who'd glanced back at me, spun on them, hands on her hips. "It's the brother and the wicked stepfamily."

"Zara!" Heart lurching, I winced.

"What? The term seems fitting, no?" She crossed her arms over her tan cashmere sweater.

James cleared his throat, his focus fixed on me, shoving his hands into his pockets and rocking back on his heels. "Sorry to drop by without calling."

"No we're not." A gray-haired woman stepped up and pushed James back. "We all know Harper would never have agreed if we'd called."

My breath caught. If that didn't sound exactly like her son…

Zara, clearly thinking the same thing, stuck her hand out forcefully. "You must be Kyle's mother. My husband plays with your son."

Vivianne dipped her chin in agreement. "We adore Asher."

"Almost everyone does." The humor in her tone was dark in a way I'd never heard from her before.

"Can we come in?" Vivianne asked.

"Why?" Zara snarled.

Quickly, I hustled around the sofa. "Yes. Please come in." I grabbed Zara's arm and forced her back, giving her a pointed look. "It's fine."

"But only if you're perfectly pleasant. Otherwise, I'm calling Lud," she threatened. Her bodyguard was in the car, waiting for her. And if she called, he'd be up here to toss everyone out in less than a minute.

The other woman cleared her throat. "Maybe it's best if we talk in private."

For the first time tonight, I took Susan in. The last time I'd seen her, she'd been cloaked in grief, having recently lost her husband. She looked better now. The color had returned to her face, and her ashy-blond hair was styled.

"I will not leave," Zara said, straightening beside me. "Harper is wonderful, and yet you've been nothing but awful to her. I won't stand by and allow anyone to try to convince her she is not worthy of all the best things in life."

Chest aching, I gaped at her.

"What?" she asked, frowning at me. "Friends have each other's backs, no?"

I smiled and nodded. It was the only response I could muster.

It had been so long since I'd had a friend. I had coworkers and neighbors and people I spoke to often because of Piper, but all my friends had faded away after I got married and had Piper. Maybe that was my fault. Maybe I'd been living with my guard up. Worried people would judge me or her. Zara, though, had forced her way into our lives because she was pushy. Kind of like Kyle had.

I surveyed his family, anxiety burning in my stomach, and reached into my pocket for a Tums, only to realize I didn't have any. It had been so long since I needed them. Not since before Kyle had started coming around.

I wiped my hands on my leggings and took a strengthening breath. "Zara's my best friend. She's staying." For a moment, I worried about how she'd take that statement. But she simply beamed at me.

"We understand your need to have your best friend around for moral support, don't we, Susan?" Vivianne crossed her arms over her chest.

"Yes." Susan sighed, shaking her head, though I thought I saw a hint of a smile.

Beside her, James chuckled, although I didn't get the joke.

"You want to sit?" I waved to my small table.

As they moved to sit, Zara whispered, "I'm going to grab the chair from your desk in your room." Then she was gone.

"We came to apologize and clear the air," Vivianne announced the moment we'd all settled.

"I'm not sure you have anything to be sorry for," I said, surprising myself with my boldness. "And James has apologized twice."

Zara dragged the chair back into the room and pulled it up next to me.

"I'm here for moral support. Like Zara," Vivianne corrected.

"I'm the one apologizing." Susan shifted in her chair, her face pained. "I have not been fair to you."

I didn't disagree, so I simply laced my fingers and waited for her to continue.

"You probably know this already, but betrayal is a hard thing. And I was hurt when I found out about you." She tilted her chin up. "Though it was years ago, I never dealt with it correctly. James and I put it in a box and moved past it." She twisted her hands in her lap and exhaled a shaky breath. "But it wasn't fair of me to keep your family from you."

When she was silent for a moment, Vivianne said, "And?"

"Your father would have liked to have seen you. To set up some kind of shared custody arrangement." She cleared her throat. "But I didn't think I could handle that. I was sure that having you in my home would do nothing but remind me that he'd betrayed me. Remind me of why I couldn't trust him."

I wanted to be mad. I *was* mad. But I could also understand how hard it was to trust a person after a betrayal. And being asked to care for the reminder of that betrayal? Yeah, that would be a challenge.

"I've been awful. I can't tell you how sorry I am. But I would like to try something else." She looked up at me, her blue eyes sad. "I'd like the chance to get to know you as the person who makes my nephew so happy."

"I don't know..." I shook my head. Lately, I was the opposite of a source of happiness for Kyle.

"Oh, I do. At Thanksgiving, he practically bit my head off over you."

My breath caught at that. Thanksgiving. That was before we were even together.

"First time that man ever yelled at me." She chuckled a bit uncomfortably.

"You should have seen him at Christmas. You would have loved the way his face lit up every time he got a text from her." Vivianne piped up.

"Wait." James tapped the table. "Before we go on to Kyle. I have something to add."

I tensed. The last time we'd spoken, he'd been angry. Was that still the case?

"My mother has also decided to stop being petty." He frowned at Susan, who glanced down. "She's no longer contesting the will." He pulled a beige envelope out of his pocket. "And in turn, the checks to you and the kids have been cut from the estate."

My lungs seized completely for a moment. When I finally forced air into them, I squeaked out an "Oh, I can't."

But Zara snatched the envelope from his hand and clutched it to her chest. "She can and she will." She pursed her lips at me. "Don't be stubborn."

I opened my mouth to argue. Instead, I blew out a long breath. The truth was, the hundred thousand dollars each would go a long way. It would pay for therapies for Piper, and I could set up a college fund for Sam. "Thank you," I said, taking the beige envelope from Zara.

Leaning forward, James put his hand over mine. "I know I've messed up too many times to count. But I do honestly want to get to know you and the kids better. I want to be involved in your life. The stress of the past doesn't have to hang over us anymore. Not if we don't want it to."

I studied his amber-colored eyes, realizing then that I had two choices. I could keep trying to be an island. Alone and safe. Or I could have people on my side. People in my life. Friends. Family.

"I'll work to make it less of a challenge," I agreed.

He stood and pulled me into a hug. The first we'd ever shared. It was more comforting than I could have imagined. For a moment, I closed my eyes and soaked in the peace he imbued.

After another minute of small talk, they said their goodbyes and left. And though much had been resolved tonight, it didn't feel like an end. It felt like a beginning.

"Well." Zara clapped, the sound loud in the suddenly silent space. "I think this takes care of the family worry."

I nodded.

"He loves you." She laced her fingers and brought her hands to her chest. "Just talk to him. Trust yourself."

And for the first time in weeks, I felt like maybe I could.

KYLE
47

GAME ONE. Only a month ago, I was certain that this would be the best game of my life. Harper, Piper, and Sam would be in the stands, cheering me on. I'd show off for them. How could I not? I'd catch a ball in the outfield and give it to them. God, I had been so arrogantly confident in our relationship.

"Dude, come on." Mason stood several yards away, with his arm pulled back, waiting.

"Sorry." I shook my head and held up my glove.

The ball snapped against the leather of my glove when he finally threw it.

"What happened? You were fine yesterday. Even fired up at the press conference. Today it's like all the life has been drained out of you."

He'd probably think it was stupid. But after my dear diary yesterday, it felt significant.

I tossed the ball back his way. "She didn't read my message this morning."

Mason tipped his head. "What do you mean?"

"I send Harper a message every morning." I sighed, deflating. "She never replies, but she always reads it. But today." He tossed the ball back. "She didn't read it."

"Shit." Mason frowned.

"Exactly." I threw the ball back at him. "Just get rid of it. I don't want to pick someone."

When we were finished warming up, we always handed off the ball to a fan. Because we were surrounded by them. This was spring-training game one. Probably the biggest crowd we'd get until opening day. But my heart wasn't in it.

Mason searched the stands, his focus fixing on a spot over my shoulder.

"What?" I asked, spinning around.

I scanned the crowd for what might have caught his eye. It only took a moment to spot the red hair. Lots of red hair.

My heart took off at a breakneck speed when I registered what I was seeing. *She came.*

For one beat, I was overwhelmed with utter joy. Maybe everything really could be okay. But just as I started to smile, Harper turned and beamed at the man stepping up next to her.

All the air was sucked from my lungs like I'd been sucker punched. Jace.

No. No fucking way. The world tilted on its axis, and I stumbled.

"Jeez, Streaks." Mason grabbed my arm, steadying me. "You're going to bust your ass. Breathe," he said, shaking me, as if to pull me from my stupor. "Don't jump to conclusions. You don't know what's going on."

But I couldn't. I couldn't breathe. I needed to move. I needed to be faster. I needed to undo the last month. Hell, go back in time and undo the last three months. Go back in time. Because fuck all of it. I should have made better decisions every step of the way. Everything that mattered—really mattered—was abundantly clear in that moment.

"Breathe," he repeated.

I sucked in hard. Yes. Breathe. If I didn't, there was no way I'd make it across this damn field to the three people who mattered more than anything.

So I was running. Because even after everything, I couldn't find it in me to want a life that didn't include them. Hopefully I hadn't already fucked it all up.

"Harper," I called.

"Kyle!" Sam ripped his hand out of his mom's and darted for the wall separating the field from the stands.

I reached him just as he flung himself over the wall at me. Security was on us in a second, but as I wrapped him up and pulled him into my chest, I waved them away.

With my face pressed to the crown of his head, I whispered, "I missed you, bud."

"Me too." He pulled back, beaming. "We came to see you play."

"I'm glad." I set him back down on the other side of the wall and turned to Piper, who'd approached too, though not as quickly. "Didn't think you were coming."

"You got us the tickets," she said, clearly unsure of why I was concerned that they might not be here.

"I know." I smiled, my heart bursting at her reaction.

"Don't lose," she reminded me, focused on the logo on my jersey. "And make sure you don't pull up on your swing."

Warmth bloomed in my chest. "Have you been watching Sports Center again?"

"No, I watched *JM Baseball* with Chris Rose and *Talkin' Baseball*."

With a chuckle at the list of podcasts, I adjusted my ball cap. "I've fixed my swing," I promised.

"Come on, guys." Jace took Sam's hand and tilted his head toward the stands. "Let's find the seats before the national anthem."

"We'll see you after the game?" Piper asked.

I nodded. Hell yeah, they would.

"Play good," Sam said as they climbed the stairs.

With a grin, I gave him a final wave. Then, finally, I turned to Harper.

"Hi," she said, her cheeks pink and her lashes fluttering.

"You brought Jace?" I winced the second the words were out of my mouth. Fuck. I didn't mean for that to be the first thing I said.

"Oh." She glanced back at her ex, who was now by the dugout, settling the kids into their seats. "He agreed to fly down and help with the kids."

My heart thumped so forcefully, I wouldn't be surprised if she heard it. "So you two aren't..."

Her eyes widened. "No."

The breath left my body in a rush, but then I remembered. "You didn't read my text."

"Yes, I did." She cocked her head to the side.

That couldn't be right. An hour and a half ago, it still hadn't been read.

"As soon as I got off the plane."

She flew in this morning. A weight dropped from my shoulders. "So what does it mean that you're here?" I wanted to hope, desperately.

"I'm here to talk. To tell you that I understand why you didn't tell me about your family." She swallowed.

I tried to beat back the hope bubbling up in my chest, but my heart was racing now, getting ahead of itself. "And?" I held my breath.

"I forgive you." The words were a whisper. "And I want to try to move past it."

"Is there a but?" Because if so, she could so easily crush me.

She swallowed thickly. "But I'm not perfect. I'm going to annoy you because I'm going to question things. Even when you don't deserve my distrust. Not forever, I don't think. But maybe for a while."

"Ask as many questions as you want, Crabby. I'll answer them all." With a trembling hand, I cupped her cheek, and when she didn't flinch away from my touch, my heart flipped in my chest. "Neither of us has to be perfect. I'm going to piss you off, I'm sure, when I butt in when you don't need me or when I give you a hard time just to see how fast I can bring your smile back. Or, you know, when I buy you a car."

"You've never bought me a car." She tipped her head, her brows pinched in confusion.

Huh. Now that she was here, that plan might have been a bit ill-timed. But I knew better than to hide a truth.

"Well..." I released her so I could scratch the back of my neck.

Her mouth fell open, and her eyes went wide. "You bought me a car?"

I slapped on what I hoped was my cutest grin. "A Cadillac XT4. Really cute silver SUV. Cam is picking it up tomorrow."

She frowned, searching my face. "I wasn't even talking to you."

"Oh, I know. But I figured if a car showed up, you'd call me to yell about it."

She sighed. "Yeah, I would have."

"And I wanted to hear your voice." I shrugged.

"You are ridiculous," she huffed, but her lips tipped up in a smile.

My heart soared at that simple expression. I lifted up on my toes so I could reach her over the fence and cupped her cheek again. "I'm only ridiculous for you, baby. Like I said, neither of us has to be perfect. We just have to work to build an us together."

"Forever?" she asked.

My chest expanded, and there was no fighting the smile that split my face. "Forever." I pulled her head down to mine and kissed her. The second our lips met, I pulled her over the wall and into my arms.

Around us, the field erupted in cheers from both the fans and my teammates.

"I love you, Harper," I said against her lips.

"I love you too, Kyle."

KYLE
48

I STUDIED THE RED HAIR, memorizing its exact shade, as I twirled a soft strand around my finger.

"Ouch," she mumbled. "I told you to stop."

But I couldn't. I hadn't been able to let go of her for the last twenty-four hours. The Revs had won the game, and as soon as it was over, I'd brought Harper and the kids back to my place. Jace was staying at a hotel nearby, and he planned to take Sam to Legoland tomorrow before they all flew home on Friday.

I hated that they had to leave so soon. But school and work were waiting for them back in Boston. And I'd be home in a few weeks too.

I released her hair, then tugged her against me.

"You're making her nuts, Kyle," my mother warned from where she sat on the other side of the living room.

It turned out that Harper and the kids weren't the only ones who'd flown down for the game. Bill was already here, of course, but my mom, along with Aunt Susan, JJ, his wife Dana, and their twin boys showed up at the field as well.

The wildest part? It had been Harper's idea. It was a good thing I'd opted for a place with seven bedrooms.

"You need to start the grill anyway." Harper nudged me, trying to force me off the love seat we were snuggled up on.

"I will in a second." No one was begging for food yet.

Bill was teaching Piper to play chess at the table. She was completely locked in, concentrating on each rule he explained. I'd give it six months before she kicked his ass at the game he'd been playing his whole life.

JJ's twin boys and Sam were in the pool. They looked so much alike, they could almost pass as triplets. Especially with the goggles. I could only pick Sam out because he wore green swim armbands, while the twins wore blue.

My aunt and Dana were watching the kids play, both wearing smiles. Dana's didn't surprise me, but Susan's? Yeah, it was hard to believe that she could be okay with all of this. I'd been clear with her yesterday that she had to be pleasant to Harper, and she'd waved me off as if the warning were unnecessary. I wasn't sure how that one-eighty had happened, but I wasn't complaining.

"Baby." Harper leaned closer to me. "The kids need food. If you wait until they're asking for it, then we'll have a whole crew of cranky humans to deal with."

I dipped lower and gave her a quick kiss. I'd kissed her at least four hundred times today, but the temptation to do it again was impossible to ignore.

"I'm here," she promised, giving me a small smile and patting my leg. "And I'm not going anywhere."

Without having to talk about it, she understood my apprehension. Instead of being annoyed, as my mom claimed, she patiently reminded me, over and over, of her presence. Of her devotion. If she ever needed her own reassurance, I'd give it to her as many times as she needed to hear it.

I slipped off the love seat and headed over to light the grill. We'd had a grocery order delivered, and because of the number of people here, we'd gone with an easy meal—burgers and grilled chicken and a salad. I trotted around the pool to the outdoor kitchen, only then realizing how similar this space was to my patio at home. Cam was usually the one grilling there, but it couldn't be that hard to figure out the grill.

I opened the lid and twisted the nobs, but nothing happened.

"Need some help?" JJ asked beside me, startling me.

I bobbled the lid but caught it before it slammed. And with a sheepish smile, I stepped out of the way.

As he messed with something in the cabinet below the cook surface, neither of us spoke, the silence growing awkward.

Itching to fill the air but at a loss for how, I rocked back on my heels. He and I had yet to really talk, and an uncomfortableness lingered between us. I wasn't sure what to say to ease the tension. I'd never apologize for falling in love with Harper. But I missed my best friend.

Before I could come up with anything reasonable, he stood and pressed a button, and the grill ignited.

"Thanks."

"So." He glanced around, maybe gauging how much privacy we had. "I just want to say a couple things."

Apprehension curled in my gut. "I'll give you the same warning I gave everyone else. You want to tell me I'm an asshole, fine. But I swear to God, I have a zero tolerance when it comes to how people speak about Harper, Piper, or Sam."

He held both hands up. "No. She is my sister. Shit, I wanted this." He shook his head. "Look, I'm sorry I reacted badly when I found out about you and Harper."

Shock stole the air from my lungs.

"I was surprised. I never thought I'd see the day you'd settle down. And I was jealous, I guess, because I had spent a year trying to get to know her, to get past her walls. Yet in two months, you'd practically moved her into your house."

I crossed my arms. Although his speech had started off okay, now I questioned where he was going.

"Kyle, look around." He extended his arm. "My boys are playing with their cousin. Harper is laughing with Aunt Viv. It feels good." He dropped his hands to his sides. "This is what I spent a year trying to make happen. This is what I promised my father I would work toward. And I have you to thank for bringing it together like this."

I studied him, confused by the change in direction. "What?"

He smiled. "There is no world in which this would have happened without you. You're the bridge Mom and Harper needed in order to move forward. So thank you. Thank you for making this happen, even if you did it in your own unique way." He held out a hand.

Rather than shake it, I yanked him in for a hug, chuckling.

"What's so funny?" he asked as he pulled back.

"Remember back in high school, when Bill joked about me marrying your sister?"

"Ugh, you were giving Dani shit about her braces, and Bill said it was because you liked her." He barked out a laugh. "I called his idea a foul or some baseballish shit like that." He rolled his eyes. "We ate, slept, and breathed baseball back then."

"Some of us still do." I pulled the burger patties out of the outdoor fridge. "You declared it would be a foul out. At the time, I agreed. Dani was never going to be the girl for me." I smirked. "But." Over my shoulder, I watched Harper where she sat, smiling at my mom.

She tucked her braid over her shoulder and wiggled her fingers in my direction.

I blew her a kiss. "I'm going to need you to change your mind, because I'm marrying your sister."

I might not need his blessing, or anyone's, for that matter, but it felt good when JJ smiled and nodded.

Epilogue

Harper

I GLANCED up from my phone as we pulled behind a building I didn't recognize.

Although I preferred to drive, especially since I'd fallen in love with the SUV Kyle had gotten me, he had insisted that Cam pick me up from Boston Lights and drive me to meet him today.

"I thought we were going to lunch. Where are we?"

"Don't worry." Cam looked over his shoulder at me and smiled. "He's inside."

I sighed. "This seems like another harebrained scheme."

Cam barked out a laugh. "You know our boy is full of them."

After we'd returned from Florida, Cam had been a lot more relaxed around the kids and me, even when we were at Kyle's place. Which was more often than not, these days.

I pulled the door to the Escalade open. And before I had both feet on the asphalt, the heavy metal door of the brick building opened, and Kyle stepped out.

"Hey, Crabby." He moved to my side and greeted me with a kiss. "I missed you."

"It's been six hours." The kids and I had stayed with him last night, and although he had crawled out of bed at six to get to practice, it was barely noon.

His hand found the small of my back. "Feels longer. I can't wait for the season to be over."

"You don't mean that." I laughed. The Revs were leading the division and would be heading into the playoffs as the top seed.

"I'm not saying I don't want to win the World Series. Because we so are this year."

Smiling, I nodded. The farther we got into September, the more important it became that I agreed with his assessment that the Revs were going to win it all.

"But I'm ready for more time with you and the kids. Baseball is a bitch when you have a family at home."

I peered up at him and gave him a reassuring smile. "It hasn't been that bad. We have a system."

A lot of which revolved around FaceTime. Especially since Kyle spent a good 50 percent of his time outside of Boston. But we were making it work. And when he was home, he was all-in with the kids and with me.

"Come on. Coach only gave me an hour off." He led me into the back door, where two armed security guards stood. Past them was what looked like a cage door.

"Where are we?" I asked, apprehension skittering through me.

"The back entrance to Tiffany's."

My heart stuttered. "What?" I breathed, peering over my shoulder. Tiffany's didn't have a restaurant inside, did it? There was that movie, *Breakfast at Tiffany's*, but I always thought that was more of a joke about eating there.

"I'll explain in a minute," Kyle promised as we moved down a long hallway.

"Mr. Bosco." A man in a dark gray suit stood by another door, dipping his chin as we approached. "Right this way."

There was a love seat on one side of the room, and a chair on the other. Between them was a small table with two champagne flutes on top, along with pieces of silky black fabric.

Without a word, Kyle led me to the love seat and pulled me down beside him.

Heart thundering in my ears, I gripped his hand tight. "What is going on?"

He shifted on the cushion beside me and tucked a strand of hair behind my ear. "You know how we've talked about moving in together officially after this season?"

I inhaled deeply, willing my nerves to calm. "Yeah."

"And you know how I love adding life points to my list."

I snorted. He was ridiculous about that theory he had. Even retirement didn't seem to upset him, because it would add to the life points.

"I'm shooting to be one hundred, and marriage definitely adds some." His grin was teasing, but my eyes widened.

Forget teasing. That word, *marriage*, had my lungs seizing and my heart stopping. Marriage. Tiffany's. Blinking, I scanned the items on the table and brought a hand to my mouth.

"Oh my gosh. Are you buying a ring?"

"We are buying a ring." He tilted my chin so I was facing him again. "Because no matter what, I want you to have exactly what you want."

I swallowed past the boulder in my throat and croaked, "I'm sure they're all gorgeous."

"Well..."

"Ready, Mr. Bosco?" The man in the suit settled in the chair across from us and set a tray with twelves rings on the first piece of black fabric.

My heart lurched at the sight. Each diamond was unique, but they were all huge and flashy. I blinked at the glittering diamonds, at a complete loss for words.

"Take your time." The man smiled politely and then moved back to the door.

"Do you like any of them?" Kyle asked hesitantly, his hand shaking where it cupped mine.

"They are all beautiful." Sleek and modern. Not necessarily what I would pick, but every single one was gorgeous.

"I have one more option." He shifted forward and dug in his pocket.

When he pulled his hand out with a sparkly item pinched between his fingers, my breath caught. My grandmother's ring. With my hands over my mouth, I blinked back tears.

I'd sold it almost a year ago. And every time marriage had come up, I'd wished I had it. After I deposited the checks from the inheritance, I'd gone back to the small jewelry store, only to find that they'd sold it. I'd hoped it would take longer than a couple of months to move an antique piece like that, but the jeweler had assured me that it had sold right away.

"How on earth did you get that ring?"

"I heard through the grapevine—"

"Zara?"

He grinned. "Actually Asher."

That was surprising after everything that had happened with them over the last several months. I was shocked she'd told him about it.

"But only that you'd sold it," Kyle said. "He didn't know where. So I went to every jewelry store in Boston, I swear, until I tracked it down."

Heart aching and hands shaking, I finally let a tear slip free. "Oh my gosh."

He lifted a hand and wiped it away, his expression soft.

I loved that ring. Inhaling, working to calm my emotions, I surveyed the others again. "But do you want—"

He pressed his finger to my lips, stopping the words. "I spent two full days tracking this down because I want you to have it."

"Will they be mad if you don't buy one here?"

He shrugged, unconcerned, as always. "We can get our wedding bands here. Plus, I bought something else."

"What?"

"Jonathan," he called over his shoulder.

The man in the suit came back, this time holding a smaller tray.

On it was a silver bracelet. The chain looked like a thin sparkling rope, and in the center was a circular piece with an H stamped on it. But there were two extra lines coming up at odd angles. It took me a second to realize what I was looking at.

"It's an H and a K." Our initials.

Kyle nodded. "It's a custom-made permanent bracelet. If you want, they'll solder the ends together."

"So it won't come off."

His lips tipped up in a shy smile that was so unlike this confident man.

"You'll have my name on your arm." I traced his tattoo with my finger, then moved that same finger to my wrist. "And I'll have yours on mine."

"That was the idea. We'll both be permanently marked." He brushed his index finger over my wrist in the same spot I'd just touched. "But only if you want it."

"I love the idea, baby." I held my wrist out.

Kyle nodded at Jonathan, who clasped the bracelet and secured it, then brought out a soldering tool and a shield to protect my skin. The heat was a little uncomfortable, but only for a moment.

Once it was in place, Kyle lifted my hand. The circle with our initials sat centered on my wrist. He kissed the spot and then dropped down to one knee.

"There is no one in this world I'd rather do life with. You're my friend, my partner, my playmate, my challenge, and the love of my life. So will you do me the honor of adding one more title to that list? *Wife*." He held up my grandmother's ring. "Marry me, Harper?"

I nodded and held out my hand so he could slip the heirloom onto my finger.

"I will love you forever," he promised. But his words meant more than just *I love you*. They were a promise to actively keep loving me, through all the good days and even on the bad days.

"I will love you too."

Curious what is going on with Wren and why she is acting so unlike herself?
Preorder Coach Wilson's story

DEAR READER

Dear Reader,

First, let me just say a massive THANK YOU for reading *The Foul Out*. This book will always hold a special place in my heart.

Harper and Piper's relationships mimics my relationship with my youngest son. Some days it felt like I was writing a dear dairy of my day on the page. (Yes that is where the idea for Kyle's texts came from, because I needed the light and cute to balance out the exhaustion of it.) I would live the meltdown with my son and then write about it that night. I worried a lot about how Harper would come across because it is draining and frustrating, and doing it alone just adds to that. For those who live it, I hope the book made you feel seen and heard. For those who don't, I hope it gave you a small understanding of how it feels, and how the kids who are struggling feel too. Balancing all that, while still making the story cute and funny, was a struggle, but I hope I achieved my goal.

Also, did you see the easter eggs for the next book? Why is Wren being so unlike herself? Did you wonder what happened on that business trip? I can't wait for everyone to get Coach Wilson's story which is coming out December 1st! And then, Asher and Zara's story in 2025!

Hopefully you'll join me on the entire Boston Revs ride, because it will be such fun!

If you haven't yet, definitely jump back to the Momcoms for Beckett and Liv's and Cortney and Dylan's stories. Then check out Mason and his trainer's story in Gracie York's (My pen name with AJ Ranney) *Back Together Again*.

Finally, remember: Live in your world, fall in love in mine.

Jenni

ACKNOWLEDGMENTS

A big thank you to my kids. Andy, you will probably never realize how much you inspired this story, but you did. And thank you for letting me use our days on the page. Spencer and Russell, thank you for all the help with the foul ball and fan interference rules, and baseball stats. I'm sure you were both sick of reading chapter 2, making sure the balance was all there with real baseball rules. Love you both! Ashely, thank you for letting me edit this while moving you into college, we got both things done and you put up with me saying 'one more minute babe' a million times. I'm so grateful for all four of you!

Thank you to my parents, who support me in everything I do all the time. I couldn't get through life without you guys. Being able to count on you both for help, support, or encouragement is the best gift. Thank you for the many many hours and days of babysitting so I can go to events and signings. I couldn't do this without you! Thank you for being examples I can strive to be with my kids and being the best grandparents ever.

Beth, thank you for being you. Detailed, and organized because I am not. And your series bibles are amazing. You are a friend and such an amazing supporter of me. I will never stop singing your praises from the rooftop. You rock at your job, and we all know it! Thank you for being the wonderful person you are.

Becca and the rest of the Author agency you all are the best. You keep up with me and always have things under control. I'm chaos and I'm sure I make you nuts with the 'wait, when is the cover reveal' messages, I constantly send your way.

Sara, thank you for everything. There aren't enough words to explain what you are. A friend, a support, a cheerleader, and an amazing visually creative gem, I'm so lucky to have you. You wear so many hats, not just for me but for all the authors you work with. You do it all and juggle so many things it makes my head spin. But whenever I need one more thing you get it done. I'm so proud of the amazing business you created and I can't wait to watch you keep flying.

Jeff, thank you for being the final nit-picky check to make sure everything is perfect. Becoming a romance reader wasn't on your to do list, but I'm grateful you did it anyway!

Britt, thank you for being you. I probably could do things without you, but I wouldn't want to. I can't believe I was lucky enough that you recognized a random beach one February day. Your support is never ending, even when you are so busy with your own stuff. Watching you soar in your success is inspiring. I love getting to be part of every new idea you have. You are the best.

Jess, thank you for being with me through the entire process for this book. Every time I was so over this story, you always helped get me writing just a bit more so you could read it. I'm so grateful to not only get to work with you, but also to call you a friend.

Shani, I can't thank you enough for all your support and expert sticker making. You never stop singing the Revs' praises and I'm so blessed to have you on my teams. You are creative and amazing!

Rick, Lauren, and all the rest of Hambright, thank you for taking a chance on me and helping to make this release awesome.

Glav, thank you for all your TikTok help, and being an amazing beta reader. You always find the perfect little spots to add something that make the hero just that bit more swoony. I'm also so grateful for all the laughs you bring to my life, and I apologize for all the spiders I bring to yours.

Amy, thank you for being the organized one, the one that keeps us on track, and the one that makes sure we get it done. For putting up with my chaos and my next 'fun' thing. I'm so lucky to get to call you one of my best friends. Daphne, thank you for all your help tweaking both Piper and Harper, and letting me vent about my kids. Anna, thank you for being a great friend and helping whenever I need a beta reader. Also, for having so many TikTok accounts that I can't even keep track and shouting to the world to read my books. I'm grateful for your support and friendship. Kenzie and Courtney you two both own TikTok and I am so glad to have your help with that!

And a big thank you to the rest of my friends and family who have helped me with encouragement and feedback. I love you all and am so thankful for your support.

ABOUT THE AUTHOR

Jenni Bara lives in New Jersey, working as a paralegal in family law, writing real-life unhappily ever-afters every day. In turn, she spends her free time with anything that keeps her laughing, including life with four kids. She is just starting her career as a romance author writing books with an outstanding balance of life, love, and laughter

ALSO BY JENNI BARA

Want more Boston Revs Baseball?

Cortney Miller

Mother Maker

Christian Damiano

The Fall Out (The Boston Revs Three Outs Book 1)

Mason Dumpty

Back Together Again (Written under the name Gracie York)

Emerson Knight

The Fake Out (The Boston Revs Three Outs Book 2)

Kyle Bosco

The Foul Out (The Boston Revs Three Outs Book 3)

Coach Wilson

Finding Out (The Boston Revs Three Outs Book 4)

coming December 2024

Asher Price

The Freak Out (The Boston Revs Three Outs Book 5)

coming 2025

Curious about the baseball boys from the NY Metros

NY Metros Baseball

More than the Game

More than a Story

Wishing for More

Made in the USA
Columbia, SC
17 November 2024

46732565R00213